The Lost Scroll

The Lost Scroll

Tahira Ejaz

&

Malik Khalid Ejaz

FACT & Lore
PUBLISHING INC

Published by Fact and Lore Publishing Inc.

ISBN 978-1-7781900-5-6 (paperback)
ISBN 978-1-7781900-6-3 (ebook)

Dedication

I wish I could get my hands on Aladdin's lamp somehow. Don't get me wrong; I don't wish for a magnificent palace, precious jewels, or unlimited riches. No! All I desire is to turn the wheel of time back and materialize in my father's garden where I used to go in the evening to collect the sweetly scented Arabian Jasmine.

It was about 20 years ago. After I had collected the moon-white flowers, I would go to my grandfather's house, right next to ours, along with my father and place the flowers on the table by his bed where he used to sit and welcome us. We called him Baba G. The strong fragrance of the snowflakes of summer would fill the room in no time. Baba G used to ask me what I had read that day. I was reading a popular fiction series at the time and used to tell him what happened next on a daily basis. Baba G loved books. Though I don't think he ever read a fiction book himself, he was more into serious non-fiction reading. Nonetheless, he loved listening to me.

He used to listen attentively to the story, and when I would be done narrating it, he would say, "I wish one of my children writes a book one day!" with such a yearning that his eyes would fill with tears. This desire was aroused by his deep respect for writers and his fascination for their ability to affect others through their words.

At the time, I never thought in my wildest dreams that my brother and I would be honored to fulfill his wish one day. I am happy beyond words that we did. The only regret is that it happened too late. He is no longer with us and would never hold this book in his hands with tears of happiness escaping through his eyes. That is the image that I want to witness, hence my desire to get the magic lamp.

With the belief that wherever he is, he would know that his wish was granted, I dedicate "The Lost Scroll" to Baba G with the words I never said to him before: "I love you, Baba G!"

-Tahira Ejaz.

Dedication

I dedicate this book to my amazing kids. You are the reason I started writing. I always had questions in my head, but when you started asking those questions, only then did I truly begin thinking so I could tell you the correct answer. In this book series, I will provide answers that make sense to me, but I want you to keep an open mind and only accept what makes sense to you. You are my next version - an upgrade; smarter and more capable.

I also want to dedicate this book to my wife. You know that I couldn't start this adventure without your support. Over the years, I have shared all kinds of crazy ideas with you. Thank you for listening, tolerating, and helping me choose the ones that were a little less crazy. Thank you for being you. I love you!

And I want to dedicate this book to my Ammi (Mom) & Abu (Dad), who raised me to have a thinking mind, allowed me the freedom to question things, and keep looking until I could understand everything. I'm sure I wasn't an easy kid to raise. After reading what I have to say, I hope you will be proud of me. :)

Baba G (My grandfather) probably never expected that I would write a book, so, unlike Tahira, he never mentioned his wish in front of me. I don't blame him, as I was more likely to be found with a cricket bat in my hand instead of a book. He loved to read books and wanted his children to be qualified enough to one day write books. I'm not sure I am as qualified as he had hoped, but I am sure that he is smiling today. He wished for it at a time when most people around us didn't even send their kids to school. He chose a different path and made it possible. Today, following in his footsteps, I am also choosing a different path - believing in myself and writing what is in my heart.

- Malik Khalid Ejaz

Chapters

Ch 01: Hello, World!

In my dream, I heard a voice say,

"Your vessel is sinking; survive the tides.

The end is coming; open your eyes."

The voice kept repeating like an alarm. I heard it but did not wake up. Suddenly, a much louder sound startled me, and my eyes shot open. I listened to the splashing of waves, but that was not what woke me up. The startling sound was gone.

I tried to sit up but lost my balance. My hand reached out and held onto something for support. I couldn't see anything. It was too bright. As my eyes adjusted, I found myself on a small boat. Waves surrounded me, rocking me back and forth and left and right. Quickly, I grabbed the other side with my free hand. The water stretched as far as I could see, and the furious waves battered my small, powerless boat, making it wobble dangerously.

With fearful eyes, a straight back, and a tight grip on both sides, I sat as the wind whipped my face and the boat rose and fell on the tides. I felt small, very small, an insignificant thing at the mercy of the waves. My mind raced to figure out what was going on and where I was.

Suddenly, a loud growl vibrated through the air. I turned around and saw an island I had just passed; with wide eyes, I recognized an Albertosaurus. Behind it was a long-necked Brontosaurus reaching for the tallest treetops, and in the background were the Rocky Mountains with snow-covered peaks. The sight of these incredible giants excited me, but I was being carried farther and farther away. I kept looking back till they disappeared out of sight.

Then I remembered the warning in my dream. A voice was alerting me to the sinking of a vessel. Did it mean my boat? In a panic, I checked for leaks. The boat didn't show any signs of collapsing. There was no water inside, and the sidewalls were high enough to shield me from the splashing waves. The voice in the dream was wrong. My boat was not sinking.

I wondered why I was in the boat. I had no memory of getting in it. In fact, now that I thought of it, it shocked me that I had no memories at all. I tried for some time, but couldn't remember anything.

"Where am I?" I asked myself in frustration. "No, let's start with a simpler question: Who am I?"

I kept thinking, but nothing came to mind. To find some clues,

I searched myself and discovered a watch on my wrist, a very strange watch, as it didn't tell time. Instead, it showed a whirlpool - which made me more anxious.

I looked around, but as far as I could tell, there was no whirlpool near me. I sat up to see farther away. But the moment I did, the boat started to rock dangerously. I lowered myself quickly, and once the boat stabilized, I continued my search. I found a piece of paper in my pocket, and on it was a poem:

Your vessel is sinking; survive the tides,

The end is coming; open your eyes.

Live and think, but don't you stall,

Catch the wizard; go past the fall.

The prophecy is cruel and very clever,

The fruitless war goes on forever.

Look to the future, but first in your past;

Know that your world is oh so vast!

I had heard the poem in my dream and then found it on a piece of paper in my pocket. So strange!

For some time, the boat moved on, and I looked around helplessly. Then, far ahead of me, I saw an island. I felt my muscles relax, and a sigh of relief left my lungs. The land was still far away, and I had no means to change direction, but that was alright—I was headed straight toward it.

The possibility of reaching the ground made me feel much better, but the thought of dinosaurs was worrying. Even if I reached the island and survived the water, how would I survive the land?

Eventually, I got close to the island, going toward the middle, where the water divided the land into two halves. A vast green forest covered most of the island, except for a darker patch that looked like it was burnt down.

Few more moments of looking around, and then there was land on both sides, and the waterway shrank till it was only a few feet wide. I wanted to stop, but the banks were rocky. The current also felt much faster now. There was no way I could stop there.

The boat moved on, and I saw a group of people who had spotted me as well. They waited for me to reach them and then ran alongside the boat. And as they were running, they were chanting:

"Your vessel is sinking; survive the tides,

The end is coming; open your eyes."

I sat frozen and watched them with a mix of fear and confusion. They kept running along, repeating the rhyme over and over again. It sounded like a warning. I couldn't wait any longer. I needed to get out of the boat.

Ahead, in the distance, I heard—and then saw—a waterfall with a misty fog surrounding it. Large stones blocked access to it, but water pushed around the narrow gaps and fell to the depths below. The path was not wide enough for my boat to go through, but I had to stop to avoid smashing into the rocks.

As soon as I found a clearing on the shore, I paddled with both hands and changed direction just enough to go over the shallow sandy area. The boat slowed down considerably, but the fast current threatened to topple it. I jumped out as soon as I felt safe enough. Some of the people ran to drag my boat out of the water. Others gathered around me.

Down on my knees, I breathed a sigh of relief. Finally, I was out of danger. Or was I? I looked up at the curious eyes surrounding me. The inhabitants of the island watched me with caution, keeping their distance. They had lean figures with delicate-looking wings protruding from their backs, which shimmered softly as the sunlight reflected off them. And as they fluttered their wings lightly, my back muscles moved too, and something rustled behind me, making the same fluttering sound. In surprise, I turned my head to look over my shoulder and discovered that I, too, had wings. I stretched them out in awe as one of the people approached me, placing a comforting hand on my shoulder. She spoke in a gentle voice, "You are safe now." I noticed the watch on her wrist and then glanced at the others - they were all wearing the same watch.

A sharp whistle cut through the air, causing everyone to step away from me. Men and women burst out of the forest, moving so quickly that they encircled me before I could even react. I stood up, trying to make sense of the situation. The strangers wore light armour, and their spears pointed in my direction. Large bows hung over their shoulders, next to their wings. For a while, they just stood there, surrounding me, their silence more threatening than any words could be. I waited, unsure of what to do next, while they simply stared back at me. The only sound came from the waterfall, utterly indifferent to the tense situation.

After a baffling silence, the sound of running footsteps finally broke through. A girl emerged from the forest holding a notebook, and one of the men stepped forward. He ordered me to follow him and started walking toward the waterfall. Others waited for me to move, and with their spears and bows, I decided it was best to obey. The girl with the notebook observed me constantly.

We moved forward, and panic set in. Why were they taking me to the falls? Would they push me off the ledge? Why had they surrounded me? The weapons in their hands scared me. Summoning some courage, I asked them, but they didn't answer. We were now very close to the edge, and I did not want to go any further.

The man in the front went closer to the edge and turned onto a muddy path. I followed, relieved that they weren't going to throw me over. The trail led us down one side of the fall, where an island was surrounded by rushing water. The only way to reach the island was via a movable bridge, which one of them moved and crossed, ordering me to follow. As I walked across the bridge, I looked at the large tree covering most of the tiny land.

The tree stood like a giant umbrella, with sides that came down to the ground. Long tresses of light blue flowers hid the trunk. The man pulled back the floral curtain to reveal a dimly lit chamber under the tree. He asked me to go inside, and as I walked in, he closed the opening behind me.

The tree trunk stood like a pillar in the center. The thick branches arched up and outwards and fell back to the ground as thin, hanging vines. I peeked through the natural walls to see what was happening outside. The man was leaving via the bridge. Once he reached the other side, the bridge was moved away, and I was left alone on the island. It felt like I was in prison.

They just left. Walked away. And when there was no one around, I walked out of the tree and glanced at my surroundings. The current around the tiny island was strong enough to prevent me from escaping, but on one side, the stream was so narrow that I could easily jump across and head into the dense forest. The waterfall was loud, and no other sounds could be heard. I checked the top of the falls and didn't find anyone watching me. I wondered why they would leave me in a "prison" that I could easily escape from. Would something happen if I tried to run?

I walked to the narrower crossing, frequently checking the top of the fall. Then jumped across the stream. With my head held low under the shade of my hands, I ran to hide in the nearest bushes. My wings spread out behind me like a shield. I expected a hail of arrows or spears, but thankfully nothing happened. Once in the bush, I peeked out and still found no one watching me escape. This made no sense. Was it not a prison? Why did they bring me to the tree and then leave?

I stretched my wings to see if I could fly away, but they were too delicate to trust with flight. They felt weak. I had no confidence that they could carry me. None of the people had used their wings—I had only seen them walk. After thinking for a while, I decided to go back and stay in "prison." I wanted to know what it was all about. I was also scared of encountering dinosaurs in the forest. Being with people felt like the wiser choice.

I walked back to the tree prison, repeatedly glancing up at the top of the waterfall, trying to understand the mysterious reason they had brought me to the island under the falls.

After entering the tree, I sat against the trunk and waited, my eyes shifting around the dimly lit chamber. My watch still showed a whirlpool. Maybe I wasn't out of danger yet?

The scraping sound of the bridge alerted me, and I immediately tensed up. From the faint sound of footsteps, I could tell that it was more than one person making their way across the bridge. I remained still, my senses on high alert as I prepared for any possible scenario.

Their footsteps drew closer. I saw two pairs of hands move the vines aside, and then three people entered my tree prison cautiously. The two on the side were heavily armoured. Their armour had strange-looking markings. Maybe they were higher in rank compared to the ones who had surrounded me earlier. I stood up and waited, wondering who these people were and what they were going to do to me.

Standing between the two armoured men was a woman without any armour. Her eyes squinted in concentration as she walked closer and said, "I am Feray, and these are my guardians. Do you have powers? Magic, to be precise?"

I muttered nervously, "No, I don't have powers... magical powers, to be precise."

"Is that so? Well, I will find out soon enough," she said, her tone filled with pride.

She called for someone named Boris to enter, and as he did, I noticed more people waiting outside the tree, including the girl with the notebook. Boris placed a large glass vial in front of me. Its softly glowing whitish contents mesmerized me. Boris asked me to sit down. I obeyed, observing the vial cautiously.

The woman, Feray, asked me to place my hands on the vial. I did not want to do that. As I hesitated to touch the vial, the guardians moved closer, their weapons at the ready. Feray gave me a stern look, and with her furrowed eyebrows, she ordered me to comply, "Go on!"

Reluctantly, I obeyed and placed my hands on the glowing orb. It felt cold but smooth to the touch. My hands disappeared under its glow. I closed my eyes and waited for something to happen, but the vial remained still and quiet. Peeking from behind my eyelids, I noticed the dim, whitish contents had changed into a greenish-white. Curious, I looked at the lady to see what it meant. Her taut expression had softened, and she appeared more relaxed now. She took the vial from my hands, and as she did, the glow turned white and blindingly bright. She returned the vial to Boris, who left with it.

The guardians visibly relaxed and lowered their spears, returning them to their sides. Feray's tone was now softer as she spoke again, "Newcomer, you were right. You have no magic. Welcome to Serenus!" It was a welcome change in her tone, but I couldn't help but feel a little disappointed at not having magic. I nodded, still feeling a little uneasy about the whole experience.

The guardians stepped back and moved the flowery tresses aside to allow Feray to walk through the opening. As she exited, they kept the vines separated like an open curtain and looked at me. I stood up and followed Feray, watching the changed expression on their faces. To my surprise, they were smiling. I wondered if they would have smiled if I had magic. Perhaps not. Lucky escape.

Outside the tree, a man stood waiting. He had an air of wisdom and confidence about him. He introduced himself, "I am Kratos. Feray was testing to see if you have any magical abilities. I apologize, but this is necessary." I nodded, still feeling a little disconcerted by the test. Kratos must have sensed my unease because he added, "Please don't worry. It is simply a precaution we take for the safety of everyone here in Serenus."

I managed a weak smile. I didn't say anything; instead, I studied him closely. He was a tall and muscular man. His broad shoulders and big arms made him stand out. His long, black, curly hair was tied up neatly. When he spoke, his voice was deep and gentle, "Welcome to Serenus! As long as you live in peace, this place will be your home." My home?

Kratos gestured for me to follow him. We went back to the top of the falls and then trekked a path to the forest. Feray stayed quiet and walked ahead of us. Kratos and I were side-by-side. The armed guardians disappeared on a different path.

As we walked, Kratos talked more about Serenus. It was a village that lived in harmony with nature and magic. They believed in protecting the forest and its inhabitants and dedicated their lives to this cause. I listened to Kratos, trying to make sense of everything. They were strangers, but I felt the sincerity in his words. I found myself trusting him.

He continued, "We have much to offer in Serenus, and perhaps you will find your place among us." I thanked Kratos, grateful for the invitation.

There was so much I wanted to ask. Where was I? Who were they? Why was I here? But for the moment, I stayed quiet to see what would happen next. Earlier, they treated me like an enemy, but now things appeared to be heading in the right direction.

When Kratos became quiet, I looked around. The grass was a fresh shade of green, decorated with an array of wildflowers looking happy in the bright sun. The trees were abundant with leaves that varied in colour, vibrancy, and beauty. With every step, I found myself impressed by the sheer beauty of this place. I felt a sense of peace wash over me.

The girl with the notebook still followed us quietly. Kratos continued to tell me about the island of Serenus. It was a place of peace, and its inhabitants were known as Seren. They had lived on the island for as long as anyone could remember. Everyone came to the island in a boat. Kratos himself had come decades ago and worked as a blacksmith.

Feray remained tight-lipped and kept to herself. Kratos appeared uneasy with her silence, stealing glances at her every now and then. Suddenly, Kratos pointed ahead and announced, "Our village!"

The first thing that caught my eye was a group of unusually wide trees bursting with colourful flowers that glowed brilliantly in the sunlight. These trees were unlike any other in the forest; not too tall, only about twice my height, but impressively wide. Tresses loaded with flowers hung down the sides, just like the tree on the island under the fall. Each tree bore flowers of a different colour and stood circling a much larger tree with white flowers.

Kratos pointed to a wooden house nearby. "Feray lives here." We turned right and arrived at a large village of wooden homes with beautiful front gardens. Ahead was a large clearing with a banquet area at its center. Many men and women sat around the tables, chatting and enjoying their food in a merry atmosphere. It was a very festive environment, and I found myself even more drawn to the place.

Kratos led me to a table brimming with food, and all eyes turned toward me. An elderly woman stood up slowly, silently welcoming me with a raised drink and a nod. Others followed her lead, bowing their heads in respect. I mirrored the gesture, and they sat down and turned their attention back to their own conversations.

We took a table, and Kratos introduced me to the girl with the notebook. Her name was Amy, and she was Feray's apprentice. As I sat next to her, she greeted me kindly and offered me a platter full of food.

I selected some ripe apricots and peaches from a platter of enticing fruits. A man then brought us bowls of soup, which had a sweet and tangy taste. Following Amy's lead, I tried the soup but could not decipher its ingredients.

Feray explained that the midday meal was traditionally eaten in the village center, although we were free to eat anywhere we wanted. I sensed that she preferred we eat there, almost as if it were an unspoken rule.

Kratos and Feray left after they finished eating. Amy stayed as I ate slowly, looking around at the beautiful place I had found myself in. She spoke kindly, "You will stay at the Serenus Lodge until your home is ready."

I nodded, surprised to know that I would get a home here. It was all very mysterious; I didn't know where I had come from and why. And why were these people being so friendly to me, feeding me excellent-tasting food, and they were even going to give me a home to live in? I was impressed by how kind everyone was. Except for Feray and the guardians, I reminded myself.

Amy noticed my thoughtful look and asked, "Is everything okay?"

I nodded again and said, "Yes, I'm just trying to understand everything."

Amy smiled warmly and said, "It's natural to feel this way."

I thanked her, feeling reassured. I had a lot of questions in my head, but I didn't want to overwhelm her. Instead, I asked, "What do people do here?"

Amy said, "Most people are farmers, but there are also artisans and craftsmen. Some of us work with magic too."

It was hard to believe what was happening. It almost felt like a dream. But it wasn't. I was really here, in this magical world, surrounded by people who had magical abilities.

After the meal, Amy walked me to my temporary residence: a room in the Serenus Lodge. I had so many questions that demanded answers, but she said she had a lot of work to finish before dark. But before she left, she said, "I understand how you feel. Every newcomer has questions. I promise I will provide answers in the morning. Until then, please stay in your room."

It was only a little after midday, and I had to wait for the following day to get more answers. I understood that they had other things to do, but it would've been better if they had allowed me to explore my new world on my own. Once again, I had the feeling of being in prison.

Inside the room, I found a note on the bedside table. In big, bold letters, it read: "Welcome to Serenus! What's your name?" And at the bottom, "Please do not roam around at night." Then there was a small sign that looked like a dinosaur. I thought this card could have been an excellent place for some text to introduce me to this world, but there was nothing else on it.

I didn't know my name. Why not? How did I lose my memories? I hoped Amy could shed some light on the matter the next day. Kratos had mentioned that everyone arrived here by boat, which made me wonder if they knew where they came from.

I tried to remember my past, but I couldn't remember anything. I even tried thinking of a name for myself, but it felt meaningless. I had to remember who I truly was. I sat down and thought about why I would head out in the water in such a tiny boat. Was I running from something? Or did someone make me leave? I couldn't remember.

As was expected of me, I stayed inside the room for the rest of the day and spent most of the time looking through the window. I could see a small section of a stone pathway. Occasionally, someone would appear on the path, and I would start watching them intently until they disappeared out of my view. People were busy in their routine lives. They looked comfortable and at ease. Maybe this was a safe place. These people could have behaved in any way, but they were nice to me. I comforted myself with the thought that wherever I had come from, this wasn't such a bad place to be. It could have been a lot worse.

The view from the window became monotonous, and I grew restless. I started pacing in the room. After some time, I stood in the center of the room and stretched my wings. I wanted to be outside and explore the world, but bound by the walls around me, I could only stretch.

I was deep in thought when a knock at the door startled me. It was a kind man who brought my dinner and left with a smile. His smile made me feel better - and safer. A smile from a person I had never met before comforted me. How amazing was that? He smiled, something changed inside my head, and I felt better. Magical!

After reflecting on the impact of the stranger's smile on my mood for a few moments, I reminded myself that it was a common and natural thing. I shook my head, trying to clear my mind of unnecessary thoughts.

The people seemed friendly, but I still couldn't help but feel unsure. It was all so new and strange, and I was still trying to figure everything out. Even though their gestures seemed kind, I knew I needed more time to decide if I could trust them.

Magic... Did people here have magical abilities? I didn't. What could they do? So far, I hadn't seen anything that felt unusual except for the vial that changed colour when I touched it. When Feray held the vial, it became much brighter. Did she have magic? I felt a little scared of her and pushed the thought out of my head.

I went to bed, still very confused and not fully believing the things I had experienced. I dreamed of a sinking vessel, a dangerous whirlpool, and a smiling Albertosaurus. And best of all, I dreamed of flying high above the clouds and over the Rocky Mountains, watching majestic dinosaurs roam underneath.

Ch 02: Introduction

The next morning, I woke up feeling refreshed but still unsure of my surroundings. As I lay in bed, I thought about the dream I had. The sinking vessel and dangerous whirlpool were the scary part. But the smiling Albertosaurus and flying over the Rocky Mountains? That was something else entirely. I was happy in my dream.

I got up and looked outside the window. The sun was shining. The birds were chirping. It was a beautiful day. I wanted to be outside. I wanted to explore Serenus, but I couldn't leave the room. I watched the stone pathway I had been observing the day before. The town was bustling with activity, and people were going about their day, greeting each other with smiles and laughter. I felt a little out of place, but no one seemed to notice or care.

When I answered the knock at my door, I found a cheery-looking Amy standing there. She had brought breakfast along with her notebook and informed me that we would be staying in for a while so she could answer my questions, and then we could go out. She took notes frequently. She looked around my room and wrote something in the notebook. I assumed it was part of her job, so I didn't question it.

Amy initiated the conversation by asking if I slept well and then proceeded to discuss her role. She was Feray's apprentice and was also responsible for introducing newcomers to life on the island. We made our way to the window, where two chairs sat alongside a table. Amy waited for me to pick a seat, and I settled on the chair that offered a view of the outside. Once again, she jotted something down, placed the breakfast basket on the table, and took the other seat.

For the first time, I observed her closely. She was young and not much older than me. Her long brown hair was intricately tied up in a bun. She was pretty slim and had various rings on her fingers. Every ring had leaves in its design, except for one. The exception was a simple ring that featured a large, white, translucent sphere. Inside the sphere, white wisps swirled around slowly, and I couldn't help but wonder what it contained. I observed Amy turning the ring around her finger frequently.

She smiled and asked, "What do you want to start with? Answers or breakfast?"

I replied quickly, "Answers, please."

Amy said, "Okay, first of all, there are no dinosaurs on the island. We have found some fossils, but never a live dinosaur."

I breathed a sigh of relief, but at the same time, I felt disappointed. As scary as the dinosaurs were, it would have been incredible to see and live among them.

She laughed. "Relieved and disappointed is how every newcomer feels after hearing this."

Before I could ask a question, she said, "Every one of us has come to this island just like you did. We heard the warning of a sinking vessel in our dream. Then we woke up to the sound of an Albertosaurus. We found ourselves in a boat and were terrified of a nonexistent whirlpool. Just like you must have, we found a strange poem in our pocket, a mysterious watch on our wrist, and no memories of our past."

She paused, and I couldn't believe what she had just said. Every single one of us came to the island in the exact same way? I couldn't help but wonder where we came from and why.

Amy adjusted her large, white ring and continued, "We have all wondered about our wings and found that the best they can do is carry us over a short distance. We can't fly high up in the sky. Am I right so far? Has that been your experience?" I nodded, and she put a checkmark in her notebook.

Once again, I had just opened my mouth to ask my next question, but she answered it without even hearing it. "No one has stopped at the dinosaur island on their way here. We all woke up only after it was too late to go there. We turned our heads back and watched it disappear behind us as the current carried us forward. Tell me, how amazing were the Rocky Mountains?"

I remembered the scene in my head and replied, "So amazing. So magnificent." Amy slid her notebook toward me and, with her finger, pointed at the text:

So amazing. So magnificent.

I read it and looked at her in wonder. How did she know I would say this?

She continued with a smile, "I have met many newcomers, and in the beginning, everyone asks the same questions. And when asked about the Rocky Mountains, everyone answers using the exact same words. We don't know why, but everyone answers this question like this."

This was so strange. With every answer, it became apparent that I was pretty ordinary. There was nothing special about me. But it also showed that we were all connected in some way.

Unaware of my thoughts, she went on, "Some people believe that the poem is a guide. We are supposed to do things the way they have been told in the poem. They believe it is our mission. But a vast majority believe that it is not like that. There is no mission, and we aren't supposed to walk a predetermined path. After all, the poem is wrong. No vessel has ever sunk. People arrive here, live their lives, grow old, and then die. But yes, it is very mysterious that we start with the poem."

I looked out the window, contemplating her words. I was not convinced that the poem lacked any deeper meaning.

As I looked back at her, she continued, "Over time, we have learned that the best way to live here is by being kind, generous, and accommodating. All of us contribute to this world and, in return, benefit from it. I am an apprentice with Feray, a healer who works with the magical trees. Kratos is a blacksmith. All of us do our part in one way or another. You will be expected to do the same. Every newcomer gets a place on the island. It is their home for as long as they live in peace. We have devised a very fair system to allot land to newcomers. Each next arriver gets the next available plot going away from the village center."

After she put another checkmark in her notebook, she offered, "Now ask me any questions you want, and I will answer as well as I can. But before that, tell me—have you picked a name for yourself? Many newcomers pick a name right away, while some wait to decide later on."

She waited patiently as I processed the information. I wasn't interested in a name. All I wanted was more answers. "Where do we come from?"

Once again, she checked something in the notebook and then gave a short and straightforward answer: "No one knows!"

I asked, the curiosity evident in my voice, "Why did we come here?"

She made yet another checkmark in her notebook. She raised her shoulders in a shrug and shook her head, "We don't know that either."

"Has anyone ever tried to go back and find out?" It bothered me that they did not know these answers. I thought these were the most straightforward and obvious questions. If they had lived here for so long, why didn't they find out?

"Many have tried, but no one has succeeded in going back as much as a single step. The current is too strong to travel against it, but it's not just the water; there is more to it. We cannot even throw a rock back in that direction. There is an invisible barrier that stops anything from going that way. We can move freely on this island, though." Her words carried a tinge of mystery.

As I leaned back in the wooden chair, I rubbed my head and tried to make sense of everything she had said.

"I know it's a head spinner," she added softly, "but in a little while, you will get used to it, and then it won't feel so strange anymore."

"If we can't go back, how about going forward?" I asked.

"Yes, we have tried that as well. And we've found that we can go forward. But no one who left has ever come back. The principle stays the same: we can only go in the direction of the current, and it never changes its direction. It never slows down or speeds up. If someone leaves the island, they leave it forever. Therefore, we don't know what lies beyond, or if there is anything there at all." Her voice carried a hint of sadness.

Every answer brought more questions. "That is so strange!"

She nodded in agreement. "We have looked from the highest points on the island but found no other piece of land around ours. All we can see is a dark curtain that blocks all probing. Those who leave, leave prepared to die, accepting that there is no coming back and that there might not be another island to stop at."

I asked, "But if there is the dinosaur island and then this one, there could be more ahead. I think it is quite possible, don't you?"

She shifted uncomfortably in her chair, the aged wood creaking beneath her. For a moment, she stayed quiet and focused on her rings. Then, with a sigh, she looked up and forced a smile, "You are right, it is possible, but we can't know for sure. And there was no black curtain blocking our view as we travelled from the dinosaur island to this one. But there is one ahead of us. So, things could be different." A sad look took over her face. "We send our dead forward in their boats with gifts and flowers, hoping that they will reach a better place. Everyone arrives in a boat and, unless there is an accident, leaves in a boat. And so, we keep our boats with us for our entire life. This island is our home. Serenus is our world."

It was a grim topic, but judging by her low tone, I felt her sadness had another reason. I asked gently, "Amy, did you lose someone?"

She nodded without any expression on her face. I placed my hand on hers to comfort her. "I'm so sorry, Amy."

She forced a smile. "Thanks. It happened a few weeks ago. I'm sorry if I made you sad. Don't let it dampen your spirits. Our world is so beautiful, and there is so much that will amaze you." She paused for a bit and then continued, "It is important to understand how to live here, and once you learn the basics, it can be a lot of fun." Then she pointed toward the breakfast. "Let's eat now. We can continue our conversation later."

We ate in silence. I kept going over all the strange answers I had received and the new questions they brought.

After breakfast, she wrote a few more things in her notebook. I was very self-conscious because of her studying eyes and constant note-taking, wondering what she might be writing and whether I was behaving as expected, so I asked her about it.

Before she could respond, a small Albertosaurus appeared outside the window. For a moment, it startled me, but then I realized that it was a flat piece of wood that was cut and painted to look like a dinosaur head.

Amy shifted the subject from the island to her notebook. She held it up and said, "This is a part of my job. I'm supposed to observe every newcomer and analyze their personalities. I'm glad you asked because it is important to understand. In the beginning, almost everyone who arrives here behaves in the same way and has the same questions, but, deep down, we are a little different from each other, and soon after our initial experiences, our small differences send us on very unique paths. We start looking at things in our own way."

She found me listening intently and continued, "For instance, when I came in, I noticed that the window was open. Yesterday, you escaped the island under the waterfall but then came back voluntarily—instead of running away, you wanted to know what was going on. Instead of focusing on choosing a name, you focused your attention on getting answers to your questions. And then your questions about going back and forward confirmed that you have an exploratory mind."

I nodded. She continued with a smile, "When I became sad, you felt my pain and tried to console me. This tells me that you are sensitive and empathetic, and your first instinct was to somehow make me feel better."

I smiled back, happy that she had felt my care. She went on, "We do our part by giving a good welcome. The first experiences in the life of a newcomer are the most impactful, and we try to do the best we can. Good experiences make good people, and it is easier to be nice today than to deal with a dangerous person later on."

She glanced at her notebook and added, "Please understand that I am not judging you. My goal is not to decide whether you did something in the right or wrong way. For example, you were awake and ready to meet me when I arrived. Instead, you could have been sleeping, as many people are, and that's perfectly alright. It is a lot to take in, so many people have trouble falling asleep for the first few nights, and that's why they wake up later in the morning. This analysis is just a starting point, and nothing we learn at this stage is certain. Over time, you will find what interests you, which will shape your life's direction. This personality analysis also helps us to give you the right job, the one that matches your interests."

I was very impressed to hear about their arrangement regarding land allotment, providing a good experience, personality assessment, and work assignment. But the presence of an invisible barrier around the island was hard to believe.

Then I recalled how guardians had surrounded me upon my arrival. They had threatened me with their spears and put me in prison under the waterfall, then they tested me to see if I had magic. That was definitely not a good experience. It wasn't friendly or welcoming at all.

I asked, "Why was I tested for magic?"

Amy responded casually, "Each one of us is different from others, and very rarely, someone arrives with abilities we cannot explain. Those people need a different starting environment and orientation."

"What kind of abilities do people have?"

"Feray can work with light. I can, too, though I am still learning to control it better. Another person here can feel what others are feeling."

Amy paused as someone knocked at the door. She carried her notebook with her, opened the door, and handed it to someone outside. Then she turned around and asked, "Do you want to ask more questions?"

Before I could answer, she opened the door just a little, peeked outside, looked back at me, smiled, and said, "Whenever you have a question, you can come to me. Let's go out now."

I was happy to hear that. I wanted to go out and see the world. I got up quickly and followed her out the door.

The moment I stepped outside, I found the entire village gathered there. Everyone screamed, "Surprise!" followed by many cheers, whistles, and horns. A rhythmic drumbeat filled the air. It startled me at first, but I recovered quickly.

With wide eyes and a puzzled smile, I watched as they split into two groups, leaving a path in the middle that led to the village center. Amy and I walked toward it as the crowd cheered and danced on both sides.

It was hard to contain the excitement that filled my heart with their generous hospitality, and I thanked everyone. There was a seating area in front of a makeshift stage. Amy brought me to the front row. Behind us, the Seren started taking seats.

I couldn't believe what was happening. It felt incredible. They were going above and beyond, trying to give me the best early experiences possible.

I sat down and asked Amy when they had prepared for this. "Yesterday evening and today while we were chatting inside," she answered with a big smile.

I looked at everyone behind me, happily thanking them with a smile and a nod.

The music stopped, and a loud voice from the stage captured my attention.

"Welcome, people of Serenus and our newest comer!"

A massive roar from the crowd followed. Goosebumps of excitement rose on my skin.

After the noise subsided, the person on the stage continued, "Welcome..." He glanced at Amy's notebook and resumed, "Welcome, newcomer! We are delighted to have you. On behalf of the entire village, I welcome you to Serenus, the land of peace. We hope you will live a happy and healthy life."

He paused for a moment as the crowd clapped.

Then he continued, "Ladies and gentlemen, our drama club is ready to entertain you with their outstanding performance. Please enjoy!"

Loud cheering and clapping followed his announcement and continued for some time but then quieted down to a sudden hush as the music started again.

Many boys and girls ran onto the stage from one side. They were holding boards with waves painted on them. Two girls arrived carrying a boat from both ends, rocking it on the waves, with a boy pretending to be sitting in the boat, asleep.

The ones carrying the waves started chanting:

"Your vessel is sinking; survive the tides.

The end is coming; open your eyes."

The sleeper in the boat moved but did not wake up. The waves continued their chant more forcefully.

"Your vessel is sinking; survive the tides.

The end is coming; open your eyes."

The boy moved again but still wouldn't wake. The crowd laughed.

After a few more attempts and bursts of laughter, a girl ran on the stage with the wooden cut-out of an Albertosaurus head that I had spotted earlier outside my window. She let out a loud scream right next to the sleeper. The crowd laughed hysterically as the noise startled the boy, and he almost fell out of the boat. He balanced himself clumsily and looked around, acting scared.

Then he checked his watch and searched his pockets. He found the poem and read it out loud, looking confused. He looked around, scratching his head, rocking in the boat comically.

The entire village laughed. And I laughed with them.

The boy in the boat leaned forward as he spotted something in the distance. With squinted eyes, he kept looking ahead.

Gradually, the waves started walking off the stage to one side, and from the other side came the trees. The newcomer watched them in amazement. He left the boat, which started heading back and out the same way as the waves. From behind the trees appeared people of the island who greeted him warmly.

It was my story, but also everyone else's story. I knew this part but was eager to see what would happen next.

The music became more dramatic, and another newcomer dressed in identical clothes ran out from behind the boy in the boat. I hadn't noticed that there were not one but two boys—or at some point, another one had somehow snuck in and hid behind the first one.

The people who had come to greet the boy, moved back and watched the boys silently.

One of the boys began to water a tree while the other picked a flower and crushed it under his feet. The first boy shook his head in disapproval, but the second one laughed without care.

Dejected, the kind boy returned to watering another tree. The cruel one formed a fireball and threw it toward the tree. The unfortunate tree immediately turned into burnt char.

It reminded me of the burnt part of the island I had seen from my boat. They must have been telling a true story.

The kind boy stared at the other one furiously, but the vile boy remained unaffected and continued laughing wickedly. The kind boy moved forward. The cruel one stepped forward proudly. They circled each other, their worried expressions hinting that something terrible was about to happen.

They lunged at each other, and a fight started. They fought for some time but eventually fell to the ground and lay motionless. The people who stood behind the trees rushed toward the kind boy and were amazed as flowers from the nearby trees began to fall over his body. He moved slowly and, in a moment, was sitting up. The crowd cheered and clapped excitedly.

The evil boy remained motionless on the ground. Some villagers carried him to a boat and placed him in it.

The good boy now stood in the center of the stage. He pointed at the one in the boat and said:

> "I tell you the tale of a miserable soul;
>
> Incarnation of greed, a foolish mole.
>
> Rejected tradition, fell from grace;
>
> His pride, no longer, could he brace.
>
> Reason or caution was not his aim,
>
> But disgust and slur and disdain.
>
> A heart so dark, no light could save.
>
> Destroy the ark, a mission he made.
>
> Blind with hate, he chose a foul play.

Grim his fate, he had to pay.

Pride is hexing, slander and poison;

Let this be a warning, reminder, and lesson."

The waves carried the boat away. The crowd went ecstatic as it left the stage.

All the characters returned for a final bow. I clapped and cheered, appreciating them along with the entire village.

The music stopped, and a girl arrived on stage, carefully positioning herself in the center. She glanced over the crowd and spoke in a dramatic, thundering voice:

"Mysterious start and options countless,

Greedy and proud or caring boundless,

Steal and offend or heal and mend;

What path you intend, my new friend?

The history we witnessed, not worth a repeat.

The comer we observed; a person so sweet.

A thinking mind,

A being so kind,

Has secrets to find,

And release our bind.

This one is a thinker, fair assessment decrees,

Like blessed ones who taught us the magic of trees,

Still only a seed and time he will need,

To unravel the mysteries, a wondrous deed.

The mission is noble and riddles to beat,

I wish you the best; it's no simple feat."

The crowd cheered and whistled as Amy whispered in my ear, "Congratulations, you have been chosen to be a thinker. You should stand up and thank the people."

I stood up and looked from one side to the other, bowing my head in respect and appreciation. The crowd responded with claps and whistles.

Music started again, and a girl sang in her mesmerizing voice. People danced to the rhythmic beating of drums, chatting happily. Many of them came over and introduced themselves. The rest of the day passed in introductions and merry laughter.

I enjoyed meeting Fabio and Misa the most. Amy said that both of them had been friends since they met. Fabio was thin and tall with a broad mischievous smile. His eyes sparkled as he laughed loudly at every small thing. Misa was equally fun but quite the opposite in appearance, being much shorter than Fabio. Framed by her long red curls, her face shone brightly as she talked non-stop. I spent most of the evening with them. They showed me their favourite trail, right in the village center, around the magical trees and back. The trees glowed in the dark, lighting the path in a rainbow of colours. It was an incredible sight. I wanted to know about the trees and their magic, but they said Amy would tell me in detail.

After some time, Fabio and Misa left. I sat with Amy, watching the people laughing merrily, and thought about my work as a Thinker. My mind was full of questions. I had no idea what a thinker was supposed to do. Amy sensed my preoccupation and asked what was bothering me. I told her.

She replied gently, "Do not worry. I will answer all your questions. We still have another day to spend together. The orientation for newcomers lasts for two days."

After the party, I returned to my room in the lodge. I couldn't wait to wake up in the morning and learn more about this island, but it was pretty difficult to fall asleep. I stayed up late, as my mind was busy with excitement, still not fully believing all the wonderful things that had happened during the day. I pondered over the actions of the two boys in the stage performance and promised myself that I would live just like the kind one. The play hinted that something terrible had happened here. I wondered who did that and why. This place was so beautiful, and the people were so kind that it was hard to believe someone could try to ruin it.

Ch 03: Orientation

The next day, I woke up early and went for a walk. I strolled along the same trail that Fabio and Misa had shown me the night before. The trees didn't glow as they had in the dark, but they still looked incredible. The sun was already high in the sky, and the village was bustling with activity. People were going about their daily routines, and I felt like I was part of this community.

I walked around the village centre, observing everything with keen interest. I noticed that everyone had a well-defined role.

Amy found me and greeted me with a smile. "Good morning, my friend!"

"Good morning, Amy. How are you?"

"I'm doing well, thank you. Did you sleep well?"

"Yes, I did."

"Great! Would you like to join me for breakfast?"

"Sure, I'd love to," I replied, curious about what Amy would share today.

"I have good news for you," she announced, smiling broadly. "Your home is ready! You can move in today."

"Really? That's quick!"

The news of getting my own place filled me with joy. She told me we would see my new home after breakfast, so we quickly finished our meal and left.

Serenus Lodge was located right next to the village center, and until now, I had not seen anything else. We followed a path heading out of the village centre. Beautiful wooden homes on both sides. All the houses were similar in size and structure. A circular fence surrounded each home, with an opening in the front for a stone pathway that connected the street to the entrance door. Every house had a front and a back yard, with enough space on the sides to walk around. The beautiful plants and trees that decorated these yards gave each house a unique look and reflected the owner's taste.

Then, I saw a glittering pond fed by a stream. Amy explained that the stream was coming from a nearby lake and that numerous bodies of water were scattered across the island, but they didn't join the water surrounding it.

Once I understood the basic layout of the village, I asked Amy about the magical trees. She replied, "I can show you the trees another day. You will have to experience the magic yourself. Words cannot explain how amazing they are."

"Alright, what is a thinker, and what am I supposed to do?" I asked.

"A thinker is someone who explores the concepts and workings of things and tries to understand how we can use that understanding to our advantage," Amy explained. "The thinkers of the past discovered how to use the power of the magical trees. But there are still so many unanswered questions. Thinkers focus on those questions and try to find answers."

"So, what questions should I try to answer?" I asked.

She laughed at my question. "The choice is yours. You'll come across many mysteries. Pick the ones that interest you. But remember, it's still early, and you have plenty of time to figure things out. Wander through the village and the forest, and discover what catches your curious mind."

"I wish I knew which question I was meant to answer. It would have been easier that way."

"Give it time. Let the answer come to you. Until then, enjoy this place, make friends, and learn what we already know."

"What about the mystery of where we come from?" I knew this was a complicated question, and as soon as I asked, I doubted I would find an answer.

Amy shared my uncertainty and said, "That's a huge challenge. There are no clues. Where would you even start? I recommend setting aside this particular question. Focus on the many things that can improve people's lives." She paused, studying my reaction before continuing, "Start with smaller mysteries, and maybe one day you'll be able to find answers to the big questions too."

By then, we had arrived at a wooden boardwalk, and across it stood a lone house on a raised mound, with no other buildings nearby. In the front was a low-lying swamp with tall, overgrown grass covering most of the land, reaching the base of a steep hill in the distance. Behind the house lay a slightly elevated, muddy forest.

Amy informed me that this was my home. I was very disappointed. I had seen so many beautiful houses on my way here that the view of my own dampened my spirit badly. It could have been the worst place for a home. Amy was also looking around, shaking her head.

Just moments ago, we had crossed a serene river, and I wished I could have a house near the soothing sound of water flowing over rocks. It was hard to feel happy about this place, but I managed an awkward smile and went inside to inspect my new home.

Inside, a large window offered a generous view of the swamp and the hillside. In one corner stood a stone fireplace facing the open space in the center, with two chairs on a circular rug. There were no rooms like those in the lodge. A table and chair were situated beneath a raised wooden bed. The space was simple but comfortable.

Amy reminded me that the process of allocating land was fair. I received the next available spot. She pointed out a few positive aspects of the location. She said thinkers often preferred a tranquil environment, and since the area around the house was so muddy, it was unlikely that more houses would be built nearby. I would have the entire space to myself.

Despite her attempts to cheer me up, I couldn't deny the reality – I had received a swampy yard with no houses for company. I tried to assure her it was okay but knew she could see through the lie.

To change the subject, she showed me a framed poem hanging on the wall that the girl on stage had read to announce my role as a thinker. Carved into the wood, it was a gift from Kratos, the kind blacksmith I had met upon arrival. His generosity shone through once again.

Amy looked out the window to the backyard and said, "Your boat is in your backyard." I walked over to the window and peeked out, her words echoing in my head: Your backyard. It was my backyard. I felt a connection to the place, grateful to have a home.

Then Amy showed me how to start a fire in the wood fireplace. She pointed towards a cabinet and said, "Pots and pans are in there. If you need anything else, you can ask Kratos. He'll help you."

I spotted firewood on the cabinet's bottom shelf and opened a hinged door above it. Inside, I saw pots, pans, and additional utensils.

Then Amy pointed to the table under the bed. "You'll find some papers and a pen there. Aidas makes paper from various plant fibres. You can go to her if you need more."

I nodded.

Amy offered to teach me how to make tea. She took some dry leaves from a jar and explained, "These are creeping snowberry leaves. Boiling them in water releases a minty flavour, creating a delicious tea. Adding a few drops of lemon enhances the taste." She added knowingly, "It's good for headaches too. It's a common plant in the area. You can pick the leaves in the forest." I examined the leaves closely, so I could recognize them in the forest on my own.

Once the tea was ready, I sipped it, savouring the minty, refreshing flavour.

As the orientation neared its end, I grew anxious about being left to figure things out on my own. Amy told me about many people who could assist me with various problems.

She concluded with, "You can eat at the village center, though most people prefer to make their own breakfast in the comfort of their home. The cooks at the village kitchen can share recipes for a simple and healthy breakfast."

A loud knock rapped at the door. I opened it and was delighted to find Fabio and Misa, who brought blankets and pillows—a gift from Azar, the wool maker.

Fabio and Misa worked at the forge. They didn't stay long, as they were on a short break from work. They invited me to visit their workplace and left.

Amy extinguished the fire and stood up, inviting me to accompany her for the final part of the orientation. We were going to visit both ends of the island.

First, she took me back to where I had come from. We stood at the water's edge. Then, she picked up a stick and threw it in the air. It flew for a moment before hitting an invisible barrier and ricocheting back. She pulled me down just in time as the stick whizzed over my head. We laughed, tossing various objects at the invisible wall, ducking and dodging as they bounced back.

Amy said this was a game people played here for fun. Then she held my hand, and we waded into the water towards the invisible barrier. We couldn't go any further as a spongy force pushed us back. The harder we pressed forward, the stronger it resisted.

"It's time to visit the other side," Amy announced. "But first, let's eat at the village center. The walk to the other side is longer, and the trip will take us the rest of the day."

After our meal, we strolled along a winding path that ran parallel to the river beyond the waterfall. I noticed a few bridges crossing the river, but we stayed on our side. We encountered many Seren during our walk. They were returning from the Dark End. That was what they called the island's end on this side.

Once we reached our destination, I understood the reason for its name. The barrier here was a dense, foggy black wall, making it impossible to see anything beyond it.

I observed people playing games here too, but the game was different on this side. Instead of bouncing back, the thrown objects made a swishing sound as they passed through the barrier and were carried away from the island.

Amy tossed a stone. It whistled through the air, slowing down to match the speed of the invisible current before continuing at a constant pace until it vanished from sight.

The current carried rocks thrown into the water while the invisible wind carried away objects tossed into the air. And soon after breaching the barrier, they disappeared into the black fog. All we could see beyond was complete and utter darkness.

A person brought some garbage and threw it into the water. Amy informed me that this was how they kept the island clean. The water carried all unwanted things into the dark.

We threw many sticks and stones, finding the activity quite entertaining. The swishing sound was pleasing to the ear, and I found myself wanting to do it over and over again.

Amy cautioned, "Remember not to enter the current. We can

move forward but cannot return."

With that, the orientation concluded. After enjoying a bit more at the Dark End, we headed back to the village center. The sun was setting by the time we reached. We shared one last meal together.

Starting tomorrow, I was to be on my own without a guide. Amy left after dinner, inviting me to seek her help whenever needed. I expressed my gratitude for her kindness.

After she left, I sat alone, looking around nervously. A whole world surrounded me. I could go anywhere and do anything, but I felt empty and lonely. What was I supposed to do? I decided to head home before it grew too dark. The long walk back to my solitary house only intensified my sense of loneliness.

I didn't feel prepared to be on my own yet. The walk in the dark frightened me, and I found myself quickening my pace. By the time I reached home, I was so scared that I couldn't shake the feeling that someone or something was following me. I knew nobody was there, but I couldn't push the thought from my mind. Fear propelled my steps, and every little sound made me jump and glance over my shoulder anxiously. My heart pounded in my chest. I hugged myself defensively as the distinct smell of the swamp served as a haunting reminder of its eerie presence. I practically sprinted to my door, flung it open, rushed inside, and closed it behind me. The safety of the walls provided some comfort.

It took some time to calm myself. Before night sucked all light,

I started a fire with some effort and then sat in a chair facing the fireplace. The fire's warm glow made me feel even safer.

When I grew tired of sitting, I glanced out the window. The darkness outside was unnerving. I closed the window and stepped away.

Exhausted and drowsy, I was still afraid of the dark. I lit a candle before extinguishing the fire in the fireplace, letting it burn for a while as I lay in bed with my eyes open.

The flickering candlelight made the room feel cozy yet eerie, casting dancing shadows on the walls. I had stayed alone at the Serenus Lodge without fear, but I felt strangely scared in my own home.

To distract myself, I listened to the sounds outside. These were the same noises I had heard the previous night, but they felt more mysterious this time. I felt vulnerable—unlike last night, I wasn't in the village center surrounded by other homes.

I knew the night sounds came from crickets, chorus frogs, and owls that hooted occasionally. But tonight, I heard other sounds, too: one resembled a squirrel or another rodent scurrying through dry leaves, and another was like tapping or clicking, as if something was bumping into another. I tried to make sense of it. There was no pattern to its repetition. Ultimately, I convinced myself it was just the wind causing these noises. Nothing to worry about, I thought, trying to reassure myself.

When my attempts to dispel my fears failed, I hid under the thick blankets and eventually fell asleep.

In the morning, Kratos and Amy arrived with breakfast. Amy was concerned that newcomers could feel scared being alone in their new homes, even when surrounded by other houses. My home was isolated and near a swamp.

She was correct; I had been afraid but didn't tell her. I thanked Kratos for his gift of the carved poem in a hanging frame. He smiled at me but glanced around with disapproval. He didn't like the location of my home either.

After breakfast, we walked to the village center at Kratos's invitation. Amy left for Feray's yard while Kratos and I continued to a larger building. Two armed men guarded its entrance. They recognized Kratos, greeted him respectfully, and stepped aside to let us in.

Inside, we met an elderly woman. She had a kind and graceful face, and her voice carried wisdom as she spoke. She greeted us warmly, and Kratos told her about the swamp near my home. He was angry at the builders for constructing my house in an undesirable spot.

The old lady asked us to wait as she sent a guardian to summon the builder to explain his choice of location.

As we sat waiting, Kratos invited me to his forge, telling me I was welcome to visit him anytime. He also introduced me to the kind old lady. She was Alev, one of the village elders. People came to her when they needed help resolving problems.

Soon, the builder arrived. He bowed his head to greet Alev respectfully. When informed about our concerns, he said, "Each house must be built on the next accessible site large enough for the building and the yards. The pathway needs to remain clear in all seasons." He turned to me and asked, "Is your house and yard not the same size as the others, or is it not accessible?"

Kratos addressed the builder, "Why did you have to build near a swamp and so far from the other houses?"

The builder responded calmly, "I remember the entire set of guidelines I must follow. Nowhere does it state not to build near a swamp. There is also no mention of it needing to be close to other houses."

Kratos was not satisfied with his answer. He turned his argument toward Alev, "How is this a good experience for a newcomer to live alone near a swamp? Our guidelines should be secondary. The primary goal is to provide a good experience."

Alev thought for a moment. Then she asked the builder, "It's clearly not a place you would have wanted to live when you were a newcomer, right?"

The builder's face turned red with embarrassment. He nodded silently. Since they agreed the place wasn't suitable for living in, I hoped they would give me a different house, but Alev's words dashed my hopes.

"We cannot move Seren around once a piece of land has been allotted. That will cause many to want a different house. It will bring more bad feelings than good." She turned toward me and said gently, "You will have to stay at the house assigned to you. I am sorry for the discomfort you must endure, but we have no other choice."

She addressed the builder, "You need to ensure that each new house is built in a place that doesn't create such a negative experience."

Lastly, she spoke to Kratos, "You are a wise man, Kratos. You understand we cannot change the allocation without creating a bigger problem. But now that this issue has been raised, it won't happen to another."

Kratos was unhappy but accepted Alev's reasoning. I felt disheartened by the decision. But there was nothing to say. We thanked the lady and left for the village center. Before parting, Kratos offered to send someone to stay with me if I was scared, just for a few nights until I felt comfortable. I assured him I was okay. It was my home now, and I had to adjust to living alone. I hid my fears and thanked him for his efforts.

After Kratos left, I stood alone in the village center. I wanted to explore the village, so I ate lunch and wandered around. I saw farmers tending to their crops, shepherds herding sheep, and carpenters sawing wood. After the long walk, I picked up some food from the kitchen for the night and returned to my home to explore the surrounding area before dark.

There was plenty of daylight left when I reached home. After putting my dinner inside, I inspected the front yard. It was bare. No plants or flowers. I planned to plant some soon.

Then I stood in the middle of the yard and spread my wings. They pushed the air down as I flapped them, creating a rustling sound. I felt lighter, but my feet stayed on the ground. I tried several times but soon grew tired. I had not seen anyone use their wings. Why did we have wings if we couldn't fly? Another mystery to solve.

I walked to my front door and sat down. The cattail grass in the swamp swayed gently in the breeze. The distinct smell of the wetland added to the spooky feeling. After sitting there aimlessly for a while, I went inside and made tea.

Then, sipping tea, I examined the backyard. A stone pathway led me from the front door to the side and back, reaching the center of the yard. Wild plants grew all around. My boat was chained to a fence post. The wooden fence was new, and it disturbed the plants, but the rest of the yard was overtaken by wild vegetation. I made a mental note to clean it up soon.

After putting the empty cup inside, I walked across the wooden boardwalk toward the unoccupied new houses. These were to be awarded to the next newcomers.

These homes looked much safer and more welcoming compared to mine. I felt jealous. I wished I had arrived just one newcomer later. Then I would have lived there instead.

I continued walking until the path ended near a forest. Builders hadn't cleared this area yet. I spotted some snowberry plants and picked a handful of leaves. Then I returned home, washed the leaves, and left them out to dry.

With nothing else to do, I sat on a chair and listened to the wind outside. It was a windy day, growing stormier by the minute, making it impossible to do anything outdoors. I decided I would go out and meet other Seren tomorrow and explore what exciting things could interest me. I needed to find an intriguing question to answer.

Outside, the wind grew louder and more forceful. Then came the rain. It was incredible. The raindrops fell on the roof in a continuous volley of musical notes. I stood by the window and enjoyed my first rain as it got heavier and more intense.

When the rain started, everything else became quiet. The creatures living in the swamp fell silent. I imagined they, too, must be enjoying the sound of the howling wind and the rain splattering in the mud.

Gradually, it turned dark and cold, so I started a fire and realized I would soon need more wood. I had to figure out where to find it.

I grabbed a paper and pen, preparing a list of things I needed to do—chores to maintain my home and unanswered questions I had encountered.

Then, on a new piece of paper, I wrote:

All of us came in a boat carrying only a poem and a watch. We have wings, but we cannot fly. We do not know where we came from or what is next. And we do not know why we are here. We can live here, grow old, and then die. I know things that no one told me. I know the names of things, I know that it is raining outside, and I know how to write and that I can write on paper with a pen, but I don't know many other things, like why I have a watch that shows a whirlpool. And how did I know that it was called a whirlpool? I need to find out how I know the things I know. And I need to find out the things I do not know.

I read the poem a few times and placed it on the table with other notes.

Then, I settled in the chair, staring at the fire in the fireplace, listening to the rain outside, and realized that Amy's assessment was correct. I was a thinker. I needed to know things I didn't know. Not knowing bothered me. But perhaps it bothered others as well; it was possible that everyone thought about these things but never found the answers.

I had to find the answers. It was my job.

I recalled the poem and decided I would ask others what they thought it meant. It sounded like a mission, instructions I needed to follow. But Amy had said that it was not the case.

The storm continued into the morning, and I woke up to the

noise of the wind and rain. I had nothing to eat for breakfast. Amy had been bringing it every day, but now I had to do it myself.

I made tea with the last of the firewood and waited for the rain to stop. Looking outside the window, I saw the swamp was filling with water. More and more water cascaded down the hillside. Soon, I could only see the tips of the cattail grass.

I peeked outside the window to check the boardwalk. Thankfully it was not flooded. If the rain didn't stop, it could submerge the path. The thought worried me, but I reminded myself that at least I had a boat.

There was no telling how long the rain would last. I needed to be better prepared, so I made a list of essential items to keep at home. Even if the rain cut me off from the rest of the village, I should be able to survive without any problems. Food was at the top of the list, followed by firewood.

Thankfully, the rain stopped soon, and I headed out for the midday meal.

In the kitchen, I met the cook, who kindly showed me how to prepare my breakfast. It was quite simple. Every meal consisted of warm bread, fresh vegetables, and fruit. Herbs and spices added aroma and flavour. The recipes were easy to make. He gave me enough ingredients to last a few days.

Firewood was collected and dried at a nearby stockpile. I carried some in a cart and then returned the cart.

Next, I went to the magical trees to meet Amy, but she wasn't there. Feray met me at the door of her house as she was heading out. I was hesitant to ask about her work because of her cold behaviour a few days ago, but my curiosity got the better of me. Gathering my courage, I asked, "Can you tell me about the magical trees, Feray?"

She responded half-heartedly, "Yes, I can, but let's be quick about it. I have a lot to do." I followed her like an unwanted guest.

We stopped before entering the circle of trees. Feray said, "These are Lighttrees. The seven trees in a circle around the white one - the Moontree. Each produces different coloured flowers and has a unique magical effect. Six of the trees in the outer circle are the same size, but the seventh has only two trunks and forms an arch that serves as the entrance to the circle. As you can see, the Moontree is much larger and taller. It is the one the other trees rely on. We believe it is the mother, and the seven are its children."

We walked to the arched entrance. The branches overhead intertwined, creating a beautiful canopy. Unlike other trees, the flowers on the arch tree were in a gradient of colours, changing from deep indigo to vibrant violet to rich red.

The entrance opened into a spacious yard I had walked on with Fabio and Misa. This area formed the inner circle around the Moontree. Each of the six trees had an opening facing the inner circle, and to our right was the tree with red flowers.

Feray walked toward it and went inside. I followed. The first thing

I noticed was that it wasn't a single tree. Six trunks stood like sturdy pillars, expanding the ceiling formed by the intertwined branches to an incredible width. These pillars made a circle around an open, brighter area.

In the center was a bulb—a single massive fruit. Branches from all pillar trees came to it from above, hanging it just barely touching the ground. Surrounding it were tables and benches. I went closer for a better look. The bulb glowed and emitted a soft red light, bathing everything in a warm, fiery hue.

I looked around in disbelief as Feray explained, "The flowers on the six pillar trees collect the light and store it in the bulb in the middle. People sit on the benches and absorb the light to receive each tree's magical benefit. Except for the entrance arch, each tree is the same. A bulb in the middle, surrounded by a seating area which is encircled by the six tree trunks."

She pointed to the shelves between the trees. "One opening to walk into the tree chamber, and the rest are filled with shelves to store the light vials."

Tall, wooden shelves stood between each tree trunk, leaving one opening from where we entered the tree chamber. Hundreds of glass vials, filled with glowing red light, lined the shelves neatly.

My curiosity was piqued, and without thinking, I went closer and touched one.

"Careful! It's fragile and very precious," Feray warned urgently.

I pulled my hand back and stood away from the shelf. "What are these?"

"These vials contain the sunset light. We store it until we need to use it. The trees continuously collect the light in the bulb until it is full. But when there is no sun for a few days, the bulb loses its glow and needs to be refilled. It's my job to collect more light in the vials for when the tree runs out or if I need to use it away from the tree."

"Sunset light? In a vial?"

Feray answered while carefully arranging the already organized vials. "The light of the sun when it sets. Where else would you put light except in a glass vial?"

I couldn't believe what she said. It seemed to defy everything I knew, but then again, how much did I know? "We can store light in glass vials?"

"Not everyone can do it, but I can. Though it's not easy—the timing is critical. A little early or a little late, and you'll get the wrong colour. I have to wait patiently until it's the right shade. The sun gives this particular hue for a cruelly short time."

Feray's demeanour changed. Earlier, she was cold, but now she was excited and happy as she started telling me about her work. She seemed proud of it. I liked this side of her.

She took a tiny vial from a shelf and held it in front of me. "This is how much I get in one sunset." The vial was smaller than my palm. I glanced at the shelves and wondered how long it must have taken her to collect this much light.

"What do you do with it?" I asked.

"I am a healer. I use the lights to heal the Seren." Feray replied.

"Healing by sunlight? How is that possible?"

She put the vial back and said, "The sun gives life to the living. It can also heal. I collect and use the lights to heal people." She spread her arms to point at the trees and said, "Don't they grow from a tiny seed into these giants in the presence of sunlight? Can any living thing go on its journey of life without it? No sunlight means no life. The Redlight helps heal ailments of the blood. If someone loses blood, the sunset light will help them regain it quickly."

Feray had now transformed into an enthusiastic teacher. "Come. I'll show you the other lights I've collected. You'll be amazed to know what they can do." She put the little vial back, and we went out. Next, it was the Orangetree.

We entered the chamber. It was a complete replica of the red one, except for the colour of the flowers, the hues emanating from the fruit bulb, and the matching glowing vials. It was equally mesmerizing. I watched the bulb in the center with swirls of orange light inside as Feray said, "Orangelight gives strength to mind and body."

She continued as we approached the Yellowtree. "These trees

are ancient. Who planted them and when is a part of lost history. They have been helping healers for as long as we remember. Yellowlight strengthens creativity and imagination. Thinkers prefer to spend time in its chamber when they need to think outside the box."

The mysterious ancient trees fascinated me. I was especially thrilled to learn about Yellowtree and decided to visit it soon. It might push my imagination enough to come up with a question worth answering.

The next tree we visited was green. I was surprised to see green flowers. I had strongly associated green with leaves, so seeing green flowers was a remarkable experience.

Feray told me about the healing effects of the Greenlight. "Green brings clarity to mind. It's another tree that thinkers like to spend time in. Sitting under the Yellowtree can make your thoughts a bit too adventurous, taking you to strange places. I recommend visiting the Greentree afterward to find clarity in your new ideas. Thinkers can receive this tree's benefits much more than others, allowing them to understand concepts that may otherwise seem beyond their ability."

I listened to the information attentively and realized that visiting these majestic trees was a part of my work. I looked forward to coming here often. I knew I would love it not just for my work but also to cherish the beauty of this place. With another look at the vials of the cool Greenlight, I walked out after Feray.

Then we entered the blue chamber, and Feray asked me how I felt. I knew why she asked that. We had just come in, but I felt different almost immediately. Calm and peaceful. The feeling struck me. I told her so, and she was satisfied with my answer.

"Yes, Bluelight brings peace of mind. The lights don't just heal the body, they also heal the soul, and different lights affect us in different ways. The villagers come here often to sit under the trees. They stay in the chambers, and these lights heal them, uplift their moods, tame their tempers, enhance imagination, provide clarity of thought, and make them energetic."

The mysterious ancient trees fascinated and surprised me. They probably intrigued Feray even more. I asked her if that was why she became a healer.

"Being a healer is not a choice. I had the ability, so this is my job. Amy also has the ability, but she is still learning," Feray explained as we entered the last tree in the circle—the Indigotree.

It reminded me of the tree on the island under the waterfall, which had been used as my prison room, though it couldn't keep me in. It seemed absurd to use such a place as a prison. I wanted to ask Feray about it but didn't want to interrupt her, so I left the question for later.

"What does this light do?" I asked instead.

"Indigolight provides self-control. This tree can be beneficial for people who have trouble organizing themselves." Her rushed answer made me feel she didn't seem very impressed by the healing effect of this tree.

Amy's voice suddenly interrupted us. "Feray! Where are you?"

We walked out of the tree chamber. I greeted Amy. She smiled and spoke to Feray, "Kratos says the project is on schedule. He wanted to know if you would like to come and ensure things were going in the right direction. And he wanted me to send the new-comer over to his forge."

We had seen all the tree chambers except the white one. It stood tall in the middle, surrounded by other large trees, still overshadowing them with its expansive size.

Feray looked at Moontree. I followed her eyes, hoping she would show me its chamber. The white flowers shone in the bright sunlight, giving it an ethereal glow. To my disappointment, she turned away from it and walked to her home outside the Tree Circle. Amy and I followed her to the wooden house.

As Amy and I followed Feray, she turned around and said, "I have work to do. Go with Amy. She will take you to Kratos."

I thanked her for showing me the Tree Circle and left with Amy.

Amy and I walked toward the village center. She pointed to a path and said, "Kratos's forge is through there. I need to get back to Feray. Do you think you can go by yourself? Just follow the path, and you will be there. It isn't too long."

I thanked her and walked on. The sounds of hammering and clanking of metal tools filled my ears, signalling that the forge was close by.

Soon, I entered an open area featuring a large workshop with a blazing hearth at its heart. Two long buildings with spacious verandas stood at the back. Kratos and another man were working, taking turns hammering a long piece of metal. When Kratos saw me, he left his work to greet me.

"How's it going?" he asked gently. I appreciated his kind tone. Though most people were welcoming, Kratos seemed especially warm.

We navigated around the metal structures scattered across the forge as he showed me around. Many people were working at various stations, crafting new metal parts. Kratos introduced me to his apprentice, Idir, a strong young man with a big smile. Together, we ventured out into the yard.

One building at the back served as an armoury, but to my surprise, it housed no weapons. Kratos explained, "We used to make weapons and armour in the past, but they are not needed anymore. The guardians already have everything they need. Occasionally, someone comes with a loose joint or a broken chain, and we fix it, but that's all. We are using the armoury to store our tools and raw materials."

The other building stored firewood and coal. With that, the tour concluded, and we returned to Idir. He was still hammering the iron piece, shaping it into a rectangle. I observed his work for a while before turning my attention to the metal structures piled around the workplace.

Kratos explained, "We are working on a big project that Feray designed. And it's about the right time too. We were getting bored of doing the routine things over and over again."

"But what is it?"

He laughed. "I've been wondering the same thing. Feray didn't explain it. She just sent me the designs. She says it is supposed to be a surprise."

"She calls it her special project," Idir chimed in. "We are very excited to see how it turns out."

Kratos and Idir resumed their work, and I went to meet Fabio. He was focused on a part but paused when he saw me. I didn't want to bother him, but he didn't seem to mind and accompanied me to an area with chairs and a table. We sat down. Misa, who was never far from Fabio, raced over to join us. She greeted me and asked how things were going.

We chatted briefly before I inquired about their thoughts on where we came from and what lay beyond the island.

Fabio replied, "No one knows for sure, but everyone has a theory. If you want to hear the most interesting ones, you should go to Qilam. He was a thinker..."

Misa interrupted him, "Qilam has gone crazy. You want him to talk to him for answers?"

Fabio defended himself, "No, I'm just saying that he is really passionate about these questions and has amazing theories." Then he looked at me and added, "But don't believe his words. These questions have made him a little soft in the head."

Misa added, "I don't think you should be talking to Qilam at all. Focus on discovering things that will genuinely help people."

Despite their warnings, my curiosity about Qilam grew. I wanted to meet him and discern the truth from the madness myself.

Dark clouds shrouded the sun, and I could hear a distant rumble. "I think it will rain today," I remarked.

"It is the rainy season. You should get used to it," Fabio responded.

Misa inquired, "Do you have an umbrella?" I shook my head. "You should get one. I think I have a spare one you can take."

As Misa fetched the umbrella, Fabio offered me my first task. "You're a thinker. Can you answer something for me?" Eager to help, I nodded. He continued, "I work at the forge. I enjoy it, but sometimes I wonder if it's the right job for me. Can you tell me how to know if this is what I'm meant to do?"

His question surprised me. I never thought I would be thinking about such questions. I was more interested in the bigger mysteries that surrounded the island. Nonetheless, I promised to think about it and return with an answer.

Misa returned with the umbrella, and I thanked them both before heading home. The day was fading, and darkness crept in.

Once home, I left the fireplace crackling and flickering as long as I stayed awake. Then, I lay in bed, listening to the symphony of crickets, my thoughts filled with magical trees. And, most importantly, the prospect of meeting Qilam. I reminded myself not to believe everything he said. What interesting theories could he have about where we came from? Maybe he knew something, or perhaps he was crazy. I needed to find out for myself.

Ch 04: Stranger Danger

I woke up to the sound of birds chirping outside my window. The rain had stopped, and the air was fresh and cool. I stretched and got out of bed, feeling ready for the day.

As I prepared breakfast, my mind was preoccupied with the thought of meeting Qilam. I poured myself a cup of tea and heated the bread. A few sips of tea were enough to spread the warmth throughout my body. Then I headed out to find Qilam.

The sun was shining, and the air was warm. I walked towards the village center and asked around to find out where I could meet Qilam. Everyone I talked to was surprised that I wanted to meet him. Most said it wasn't worth it. It felt like they were trying to protect me from something he might say, but this made me want to meet him even more. What were people so afraid of? Words didn't scare me. I knew it was my choice to believe him or not.

I learned that Qilam no longer lived in his home. He abandoned it a few weeks ago and now lived in the deeper part of the forest, as he preferred to be alone. He used to be a thinker like me, but his thoughts had become unbearable for people, and gradually, he moved away.

Finally, the cook in the village kitchen provided the information I was looking for. He told me I could find Qilam on a walking trail that led to the deep forest. He asked if I could take some food for Qilam as he had not come in for some in the past few days. I was happy to help. I took the food and left for the trail in the forest.

The Seren probably came here often. The trail was easy to follow even as it twisted and curved around the trees. The dense tree canopies above me didn't let much sunlight reach the ground, and the vegetation was sparse. The forest was more open than I expected. Looking from outside, it looked much more thickly populated, but once I had walked for a bit, there were a lot of open spaces, although the sky was barely visible.

A constant hum surrounded me as I continued walking the trail, looking for Qilam. It was the sound of the wind, birds, and bugs - the sounds of life in a living forest. I had never asked anyone if there were dangerous animals in the woods, and the thought bothered me now that I was all alone.

Thankfully, it wasn't long before I found Qilam sitting under a tree in front of a campfire. He looked up and saw me, and his eyes seemed to penetrate my soul. He was old but looked even older than his age. An unkempt beard and messy hair made him look like a sad, dejected fellow. As I got closer, I was surprised to see that Qilam was not alone. A few men and women sat in a circle nearby, holding each other's hands with eyes closed in meditation. In the middle of the circle were candles and markings on the ground.

Paying no attention to my arrival, they started chanting and humming. I questioned my decision to visit Qilam. Were these people crazy? Should I not have come here? I hesitated for a moment, but my curiosity got the better of me, and I moved closer.

Qilam motioned for me to sit. "We are communing with the spirits of the island," he explained. "They have much to teach us if only we are willing to listen."

I listened to their chanting but couldn't understand the words.

Qilam began to speak, his voice low and hypnotic. He spoke of the ancient spirits of the island, of their wisdom and power. He spoke of the connection between all living things and the importance of respecting the natural world.

As I listened to Qilam's words, I felt a sense of clarity and understanding. He wasn't crazy, as Misa had suggested. He was simply attuned to a different way of seeing the world. And perhaps, just perhaps, he held the key to unlocking the mysteries of the island.

I sat and waited for them to finish so I could talk to him privately. When the ritual ended, and the others left, I moved closer to Qilam.

"So, you want to talk to me?" he asked, his voice deep and gravelly.

I nodded, feeling slightly intimidated. "Yes, I have a few questions."

Qilam gestured for me to take a seat on a nearby log. "I don't have many visitors, especially not ones who bring food," he said, taking the container from me and opening it. "So, what do you want to know?"

I hesitated for a moment, unsure of where to start. "Well, I've heard that you have some unique perspectives on the mysteries of the island. I'm interested in hearing what you have to say."

Qilam chuckled. "Unique perspectives? That's one way of putting it. Some people would say I'm crazy."

I shrugged. "I'm willing to listen and make up my own mind."

I sat by as he ate. I could tell he was hungry, but still, he was more interested in talking. I told him I was a newcomer and was supposed to be a thinker. He stared at me and said, "There are many better things to do. Don't be a thinker."

I didn't expect this answer. "Why not? I like to know things."

He replied, "Everyone likes to know things. What are you interested in knowing?"

I said, "I want to know why we came to this island and what is next. And where do we...."

He interrupted, "People already blame me for Alfred. Do you want me to get in more trouble?"

"Alfred? Who is Alfred?" I asked.

"Who was Alfred? He was a brilliant young man, but he is gone now. Didn't they tell you about him?" I shook my head, and he continued, "He was a woodworker. The best there ever was. Someone so young rarely gets this good at something. And even though he wasn't a thinker, he liked to know things."

I sensed sadness in his words. "Then what happened?"

"He made the biggest boat he could make and left the island in search of what is next. You see, people think I filled his head with these ideas. No, he was way ahead of me in his passion for finding out if there were more islands ahead of us."

He seemed to regret something, or maybe he was defending himself against what others thought of him. Qilam continued, "The entire village thinks he left because of his conversations with me. They don't believe me that it wasn't the case. Didn't they try to stop you from meeting me?"

I told him how people thought his ideas were crazy and that I shouldn't believe what he had to say.

He laughed. "Yeah, crazy theories to explain a crazy world. Maybe the people are right. You are too young. You shouldn't worry about these things."

I explained, "Listening to someone's opinion is not dangerous. No one can force me into believing something I don't want to believe in, and I only believe in things that make sense to me."

He laughed heartily and said, "Ideas can be scary. You are too young to understand. An idea can cut deeper than the sharpest sword. Words are powerful." He paused and then continued in a firm tone, "With words, you can motivate people to believe in lies. You already believe in many lies that they have been telling you. It is amazing how we are so blind yet so proud of our beliefs."

I was confused. Was I proud and blind? "What do you mean? What lies?"

"Go and live an easy life. Don't get entangled in these questions." He tried to push me away, but now I wanted to know even more.

"The more you hide, the more I want to know. I will talk to someone else if you do not tell me."

He replied knowingly, "I know the type... The need to know." He sighed loudly and continued, "But if you talk to them, they will only tell you lies."

"Who are they?" I asked.

Qilam almost yelled, "All of Serenus. The villagers. Every one of them has either been brainwashed or is on the mission to tell lies."

My curiosity was piqued. I needed to know what lies he was talking about. I begged, "Tell me the truth then!"

He frowned and watched me with sharp eyes for some time. I could see that he was fighting an inner struggle about whether to tell me or not. He stayed quiet for a moment but then sat up and said, "Do you know the story of the evil wizard?"

"No! What evil wizard?" I replied.

He breathed out a deep sigh and shook his head. "A powerful wizard lives on this island. His magical abilities are so great that he evades death. Nothing can kill him. He has been caught many times and has been killed too. But he comes back. His goal is to send people in search of more islands. People say he steals the souls of the unfortunate ones who fall for his tricks, which is why he cannot be killed. The prophecy mentions him, remember? 'Catch the wizard; go past the fall.' And to catch the wizard, first, you must know who the wizard is. So many have tried to catch the wizards, thinking it would lead them to another land past the fall. Of course, no one who went can come back to tell us if they did find a new world."

He stopped and found me waiting intently to hear more.

"I believe, and mind you, I am not the only one—many have believed that there is more to this world than we understand. Gods have created more lands, and our purpose is to find a way to those islands. Only the chosen few will ever reach the end. Why else would the gods give us the poem?"

"I don't know. It must mean something," I said.

"Exactly. The villagers want you to live here as if that is the purpose of life. That doesn't make any sense. Why would the gods give us a message that says your world is so vast?" His voice was full of passion now.

His words were so confident that they puzzled me. Why didn't anyone tell me about the evil wizard? But then, Qilam might really be crazy. Or he might be tricking me with his words. I didn't know if I could believe him. Still, I wanted to know what else he had to say.

"What do you think the gods are telling us?" I asked.

He continued in the same passionate tone, "Think about it. Someone created us. They sent us in a boat, and the only things they gave us were a poem and a watch. Why? If I send someone to a world, why would I give them these things? Right? Because they hide answers in them. I would want them to find their way forward by understanding the instructions in the poem. Now, this is where most people differ from my views. I don't think the poem contains hidden clues that must be found. No, the gods wanted to make it easy to understand, so they wrote it simply. I think that the poem's meaning is understood by reading it literally; Our vessel is sinking. This one is obvious. It's not the boat, or they would have said our boat is sinking. The vessel is another word for our body. It's the body that is dying. Surviving the tides means lasting long enough to reach what is next. Some people say tides are the hardships we face in our life. I think it's the tides, literally. The waves are bigger ahead of this island, so we must prepare to survive those dangerous waters."

He stopped and checked to see if I was following. I nodded, and he continued, "The end is coming; open your eyes—this part is a warning that we will not live forever. Our vessel is sinking, after all. Then it tells us to 'live and think, but don't you stall.' We are supposed to do something and not take too long. And what is it that we need to do? 'Catch the wizard; go past the fall.' Is it just a coincidence that a wizard lives here? No! We are supposed to catch him and go forward."

I interrupted his enthusiastic speech. "Why do you think people don't believe in all this?"

His excited tone was replaced with a sombre one. "They have given up. So many used to believe it, but when the wizard proved too powerful to be captured or killed, they started to think that the poem was misleading and the mission was impossible. I don't blame them. We have caught the wizard so many times. We kept him in the prison tree under the fall, but we didn't know what to do with him. He would come back if we killed him or sent him in the dark. Eventually, people stopped believing, and now no one is trying to catch the wizard. And when we are not trying to capture him, he is not attacking us either, so there is peace. Villagers prefer peace over finding answers."

"But you think we should believe in the literal meaning of the poem?" I asked.

"Yes, but I am not claiming to understand it fully. Alfred thought we were supposed to go past the fall since we had already captured the wizard many times. He was a woodworker. He built the biggest boat he could and left the island searching for another land." Qilam's voice became sad.

"You worry that it was a mistake?" I asked.

He responded grimly, "I don't know. It's possible I am wrong about it, and I encouraged Alfred to go into the Dark End. It weighs heavily on my conscience that he may have died in vain. He was friends with Feray's apprentice. Everyone listens to what they think, so they say my words are dangerous for peace on the island. I try to stay away unless someone wants to know what I think because, you know, there is a good chance that what I am saying is right. This island could be a stepping stone to more amazing worlds ahead."

"Where is the wizard now?"

"I believe he is still here, hiding and scheming. He keeps trying to find a way to go forward. While he is mighty in his abilities, you should know that he is basically a coward. He wants others to try to go forward in unique new ways, and only when he is sure that it works will he go forward himself." Qilam finished the story and asked me to head back to the village before it got too dark.

I wanted to hear more, but I did not want to roam in the forest after dark. I left with my head full of new answers and even more questions.

I reached home and stayed in for the rest of the evening, thinking about Qilam's words. If he was right, this island was a temporary place, and we were supposed to go to the next one. But that was risky. It would be a safer choice to stay here, but then I may never find the answers.

After thinking for hours, I decided I was too young to go on a mission to find new lands. It was a fact, after all, that even the critters in the swamp scared me at night. Catching a powerful wizard and discovering new worlds seemed an impossible task for me.

I stopped thinking about these matters, but before that, I wrote down my newfound understanding on a piece of paper.

Qilam thinks the gods have sent us on a mission. We must catch the wizard and go past the fall looking for new worlds. We are not supposed to stay here for long. The waves ahead are bigger and more dangerous, so Alfred made a big boat and left. He may have died, or he may have found the answers he was looking for. He was Amy's friend, and she thinks he might be dead.

Then I started a fire and sat by it, listening to the sounds outside to take my mind off the topic. It had started raining again, but I was not worried. I had prepared for the rainy season with enough food and firewood to last me a few days in my home. And I had an umbrella to keep me dry if I needed to go out.

It was still early, but the rain made me want to snuggle up in the blanket. The fire burned brightly and kept me warm, and the soft, warm blanket around me felt comforting, even protective.

The sound of footsteps startled me. Someone was coming. I looked through the window and saw a person carrying a lantern walking towards my home. My mind played tricks on me and filled me with sudden fear. The thought of an evil wizard coming to steal my soul made my breathing grow faster. I tried to push back the irrational thought and kept my eyes on the person outside. Soon, I recognized the visitor and was relieved to see that it was Amy. I opened the door to let her in. She left her umbrella on the side and asked if she could stay for the night. I was surprised and happy at the same time.

She made tea as we chatted casually and then came to the reason for her visit. "I heard you were looking for Qilam. Did you meet him?"

"Yes, I met him. He told me about Alfred," I responded.

"Listen, I don't want to tell you what you should or should not do. I just want to share some things that Alfred told me. He was my friend, and we talked about his conversations with Qilam in detail. I tried to stop him from leaving, but he had made up his mind. I'm worried you are on the same path."

I quickly assured her, "Don't worry. I have no intention of leaving the island."

She raised her eyebrows and replied, "That's great to hear. However, I want you to know that Qilam is not as he seems. Alfred told me how Qilam suggested different ways to leave the island and convinced him to build a big boat to survive the big waves. Although Alfred liked the idea, it was Qilam who was behind it."

I interjected, "But Qilam made it sound like he was concerned for Alfred, yet Alfred still wanted to go."

Amy responded firmly, "That's not what happened. I want you to understand that you cannot trust anything Qilam says. He is full of lies. Did he talk to you about reading the poem literally?"

"Yes," I replied.

I was curious to know Amy's thoughts on the matter. Qilam had told me that the villagers were lying, and now Amy was saying the same about him. As I looked at her kind face, I hoped that Qilam was the liar and not her. I had taken a liking to her, and the thought of her deceiving me troubled me more.

Amy continued forcefully, "It's all nonsense! If the gods wanted to give a literal instruction, why use the term 'vessel' for the body? Why say that it is 'sinking' instead of 'dying'? I don't claim to have all the answers, but I want to make it clear that Qilam doesn't know either. Nobody does. I've had numerous conversations with Alfred, and I know how Qilam manipulates people into leaving the island. I don't think Alfred is the only one. Since Qilam started talking about finding more lands, four other people have left the island to light-knows-what fate."

Amy spoke with such conviction that I felt she really cared for my well-being. We continued to chat late into the night, but Amy made it clear that she had come to protect and warn me.

I shared what Qilam said about the evil wizard. She nodded in agreement, "Yes, that is correct, but the wizard hasn't been seen in a long time. The Seren think he may have left the island, or perhaps he's still here, hiding and waiting for another victim to trap. Both the wizard and Qilam are equally dangerous. Both want to send people off the island to see what's next, and both are scared to try it for themselves."

A chilling thought crossed my mind. Qilam had said that the wizard wanted others to try going forward, and only when he was sure it worked would he go forward himself. According to Amy, Qilam was the one convincing people to leave.

"What if Qilam is the wizard?" I voiced my thought in a shivering voice.

Amy laughed. "Honestly, I have thought the same thing many times, but we have known Qilam all his life. He came before me, but people have seen him live among us since he came to the island in a boat. He is a coward and has the same ideas, but he is not evil. He hasn't hurt anyone except with his words. And he does not have magic, so he can't be the wizard."

"How does this test for magic work? And why is the tree under the falls used as a prison?" I had thought about this question so often that I was surprised I hadn't asked it yet.

She explained, "The magic of the tree under the fall stops magical beings from leaving it. Anyone without magic can come and go freely. And it is a prison only in the daytime. At sunset, the barrier disappears, so we cannot keep anyone imprisoned forever."

"But Feray has magic, and she can go in and out?" On the day of my arrival, I had seen Feray enter the prison tree. It was still daytime, and Feray could leave freely.

Amy smiled proudly and said, "That's an excellent observation. Feray could enter and leave the tree because she was wearing a small Moonlight vial in her necklace."

"You are her apprentice. Does that mean you also have magic? What can you do?"

She smiled and said, "Yes, Feray and I can, for lack of a better word, call the light. This ability is our magical power, and through it, we can capture and store it in a vial and then use the light to heal others. We cannot do any other magic."

We continued chatting late into the night, and Amy told me she was very excited about a new project that Feray and Kratos were working on.

She had to go to work early in the morning, so we had to sleep. I slept on the rug in front of the stone fireplace and asked her to sleep in the bed. She hesitated but agreed when I insisted. It was the least I could do to repay her.

As I lay on the rug in front of the fireplace, I couldn't help but think about the conversation I had with Qilam. I wondered what his true intentions were. Dwelling on these thoughts, I drifted off to sleep.

Suddenly, I found myself standing in a dark and ominous forest, feeling the presence of something or someone evil nearby. A voice called out to me, "Come to me, my child. Come to me, and I will show you the way. Do not trust anyone on this island. They are all hiding something from you."

I followed the voice and soon found myself standing in front of an old, decrepit castle. The voice spoke again, "Enter the castle, my child. Enter, and you will find what you seek."

Without thinking, I entered the castle. Inside, I found a dark and gloomy hallway that seemed to go on forever. As I walked down the hallway, I felt the eyes of something watching me. Suddenly, a cackling laugh echoed through the hallway, and a figure appeared before me.

It was the evil wizard from Qilam's story. The wizard had a magical staff. He spoke in a menacing voice, "Welcome, my child. I have been waiting for you. You have something I want."

I tried to run but found myself rooted to the spot. The wizard raised his staff and pointed it at me. A blast of dark energy shot out and engulfed me.

I woke up with a start, covered in sweat. Relieved to realize that it was just a dream, I lay back down, but the image of the evil wizard was still fresh in my mind. I knew that I had to be careful and stay away from Qilam's schemes. The thought of leaving the island now seemed more dangerous than ever.

Ch 05: Friendships, New and Lost

I woke the next day to find that Amy had already left for work. However, before she left, she had prepared breakfast for me and set it on the table. Her kindness made me start the day with a smile.

I thought about the reason for her visit. She wanted me to stay away from Qilam. Last night, I had already decided that I was too inexperienced to go looking for new islands. Now I needed to find something else to occupy my mind. I remembered Fabio's question about how to know if he was doing the right job. While I attempted to think about it, I quickly became bored and decided to think about it later.

The rain had stopped, but water still flowed over the steep wall of the hill, forming a temporary waterfall. The swamp had vanished, and in its place was a pond. I was delighted to be rid of the swamp, even if it was temporary, and I wanted to enjoy the new landscape. I dragged the boat from the backyard and placed it in the pond, using a tree branch as an oar to move around the water. It was so much fun.

I lay down in the boat and tried to recall how I must have felt when I woke up near the dinosaur island, but there wasn't much to remember. It wasn't too warm, and the sunlight felt good on my skin. The waves in the pond were small, but the boat still kept moving. The sound of the waterfall added to the relaxed atmosphere. I wanted to make the most of it before the pond reverted to a swamp, so I stayed on the boat for quite a while.

Lying in the boat and gazing at the sky felt like a luxury. My empty mind kept going back to my work as a thinker. What was I supposed to think about? The only things that I found interesting were dangerous. I had to meet more people and explore the island to find an intriguing question to answer.

Why do we have wings but can't fly? The question flashed in my mind, and I decided to focus on it in the days to come. First, I needed to know what people already knew about wings.

I closed my eyes and imagined I was flying. The slight movements in the water gave my imagination a realistic touch. I felt like I was floating in the air. Small tremors ran through my shoulders as my wings ached to take flight.

Sometime after midday, I got out of the boat, tied it to a tree, and went to the village center for food. I questioned the cook about wings. I was amazed to know that he had been practicing and could hover in the air and cover small distances. He advised me to exercise my wings often so that the muscles could grow strong and carry me in the air for longer.

Later, I met an old lady in the village center. She welcomed the question and gave quite a lengthy response. It was a story that she had heard in her childhood. She said there was a time when we could fly, but slowly, as we became lazy and preferred to stay on the land, we lost the ability. She thought that with some training, we should still be able to fly. With a shake of her head, she concluded soberly, "We have wings, but we don't fly."

After talking to a few more people, I realized that most believed that our lifestyle was too sedentary. We did not exercise enough, which was why our wings could not carry us. But then I met another woman who had been very active all her life. She thought there was more to it. I wanted to hear her theory in detail.

She explained, "Look at the birds and animals. Most living things have so much in common with us: two eyes, one nose, one mouth, two ears, two arms, and two legs. Yes, there are differences, but why are we so similar?" She paused to let the question sink in, then continued, "I think people and animals started from the same thing. Whatever it was, that creature had two eyes, one nose, two ears, etc. Over time, we changed in different ways, and over a much longer time, we have become quite different. I think the creature that we started from had two arms, two legs, and two wings. Later, some of us lost our wings and became animals, yet others lost their arms and became birds. We kept arms and wings too. But as we became bigger and heavier, the wings could no longer carry us. I think eventually we will lose the wings entirely."

Another Seren explained that we were actually sons and daughters of gods. We had wings like gods and could fly around between heaven and land. But when we became mischievous and misbehaved, we were sent down to live on the ground as punishment. The gods ordered the wings to no longer carry us back to the heavens, so they remained with us only as a reminder that we should have behaved better.

The more stories I listened to, the more difficult it became to find the truth. It felt like a dead end, but I couldn't give up. I wanted to find an answer to at least one crucial question. What good was a thinker who couldn't answer anything and just gave up? Of course, I understood that I wouldn't find the answers in a single day. It needed time.

I remembered what Feray had told me about the thinkers spending time in the yellow and green tree chambers. Maybe it was time to take help from the trees. I walked to the Tree Circle and entered the Yellowtree chamber.

Amy and a few others were sitting there quietly. Without disturbing them, I sat on the side and closed my eyes, just like them.

I sat quietly, waiting for the magical effect of the tree to take hold. My focus was on my breathing and the question in my mind. Gradually, my head began to fall backward, and I fell asleep with my mouth open.

I dreamed about the ancient creature that we all began from - the one with arms, wings, and legs. The creature rose from the ground and stretched out its arms, revealing the magnificent wings that it possessed. Suddenly, a brilliant halo of light encircled its head, and I realized that I was looking at a powerful deity. Its eyes bore into mine with anger as it spoke in a language I could not comprehend. In an instant, it banished me to a distant, unknown land far below. I cried out for mercy, but the deity ignored me, disappearing into the light. As I tried to spread my wings and fly back to the heavens, I realized with dread that my wings had lost their power, and I was trapped in the land below.

I was alone in the tree chamber when I woke up; it was getting dark outside, and I had lost track of time. I quickly went to the village kitchen, picked up some food, and hurried home. As I was walking, it started to rain, and by the time I reached home, I was fully soaked. After changing into dry clothes, I started a fire and sat by it, lost in thought about the dream. Unfortunately, I couldn't recall most of the details. I went to bed late that night, still thinking about the mysterious dream.

Once again, I was transported to a strange world. This time, I flew high in the sky with wings as wide as an eagle's, soaring over mountains, forests, and rivers, feeling free and weightless.

Suddenly, the scenery changed, and I found myself in an underwater world. The sky was dark, and the water was murky. A massive creature swam towards me, with the same features as the ancient creature I had dreamt of before. Its wings were enormous, flapping like a bird's. It stopped in front of me and stared at me with its large, glowing eyes.

The water started to rise rapidly, and the creature's wings wrapped around me. It lifted me up, and we flew high above the water. The rain poured down heavily, and the wind was fierce. Villages below me were engulfed by the flood, and people were screaming and running for their lives.

My heart pounded in my chest as the world changed again. I was now standing in front of a witch who told me what my dream meant.

"The flood is a symbol of change and transformation," she said. "Your dream might be telling you that a great change is coming, and you need to be prepared for it."

Her words gave me chills, and I wondered what was coming my way. The witch continued, "The ancient creature in your dream represents your inner self, the one who guides you through life. Its wings symbolize freedom, and the fact that it lifted you up during the flood shows that it will guide you through any challenges that come your way."

I listened intently, feeling both afraid and comforted at the same time.

"Remember to trust your instincts and listen to your inner voice," the witch said before disappearing into thin air.

I woke up with a start, my heart racing from the intensity of the dream. The sun was shining outside, and I could hear birds chirping in the distance. As I got out of bed, I felt a sense of excitement and anticipation for what was to come. The dream had given me a newfound sense of purpose, and I was ready for whatever changes lay ahead.

Someone knocked at the door, and I found the builder standing outside. He had come to check if my home was in danger of flooding. The river had changed direction. The heavy rain overnight had caused the water to overflow the river banks and change its path over the hill toward my swamp.

After a thorough inspection, the builder said, "Congratulations, your swamp problem is over. I believe the change in the direction of the river flow is permanent. The river will now flow over the hill in three waterfalls, each dropping into the swamp, turning it into a forever pond. But there is no danger to the house, as it is on raised ground. The overflow from the pond will go into a ditch that travels under the boardwalk and will meet the existing river, connecting back to it."

It was unbelievable. The swamp in my yard was replaced by a permanent pond and waterfalls. I loved spending time in the water, and the prospect of doing it whenever I wanted was a fantastic surprise.

The surprises for the day were not over. The next one came with Idir. He came to talk to me about adopting a pet. I had never seen a pet in the village, so it surprised me. He said the pets were tiny and had to be kept inside the home at all times. Many people had pets, but I had never visited anyone, so I had never seen one.

I wasn't sure if I could take care of a pet, but Idir tried to convince me, saying it could be a great way to have company when I was alone. I was still unsure but agreed to visit the pet keeper. If I didn't want one, I could leave without adopting.

Idir and I walked to the pet keeper's house. It was full of glass boxes with different animals scurrying in them. All the animals were tiny, so small that I could carry them in the palm of my hand, and they were so cute that I wanted to adopt every single one of them.

The pet keeper said that these animals were too small to survive in the wild. I had to provide for all their needs. They didn't ask for much. Just some attention, regular feeding and cleaning routine, and a box inside the house provided enough for them to enjoy life.

It became tough to choose between them. Eventually, I narrowed down my search to only a handful of options.

Lenni the Llama had light brown fur. It was so small that it slept on the palm of my hand.

Ice Cream was an all-white dog with icy blue eyes and a fluffy tail.

A jaguar was playing in its tiny pond and was very active and fun to watch. I read the name tag on its box and smiled. It was named Patches.

Then there was a monkey named Monkey, a green-eyed owl named Twig, a kangaroo named Pouch, a parrot named Hush, a glass octopus named Sprinter, and a sheep named THE GOAT.

The pet keeper was quite a character and made sure to find the most amusing names for his pets.

In the end, I couldn't decide which pet I wanted and decided to come back another day to make a selection. Idir and I laughed as we remembered what I had said earlier, that I wasn't sure if I wanted one. Now, I wanted many, but as the keeper had explained, it was a big commitment, and I should only pick the one I really cared for. The keeper preferred that we keep the adopted pets forever because they bonded with their owners.

I thanked Idir for bringing me to see the pets. He replied, "Thank Kratos. It was his idea."

I wanted to thank him in person and went to the forge with Idir.

Kratos had been nice to me since the day I arrived, and I wanted to do something nice for him, but I didn't know what. He was hammering a piece of metal while his companions were laying out the finished parts in the yard.

I thanked him for the idea of adopting a pet and then asked directly, "I want to do something nice for you, but I don't know what I can do."

He smiled and said, "You are a thinker, and I have many questions that you can help me with."

I couldn't believe I'd be of any use with my limited knowledge, but I said, "Yes, I would love to help."

He moved away from his work, and we sat on the chairs outside. He said, "I have lived here for a long time, and I try to always do the right thing. I help people when I can, and I work hard at my job, but I am not sure if I am successful in life or not. How can I know?"

I looked at him with wide eyes as he finished. I had not expected such a question, and it reminded me of what Fabio had asked earlier. These questions were very different from what I had hoped.

Kratos and Fabio were much older than me. If they couldn't find an answer, how could I tell them?

Kratos watched me for a bit and said, "You don't have to think about it now. Tell me later when you have the answer."

I promised I would though I worried I might not be able to tell him something he didn't already know.

Kratos moved in his chair and settled comfortably. It was an excellent opportunity to ask some questions. I started by asking him about the watch on everyone's wrist.

"Why do we have a watch? What do you think?"

Kratos raised his wrist, looked at it, and replied, "We don't know."

I wanted more details. "Is it made of metal? Did you try to pry it open and see what is inside it? Maybe we can find something interesting."

"Many have. I have, too. It stopped when I removed the glass from the metal case. There is nothing inside it. Just an empty shell. I'm sorry, but I didn't find anything interesting to tell you."

"Hmm, okay," I said disappointedly.

Kratos continued, "The watch and the boat are very mysterious. We've tried to probe but found no clues."

"What is mysterious about the boat?"

"All the boats look exactly the same. We have put many boats together and inspected them in detail. To the smallest detail, all boats are identical clones and totally indistinguishable from others. It is so strange because we have never found two pieces of wood that look alike. There are always small differences. The lines formed by the wood grain, the position of the knots, etc., give each piece of wood a unique appearance. Whoever made these boats has otherworldly powers and is way more capable than us. Maybe they used magic to create them."

I was getting used to receiving strange information that provided no answers and raised more questions. I listened quietly.

I was a thinker. I was supposed to understand things that others couldn't. So far, I couldn't even come up with a new theory to explain something. Everything I could think of had already been thought of and proved useless. I thought I could try thinking about these things in the Yellowtree or Greentree. I might come up with something new. But then I remembered that I was not the first thinker here. Many must have tried that too. I asked Kratos, "Have the trees helped find any answers?"

He said soberly, "No. Many theories but nothing for sure."

I felt useless. I wanted to play a meaningful role in this world, but I didn't know how I could find a new answer. Everything had been thought about, and there were no clues to follow that could take me on a new line of thought. It felt hopeless. Maybe I could contribute in some other way. I asked, "Can I help around the forge? Is there anything I can do here?"

Kratos replied kindly, "You don't have to do that, but if you want, you can help others move the big pieces."

I thanked Kratos as he returned to his work. I joined Fabio and Misa and helped them move the heavier parts. Every now and then, they would start giggling at a joke the other made. I felt much better now that I was actually helping.

Fabio and Misa were always fun to be around and very easy to talk to. I told them about my dream in the Yellowtree chamber. They laughed, and Misa said, "The Yellowtree is the most fun of all the trees."

I told them I saw Amy sitting there, and suddenly their faces turned sober. I couldn't understand what was wrong, so I asked.

As Fabio stood by with a solemn expression, Misa replied, "She is so sad. I wonder if she will ever go back to how she used to be."

"What do you mean?" I asked.

Fabio answered this time, "Amy had a friend, Alfred. Although they had different jobs, we almost always found them together. They were the loudest and most fun people in all of the village. And they were always up to something adventurous."

I thought of Amy and was surprised that her image in my head did not match what he was telling me. She had always been calm and composed. I just could not picture her as loud, fun, and adventurous.

Fabio continued, "Alfred used to call her Kaur because she was never afraid of anything."

"Kaur?" I asked.

Fabio replied, "Yes, Kaur, meaning the lioness. Kaur was a fearless woman who lived on this island long ago. It's an old story. She defended the village against a powerful wizard."

I nodded, and Fabio continued, "You know how most Seren stay in the village even though the island is so big? Amy and Alfred were not like that. They explored the farthest reaches of the land, always looking for a new experience."

"Then what happened?" I asked sadly.

"Qilam happened," Misa growled. "He became friends with Alfred and convinced him to explore the world beyond this island. Amy tried to stop him, but he left."

Fabio added, "And since then, Amy has changed into this new person. So grown-up-like, boring and serious."

Misa continued, "And it's not only that she is mad at Alfred for leaving, but she also blames herself for not going with him."

We stood in silence for a while, shaking our heads in sadness until Kratos's voice interrupted us, and we returned to work. However, the image of a cheerful Amy lingered in my head, and I couldn't help but think that Fabio and Misa's description of her and Alfred was something special. A strong sense of dislike for Qilam began to take root in my mind.

After we finished our work at the forge, we gathered all the tools and put them away in an organized manner. Idir invited me to join them in Bluetree, their go-to place to unwind after a day's labour, and both Fabio and Misa insisted that I come along. They promised to walk me home after dinner.

As soon as I entered the blue chamber, my melancholy mood

dissipated, and I felt happy and at peace, just like my newfound friends. Idir then recounted our visit to the pet keeper, and we laughed at how I didn't want to adopt a pet initially, but later on, I wanted to take them all home.

The more time I spent with my friends, the more connected and content I felt. It was a wonderful feeling to be part of a group, and I slowly felt like I belonged there. However, my thoughts drifted back to Amy, and I couldn't help but wonder how she felt after losing her friend. The memory of their story made me sad again.

Idir's singing stole my attention.

"Under the Whitetree's gentle sway,

All of our troubles fade away

Its leaves and branches, pure and bright

Heal our hearts, restore our might

With every breeze, it whispers hope

And all our fears, it helps us cope

Its magic spreads across the land

Bringing peace with a loving hand

No evil force can stand a chance

Against the Whitetree's joyful dance

It breaks the barriers of our pain

And shines a light on the darkest lane

In its presence, we find our way

To a brighter and happier day

For the Whitetree is more than just a tree

It's a symbol of love and unity"

Idir's talent was awe-inspiring. I loved listening to him sing. Fabio and Misa also listened quietly as he started singing the next song:

"Beneath a red tree's canopy,

All wounds of blood will surely flee.

It has the power to heal us all,

Making us rise and never fall.

Trees of colours, strong and true,

Gifts of nature, pure and new.

A healing balm, both pure and rare,

For mind, body, and soul to repair.

The orange tree bears fruit so bright,

A strong and sturdy tree in sight.

It helps us gain strength from within,

Our minds and bodies can never thin.

The yellow tree is full of surprise,

It sparks creativity in the ones it likes.

Our minds run wild with ideas galore,

Enabling us to create more and more.

The green tree is a sight to see,

It brings clarity and sets us free.

Our minds are sharp, and we can think,

Making us strong and far from the brink.

The blue tree stands tall and strong,

It gives us peace, and we can hum a song.

It brings us joy and calms our nerves,

Our minds at peace, our souls preserve.

Indigo tree, oh, how it glows,

Its power of self-control it shows.

It guides us through the toughest days,

Our paths illuminated in many ways.

Violet tree, full of grace,

Brings a balance to this place.

It realigns us and makes us whole,

Making us feel more in control.

Finally, the white tree of life,

It brings hope and removes all strife.

It heals the soul and gives us light,

Making everything pure and bright.

Trees of colours, strong and true,

Gifts of nature, pure and new.

A healing balm, both pure and rare,

For mind, body, and soul to repair."

His superb singing drew a round of applause from us. Then we started chatting. I told them that I was having trouble with my job as a thinker, and Idir responded with a philosophical answer: "Thinkers don't have a day job. Your job will keep you busy even while you are aimlessly resting. There is a saying about thinkers: 'For ninety-nine out of a hundred days, a thinker appears to be doing nothing, then on the hundredth day, they surprise everyone with a mind-blowing discovery.' The ninety-nine days are hard on the thinker, but the hundredth day pays off."

Misa comforted me, saying, "Don't worry too much. It takes time. For now, just enjoy life."

I recalled Fabio's question. I still hadn't found an answer to it. Maybe it was time to visit the Greentree. "I want to sit under the Greentree for a little while to think about something," I said.

Misa laughed and replied, "Looks like we won't have to wait for a hundred days!" I left them, promising to come back in a bit.

I heard Idir singing another song as I headed out,

"In the land of the magical light trees,

A wizard lived with powers to freeze,

He created a staff, mysterious and rare,

That could take you anywhere.

But beware the invisible barrier,

Around the island, it's a terror,

Beyond its bounds lies the dark end,

Where evil forces descend.

In the heart of the forest, there's a tree,

Yellow its flowers, oh can't you see,

It makes you imagine without a filter,

And your mind races like a helter-skelter.

But beware the invisible barrier,

Around the island, it's a terror,

Beyond its bounds lies the dark end,

Where evil forces descend.

But fear not, my friends, for we have each other,

And the joy of our companionship, like no other,

Let's dance under the light of the Bluetree,

And sing songs full of glee."

Sitting in the chamber lit in green, I focused on a single question: how can one know if their job is right for them? Without thinking,

I closed my eyes and lifted my head up. The Greenlight began to take effect, and I experienced a level of mental clarity I had not felt before. I continued thinking for a long time.

Idir shook my shoulders, and I returned to the chamber, opening my eyes. I was surprised to realize that I not only thought about Fabio's question but also had the answer to Kratos's. I had lost myself in thought and had a conversation within my mind. As I considered one thing, the other me checked the reasoning behind it, corrected me if I was wrong, and showed me a better logic. I accepted the new line of thought.

The experience was so vivid in my head that, unlike the dream under the Yellowtree, I fully understood and remembered it. I contemplated both questions with such a clear understanding that everything became simple and straightforward. It was all so strange, and I felt as though these thoughts were not my own, as if I was thinking with another mind, one that was far more capable and experienced and could see things so clearly. Was it the tree? Was I talking to the tree, and was it sharing its infinite wisdom with me? I didn't know how, but I had the answers I was seeking.

I left with Idir to share the answer to Fabio's question, feeling a renewed sense of purpose and clarity.

Fabio and Misa were waiting outside the tree, and we started walking towards the village center. On our way, I addressed Fabio, "Fabio, I have the answer to your question."

"Really? That was fast," he replied with an amused grin. "What is it?"

Misa and Idir were also curious about the answer, but first, they wanted to know the question. Fabio repeated it, and I began to answer: "If you feel accomplished when you go home after a day's work, then you may be in the right job. And if you find yourself eagerly looking forward to the next exciting thing you will do at work, then you are definitely in the right job."

The three of them remained silent, and I felt a tinge of uncertainty. Did they think my response was valuable or foolish? I awaited their thoughts with bated breath. As we reached the dinner table, nobody spoke a word. We ate in silence, and I pondered whether my answer had been worthwhile.

Finally, Idir broke the stillness with excitement, "I am definitely in the right job!"

Fabio and Misa remained silent.

Following dinner, we strolled along the trail that encircled the light trees. We were no longer alone, as numerous groups of people walked alongside us, relishing the refreshing night air. The breeze generated a soft swishing and howling sound as it drifted through the adjacent forest. The rustling of the leaves and the swaying, sparkling vines of the light trees intensified the enchanting ambiance. The night was captivating, and the unclouded, starry sky appeared magnificent.

The waterfalls in front of my home were also beautiful, and my friends had not yet seen them. I wanted them to experience the beauty with their own eyes, so I told them about the pond and the falls. They were astonished by the exciting turn of events. I invited them to come and enjoy the pond sometime, and they said they would after Feray's project was over.

It was strange that they didn't know what they were making. Idir said it was always like that with the healer's projects—there was an element of secrecy. She only shared the design of individual parts and never told more than what she thought was needed to build the components.

As it was getting late, we headed home. First, we walked to Idir's home. He invited me to visit him sometime, and I promised I would. Misa and Fabio lived closer to my home, so they accompanied me all the way back before leaving. They couldn't see the falls in the dark, but as we heard the sounds of the falling water, they raised their heads a little, and a smile appeared on their curious faces.

After they left, I sat in front of the fireplace and kept thinking about my new friends. It had been a long day. I pictured Amy and Alfred happily exploring the island, although I still couldn't imagine her being fun and loud.

I thought about which pet to get, and finally, before drifting off to sleep, I made up my mind.

The next moment, I found myself in the middle of an exciting adventure with Amy and Alfred. They were bursting with enthusiasm as they embarked on their quest to find the legendary troll cave. Together, they trekked through a dense forest. The towering trees were so tall that their canopies seemed to touch the sky, casting a surreal glow on the forest floor. The leaves rustled gently in the breeze, and the sweet sound of birds singing echoed through the trees. The forest was teeming with life, and every plant and tree seemed to have a story to tell.

In the midst of our journey, they stumbled upon a small white dog. The pup's fluffy tail wagged so hard it was almost a blur. Amy and Alfred were overjoyed to meet the dog, and without hesitation, they decided to bring him along on their adventure. As they continued the trek through the forest, they came across a towering mountain that reached the clouds. They climbed higher and higher until the world around them looked minuscule. Watching the clouds drift by gave them a sense of peace and tranquillity. At the summit of the mountain stood a cave, rumoured to contain all the treasures of the world.

They entered the cave and found themselves in a colossal chamber with piles of glittering jewels and gold scattered about. Alfred's eyes widened at the sight of all the treasure, while Amy was fascinated by the sparkling gems. They ventured deeper into the cave, searching for the troll. Suddenly, they heard a low growl coming from the back of the chamber. They approached the sound cautiously and saw a massive, slumbering troll. The troll had a golden key around its neck, which Amy knew was the key to the door that led to the next part of the adventure.

Alfred was about to grab the key when the dog let out a loud bark, startling the troll and waking him up. The troll was furious and started chasing them. Amy, Alfred, and the pup ran as fast as they could, trying to escape the troll's wrath. The chase led them into a dark forest, and they lost each other in the chaos. They called out to each other, but their voices were swallowed by the darkness. The atmosphere around them was eerie and unsettling, and the wind howled through the branches, making it seem like the forest was alive and angry. Suddenly, a fierce storm raged, and Alfred was whisked away by the strong winds. Amy searched frantically for her friend, but he was nowhere to be found. She was left alone to wander in the darkness as she lost Alfred and the dog.

Ch 06: Intruder in the Sanctuary

The following day, I woke up feeling uneasy about the dream. It felt so real that I couldn't shake off the feeling of dread. I couldn't help but wonder what happened to Alfred and the white dog after they got separated in the dark forest. I tried to put the dream out of my mind as I got ready for the day ahead, but the feeling of unease lingered.

After breakfast, I went to the forge to see if I could help with anything. Feray's project needed just a few more days to complete. There wasn't much for me to do, so I wandered around, gazing at the odd shapes of the metal structures scattered around the clearing. When I grew tired, I sat under a shady tree and listened to the rhythmic sound of the hammer striking the metal over and over again.

Kratos noticed me and came to sit with me. After greeting me, he patted my back and said, "I have never felt so certain that I am doing the right job." I looked at him in surprise.

He explained, "Idir told me about your response to Fabio, and I am very impressed."

I felt pleased but also a bit shy. I had come up with an answer to his question too, but I wasn't confident enough to say it.

"Did you also think of an answer to my question?" he asked, the words I had been apprehensive of hearing, and looked at me with such interest as if I was some wise old man who knew everything.

He liked my answer to Fabio's question, which boosted my confidence. I resolved to tell him what I thought, even if there was a chance he wouldn't believe it was the correct answer.

"You are successful in life if you have people who respect and care for you. You are successful if you can make time to be with those people. You are successful if you can relax and enjoy the food you eat. You are successful if you can complete your work and still have time to do other activities that you enjoy. Finally, you are successful if you can sleep with a clear conscience."

Kratos's face was full of surprise. He put his hand on my shoulder and said, "I have met thinkers before. The way you say things is so simple and easy to understand. Thank you!" He got up and walked away, nodding in such a content way that I felt he truly liked my answer. I stood up happily, patted myself on the shoulder, and left for the village centre for the midday meal.

I had only just started eating when the bells rang. I didn't know what it meant. I looked around, puzzled, and saw a group of guardians run toward the river. Soon after, Amy came out of the Tree Circle, running after the guardians with her notebook. I followed her quickly as I realized what was happening. By the time I reached the river, the guardians had surrounded a newcomer. Another boat had arrived. This one carried a girl who looked around as perplexed as I was on my first day.

I watched them go through the same routine they had with me. The newcomer was taken to the prison tree under the fall and was left alone as everyone hid and waited to see if she would do something. She stayed inside the tree. Then, Feray tested her for magic. She did not have any abilities either. In the end, Kratos welcomed her to Serenus and brought her to the village centre.

The village centre was busier than usual as she ate her first meal. She was greeted by the same lady and sent to stay at the same lodge as me. It was all standard practice. As she waited inside and wondered about the strange world, we prepared for the party outside. The next day, we surprised her outside the lodge. I remembered how I had walked between the two groups toward the seating area, nodding and thanking everyone. She was much more active, jumping around with excitement, her wings fluttering behind her, shaking people's hands. We were very different.

After the performance on stage, a girl declared that the newcomer would be a material researcher. Later, I asked Amy what it meant, and she said, "The newcomer is very interested in how different things look and feel. When she was in the boat, holding the sides to keep her balance, she kept feeling the grains of wood with her fingers. Since then, she has wanted to know about all kinds of materials. She asked me questions about what the spears that the guardians pointed at her were made of. She was also very interested in the note on the bedside table and how it could be folded without breaking apart and the basket in which I carried her breakfast. You know, that sort of stuff, so we think she will be good at studying materials."

I asked Amy about the reason behind surrounding a newcomer with armed guardians. I believed it to be a negative experience. She explained that it was all a tradition, and there was a reason for every step. Some newcomers had behaved aggressively in the past, so it was best to take precautions.

Amy agreed that many things could be improved, but changing the old ways was difficult. She reminded me of Feray's cold attitude the day I arrived. I was surprised that she had felt it too. She said Kratos had talked to Feray, requesting that she be friendlier to newcomers.

There was no doubt that Amy liked her teacher. She tried to convince me that while the healer wasn't good with words, she was a good person and a great teacher. I understood what she meant. I felt the same when Feray had talked to me about her work and showed me the magical trees.

After the party, I left for home and decided to meet the newcomer in the next few days to help her understand and adjust to life on the island.

Once she had her own house, I went to her with some firewood and the essentials for preparing her own breakfast. She had already picked a name: Pari.

Pari asked me questions about what different things were made out of. She would point to an object, and I would tell her what materials were used to make it. She would listen intently and then point to the next thing. Amy was right—Pari was obsessed with different materials and how each was used.

Pari and I spent many days together, exploring her new world and showing her around. And in a few days, I felt that she was more sure of her role in this world than I ever was. She had a long list of materials that she had learned about. She came across a calcite piece that looked like a dragon scale. It sat proudly on the mantle of the fireplace in her home. She could spend hours looking at it intently, studying it with her eyes, imagining all kinds of uses for the mineral.

One day, I took her to the forge and introduced her to my friends. She was thrilled. As she went from station to station, watching the workers perform various tasks, I sat with Fabio and Misa. They laughed and said they liked the pet I had adopted and pointed to Pari. I smirked at their comment and explained that I had totally forgotten about a pet since I was busy showing Pari around. I told them I intended to adopt one soon.

Fabio revealed that the healer's project was finally finished, and a party was organized at the village center to celebrate the completion of the lengthy project. As the evening came, the metal forgers went through the pages of instructions from Feray and then put down their tools. The project was officially complete.

"Let's head to the village. The celebration will start soon," Kratos announced. I walked over to him and waited as the forge was cleaned and organized, ready for the next day.

The working men and women left in groups, chatting and laughing excitedly. Everyone looked happy.

I accompanied Pari, Kratos, and Idir back to the village center. Kratos explained that while their part of the job was finished, it was yet to be assembled, but that was to be done by Feray.

After the meal, we got up and rearranged the tables. All the furniture was carried to the edge of the yard, making a wooden circle with the benches in front. We sat down, facing the clear space in the middle. It was getting dark, and some villagers lit torches to illuminate the atmosphere.

The celebration started with a slow song. Everyone joined in and sang in a deep, soft tone. The words were strange, but they had a strong effect on me. It sounded like they were paying tribute to someone or something. I sat quietly, enjoying the peaceful experience. It was a perfect transition from the excitement and urgency of their day's work.

As the song ended, Kratos explained it to me. It was an ancient song and was, indeed, a tribute to everything that nourished us - sunlight, trees, rain, fruits, just about everything. It was a custom to express gratitude for every blessing before starting the celebrations.

After that, the party picked up. Many Seren men and women stood and sang beautiful songs. The music came from the wooden instruments of the musicians sitting in the middle of the yard. Gradually, it changed into a merry, frolicking tune. A group dressed in similar colours got up and started a mesmerizing dance. In the beginning, they held hands and danced in a circle around the instruments. Then, all at once, they spread their shimmery wings and took flight.

I was spellbound; it was the first time I had seen the Seren in the air. They looked so graceful as they hovered up together and danced in a circle above us. The audience clapped and cheered loudly, singing along happily. They ended the dance with a sudden plunge to the ground, with their wings pinned back to their bodies. As they came closer to the ground, they opened their wings and hovered a foot or so above the ground. I trembled with excitement.

I was surprised to learn that, with some practice, our wings could carry us for more than just a hover. The dance moves were proof that the wings were more capable. I couldn't say they were flying; it was more like rising up in the air and performing some acrobatics, but even that was much more than I had expected.

After that, every song was accompanied by a breathtaking dance in the air. I caught Kratos glancing around; he was looking for someone. "What's the matter, Kratos? You were expecting someone?"

"Feray is not here." He frowned.

"She might be busy preparing for her part of the work."

"I don't think so. She wouldn't miss a celebration in the past. But then, she...." He trailed off.

Concern grew inside me. If Kratos was worried, it must be serious. "What is it? Do you think there might be a problem?"

He sighed and whispered his concern to keep it between us. "Feray is not herself. Lately, she has been acting differently. I don't know what, but something has changed. I should go talk to her."

He stood abruptly. Before he could leave, the song ended. Idir called for him to dance with him. Kratos looked conflicted, but he couldn't refuse an excited-looking Idir.

Kratos joined Idir in the dance, and the crowd cheered and whistled. He was very graceful in his dancing, while Idir was more energetic. They were compatible with each other even though their styles were quite different.

As the night grew darker, the celebration ended. Idir laughed loudly while recounting the performances of the people. Everyone returned to their homes. Pari had already left with another Seren. I walked back alone, but I was not afraid of the dark this time.

In the morning, Qilam surprised me with a visit. After my conversation with Amy, I did not want to talk to him, but he had come to my home and was a guest. I couldn't be rude and tell him to leave, so I listened to what he had to say.

He had come with terrible news and a warning. He told me that someone was planning to attack the village and steal all the vials of light from the tree chambers. I asked him for more details, but he said that was all he knew. He left in a hurry, and I wondered why he came to me with this news. I didn't know if Qilam was telling the truth, but the warning was so dire that I had to inform the village quickly.

I ran toward the village centre, still thinking about who I would tell. I decided to go to Alev, but then I remembered that the guardians had only allowed us in after recognizing Kratos. It was better to inform Kratos, so I ran toward the forge.

I arrived out of breath and found Kratos having tea with his fellow workers. They were usually very busy with work, but now they were sitting like they had nothing to do. Kratos asked me to sit down and catch my breath. When I calmed down, he demanded that I tell him what had happened. I started talking immediately, but they couldn't understand a word. I paused, took a few deep breaths, and started again: "Someone will attack the village and steal all the vials of light."

I told them how Qilam came to my home and delivered the warning. Everyone was shocked. At first, they didn't want to believe that Qilam was being honest. Their mistrust of his words was evident, but it was also not easy to ignore him. Kratos wanted to know how Qilam knew about it. I did not know that.

Everyone was uneasy, but Kratos was furious. "Qilam definitely knows more. Who told him someone would steal? How did he come to know about it? He is hiding something. And what kind of attack? We need to gather more information as soon as possible." He instructed everyone to keep the news to themselves before asking me to follow him, and we headed to the village centre.

Once we arrived at Alev's house, Kratos asked me to tell her what had happened. I delivered the bad news. Her jaw dropped in disbelief. She called Boris and told him to increase the number of guardians around the trees, and then she called Feray. Her reaction was similar.

Kratos asked Alev if she thought it could be the wizard. She replied, "He has no accomplices. Since we started the tradition of giving a good experience, all the newcomers have stayed in the village and are accounted for. No one has joined him. I doubt he will try to do something like that himself. He will want an accomplice. It could be him but through another. We need to find out who is helping him. I suspect Qilam. We must arrest him immediately."

Feray and Kratos agreed as Alev decided that the matter should be kept a secret until more information was known. She asked me to keep quiet about it, then ordered Boris to find and capture Qilam.

When we left, Feray was beyond herself. Kratos and I tried to calm her down. We understood that she was the one most affected by the news. It was her life's work that was at risk.

Kratos suggested that they would halt the work on the project until this mystery was resolved. Feray agreed. They wanted to focus all their attention on finding out whether it was true and how they could stop it from happening.

Before this day, I had only seen happy faces on the island. Now, it was different. Everyone was tense and afraid. Feray told Amy about Qilam's warning. She needed to know because of her involvement with the light and the magical trees.

A group of guardians passed by, running toward the Lighttrees. Everyone in the village centre stood frozen, watching them.

We could keep the news a secret, but we could not hide the worry on our faces and the alarmed guardians protecting the trees. Villagers figured out that something was wrong and started to whisper amongst themselves.

The only hope of getting more information was by finding Qilam. The day passed without any news of him. The guardians searched deep in the forest, but he was nowhere to be found.

I was at the forge with Idir when Feray arrived. It was evening. She was there to discuss her project with Kratos. Idir and I heard the entire conversation. She had changed her mind about delaying it.

Kratos disagreed with her. He believed that, at the moment, it was better to not start something new and wait till things became clearer.

Feray insisted that her project was needed now more than ever before. Kratos demanded to know the reason for the urgency, but Feray wouldn't tell him. Their conversation ended in an argument, and she left furious.

I didn't understand why completing the project was so important at such a taxing time. I thought Amy would know the reason for Feray's insistence and decided to ask her.

I went to look for Amy in the tree chambers. The guardians stationed outside did not allow me in but informed me that Amy was not there. I thought she might have left for her home already, but I wanted to be sure, so I went to check Feray's house before leaving for the village.

As I walked to the healer's house, I wondered if Feray would ever show me what was in the Moontree chamber.

I reached her house but stopped as I heard voices coming from inside. Feray was arguing with someone. My instincts told me to hide, so I went to the back of the house and stood by a window. The voices were low but still clear. A shrill, menacing voice travelled through the window.

"Have you lost your mind? We have come this far, and now you say you are not sure?"

Feray's voice was weak and tired. "I don't know if this is what I want."

I moved closer to the window to peek inside. An old lady with silvery-white hair stood in front of Feray. Her face betrayed her desperation.

"Of course you do," the old lady insisted impatiently, then she walked away from Feray and stood by a table stacked with rolls of paper. The lady studied something on the table for some time. Then, she turned to Feray again. Her voice was calm and relaxed now and showed no hint of anger. "You are the most talented healer I have ever seen. I shared my knowledge with you because you showed so much potential. It would be silly to step back when greatness is just a step away."

Feray pulled herself together. The old lady's praise softened her tense face. She said in a firm tone, "I value your faith in me. You know I am grateful for all you have done for me. I feel troubled only because none of the healers before me have attempted such a thing."

The old lady laughed sweetly. "Oh! Now I understand what's happening. It is not you. It's the nerves. They create doubt in the heart of the one who is attempting something new, something exceptional." She patted Feray's shoulder and continued, "Now, now. Don't overthink. I promise you everything will go smoothly. You have a duty to your land. And only you can protect it. Remember! I believe in you."

The old lady was really good at encouraging Feray, who now stood stronger with a proud smile on her face. "You are right. I am so thankful for what you have done for me. I don't know how I will ever repay you."

The old lady patted Feray on the shoulder and said, "No need for such thoughts. Show the world what you are capable of, and surprise everyone. Do your duty... that's all I want!" Feray smiled broadly and said she would check on the things she needed for the morning before leaving. I waited to see where she was going, not wanting her to see me hiding outside her house.

Feray walked to the Tree Circle and disappeared inside the Moontree. I wasn't sure what to do. I had no idea how long she would take in the white chamber, so I stayed where I was.

"Cursed place! When will I get out of here?" The old lady's voice was full of disgust. The sudden change in her tone shocked me. I peeked inside through the window.

She was tense and kept mumbling something inaudible. "Just one more night," she muttered slyly under her breath many times.

Something strange was going on. I wondered what she meant by getting out of here. And what did she expect to happen after this one more night?

The more I thought, the more sinister the lady seemed.

I couldn't understand what was happening there and decided to go back and tell Kratos, but I had to wait for Feray to come back. I couldn't risk getting caught. I was also worried that the guardians might tell Feray I had come to her home.

Confused and scared, I slumped down with my back to the wall and waited. After what felt like an eternity, Feray returned to her house. Without making a noise, I got up and peeked inside. She entered the room and stood by the table, studying the papers carefully as the old lady observed her. This was my chance to leave.

I snuck around the house with quick, careful steps. Without looking back, I crossed the yard and left. The guardians had seen me go to Feray's home and leave, but they had no reason to doubt my intentions.

I walked briskly to Amy's home and asked her to take me to Kratos. She saw the worried look on my face and led me to his place without question.

Kratos looked at Amy and me uneasily. He could sense that something was wrong. He let us into his dimly lit home, and we sat down on a bench by the fireplace.

Kratos lit a torch, and I looked around. The home was the same size as mine. Some chairs were facing the simply-built stone fire-place, and a large table stood next to a wall with a raised bed.

Kratos looked at Amy, who was looking at me, waiting for me to say something. He turned to me and asked, "What happened?"

I whispered in response, "I have to tell you something important and strange. It might be nothing, but I have a bad feeling about it."

Kratos spoke in a kind voice, "Don't worry. Just tell me."

Amy watched me with a tense face. Kratos sensed my hesitation and said, "You are safe with us. There is nothing to worry about. Tell us what happened."

I recounted everything, starting with how I went to look for Amy to the conversation I overheard at the healer's house. Then I told them how the white-haired lady was full of disgust for this place and wanted to get out of there and that she thought she had to wait one more night.

Kratos's expression told me that I was right in thinking something was not right. He asked me to repeat the entire thing. I narrated the whole story again. He stood up and started pacing, deep in thought. His silence grew longer as I waited for him to say some-thing.

Amy also stayed quiet, thinking.

I couldn't wait any longer. "What do you think is happening? Who is the old lady?"

Kratos spoke first: "I have never seen a white-haired lady in the village."

Amy added, "That's why Feray wouldn't let me in her home. What is she up to?"

Kratos sat down on a chair. "I don't know who the lady is. I don't think anyone knows about her. Feray has been hiding her from us. But why would she do that? They were probably talking about the project we were working on. It seems of great importance to Feray, and she argued with me earlier in the day, but she wouldn't tell me the purpose of the thing." He sighed and rubbed his head anxiously. "What are they up to?"

He stood up and started pacing again. Eventually, Kratos said, "You did a great job coming to me. Keep it to yourself for now. I will talk to Feray. I trust her. She may have a reason for what she is doing." Amy nodded in agreement.

I was not happy with what they were saying. I didn't think there could be a reasonable explanation for Feray's actions. Kratos saw the look on my face and said, "Whatever they are doing is not happening tonight. I will go to her early in the morning and confront her."

We left Kratos's home, and Amy walked me back to mine. She was surprised to hear the sounds of the waterfalls and to find a pond in place of the swamp in my yard. I was very uneasy with what I had witnessed. Amy offered to stay with me, and I readily accepted her offer.

We sat by the fire as she talked about how Feray had changed in the past few weeks. She was different and secretive and had lost interest in teaching Amy. All she cared about was being alone, and she constantly found reasons to send Amy away.

We also talked about Alfred. She was still sad about losing him and talked about their long walks and endless discussions on the trails. Alfred was very passionate and wanted to be the best at everything he did. She told me about the wooden towers that people had built in the past in an attempt to spot a piece of land ahead. Alfred had constructed the tallest one. He didn't find another island, but they were happy to spend time looking at the beautiful world from the very top.

I asked, "If you could say one more thing to him, what would it be?"

She replied without a thought, "Don't leave... but if you must, take me with you."

"Why do you think he left?" I wondered.

"The lost scroll." Amy stopped abruptly and looked embarrassed, making me wonder if she had done something wrong.

"What's the lost scroll?" I asked, curious. "I've never heard anyone mention it before."

Amy answered in a flat tone, "It's a story about ancient knowledge that was lost forever. Legend has it that whoever finds it will become an all-powerful wizard. I think it's just another tale spun by

Seren in the past, but people started believing it to be true. That's why everyone leaves the island – to search for the lost knowledge. Alfred left to find it in other lands. He believed that once he found it, he would become powerful enough to come back for me. It makes people want to leave the island, so we decided not to mention it to newcomers."

"I see," I said, intrigued. "What kind of power does the scroll contain?"

Amy hesitated before answering, "According to the story, the scroll contains knowledge so powerful that the owner becomes a god and is free from all fears. It's supposed to be pure knowledge that can't be used for evil. But people still search for it for all kinds of selfish reasons. Alfred wanted to be the most powerful person in the world but only to do good things with his power. Unfortunately, most people think they're doing the right thing, even when they're not."

Amy continued to bring up memories of Alfred, and while I empathized with her grief, I decided to shift the conversation to something more uplifting. I shared with her my joy of having the waterfall in my front yard, recounting how calming it was to listen to the water cascading down from the comfort of my boat. This piqued her interest, and she eagerly expressed her desire to spend the night on the boat, listening to the tranquil sounds of the falls.

Without hesitation, I agreed to her request, and we secured the boat so it wouldn't move around at night. As Amy settled in for the night, I retreated to my own bed, grateful that I could provide her with a sense of comfort and peace of mind. Amy didn't care about the darkness that surrounded her. She was fearless like Alfred, and it explained why they were such good friends.

As I drifted off to sleep, I looked forward to what the morning would bring.

In my dream, I found myself walking down a dark path. It was dimly lit, and I could see the shadowy figures of trees on either side. Suddenly, I heard a loud noise that startled me, and I looked up to see a woman standing in front of me. She had long, silver hair that glimmered in the moonlight, and she was dressed in a long, flowing dress that trailed behind her.

The woman looked directly at me, and her piercing gaze made me feel uncomfortable. She began to yell at me, but I couldn't understand what she was saying. She spoke a language that I had never heard before, but her tone was aggressive, and I could tell that she was angry.

As she continued to yell, her voice grew louder and more intense. I tried to back away, but I couldn't move. I felt a surge of fear wash over me as the woman's eyes seemed to bore into my soul.

Suddenly, the woman stopped yelling, and her expression softened. She reached out and touched my hand, and I felt a strange energy surge through my body. It was a feeling unlike anything I had ever experienced before, and I felt both exhilarated and terrified at the same time.

The woman smiled at me, and I could see a glimmer of kindness in her eyes. Then, she turned and walked away, disappearing into the darkness. I woke up feeling confused and disoriented, unsure of what the silver-haired lady wanted from me.

Ch 07: Betrayal in the Woods

When Amy woke up, we headed to Kratos' place. He invited us to join him for a simple breakfast of bread and apricot jam, which we enjoyed together before Amy left for the healer's yard. I left for the forge as Kratos left to talk to Feray.

I met Idir on the way, and we walked to the forge together. Although Idir kept talking to me, I couldn't focus on his words, as my thoughts were elsewhere. I nodded occasionally to feign interest.

The forge was bustling with activity as people worked on repairing a cart used to transport firewood from the forest to the stockpile, along with a few other small jobs that had been put on hold while they worked on Feray's project.

Amy arrived soon after, armed with instructions from Feray to organize the metal structures according to her designs. She had left just as Kratos reached to speak with Feray.

Amy and I examined the designs with curiosity, eager to see what the final project would look like. However, we were disappointed to find that the papers only depicted how the various components fit together, with no indication of the finished product.

Amy shared instructions with the workers at the forge, and they started placing the pieces in their proper places. As Amy supervised the workers, I stood under a shady tree with my back against the trunk, absentmindedly watching as the scattered pieces started forming a shape. As the last part of the metal puzzle was carried closer to the almost-solved figure, Idir joined me under the tree.

I had been constantly thinking about Feray and Kratos. What was happening there? Why did it take so long for Kratos to come? Was something wrong? Too many what-ifs were swirling in my head, and every passing moment made me worry even more. I made a conscious effort to divert my attention away from Kratos. I had seen Idir use his wings during the dance last night, so I asked him if he had ever used them for longer flights.

"Let's just say I don't use bridges to cross the river." He smiled, then continued more seriously, "We don't use the wings too often. They are delicate and precious."

I nodded. "What if the wings get damaged? Can the healer fix them?"

"Yes, she can, but she needs Moonlight to do that. Moonlight is precious. Amy must have told you about it."

She hadn't. In fact, I had not seen the Whitetree chamber. I asked Idir to tell me more about it.

"Well, I am not a healer. I might not explain it properly, but I understand that Moonlight is the most precious of all lights. It's quite challenging to acquire in large quantities, as it is only captured during a full moon. We keep the Moonlight safe and only use it when absolutely necessary."

"How is it used?"

The workers dropped a piece with a loud bang, and Idir went to inspect the structure. After a few moments, he came back satisfied, "No harm done."

"You were telling me how Moonlight is used," I reminded him.

"Yes, right. So, one of the men fell off a tree during harvest time. His wing was badly injured. We carried him to the Whitetree chamber. Feray put her hand in a vial full of Moonlight and brought it out as if it were a thread. She used some strange tools and built up the injured part all by herself. It was magic," Idir recalled, the memory lighting up his face. "The Moonlight is special. Everything that has the Moonlight threaded into it is alive. I have witnessed it. The wing of the poor man was as real as it could be. That is why it is so precious."

The magic of Moonlight filled me with wonder. Idir interrupted my thoughts, offering me an apricot. I accepted, and he pointed to the tree where the fruits hung. He was about to climb it when I stopped him and offered to do it instead. Climbing trees sounded fun, and Idir agreed.

It was easy to climb, and once I reached the top, I glanced around and saw all the pieces of metal forming a familiar shape. I couldn't believe my eyes.

The metal structure had a long, thin body that narrowed down into a whip-like tail. Large wings spread on both sides. On the front was a head with a flat snout, and two holes in the head replaced the eyes.

I was terrified to see a metal creature, much like a dragon. It was too large to recognize from the ground, and the workers walked around it without noticing what it was.

My mind worked quickly as I picked some apricots on my way back down. I handed some to Idir, then paused, wondering whether to tell him about the metal dragon. Should I wait for Kratos to come? I couldn't decide.

Feray arrived at the forge, pushing a wooden cart covered with a large cloth. Amy walked over to her, and they began inspecting the metal creature. Idir approached Feray to see if she needed help. After a brief conversation, Feray continued examining the parts. When she was satisfied, she declared that it was time for her to work and asked everyone to leave her alone. "It would spoil the surprise," she insisted.

The workers left slowly. I kept my eyes on the path leading to the village, hoping that Kratos would arrive any minute.

Idir called me over and pointed towards the village. He wanted me to leave. I walked over to him and asked about Kratos. Feray had told Idir that she had finally convinced Kratos to let her proceed. She informed him that Kratos was feeling tired and staying in the orange chamber but would be back soon.

I accompanied Idir back to the village center and sat there waiting for Kratos. The yard was noisy and busy. A large group of trainee forgers surrounded Idir, asking questions about the project. He was happy and gave a detailed description of the techniques they had used. I listened without any interest and kept glancing at the guardians stationed outside the trees.

The sun rose higher in the sky, and the day turned into a pleasant one with white fluffy clouds floating in the blue sky. The cool breeze gradually picked up the pace and scattered delicate flowers that fluttered off the trees. The beautiful scenery did nothing to calm me down.

I was drained from worrying about Kratos and the realization at the forge. I wanted to see him immediately, so I decided to try my luck with the guardians and hoped they would let me see him.

"I'm going for a walk, Idir!" I said before walking away. Idir nodded and turned his attention back to his audience.

I headed to the Orangetree and asked the guardians if I could see Kratos. To my surprise, they said he wasn't there. I thought he might be in another chamber, so I went to all the trees one after the other, but the guardians said the same thing every time. Kratos had not come to any tree. Panic set in. Why did Feray lie about him coming there? An unknown fear crept into my thoughts. Was Kratos in danger? I needed to find him immediately.

I went to Feray's home to look for him. Maybe he went to talk to the white-haired lady. Once there, I waited outside for a bit, wondering if the lady was inside. I didn't know if she could harm me if I encountered her.

A soft moaning sound came from inside. There was something wrong, but I couldn't figure out who it was. The sound came again. I went forward, opened the door carefully, and gasped with horror. Kratos lay motionless on the floor. I rushed to his side and called his name, but he was unresponsive. My mind was numb with fear and worry. I kept saying his name over and over again, but he did not wake up from the strange sleep.

An idea flashed through my disoriented thoughts: I had to take Kratos to one of the tree chambers. Feray had told me the lights could heal the body and soul. He might recover if I quickly brought him to the right tree. I tried to remember. Redlight for ailments of blood, orange was good for... I couldn't recall.

I was exhausted from my efforts to lift Kratos. Despite his weight, I persisted, straining my muscles until I was able to drag him along. Once outside, I called out to the guardians at the top of my lungs, and they quickly came to assist me. They moved me aside and carried Kratos towards the trees. Nervously, I followed them while one of the guardians whistled to summon others to the healer's home.

I stayed with the guardians who were carrying Kratos to the Orangetree. They took him inside, but I wasn't allowed to go in. I rushed to find Amy and found her coming from the forge. I grabbed her arm and pulled her towards the Orangetree while explaining what had happened to Kratos.

Amy ran inside the tree, leaving me outside with the guardians. I waited anxiously, my breathing heavy with worry. Meanwhile, the commotion of the guardians' whistles had drawn everyone's attention in the village center, and Idir saw me from the crowd. I signalled for him to come over.

He rushed towards me, and I collapsed on the ground, out of breath and unable to stand. Idir sat beside me, holding my hand to comfort me. After a moment, I managed to recount the events to him, and as soon as he understood what had happened, he dashed towards the tree chamber. However, the guardians stopped him from entering, and he stood rubbing his hands nervously.

Newly arrived guardians prevented more Seren from coming to the trees, and I waited patiently for news from Amy. Idir also sat on the ground now, and we both anxiously awaited any updates. The search for the old lady in Feray's home had finished, but she wasn't found. The guardians then ran towards us and surrounded me.

Their commander approached me and asked how I knew that Kratos needed help. I explained that I had heard him moaning, but he was not satisfied with my answer. He wanted to know why I was wandering around near the healer's house.

"I was looking for Kratos," I replied. "Idir told me he was resting in a tree chamber, but the guardians outside all the chambers told me that he wasn't there. So, I thought he might be at Feray's home." Idir nodded in agreement, and the guardians stepped back.

Suddenly, a loud swishing sound interrupted us, and everyone turned toward the village center. Screams of terror erupted, shattering the peace of the day. People scrambled to get a clear view of what was happening.

As we exited the Tree Circle, I saw a monstrous creature hovering high above the forge, flapping its wings slowly. The Seren ran in terror as the creature remained in the air, its scales shimmering in the sunlight. Its long tail cut through the air with an angry swish.

The trees near the monster caught fire, and it swooped low to grab the trunks with its iron claws. The creature pulled them out of the ground, and with a thrust of its mighty wings, it flew towards the village.

The villagers ran in different directions to escape the imminent danger. I took cover behind the healer's home but couldn't resist the urge to peek out and see what was happening. The guardians ran towards the forge and whistled for reinforcements while the bell in the village center rang, announcing the threat.

The burning trees rained down on the village like arrows. The wooden houses provided fuel to the eager flames, which spread around, consuming everything they could find. More and more guardians appeared and shot arrows at the beast, but with a quick flap of its wings, the villain flew away, leaving its fiery army behind to devour the village. The past few moments had transformed the peaceful village center into a war zone. I rushed toward the magical trees to check if everyone was safe. There were still guardians outside who had not left their stations. I ran to the village where the burning trees had fallen. A large tree sprawled over an unfortunate house. Its branches spread all over the front garden while the thick roots stretched toward the sky like a bony hand. Then, with a loud noise, the roof collapsed under the weight of the tree. I looked around with a numb feeling. The once-beautiful village was now broken, burnt, and unrecognizable. The wooden furniture in the village center was on fire, and black smoke rose from the burning houses around it. It must have been late afternoon, but the sky turned dark with smoke and grey clouds that blocked the sunlight. A storm was coming. A deafening silence echoed through the village amid the shuffling of running steps and the urgent words of people trying frantically to put out the fire. But the flames were angry and hungry, wanting to consume everything they could reach. The flames licked at the house next to me, and the heat was too much. I moved away from it, keeping my eyes on the ground. The smoke rising from every side made it difficult to breathe, and the cough hurt my lungs. I sat down, hugging myself tightly.

Then, I saw Idir running toward the village centre. I shouted loudly to let him know where I was. We ran toward each other, and I looked at him, waiting to hear about Kratos. His face told the story of the horror that surrounded us, but he was relieved to find me safe.

Idir wanted me to go with him. I followed quickly and without question. As we walked away from the burning village centre, I kept looking around in disbelief. It was unbelievable how much destruction had taken place in such a short time.

The healer's yard was full of people. Many wooden cots had materialized, carrying the injured who were being taken to the chambers by the lucky survivors. We threaded our way through the groups of men and women standing together with empty eyes. They kept looking around nervously.

I was worried about Kratos and couldn't wait any longer. "Idir! How's Kratos?"

Idir's words were full of worry. "Amy has moved him to the Moontree chamber. No one is allowed to see him."

He took me to the Redtree. Amy was already there, busy with

some injured people. As we stood there, more and more wooden cots appeared. A girl was helping Amy. An assortment of jars with powders and liquids of different colours filled the tabletops.

It was getting crowded. Amy announced that everyone not injured should go to the Bluetree. Her helper informed her that it was already full. Villagers were agitated and needed to calm their minds.

Amy announced, "If you are not hurt, go to the Greentree. The Greenlight will soothe your senses. I will be there shortly."

I left with Idir and a few others for the Greentree. Boris was walking to Feray's house with more guardians. They looked alert, moving slowly. I wondered if they had found the old lady.

Idir pushed back the green curtain to let me in. Some people were sitting inside, but there was plenty of room. No one looked up as we entered. We found a quiet corner and sank to the ground side by side with our backs against a thick trunk carrying the green ceiling.

I watched as the cool Greenlight washed over me. It gently touched my mind, soothing it. I was on edge and looking around frantically, but the light started to work its magic. I closed my eyes, took a few deep breaths, and felt my head become lighter and more focused.

After a few moments, I opened my eyes and looked around with a fresher mind. Idir was also looking better. I closed my eyes again.

It seemed like a lifetime had passed since Feray stood here with me, excitedly talking about how the Greenlight provided clarity to an anxious mind. After all, it is nature's most preferred colour. She had turned around to smile at me. I shook her image from my mind. I didn't want to think about her, not after what she had done.

The cracking of thunder brought me back. Amy was there with us. I had not seen her come in. I asked, "Amy, how's Kratos?"

"I am not sure. Kratos is not injured. Nothing is broken, but he is still unconscious. I have tried everything I know, but nothing worked. We are keeping him in the Moontree. But we need to figure out what happened." She turned toward Idir. "I need your help. Since Feray is not...." She stopped mid-sentence. Her eyes filled with tears, and she rubbed them off with her hand. "Idir! Please go and bring Alev here. She might be able to help us."

Idir left quickly. Amy sat down on a bench and rubbed her forehead slowly. She was tired. I let her rest and sat on the bench next to her. She looked at me after a while and said softly, "I am so glad you went after Kratos. Whatever happened to him affected his heart. The Orangelight gave him strength and kept his body warm. You may have saved his life."

I nodded and hoped she was right. Amy left to check on the injured. Idir hadn't returned yet. The waiting would have been vicious if I hadn't been in the chamber lit in dim green. I put my head down on the table and closed my eyes. It felt good.

Footsteps approached me, and I looked up to find Boris, the

head guardian. He said soberly, "You are needed at the healer's house. Come with me."

Outside the chamber, it was already dark, with the grey clouds taking over the blue sky. The fire burned brightly in the tall torches erected all around the yard. The air smelled of smoke, and a glance toward the village revealed the source. Boris told me that the fires had been put out. Some people were injured, and others were shocked, but no one died.

The yard was almost deserted now. I followed Boris to the healer's house. Once inside, I saw an elderly man sitting in a chair beside Alev, who sat with a blanket covering her legs. Idir sat on one side. Boris offered me a chair next to Idir and pulled himself one too.

I sat nervously under the steady gaze of the elders. Alev started, "This meeting has been called to make sense of the incident. Idir considers you to be innocent. We believe his word but can't leave anything to chance. I have to ask you to go through the details of how you came to find Kratos."

I told them everything I had told Kratos the previous night and then about how I found him in the healer's home. Idir was in shock, as he knew none of it. The elders noticed it, and Alev demanded proof that I was telling the truth. I told them Amy was with me last night when I went to tell Kratos about the white-haired lady.

Boris left to get Amy, and I noticed the burning stare from Idir.

He was disappointed in me. He had trusted me, but I had kept everything from him. We were together all day, yet I revealed nothing. I tried to explain myself, "Kratos asked me not to tell anyone."

Idir crossed his arms and looked away. Amy arrived, and the elders asked her to tell them about last night's meeting at Kratos's home. She narrated the same story that I had told them.

The elders asked more questions, and we responded honestly. When they were satisfied, Alev demanded that I repeat the conversation between Feray and the old lady. I told them all I knew. They sat silently, brooding over what I had told them.

The older man asked Alev to voice her opinion. She answered in a gruff voice, "Jinyan, I am afraid it must be Esmeray trying to achieve what she couldn't last time."

Everyone gasped in horror. The room's atmosphere changed. Its grim, sad tone turned into one vibrating with anxiety. The elders exchanged glances and started whispering urgently amongst themselves.

Idir cleared his throat loudly. "Who exactly is Esmeray? I know a bit of the story, but it doesn't make any sense."

"That's because no one knows the whole story," Alev explained.

"Who is Esmeray?" I asked.

Jinyan nodded gravely and said, "Esmeray was one of the best healers we ever had. She made brews and potions unlike any we had seen before. But she was very ambitious and wanted to use the magic of trees for her own selfish reasons. We don't know exactly what she wanted to do. She had us fooled with her charming ways, everyone except for Conrad, who figured out her intentions were not good. He tried to warn us, but we were under her spell. Esmeray attacked him when he stopped her from misusing the lights. They both died in the fight. Or so we thought. She was never seen again after the attack on Conrad."

Alev concluded, "If it really is Esmeray, we need to find the answers to two questions. What does she intend to do, and how did Conrad stop her the last time?"

The elders' meeting continued, but Idir, Amy, and I were told to leave. Amy returned to attend to the injured. Idir and I left for our homes to pass the ill-fated night.

I asked Idir if he was still mad at me. He replied honestly, "I would have preferred that you told me once Feray lied to me, but I understand you were obeying Kratos."

"I didn't know Feray was capable of hurting him," I clarified.

He knew what I meant. Everyone was shocked by her actions.

"Why did Amy need Alev?" I asked.

"Alev is the old healer. The one before Feray. In fact, she taught Feray. Old age is cruel. Her hands started to tremble badly, and it got so bad that working with the lights was impossible. Then one day, the power to manipulate the Moonlight left her entirely. Feray has been the healer ever since."

We fell silent. Talking about Feray was not comfortable anymore. I had not known her for long. She came across as a proud person during most of our interactions, except when she talked about her work. I had actually liked that side of her personality. But it was different for everyone else. They had known, respected, and trusted her. Now that she had betrayed them, even saying her name was agonizing. Their wounds were fresh and raw.

Idir left for his home, and I continued on to my own. It was a terrible night. The storm had arrived, accompanied by the angry crackling of lightning. The air shook as the thunder growled, and the angry rain beat the windows frantically. I pulled my blanket around me tightly and fell into a fitful sleep. I dreamed about fire-spitting monsters and dark, mysterious places.

Ch 08:
Mirror's
Judgement

Early next morning, I went to the village centre to see how Kratos was doing. I still couldn't see him, but the guardians told me he was awake. An excellent start to the day.

The village centre was in ruins. The storm was long gone but left puddles of water everywhere. I joined the Seren, who were clearing the rubble. After a while, a crowd started to gather in front of the elder's house. The guardians told us that Feray had been captured late last night, and Alev wanted the villagers to gather for an update on the situation.

Once everyone had gathered, Alev spoke to the crowd. "Last night, Esmeray attacked the village."

The crowd gasped, and whispers echoed among them.

"This is what we know so far: Esmeray tricked Feray into helping her make that monster, and once she had it, she tried to kill Feray. Esmeray knew that Feray could stop her with her powers to manipulate light. We are lucky Feray escaped the fire, and the guardians found her. She is being held for further investigation, and we will share all findings with everyone. Until then, our focus will be on protecting the village from further attacks. Rest assured that we are doing our best to prevent further damage and rebuild as fast as possible. We will gather again when we know more." Alev left, and the crowd started whispering in anxious disbelief.

I walked toward the Tree Circle to find Amy in the Redtree. I waited outside, and when she came out, I inquired about Kratos. She led me to the Moontree in the middle of the Tree Circle.

This was the first time I saw the Moontree chamber. It was much larger than the others, and the fruit bulb in the middle was massive.

Kratos was on a bed right next to the bulb, awake. Amy and I asked him how he was feeling. He looked weak but smiled at me and said, "Much better. You saved my life. I can't thank you enough."

I smiled back. "Don't worry about that. Just get better."

Amy briefed Kratos about the situation, "The elders think Feray is telling the truth. Esmeray tricked her into making the beast.

They believe Feray did not intend for anyone to get hurt, and once she found out what Esmeray really wanted, she tried to stop her. Esmeray attacked Feray with a fireball, but she was lucky to survive. Guardians found her late at night, and now the elders are holding her to investigate further."

Kratos asked in evident frustration, "What does Esmeray want?"

Amy replied, "Based on what Feray has said, it appears Esmeray wanted to steal all the vials of light to keep her beast strong. After Qilam's warning, the guardians were placed to protect the trees. Therefore, Esmeray couldn't get the chance to steal the vials. We believe she will try again with her newfound weapon."

Kratos sighed. "Feray knew of this plan?"

Amy replied quickly, "No. She is putting it all together now. She thought she was building a guardian to protect the village against the evil wizard. Esmeray tricked Feray into thinking that this was the only chance that the village had against the wizard's upcoming attack."

"Esmeray is working with the wizard?" I asked.

"Well, we think Esmeray is the wizard," Amy said. "Or she is under his control. We don't know what it is, but the elders think Esmeray is the wizard who wanted to attack the village and steal the light."

Kratos asked, "What happens next? Where did she go after attacking the village? Do we know anything?"

Amy responded in a stern voice, "Everyone thinks she will come back. If she wants the vials, she will take them by force. It's just a matter of time."

We looked at each other anxiously and fell silent. Amy was deep in thought as she fidgeted with her rings.

Idir entered the chamber and stopped when he saw our worried faces. Kratos asked him about Feray. He informed us that Feray was here in the Tree Circle, and it was decided that she would be tested by the Mirror. Kratos sighed, and Amy shook her head.

"What does that mean?" I asked.

"You'll see. Let's go outside." Amy tried to stop Kratos as he needed to rest, but he got up slowly. Idir gave him his shoulder to lean on. With slow steps, they walked out of the Moontree chamber. Amy and I followed.

It looked like the entire village was gathered in the Tree Circle. I saw Feray sitting alone, halfway between the arch and the Moontree, and in the arch sat Alev with an old lady I didn't recognize. We went and stood next to the elders.

Feray was on her knees, sobbing like the one who had lost everything. She was holding a vial of white Moonlight in her hand. Her head was bowed. The Tree Circle was in complete silence except for her regretful sobs. The mourning echoed back from the rigid walls of the audience. Most of them had averted their eyes from the unfortunate woman they had respected so much.

Amy stood next to a tense Idir, staring down at her feet. Tears ran down her cheeks silently. She kept wiping them off.

Everyone was angry with Feray, yet it was painful to see her in this state. We didn't know what we could do to end it, so we just stood there and heard her wail.

Alev welcomed Kratos and said, "I am happy to see that you are alright. If something were to happen to you...."

Feray sobbed and broke down into hysterics.

Alev looked at me and said, "You saved Kratos's life. Accept our gratitude... what is your name?"

"I have not picked a name yet," I responded meekly.

"Picking a name isn't that hard," Alev reprimanded.

"I am not yet sure what name will suit me." I felt the eyes of the entire village on me.

Alev shrugged dismissively, "You thinkers overthink everything."

Then, Alev walked over to Feray and extended her trembling hands, taking the vial from Feray's hand. Amy then walked over and took the vial from Alev. The Moonlight vial started to glow brightly, bathing the surroundings in white light. I looked at Amy's face as if in a trance. She looked like an angel carrying a full moon in her hand, and Feray's sobbing intensified.

Alev spoke sternly, "The Moonlight has rejected you. It has started to glow for Amy. Now, she is the Seren healer. The magic itself has made its decision."

Alev looked at the old lady, then back at Feray, and said, "It is time to tell the truth, Feray!"

Feray shook her head fiercely. "No, no... Let me explain. At least... please, give me a chance."

"Then tell us what you have to say for yourself. Why would you do such a thing?" Alev said.

The village waited quietly as Feray caught her breath and calmed herself down. Then, she recounted the events that led to the devastation Serenus had gone through.

"I was out in the forest one day. That place is rarely visited. I was looking for some mushrooms and herbs for making medicines. There were plenty, and I was busy collecting them when someone approached me. It was the old lady, limping badly."

Feray sighed, shook her head, and continued in a coarse voice, "I left my things and helped her sit against a tree trunk. I had never seen her before. It was strange, as everyone here knew each other. I expressed my surprise, and she said I was right. That we had never met before. She told me her name was Savita, and she had been a healer before Alev. I had heard the name, so I thought she was telling the truth. I asked her why she wandered in the forest and did not live in the village. She told me the story of how she had been captured by the wizard, and the people thought she was dead. She stayed in captivity for a long time, and during her time with the wizard, she figured out his plans to attack the village. She said she had just escaped the wizard and came to warn us. I was foolish. I believed her words. Her old age made me think that she could not be a threat. She said she had a plan to defeat the wizard by creating a powerful creature to fight him off. I trusted her. She asked me to keep her hidden so the wizard wouldn't know she had escaped. I thought it made sense."

Alev interrupted her story, "You thought Esmeray was Savita, my teacher? And you never thought to ask me about it? Savita died in front of my eyes. If you had talked to me, we would have found out that it was actually Esmeray."

Feray sighed and continued, "I see now that I was wrong. But at the time, I thought I was doing the right thing. I had no reason to doubt she was not Savita. She taught me things that only an expert healer could know."

"Esmeray tricked you into creating a weapon for her. What does she intend to do next?" Alev asked.

Feray replied, "When we heard the warning from Qilam, I thought the attack was imminent, and so I helped her, putting aside all the concerns I had. I thought I was protecting everyone."

"What does Esmeray intend to do?" Alev repeated.

Feray continued, "Esmeray needs the vials of light to keep the creature alive and strong, and that is why she will attack the Tree Circle with her beast."

Everyone tensed on hearing the possibility of another attack, and the elders whispered amongst themselves. Feray started sobbing again but finally got hold of herself and spoke. Her voice was teary. "I was stupid enough to believe her. She tricked me, and I fell for it. I brought her here with the best intentions. She provided me with detailed illustrations, and Kratos and others trusted me and followed my directions. If only I had known...."

Alev was stern and not going to show kindness to Feray. "But you did, didn't you? You know the laws of Seren magic. Our magic is not to be used to create such a creature. It is unforgivable. Moreover, you defied the laws by keeping her hidden. You were supposed to inform the elders no matter what you thought or believed," she continued harshly, "I have known you since you were young. I know how ambitious you are. I taught you humility when you craved recognition and praise, but you didn't learn to subdue your desires. Don't act as if you never knew what you were doing. You did. You wanted to do something others couldn't, and you didn't care about the laws."

Feray's bowed head said it all. She knew the laws, yet she chose to perform the unspeakable act. Jinyan, the elder sitting next to Alev, was equally strict. "Kratos came to talk to you. How do you explain what you did to him?"

"I didn't do anything. It was Esmeray. She didn't want him to mess up our plans. She said he would stay unconscious long enough to finish our work. I meant him no harm." Then Feray looked at me and continued, "You saved Kratos. I am in your debt forever. If something were to happen to him, I could never forgive myself."

Jinyan interjected, "What about the ones who got hurt in the attack? Have you forgiven yourself for inflicting misery on them?"

Feray continued with a bowed head, "I never meant any of it to happen. I thought I was protecting everyone."

Alev looked at the elder I had not met before. Her light blue eyes made her look different from the rest. "Alia," she said, "are you ready to test Feray?"

Feray sobbed as Alia replied in a cold, distant voice, "I am." She stood up slowly.

Boris signalled for everyone to sit down, and they moved away from Alia. Alia sat down on the ground under the arch.

Amy walked over to the Moontree and picked a white flower. She put it inside the Moonlight vial, and it started to move around ferociously, creating a bubbling mist.

Amy placed the vial in front of Alia, who looked so calm, as if in deep meditation. Slowly, Moonlight started to calm down and glowed gently on Alia's face.

We waited quietly. I was curious about the trial. How were the elders going to judge Feray?

After some time, Alia opened her eyes and said, "I am ready. Bring her close."

Feray raised her head and looked at Alia, then addressed Alev angrily. "How can you do this to me? I have spent all my life here among my people. I have made one mistake, JUST ONE! And you are going to test me? Have you forgotten all that I have done?"

Alev stayed quiet, but her expression said it all. She didn't trust Feray.

Amy asked Feray to go ahead and sit by Alia. She lashed out at her. "I won't take this insult. I refuse to be tested." She turned and tried to walk away, but the guardians stopped her, holding her arms firmly. She resisted, but they did not let go.

Kratos went to Feray to try to calm her down. "Feray! Don't be difficult! No one is trying to insult you. We just want to be sure. It is better for you. Once your innocence is proven, no one will ever point the finger at you."

Kratos' words made it clear that he trusted Feray and believed she had unintentionally made a mistake. Feray kept looking at Kratos with fear in her eyes, like a bird in a cage fluttering around anxiously with no hope of getting out. She pleaded, "Kratos! You are my friend. You know me. Don't let them do this to me."

Kratos consoled her, "There is nothing to worry about, Feray. You know you are innocent, then why are you worried? Go on. Sit with Alia!" Feray shouted at him, trying to push the guardians away. "I can see what you are trying to do. You are no friend of mine." She looked around at the elders. "I do not accept this."

With a seething look at Kratos, she tried to break free, but the guardians were too strong. Boris asked them to take her forward. She kept resisting as they dragged her to Alia and tried to make her sit next to her. She shouted at them to leave her alone and fought with all her might. Kratos kept trying to calm her down, but she was senseless with anger.

It was difficult for the guardians to control her. Amy walked to the Bluetree and brought two more vials. One was blue, and the other was indigo. She put her hand in the blue vial and removed a strand of light. Then, she took a strand from the indigo vial and twisted the two strands together to form a rope. She combined the ends, and the lights merged to form a glowing crown.

Kratos and Boris helped the struggling guardians hold Feray down while Amy put the crown around her head. Her anguished expression slowly mellowed, and she stopped resisting. Her eyes softened, and she stared into space. Kratos and Boris helped her sit in front of Alia and put her hands on the vial.

Alia put her hands on Feray's. The crowd became very silent in anticipation. A bright yellow flame erupted above the Moonlight vial and flickered in a non-existent wind. I sensed an alien emotion but couldn't understand it enough to name it.

Slowly, the flame turned orange. It spread an uncomfortable ambiance around us. I looked at others to see if they had felt the change. They had. I turned my attention to Alia and was shocked to see her expression. She looked angry.

The flame quickly deepened into a red one, burning furiously and creating an eerie atmosphere. I felt the heat and was bothered by it, becoming angry with its presence. The feeling rushed through my veins and spread everywhere, fueling my anger with each passing moment. The intensity of the emotion shook me, causing me to clench my hands into fists.

Looking around, my eyes rested on Amy, and I realized that she was the reason for my anger. I hated her for having what I couldn't have and believed she didn't deserve the treasure she possessed. Only I was worthy of it, and she had snatched it from me, which increased my fury with an overwhelming sense of injustice.

As the flames turned into a roaring fire, I heard Alia sneer at Amy, and I realized that everyone was furious with her, though not as much as I was. I loathed her beyond words.

Searching for Alev, I found her sitting pompously in her chair, and I believed she must have been jealous of my achievements. Smirking with disgust, I thought she could only dream of the power and intellect I had. The more I looked at her old, wrinkled face, the angrier I became, and I wanted to hurt her. I clenched my fists even tighter, feeling my nails dig into my palms as I growled, and with a leap, I lunged at her, seething with anger. Strong hands pulled me back as I struggled to break free and attack her, screaming uncontrollably. Someone forced me down to the ground, holding me there as I kicked and punched wherever I could, but they wouldn't let me free. The rage grew inside me until I felt that my body wouldn't take it anymore. Then, it stopped suddenly and started to subdue.

Slowly, my anger transformed into an emotion I couldn't understand, and I trembled violently in its claws. Looking at the faces around me helplessly, I realized that none of them could help me, and behind them, the fire burned blue above the white orb. My heart ached as the anger drained out of my body, and instead, I drowned in raw pain. What had I done? I wished time could go back so that I wouldn't think of it ever again. NEVER! But the time had gone, and there was nothing I could do. Wrapping my arms around my legs, I rocked back and forth in hopeless agony, my face drenched with tears. Why did I do it? What for? No answer came forth, and I couldn't breathe. The air was suffocating me. Looking around in exasperation, I saw my pain reflected on the desolate faces around me. Tears ran down their flushed cheeks, and a sob escaped my mouth. The white orb with blue fire danced in front of my eyes as the sobbing rocked my body, and my mind went dark.

I felt weak and tired as I opened my eyes and saw the flickering light from a torch lighting the dim room. I could see the room's wooden ceiling while lying on a bed. The place was familiar. I tried to remember where I was. My mind was clouded. How did I get here? It took me a long time to recover an image inside my head — a furious fire burning above a softly glowing white orb.

I remembered everything and felt sick. What had happened?

I recalled feeling jealous of Amy and was confused. I had always liked her, but earlier, I wanted to hurt her. I was furious at everyone in Serenus. I felt cheated out of my fair right. I tried to attack Alev. The memory of it shocked me. What was it that came afterward? An emotion that was so strong and painful that my mind couldn't take it, and I fell unconscious. There was no reason for me to feel what I had. Yet I felt it deeply.

The door opened, and Kratos entered the room. His face was drawn and tired.

"Thank the Light! You are awake. We were worried for you. How are you feeling now?" He sat next to me and watched me with concerned eyes.

"Tired but fine," I said.

He sighed in relief.

"Kratos! What happened to me? I attacked Alev!" I asked him. My desperate voice betrayed my feelings of shock and shame.

He shook his head and said, "What do you think happened to you?"

I went over the memories again, trying to find the reason for the incredible experience. There was no reason to feel the way I did. I knew those emotions were not mine. They couldn't be. I couldn't feel like that for Amy. If anyone could feel that way... it was Feray.

"Did I feel what Feray was feeling? Jealous of Amy for taking her place. Proud of her own talent and angered by Alev's decision to test her."

Kratos nodded. He looked sad. "That's right. You felt what Feray was feeling at the time. At first, I was surprised by her resistance to being tested because I believed with all my heart that she was innocent. But now, it is clear that she wasn't. She helped Esmeray because she was too proud of herself and wanted to do something no one had ever done without regard to right and wrong. She was jealous of Amy and hated her. You attacking Alev was, in fact, a reflection of the despise Feray felt toward her."

He paused and sighed loudly. I felt sad for him. He had believed in Feray and truly cared for her, but she had let him down. It was not easy to deal with such a blow.

"I am sorry, Kratos. I know how you must be feeling."

He gave a slow, tired smile and nodded. "Do you remember what you felt before you fell unconscious?"

"I do, but I don't understand that feeling."

"Regret. Feray regrets her decisions and her actions." He was right. I nodded. She was not innocent, but she realized how much damage her actions had caused. I knew it without any doubt, as I had experienced her feelings as my own. My body shuddered as I remembered the emotion.

"How did it happen? How could I feel what Feray was feeling?"

"It wasn't just you. All of us experienced her feelings, though they affected you much more than us. It was Alia. She is the Mirror. She has this strange ability to reflect a person's feelings. She can feel what her subject is feeling, and she can make others around her experience those feelings as their own. No one knows how it works or why, but it does."

"What did the elders decide about Feray?" I asked.

"Alev called off the meeting after you fell unconscious. It was proven that Feray was not innocent, but the decision about her fate is still pending. The elders will meet again soon to announce it. But before that, there is another pressing matter."

"What is that?"

Kratos continued, "Looks like there will be another attack. Esmeray wants to steal all the vials of light to keep her beast strong. The elders are meeting again. You should rest now. I will let you know what happens."

I did not want to rest. I wanted to attend the meeting. "Can I come with you?"

"If that's what you want," Kratos replied gently.

We left the lodge for the meeting. It was raining again, so it was held at Alev's place. Kratos and I were the first to arrive at the sitting room for the meeting.

Soon, the elders arrived. Jinyan was the last one to be carried in by two sturdy guardians. Alev waited until everyone was seated and comfortable. Then she started the meeting.

"Yesterday was a terrible day. We witnessed betrayal, deceit, and cruelty. Our own let us down. But today is a new day. Let's pull ourselves together and prepare for the inevitable battle. The sooner we fight it off, the quicker the peace will be restored."

She paused as everyone listened to her with respect and attention.

"Alia has shown us that Feray was indeed telling the truth. Her actions were misguided and full of pride, but she was tricked by Esmeray to do such a thing."

Jinyan nodded and said, "You are right, Alev! I am sure Feray created the creature as the Seren defender. But it is now in the hands of Esmeray, and she wants to take all the vials. We cannot allow this. We need to stop her."

Boris was next to share his thoughts. "I have read Conrad's journals. I believe he stopped Esmeray using some kind of weapon. He did not survive the fight, or we would have known how to make such a weapon. If we could find out what it was, we would be in a better position to fight back."

Everyone nodded. After a while, Jinyan said, "There is only one place to find what we don't know about Conrad's weapon."

Alev thought for a while. Then she said decidedly, "We will visit Sere!"

Instantly, the atmosphere in the room changed. Loud gasps followed by whispering among the Seren elders and guardians. Alev ignored the reaction and continued.

"We will leave early in the morning. Boris, make preparations for the journey. The weather is bad. We must be back before the evening falls."

Ch 09: To Find the One

Kratos and I went outside before anyone else. The weather was sad and gloomy, and it was already evening. After Kratos left to rest in the Orangetree chamber, I wandered around the village center for some time, but I was not comfortable out in the open. The rain had left big puddles behind, and there was no place to sit. I was about to head home when Amy came and asked for help, and I was more than happy to oblige.

We walked toward the glowing Moontree, which looked even more impressive in the dark, and the raindrops hanging on its leaves and flowers gave it a surreal look. Amy invited me into the chamber, where the walls were lined with the usual backless shelves containing Moonlight vials. Glancing up at the ceiling, I saw a wide opening in the roof. The heavily entwined branches shied away from each other to make the circular opening right in the middle, above the bulb.

Another look at the bulb startled me. The light inside was fading. Amy understood the look on my face and said, "It has been raining a lot. On cloudy days, the trees cannot generate enough light to store in the bulb. We used the light to heal Kratos and for the mirror's test. The Moontree needs more light. It is dangerous for the tree to run out of its light. We need to pour the light from the vials on the shelf onto the bulb, being careful not to spill any. We cannot afford to waste any amount."

Cautiously, we brought the vials to the bulb one after the other and poured them onto the top, middle part, where it connected to the branches. The fruit absorbed the light and stored it inside, slowly filling the bulb.

As we did this, Amy surprised me with a new revelation. The seven trees around the Whitetree provided their beneficial healing effect when the Moontree had Moonlight in its fruit. If the Moontree ran out, the others stole the light from all living things nearby and refilled the bulb in the mother tree. Without the Moonlight, the trees would destroy instead of heal.

Amy didn't know how long the clouds would continue to darken the sky, and then there was an upcoming battle to think of. She was worried that the trees could turn against us if the Moonlight ran out.

She pointed toward the shelves, "These shelves were glowing with Moonlight yesterday. Now, they are empty. Deserted. Feray used most of it for her ambition. Moonlight is difficult to collect, and it is vital for the Seren, yet she wasted it so callously. She didn't care for her people. Alev is right. She doesn't deserve our kindness."

I was sad for Amy. She deserved loyalty, yet she received indifference and cruelty from her mentor. I didn't try to console her. I understood that nothing could comfort her at the time.

The guardians stayed outside the trees as we walked out toward our homes. On our way, I asked Amy about the place we were going to in the morning. She reminded me of its name, "Sere." Then she added, "It's a cursed place, a ruin. A place that has seen a battle between Conrad and Esmeray and was destroyed by it."

"Why do the elders want to go there?" Sere sounded dangerous and scary.

"It is cursed, but it is where Conrad recorded his memories. If there is any hope of finding any answers, we will find them there," Amy explained.

Amy left on a different path for her home, and I continued on to my own as the rain started again. The rain was gentle but loud, the waterfalls ran aggressively, and the nearby forest was full of the sounds of the night. As I stopped outside my home, I noticed footprints in the mud. Someone had been there. I walked slowly on the boardwalk to avoid making any sound, went over the fence to the backyard, and reached the back window as silently as I could. Peeking inside, I saw a figure sitting on a chair, looking toward the lit fireplace inside the house. His back was towards me, and a cloak hid his head. Without turning or looking at me, he said, "Come inside! Let's talk."

My knees weakened, and I gasped in fear. I started shivering and felt sweat forming on my body, even as the rain washed it away. The hooded figure spoke again, "Come inside. We need to talk."

Scared, I asked, "Are you the wizard?"

The hooded figure slowly turned its face toward me and moved the head covering back to expose himself. "It's me, Qilam. It is cold outside. Come in. We need to talk."

I knew that the guardians were looking for Qilam. For a moment, I thought of running to the village to tell them he was in my home, but then I decided against it. He could easily run away and disappear into the forest by the time I came back with the guardians. He had chosen to come to me because I lived alone. I decided to hear what he had to say. His past warning had helped the Seren, after all. I walked to the front, entered the home, dried myself, and sat next to him. We looked at each other silently, and the fire crackled loudly in the fireplace. I stayed quiet, still nervous, as I waited for him to speak.

"Esmeray..." he said and stopped abruptly.

"What about her?" I inquired.

He thought for a moment and then responded in a monotonous

tone, "She has been talking to me. She wanted me to join her. She thought I would be mad at everyone for blaming and ignoring me after Alfred left. She told me about her plans to take the vials. I did not want to hurt anyone, so I told her that I would not join her. She threatened me. That is why I have been hiding. I had to inform the village of the impending attack. After that, I ran and hid in the forest."

I nodded. It made sense. Qilam leaned forward and spoke urgently, "I did not want to come to you and put you in any danger, but I have nowhere else to go. Esmeray is looking for me. I had to come here to tell you about her next plan."

The fireplace crackled, then a loud boom of thunder outside shook me. The atmosphere added to my fears. I tried to calm myself and asked, "What does Esmeray intend to do?"

"Firstly, I believe that she could very well be the wizard. It makes her way more dangerous than we anticipated. During my research, I found many things about the wizard. These things help me understand her mindset. Therefore, I can predict her next move."

He looked right into my eyes and said the horrible words, "She will burn down the Tree Circle if she cannot have all the vials. You need to convince the elders to let her take them. This is the only way to get rid of her. It's a price we have to pay to protect Serenus."

"She is already so dangerous. Why would the elders do that?"

"Because once she has the vials, she plans to leave the island."

"And what if she takes the vials and doesn't leave the island? She will be more powerful than ever, and we will not be able to do anything."

He responded casually, "If she is the wizard, which I believe she is, she doesn't care about Serenus. She wants to go to the next islands and find the lost scroll. She wants ultimate and unchallenged power. Nothing less will satisfy her. To her, the Seren and their lives are meaningless. Her ambitions are everything. If she can go, she will. But if she can't, she will burn everything and destroy everyone who stands in her way."

The elders were already worried about the same thing. I agreed with Qilam's words and told him about the meeting with the elders. I skipped the part about the visit to Sere the following day but assured him that the elders were planning to fight her and they wouldn't give up the vials.

Anger twisted Qilam's face. "They are so irrational. They cannot fight her. She will destroy the Tree Circle. They should hand over the vials and let her leave forever. It's a small price to pay to save the island." He paused and then reinforced his words with another argument, "It is an opportunity for us to get rid of the wizard forever. I think we should take it."

His argument was sound, but I understood that we couldn't trust that Esmeray would leave after she had all the power.

Qilam said, "The elders won't listen to me, and I have important things to do. You need to persuade the elders." His words worried me. I asked, "What are you planning to do?"

Taken aback by the question, he said, "I need to find a new hiding place. I am just saying that we should take the offer, but I don't intend to play any role. I have already put my life at risk by warning you about the attack. I have made her my enemy. Yes, I want her to leave forever so that I can live in peace, but it is also in the best interest of everyone in Serenus."

We sat quietly for a while. Then I asked, "Are you hungry? Would you like something to eat?" He nodded. I brought him fruit and some bread with soup. As he ate, I thought about his words.

"How are you so sure that she will take the vials and leave the island?" I asked.

"People like her are power-hungry. The power of the beast is not enough for her. She wants the lost scroll. We have searched this island for generations, and we are quite sure that the scroll is not here. She needs to go to the lands past the veil. She wants a position of power in the next world, which is why she needs the beast. Now, she needs the light vials to make the journey. If we let her go, it would help her, but it also helps us. Think about it. Never having to worry about the evil wizard again. Isn't that the best for Serenus?"

"Yes, but what happens if she doesn't leave?" I asked in exasperation.

"Then we are in big trouble, me more than others," he responded with a shaky voice.

He had risked everything to warn us of the attack on the village. His warning triggered the elders, who placed armed guardians around the trees. That was probably why Esmeray had to leave with the beast without taking the vials. He had done everything a scared and honest villager would do. But I knew what others thought of him. They knew him better than I did, and I couldn't ignore their suspicions so easily. I felt obliged to him for his role and expressed my gratitude.

Qilam said, "I am as much a part of this island as anyone else. They may think my ideas are crazy or even dangerous, but I can't allow anyone to harm Serenus."

I asked him to stay for the night. He agreed. "I am very grateful. I will not bother you too much and leave early in the morning."

We sat quietly for some time, listening to the rain and watching the fireplace. I put more wood on the fire and asked Qilam, "What do you know about the lost scroll?"

His eyes shone with excitement as he replied, "The lost scroll? It is very powerful knowledge that was lost in time."

"Most of the Seren seem to think it's just a story. Do you think it's real?" I asked.

"Yes, I do. As real as you and me. More real. It is the only thing that is real in this world," Qilam chanted passionately.

"What do you mean by that?" I asked.

He spoke prophetically as I looked at his glowing face. "I don't think this world is real. It is just a test. Real life starts after you pass this test. I think the finder of the scroll will move on to live a real life that will be everlasting. Everlasting life for an all-powerful wizard."

He pointed at himself and me. "You see, we are not just this. We are so much more than this body."

"You want the lost scroll?" I asked directly.

"Every sensible, smart person should want the lost scroll. Finding it is the goal of this life, and once found, it will wake us to the world beyond all worlds."

The more I listened to him, the less I trusted his words. I wondered what the source of this information was. "How do you know this?"

"Oh, I know. Trust me. I was born with this knowledge. You know how some Seren come to this island with magical abilities? I came with a voice that speaks in my head."

His words were absurd. "And what does this voice tell you? Where do we come from?" I asked mockingly.

"You don't believe me? Didn't you hear the warning in your

dream when you woke up in the boat? Didn't you hear the voice?"

"Yes, everyone hears that. The voice in the dream wants to wake us up," I replied.

"Right." He moved forward on his chair. Now he was sitting at the edge, leaning toward me, looking straight into my eyes. "I hear it every day. And this voice talks to me about things you cannot imagine."

"Like what?"

"It speaks of a world beyond all the worlds. The one where we are gods. It calls me to itself. It is waiting for me there." He paused, running his hand through his messy beard, "The voice wants me to go after the lost scroll and become an all-powerful wizard. It says it is my mission, everyone's mission."

Qilam was past his middle years and had clearly failed at his job as a thinker. I thought he was going mad, and that's why he heard these voices in his head.

He continued speaking passionately, "You know, you and I are not different. We are the same. You question the things that other people don't question. Everyone in the village lives this life as if it is the real world. It is not. You and I know that we have come from somewhere and have to go somewhere. We have not yet reached our destination. Our future is wide open and full of amazing journeys. It is such a loss that people waste their lives here."

He was not hiding behind his words anymore and spoke clearly, so I asked, "What if you are wrong and there is no next world? What if anyone who left Serenus died without ever reaching another land?"

All his excitement vanished, and he moved back in his chair. He stared at the fireplace and spoke in a monotonous voice, "Then I am the biggest idiot who has ever lived, and the voices in my head are lying to me. But I have no way of knowing for sure. I only know what I know, and there is only one way to know more." His voice became confident once again, and he perked up in the chair. "I will go looking for the next world to find out. Oh, and I have one more reason for you to believe me. I have never told anyone about it, but I want you to know."

I didn't believe him, but at the same time, I wanted to know what he was talking about. "What is it?"

He said, "I woke up with the poem like everyone did, but I also had another page with me."

My eyes opened wide as he searched his pockets and produced a badly crumpled paper. He straightened it and handed it to me, then asked me to read it. I read it out loud:

"Train from the pod, prove your worth,

Grow into a god beyond this earth.

Very few are winners, and big is our need,

Overcome the failures and then proceed.

There's more to try if a branch will fail,

No reason to cry and nothing to wail,

We'll trace back to one and then reseed,

To find the one who will succeed."

I looked at Qilam in disbelief. He said, "I've never met another person who came with this poem. I have it. It must mean something. I am supposed to play a role. Though I don't know what."

I was shocked at what he was saying. He had another poem that nobody else had. How could I trust it? What if he wrote it himself? He could be crazy enough to believe in his own made-up stories.

One thing was clear: Qilam believed in it blindly, but there was no way for me to know if any of this was real.

I asked, "Everyone started in a boat with a poem. Someone gave it to us for a reason. The watch is also mysterious. No one seems to know what it is about. This much I understand, and I agree that there could be much more than we know, but how you leap from this to the desire to try going into the dark is beyond me. The island is quite large, and there are mysteries in even the smallest things. How do you know that the verse, 'the world is so vast,' refers to other worlds?"

He read the verses from the poem: "'Grow into a god beyond this earth.' 'Catch the wizard; go past the fall.' These are all very clear instructions."

"So, why are you still here?" I was annoyed by his beliefs and efforts to convince others while he was afraid of trying it for himself.

"I guess I lack the courage to find out if I'm right or wrong. You are right in your observation. I should have gone past the veil a long time ago."

"No, I don't mean you should have gone into the dark. I mean, you shouldn't preach to others what you don't fully believe in yourself. And if you really believed in it, you wouldn't be here."

I had made up my mind about him, and I knew that he had convinced Alfred and four others to go into the Dark End with his words while he was still here sitting in my warm and comfortable home, trying to convince me that it was worth going.

He confused me with his next words. "You are right. I should do what I believe in. I will go to the next world. I just need to do one thing first." He relaxed considerably as if he had really made up his mind.

"What is it that you need to do?" I asked.

"I want to see Esmeray defeated, only so I can leave with the peace of mind that Serenus is safe."

We sat in front of the fire for a long time, immersed in our own thoughts. I got up when I was too tired to think clearly and asked Qilam to rest as well.

Once again, I was teleported to another world. I saw the wizard standing on the edge of a cliff, overlooking a vast expanse of rolling hills and valleys shrouded in a thick, impenetrable mist. He knew that beyond that dark wall of fog lay the object of his quest: a weapon that could break down the barrier and reveal the secrets hidden within.

The wizard closed his eyes and began to concentrate, channelling his magical energies into a spell that would reveal the path he must take. Suddenly, a burst of light erupted from his fingertips, illuminating the surrounding landscape with an otherworldly glow. The light coalesced into a shining beacon that pointed the way forward, and the wizard set off toward it with purpose.

As he journeyed through the mist, the wizard encountered many dangers and obstacles. Strange creatures lurked in the shadows, their eyes glowing with malevolent intent. The wizard summoned his magic to ward them off, blasting them with bolts of pure energy that sent them scurrying back into the darkness.

Despite the challenges, the wizard pressed on, driven by a fierce determination to reach his goal. Finally, he arrived at the foot of a towering mountain, its peak lost in the swirling mists above. The wizard knew that the weapon he sought was at the summit, and he began the arduous climb up the rocky face.

As he neared the top, the wizard's heart raced with anticipation. He could feel the power pulsing through the very rock beneath his feet. With a final burst of energy, the wizard reached the summit and stood before a massive, ancient staff embedded in the stone.

The staff glowed with an eerie light, and the wizard knew that this was the weapon he had been seeking. With a deep breath, he grasped the staff and pulled it free from the stone. The staff glimmered in his hand, radiating a powerful energy that filled the wizard with confidence and strength.

With the staff in hand, the wizard turned and made his way back down the mountain, slicing through the mist with ease. The dark wall of mist that had once seemed impenetrable now parted before him like a curtain.

Ch 10: Wanderings Alone

A knock on the door woke me up. Before opening it, I looked around for Qilam, but he wasn't there. He must have left already. He had cleaned up after himself, and there was no sign of him ever being here. I opened the door and invited Idir inside.

"We will be leaving for Sere soon," he reminded me as he came inside.

"Yes, I will get ready quickly," I replied.

He helped me start a fire to make breakfast. We ate together, and I kept thinking about my conversation with Qilam. I did not want to tell anyone about what he said about the other poem or his plans to go into the dark, but I had to reveal the threat of the attack.

"Qilam came to me last night," I said softly.

Idir jumped in surprise. "What? Why? What did he want?"

"He said Esmeray will destroy the Tree Circle if we don't hand over all the vials of light," I answered soberly.

Idir gasped and stood up abruptly. "We need to leave right now. The elders should know Esmeray's plan before it's too late."

We left everything as it was and ran out toward the village center. The warning, once again, was dire.

We found Amy on her way to the trees and Kratos in the elders' home. The worry on our faces frightened everyone. I revealed the news of another attack.

"Qilam came to me last night and told me that Esmeray will burn down the Tree Circle and kill anyone who stands in her way unless we give her the vials of light. He believes that once she has the vials, she will leave this world forever and go into the Dark End," I tried to be as concise as possible.

Alev raised her brows. "Esmeray will take everything she ever wanted and then just go into the dark? Why would she do that? That makes no sense."

I tried to explain. "Qilam believes that Esmeray wants to go to the next world with a weapon that could ensure her a place of power there."

Alev interrupted me. "And why is Qilam not coming to us with this information? Why is he hiding?"

"He warned us of the attack on the village. Because of that, Esmeray could not take the vials before the beast came alive. He is afraid she will kill him. That is why he is hiding," I clarified.

Boris spoke up this time. "I wonder why Esmeray can't kill him when she goes to tell him her plans?"

"No, it's not what you think. Esmeray wanted Qilam to join her. She thought he would not care about Seren because the villagers didn't believe him and left him alone. He didn't join her but knew her plans. He shared her plans with us. That's why his life is in danger. We shouldn't doubt his intentions. He already saved the vials from Esmeray," I defended Qilam and tried to show them his perspective. "We should be grateful for what he has done for everyone."

Boris laughed a smug laugh. "And why does a powerful wizard want Qilam to join her? What could she get out of his companionship? Some crazy thoughts and a life void of any useful action? In what way has he ever contributed to Serenus? He is a complete nuisance. No one wants to be with him." He turned to me. "You are too naive." Alev addressed us sternly. "Stop arguing, both of you! It is great that Qilam came to...." She looked at me and asked, "Have you picked a name yet?" I shook my head. She was clearly disappointed but continued, "For now, nothing changes. We will continue with our plans. We need to find a way to stop

Esmeray. Boris, do what you can to defend against another attack. And hide two guardians near No-Name's house. I want Qilam captured if he shows up again." I left with my head held low and waited outside as the caravan got ready for the visit to Sere. Idir joined me, and we zigzagged around the puddles in the village center. The rain had put out the fire and smoke but couldn't wash away the memories of the terrible day. The broken, burned houses reminded me of the vicious attack. The Seren were working diligently to revive the village. The destroyed trees had been dragged away. I walked on the freshly cleaned paths without any fear of sharp broken glass hurting my feet. The damaged houses were being repaired or reconstructed. I admired my fellow Seren for not giving in to despair. They kept their hopes alive, which gave them the strength to go through the tragedy. Finally, it was time to go. Once the elders were comfortable in a four-seat cart, the strong guardians pushed it ahead. Another two coaches followed them. On our way out of the village, we passed through the forge. The sunlight squeezed through the dark clouds in a feeble attempt to brighten the landscape, but the forge was sad, grey, and silent.

Idir, Amy, Boris, and I walked alongside the elder's cart while some guardians led the party and others stayed at the rear. They were dressed in delicate-looking armour, like those who had arrested me on the day I arrived in Serenus. I wondered how such armour could protect anyone.

As I asked Idir about the armour, he smiled and explained, "This armour only looks delicate. The forgers are quite skilled at making it light enough to carry but as strong as any. The only problem is, it is useless in protecting them against magical adversaries."

The guardians pushed the cart towards the buildings at the back of the forge. Boris and Idir used scythes to cut through the overgrown grass between the two buildings, and soon a path began to take shape, allowing the cart to move on.

The scent of the freshly cut grass was soothing to my fidgety nerves, and I felt light and refreshed. The thought of our dreary destination slipped out of my mind, and we kept walking in sync with the rolling spokes of the elder's cart.

Idir and Boris worked hard to clear the old walkway, which had been buried under wild vegetation and had not been walked on in a long time. Idir confirmed my observation that the Seren had abandoned it, and no one walked over it anymore. Nature had reclaimed it and breathed life back into the ground.

It was a slow and tedious walk through the forest, and we were relieved as we approached a clearing. The forest had grown thin, announcing the end of the forested land. A furious river ran noisily right next to the forest.

Beyond the river was a strange terrain, black and bleak. Its presence took away the relief of getting near the journey's end. With every step, the Seren grew tense. I sensed it in their silence and their nervous eyes fixed on the grey horizon.

An old, worn-out bridge appeared ahead. The guardians brought the cart to a slow stop near it, and Boris went to check the bridge. It creaked loudly under his feet as he walked over its length, but he declared it safe for the cart.

Across the bridge, a wasteland spread between the river and the horizon at the other end. Tall, towering clouds hung over it, confident of their supremacy over the land. We had reached Sere.

The whole place had burned down in a battle between Conrad and Esmeray. The charred tree trunks stood like dark pillars, guarding a secret in the depths of the charcoal forest.

We advanced slowly, leaving footprints on the damp, ashy soil. The lifeless stumps were still mourning whatever tragedy befell the once-alive forest.

I looked around, searching for a tiny seedling, a blade of grass, or a mushroom, perhaps. The place was devoid of life.

I was surprised at the dark grey, empty vastness. It was unnatural. I would expect a burned forest to be overcrowded with grasses gushing out of the ground and seedlings sprouting through the fire-fertilized land. I would expect it to be rich and green. Amy was the one to sense the cause of its eternal destruction. She was sure it was the work of some evil magic. Was it a spell cast by Esmeray? Everyone believed so, though they couldn't prove it.

The cart staggered over the uneven, pathless land. We had to go slower. Time passed silently between us.

A large tree grew out of the horizon slowly. It grew larger and larger as we got closer. Alev pointed toward it, saying it was our destination.

We looked at the massive tree in amazement. It was still standing, but most of its bark was gone, burnt away. Only a few thicker branches still remained on it.

Under the tree was a heap of thin, wrinkled, black branches that looked like all life was sucked out of them. What power could have destroyed such an enormous thing? I felt small and vulnerable in the dark, black world.

Alev described the entrance to the tree, and Boris searched for it with another guardian. It took some time to move the branches out of the way, but they found the opening eventually. It was a hollow in the tree trunk, large enough for one person to go through at a time.

Alev insisted on leaving some guardians outside with the cart while asking others to go through the hollow. The Seren lit the torches and went inside the dark tree trunk. I followed Amy and walked into an open space inside it. Alev and Jinyan sat down on dusty wooden chairs inside.

The chairs were already there, along with a large table. Someone had left them there a long time ago. Judging by their size, they had been made right there in the hollow. It was impossible to bring them in through the narrow entrance.

Boris brought some scrolls in and spread them on the table. Others erected the torches in the brackets fixed in the tree walls. Conrad had stayed here and made the room comfortable. There were dusty scrolls and books on shelves on the tree wall.

"Conrad was a thinker," Alev said, "and this is where he used to come to be alone with his thoughts for days at a time. He recorded many of his thoughts here before he was lost. Search the place and see what we can learn from here." Alev pointed to the walls. "These walls are the keeper of Conrad's memory and the history of Serenus. Read aloud whatever you deem important and note everything. Nothing should be ignored."

The Seren got busy. Everyone went toward the bookshelves while the elders stayed in their chairs. I tried to study the signs and symbols that were drawn on the walls, probably with a sharp tool.

As the words were read aloud, fragments of an untold past began to emerge. Most of the shelves were covered quickly by the diligent Seren, who were busy analyzing and recording information. Boris was engrossed in studying the illustrations and drawings in a notebook. I stood by him, observing as he examined them with great care.

As we delved deeper into Conrad's thoughts, we realized that some of the writings were unrelated to the incident we were investigating. Perhaps, Conrad had used this place to contemplate various matters. However, we continued our search, hoping to uncover more clues.

Suddenly, Boris saw a note and read it out loud. "A line in the line of thought. It thinks what I think." The note was encircled by a deeply etched line. Boris repeated it over and over again, but it didn't seem to fit anywhere in the story we were piecing together. Jinyan thought it might be essential and asked Boris to note it down for later consideration.

Amy read the carved words on the tree wall, which had an almost poetic quality to them:

"A beautiful world, so fascinating!

Its colours and shapes mesmerizing,

Scents and sounds bewitching.

Its blueprint - A master plan, or systems glitching?

Harmony and sameness bring order and perfection,

Or difference is beauty, and balance in friction?

Patterns repeating, very calculating,

Wonderfully symmetrical and yet deviating."

We listened to the words, lost in thought. No one said anything for a while. Idir read the words he was looking at:

"From a seed, to a tree,

Precious yet carefree,

Does it matter if it grows,

Or, as a seedling, it goes?

Does it have a heart, or forever unrelating?

Cruel, and indifferent, Its methods un-abating."

Although I couldn't grasp Conrad's intentions, his words intrigued me. As I walked past Idir, I read the inscription on the adjacent bookshelf:

> "I found myself, but is this reality?
>
> There is more to me, or just an oddity?
>
> An accidental circumstance, or a purposeful soul,
>
> A longing in my heart wants it to be more.
>
> A meaningless existence, or to-God elevating,
>
> A beautiful world, so fascinating!"

Alev got up to read next:

> "Looking for something in wanderings alone,
>
> Disturbance in nothing, to flesh and bone.
>
> Head raised high, my passion knows no limit,
>
> The depths of the ocean, or a perilous summit.
>
> Brave in my heart, and, at times, imitating,
>
> A beautiful world, so fascinating!"

Boris continued:

> "A desperate hope that I won't drown,
>
> But troubles and doubts do cut me down,
>
> I cry and whine and carry a frown,
>
> But only for a while, and then turn around.
>
> Painful, and sad, but also elating!
>
> A beautiful world, so fascinating!"

Conrad's words had clearly sparked everyone's interest, but it was the elders who seemed the most captivated. Jinyan read next:

"What is the point? Where am I going?

Coming to an end, or am I still growing?

I'm thinking it right, or in the wrong context?

Is there a stop? Or always a next?

I'm looking for more, but also debating,

A beautiful world, so fascinating!"

A Guardian stepped aside as he saw Alev approach to read the final passage:

"Make my own path, or walk predetermined fate?

A part of me questions every detail.

Yet other wants to just believe in magic.

Not comprehend? Blind faith can be tragic!

I have a reasoning mind, not logic-negating,

A beautiful world, so fascinating!"

We exchanged glances, impressed and curious, and Alev nodded meaningfully to Jinyan, who returned the gesture. Conrad's words struck a chord, especially with the elders. I couldn't fully comprehend the deeper meaning behind them, but that only added to their mystique. I was a thinker. Was I a thinker like Conrad? Clearly not, I realized with a hint of envy.

After reading the words on the tree wall, we moved on to Conrad's writings in his scrolls. Idir was holding a notebook with a bitter expression on his face. Concerned, I moved closer and asked if everything was okay. He handed me the notebook, and as I began to read it, I was shocked by the words. It was Conrad's journal. The elders were impressed by Conrad's thoughts, and we were here to look for help from his records, but it was clear that Conrad did not think highly of himself. His words painted a stark picture, writing of his failures and struggles in life. He believed he was a disappointment at everything he tried, as if there was a darkness within him that kept him from greatness. I had imagined a heroic thinker who defeated Esmeray and saved Serenus, but it turned out he was consumed by self-doubt and negativity.

Idir saw the sadness on my face and explained, "It's true. Conrad lived a difficult life. People called him lazy and useless, and he believed it to be true. He felt incompetent, unsure of himself, and had trouble keeping up with life. He was a depressed Seren."

I sat down with the journal and continued reading. Conrad had written about how people around him didn't understand him, and he was frustrated and felt alone in his depression. Many pages had incomplete thoughts and stories, as if they weren't important enough or he didn't have the energy to finish them. On one page, he wrote about a horrible dream he had while sitting under the Yellowtree. He saw himself covered in filth on the ground, with all the troubles of his life keeping him down. His problems appeared as a monster keeping a foot on his neck, making it impossible for him to get up. It was just too sad. I couldn't read anymore and returned the journal to Idir.

Idir consoled me, saying, "Don't worry. He was eventually able to get rid of it. He lived up to his full potential. Imagine if he had known then that his actions would one day save the world from a powerful wizard. He spent all that time in misery, thinking less of himself."

Boris found something and called everyone over to look at it. We left Conrad's journal and went to see what he had discovered. It was an illustration with six circles arranged on an arc, with straight lines extending from each circle and converging at a single point ahead. The meeting point was the center of a smaller circle that emitted a thick, wavy line. That was all we could discern from this illustration.

Amy thought it looked familiar. She couldn't be sure, but she remembered seeing something similar in the scrolls at the healer's house. Alev was also intrigued by the circles. "They do look familiar," she said. "Six circles on an arc, with one in the middle gathering something from the others and sending it out."

Nothing came of it. Alev asked everyone to recheck the walls for anything we might have missed. The Seren walked around the room again and confirmed that everything related to the incident had been recorded in Boris's scrolls. "It's time to leave," Jinyan said urgently.

Alev instructed the guardians to place everything containing Conrad's writing in the cart with the supplies. Gathering the scrolls and notebooks didn't take long. Soon, we were out of the tree room and on our way back.

The last rays of the sun shone brightly before evening arrived. We must have missed a strong wind while we were in the tree room, as the towering clouds had dispersed, allowing the sun to warm the damp ground before the colder night set in.

As we returned to the village, dusk was beginning to fall, and everyone needed a thorough wash. Sere had left dark marks on our hands, feet, and clothes. I tried to rub the black stains off my hands with my clothes, but they were stubborn.

When we reached the village center, our companions went their separate ways. Alev announced a meeting for the next morning, and the elders departed. Boris, Amy, Idir, and I went to the healer's home.

The warm aroma of a tangy soup welcomed us as we arrived, and I felt great after a long, warm bath that washed away the charcoal stains. Idir and Boris had also returned from their homes, looking fresh and clean.

Kratos walked in with a curious smile. He had not joined us on our journey to Sere, as Alev had strictly forbidden it due to his health. He had spent the entire day in the Orangetree and had come to ask about our trip.

"Hey!" I shouted excitedly upon seeing Kratos walking into the kitchen with slow, steady steps.

He asked me if I was alright, and I nodded happily. Kratos had a special place in my heart, and seeing him healthy and safe was a great feeling. He demanded that we tell him everything he had missed. Idir recounted everything that happened in Sere, and Boris and Amy joined him. I sat quietly and listened.

Then Boris asked, "Kratos, you never told us how you confronted Esmeray and got hurt."

Kratos replied, "I had gone to Feray to talk about the old lady and the conversation this one heard that night." He pointed to me and asked, "Have you picked a name yet?" I shook my head, and everyone laughed. Kratos smiled and resumed his tale. "I met Feray at the front door and told her that I wanted to talk to her. She wanted us to sit outside, but I insisted we go into the house. She was quite hesitant, but I didn't listen to her excuses and entered the house despite her protests. The old lady was there by the front door, eavesdropping on us. Feray panicked when I asked who she was. She had no answer. I decided to confront the old lady myself. I demanded to know who she was and how she had come to Serenus. She didn't answer. Instead, she muttered something under her breath, and I felt like I was hit in the chest with a burning ball of fire. That's all I remember."

The narration disturbed everyone. Boris noted down Kratos' statement along with the other incidents recorded previously. Idir changed the subject. "So, what now?"

Amy looked at the illustrations in Boris's scrolls. "We must look up this illustration in the healer's scrolls. Tidy up the table. I will bring the scrolls here. I am sure I have seen this before."

I got up to help her with the scrolls. The healer's library was small, with shelves lining three walls from the ceiling to the floor. Amy picked dusty scrolls from one shelf, and we carried them to the kitchen table in our arms.

The torches flickered on the symbols on the scrolls as I looked at them absentmindedly. The others were going through them one by one, trying to find anything that could explain Conrad's illustration.

"Why don't you go and get some rest, Kratos?" Amy suggested. "You need sleep. We will come get you as soon as we find something."

Kratos argued that he had rested a lot already and it was time to work, but Amy ignored his grumbling and made him leave. I followed him out of the healer's home and into the Orangetree. I returned once he was comfortable in bed.

The search through the scrolls took all night. At some point, I fell asleep on the bench. Bright sunlight came through the window and woke me up. I stretched and sat up.

Kratos was sitting quietly nearby, looking healthy. He asked, "Did you sleep well?"

"Yes. I slept like a log. I just woke up," I replied.

He watched me with concern. "How have you been? It must be

difficult for you to witness such troubles."

"Honestly, it was quite scary. But most of all, I was scared for you. Amy and Idir have been very good to me."

"You are strong. I am really grateful for what you did."

Idir called us loudly from the sitting room, his voice carrying excitement. We went out quickly, eager to learn the reason for his enthusiasm. "Amy has an idea. We believe it will work."

We went to the kitchen, buzzing with excited voices. A look outside the window reminded me of the unfortunate incident we had all suffered. I saw two Seren leaving the Redtree, accompanied by their friends or loved ones. They had recovered and were going back to their homes. Life was getting back to normal.

We ate breakfast while Amy showed us the illustrations from the healer's library and Conrad's tree wall. The illustrations were similar, except that the one from the healer's library had symbols written next to the circles sitting on the arc and the one ahead. Idir and Boris had stayed up all night to help Amy with the search. When they finally found the right scroll, the ordeal of understanding the symbols took up the remaining night. They had called the elders to discuss their findings, and we waited for them to arrive.

Idir, Kratos, and Boris discussed making the equipment in the drawing while Amy checked the scrolls continuously.

The elders came to hear the news, and Amy started sharing the conclusion. "This illustration was found in the scrolls from the time of Savita. We believe that Savita and Conrad must have designed it when they thought of ways to deal with Esmeray. Its presence in the library and in Conrad's journal is important. I think Conrad recorded it because it worked."

"What exactly is it?" Jinyan voiced his curiosity.

"It looks like a weapon. The illustration from the healer's library has some symbols written next to the six circles. It took a painfully long time to understand. But we believe the circles are, in fact, vials containing light from the light trees."

She spread the scroll on a small table that Idir had placed in the middle of the room. Everyone leaned forward to see.

Amy explained as she pointed to the illustration, "The six circles here on the arc are the vials of red, orange, yellow, green, blue, and indigo, while this circle in the middle is violet. The arrows show that the light from the six circles is focused on the violet vial. As it passes through it, a single beam of light is released."

Alev nodded in agreement, her face glowing with excitement. "We know that every light has its distinct power. This weapon joins the powers, and I believe this new light must be more powerful than any magic."

I asked quickly, "What is the violet light for? There are no bulbs or shelves on the violet tree. Isn't it just an entrance arch?"

Amy answered, "The violet light is too scarce, so the tree doesn't grow enough to produce fruit, but we can still collect the light and use it."

"What is it used for?" I inquired.

"It is hard to explain, but basically, it brings balance and order to things," Amy said.

Alev listened attentively, then asked, "Amy, do you think this new light could have defeated Esmeray?"

Amy replied, "I do. And if we remake this weapon, we might be able to defeat her once again."

"What do you know about this new light?" Jinyan questioned her.

"Well, I don't know. I have been thinking about it. There are two possibilities. It could have all the properties of every source light, or it could have a completely different power of its own."

Jinyan was reluctant to experiment with the lights until the effect of the new light was known.

Alev asked Amy for the illustration and studied it for some time. Then she looked up from the sheet and said, "Savita was fascinated by the lights and their effects on us. Before Esmeray came, she had started experimenting with them. I had worked with her in her experiments. We mixed lights together and made new shades and hues. But we always added the Moonlight to keep the effects positive. Without Moonlight, the lights became aggressive."

Amy continued, "I think since this device doesn't take any Moonlight, it must be a weapon that can be used to attack instead of heal."

Jinyan said, "This light could be dangerous. We saw what happened to Sere."

Alev responded, "We will be careful and understand it before we use it. And I am sure it was Esmeray's fire magic that destroyed Sere."

Jinyan nodded, "What colour would the new light be?"

Others began to discuss different possibilities about the new light. I listened to their discussion while studying the illustration. Red, orange, yellow, green, blue, indigo, and violet. All colours of the Light trees. All except white. What could it be that has all the colours? I kept repeating the question in my head. And then, I rephrased the question. "What could it be that is all colours?"

The realization came suddenly, and without thinking twice, I said out loud, "Black! It will be black."

Jinyan huffed in annoyance. "Black is darkness. It is the absence of light. There can't be a black light."

I rephrased my words to better convey my thought, "I don't know if I am right or not. I am sure you know that black is not a colour in itself. It is all the colours. Perhaps Savita used all the colour lights and created something black."

Alev nodded slowly. "I think No-Name might be right. We have worked with the lights for so long, and we still don't fully understand what they are capable of." Then she addressed Amy, "I would say we try it and see what happens. We will carry out the experiment away from the village. I will accompany you. Everyone else must stay back."

Jinyan agreed reluctantly as others gave their approval. They wanted to test it quickly, so Amy left to collect the vials for the experiment. It was decided that everyone else would wait in the healer's house.

Waiting was agonizing. We were excited about the experiment but, at the same time, anxious about the result. It might not turn out as we thought.

We stayed inside and paced in the room. When I couldn't take it anymore, I left the house and went for a stroll in the yard. The weather was pleasant, with beautiful sunshine and a clear blue sky extending from horizon to horizon. The floral trees swayed gently in the occasional light breeze.

The guardians made sure that no one could go near Alev and Amy as they experimented with the lights in the forest.

We ate our midday meal at the healer's house. There was still no news of Alev and Amy.

As time passed, the excitement and thrill turned into worry. We whispered amongst ourselves nervously. Kratos wanted to go and check on them, but Jinyan forbade him from leaving the room. He was even more strict than Alev.

The front door opened, and we rushed toward the sitting room. Amy was back, and two guardians were bringing Alev in. They smiled at us broadly.

"We did it," Amy said with excitement. "We created the black light."

I watched Amy's sparkling face as she explained how they had to experiment with distances between the vials, and eventually, it worked. She continued, "The moment I arranged them one last time, the lights sent their rays out in thin, straight lines. They fell on the violet vial without entering it. A beam of glittering black light came out of the vial. I don't know if I should call it light—it looked more like a silk fabric but intangible. It fell on a plant we chose as our target and completely engulfed it. Then the plant started to wither as the ribbons sucked the life out of it. We had to stop to save the plant, but now we know that it drains life from its target. Both Alev and I studied it carefully. We have no doubt about it being powerful."

Alev agreed. "I am confident about using it against Esmeray. It is pure and mysterious. It exudes a sensation of great power. All we need now is the equipment to carry the source lights in. Amy has recorded the amounts of lights and the distances carefully. We already have the illustration to follow. Let's get to it."

Jinyan was happy now that it had been tested. The elders left satisfied. Amy explained the recordings she had noted for making the equipment. She wanted a way to keep the violet light vial aside till it was needed, a movable trigger perhaps. It should align the vial with others when the equipment is ready to be used.

"It is easy," Kratos assured, "We won't take long to make the equipment. Just keep the vials ready. Let's give Esmeray a hard time."

Amy said worriedly, "The violet light is in an awfully small amount in the Indigotree chamber. We don't have a lot to use."

Kratos provided some much-needed hope, "We will do with what we have. Let's hope it will be enough."

Kratos sat back in the chair and discussed how to make the equipment. Idir moved closer to him, and they were lost in their discussion about finalizing its design.

Boris insisted they call it a weapon. He said it gave him a good feeling. "Alright, Boris! Weapons they are," Idir laughed happily.

Ch 11: Prepare For Battle

The following two days passed slowly. I stayed at the healer's home most of the time, worried that Qilam might come looking for me if I went back to my home. I didn't want him to be captured. Though I believed he had done the right thing, the elders still doubted his intentions. Idir often visited me, explaining the different techniques metal forgers used to make weapons.

The best part of the day was mealtime. I ate with Idir and Boris in the healer's kitchen, and they talked about their progress on the weapons. They had made a prototype that Kratos approved after many measurements and questions. Now they were making more.

We needed a total of nine weapons. Amy calculated and informed us that only that much Violetlight would be available.

I left the healer's home for a walk, and a light breeze lifted my spirits. It felt good to be outside. The village centre was clean and organized. It was surprising how quickly the Seren completed the repair and reconstruction work. It was like nothing had happened to it except that it still looked deserted. They still had to make benches and tables for midday meals and gatherings.

Some Seren gathered around me and warmly greeted me. They wanted me to tell them how I saved Kratos. They listened intently and asked many questions while I recounted the unfortunate incident. They begged for more details, and I repeated the story with as many details as I could. Eventually, they were satisfied and began to leave.

Then, I left for the forge to see how the weapons were being made. Fabio and Misa met me on the way as they were heading to the village center to get food for the workers at the forge. Instead of going to the forge, I walked back with them.

We had a lot to share as we had not met since the fire. They had been busy with the repairs in the village. We chatted pleasantly as we walked through the village. Suddenly, Fabio stopped and said in a singsong voice, "Here comes Duncan!" He shared a meaningful smile with Misa.

I watched the thin man walking toward us. His eyes moved around constantly, touching everything for just a moment before moving on to the next. He rushed toward me the moment he saw me, almost gliding above the ground, his wings flapping in excitement.

He approached us and asked me with exaggerated surprise, "Are you...?" Then he came closer and asked Misa, "Is he...?" His excitement didn't let him complete his sentences.

Misa patted him on the shoulder with a smile. "Yes, Duncan. He is the one who saved Kratos."

Fabio put his arm around Duncan's shoulder and introduced him. "This is Duncan, the most intelligent Seren you will ever find."

He looked intelligent with sparkling eyes. Fabio asked, his voice full of respect, "What are you going to enlighten us about today, Duncan?"

Duncan straightened his shoulders and rubbed his hands together. His gaze fell on me. "Let me tell you how you got here!"

Misa interrupted, "O enlightened one! He came here like everyone else. In a boat."

Fabio tied his hands behind his back and stood with a bowed head. Something was going on here, but I couldn't understand it. Fabio and Misa were definitely up to something.

Duncan looked at them indignantly. "True, but it is never that simple. A lot goes between leaving and arriving." He turned to me, smiling brightly. "I will tell you how you came here." He paused to think for some time, rubbing his chin. "Aha! I've got it!" he announced excitedly. "Move back! Make some space. I need to draw it on the ground for you to understand. You see, such things are not easy to grasp."

Fabio and Misa smiled, and we moved back and stood in a semi-circle. Duncan picked up a stick and started to draw something on the ground. First, he drew a circle with the stick, leaving a tiny break where the ends should have joined together.

"This is us, Serenus. Now, you would ask where exactly is Serenus?"

He extended the open ends of the circle in straight lines in opposite directions. He walked quite a bit in both directions to draw a long line. It looked like a long line with a circle near the middle. Next, he divided the straight line into many parts by marking short lines.

He continued, "These parts here are the lands. In the beginning, Serenus was on the line, just like all the other lands. Later on, the circumstances demanded that our land drift away. We couldn't leave the line, of course. So..."

Misa and I were as puzzled as Fabio, but he couldn't stop himself and interrupted Duncan's narration with, "What exactly is the line?"

Duncan replied earnestly. "It is The Line, of course. Where the lands exist."

Clearly, he believed in what he was saying, though it did not make sense to me. I listened quietly in the hope of understanding his complex idea.

Duncan picked up again. "So, what did we do? We made the land so heavy that the line itself started to curve inwards under its weight till it encircled it completely. See this place?"

Duncan pointed to the opening in the circle. "This is where the opening to this world exists." We looked at each other with amused surprise.

I smiled at Fabio as I slowly understood the reason behind their secretive smiles. Fabio nodded to affirm my observation, but we stayed quiet and listened.

"You cannot just walk through this opening. Till you go around the circle." Duncan got up and clapped his hands to dust off the invisible dirt. "After you went around, you walked the length of the circle around the line. No one can imagine the hardships you faced and the places you saw. You proved your worth by staying steadfast. And finally, your labour paid off. You were deemed worthy of getting in the most magnificent land of all, Serenus."

Fabio and Misa burst into laughter as Duncan completed his absurd tale. He ignored their laughter and asked me, "That's how it was, right?" His eyes twinkled. He waited in hopeful anticipation for my response.

I hesitated. He had narrated the story with such excitement and conviction that it was difficult for me to discourage him. I fidgeted with my hands. Duncan was now hovering a foot or so above the ground, his wings flapping in excitement. Fabio and Misa were still laughing uncontrollably.

Reluctantly, I replied, "I am sorry, but no. This is not how I came here."

His eyes lost a bit of lustre, but he craved affirmation. "Don't just deny it. Tell me where I am wrong. I was close, at least, right?"

I felt terrible for the poor fellow who wanted so badly to be correct. I hated to answer, but what else could I say? "Not even close."

His wings slowly brought him back to the ground. He thought for a moment, then shrugged off the disappointment. "I can think it over. I'll be right next time."

Fabio had gotten over the laughing fit by now. He patted Duncan's shoulder. "Enough for today. Think about it and tell us another time." Duncan walked away, muttering under his breath.

"That was fun," Misa said with a laugh.

Fabio laughed back. "Someone has been sitting under the Yellowtree for far too long."

We picked up food from the village kitchen, and Fabio and Misa talked about Duncan's absurd stories on our way back to the forge. The clanking of metal welcomed us as we reached the forge. I strolled leisurely, looking around at nothing in particular.

Fabio and Misa left me to start their work.

The forge had been repaired. There was no sign of the terrible metal structures I had seen the last time I was there.

Idir waved for me to come over and exclaimed, "Hey, come quick! See what we have made?" He led me to the hearth, where other forgers were helping him. "The Blacklight bows are ready. Boris named them." Idir showed me how they worked and asked me to try one. I picked one up and tried it. It was lighter than I had expected.

The Violetlight vial sat off-center, and pushing a small lever moved it in place. We checked every one of them, pushing the lever many times. The mechanism worked perfectly. "Great, the bows are ready. Let's carry these to the healer's yard. Amy would be happy to see them." Idir and I carried them to the healer's yard and carefully stacked them on the table in the sitting room.

Amy was in the kitchen preparing a meal and looked anxious. I helped her chop vegetables and wash fruit before asking, "What's the matter?"

"It will be a full moon in two days. Esmeray will be at her strongest. I fear that is when she will attack. Today, it is cloudy. If we could fight her tonight, we'd have a better chance at winning."

"But we can't fight her until she attacks. She has to come to us," I reminded her.

Amy quickly responded, "There might be another way. As a healer, I can call the light. The beast is alive by the power of Moonlight. I can sense it on the island, and I believe I can call it to come to us."

Shocked, I asked, "What? You can call the beast? Are you sure it will listen to your call?"

"The Moonlight. I can call the Moonlight, and the beast will be forced to come, and with it, I think Esmeray will come to protect her weapon."

Idir and Boris left their chairs and dashed toward Amy as they heard her plan. "You can call it?" Boris asked with wide eyes.

Amy explained, "Every healer can call the lights. That is how we capture them."

Soon, they were convinced that it was better to surprise Esmeray with an attack instead of waiting for her to pick a time that suited her.

Boris left to discuss it with the elders as Idir brought Kratos and told him about Amy's plan. In no time, the elders arrived and asked about the weapons. Kratos assured them that they were as ready as possible with the available vials of light.

It was decided that Amy would call the beast tonight. Amy's idea of calling the Moonlight thrilled me, but at the same time, I was scared. Everything might not go according to plan, and no one knew how strong Esmeray was. If the Blacklight bows couldn't take her down, what would happen?

"We need to evacuate the villagers into the forest," Boris said hurriedly. Alev nodded, and he left to make the necessary arrangements. I walked out with Boris, who was now talking to his guardians about making a plan to evacuate the Seren villagers. They would be sent to the deep forest before dark.

Boris continued, "We need a group of armed guardians hiding around the yard. We have nine Blacklight bows. I need the bow bearers to be hiding closer to the yard." He turned to Kratos, Idir, and me and said, "We will each take one bow." He then looked at me and asked, "What about you? Will you go with the villagers?"

I didn't want to go anywhere. As scary as the idea of being close to the action was, it was also exciting and full of adventure. I wanted to be there to witness whatever happened. I begged, "Can I stay here?" Boris nodded.

No one slept throughout the night. The village was awake and busy. The guardians gathered the villagers in the village centre, and they were asked to bring provisions in case they had to stay away for longer. When the guardians were satisfied that everyone was there, the evacuation started in small groups. Every group was accompanied by two guardians, and the elders were the last to leave. Alev had decided to stay with Amy and was taken to the healer's house.

Everyone was on edge now. Amy wanted to practice calling the Moonlight. It was overcast, but we could still see the moon between the cracks in the clouds. It wasn't a full moon, so she couldn't collect a lot of light, but she could practice her skills and be ready for the fight. I asked if I could go with her, and she signalled for me to come.

I followed her out of the healer's home. She had requested Alev to be there in case she needed any help. Once we were alone near the Moontree, she revealed why she wanted to practice. Feray had never allowed her to capture Moonlight, but she was convinced that it was the same process. She just wanted to practice once before she tried it in the fight.

I accompanied Amy inside the Whitetree, and together, the three of us waited for the moon to appear from behind the clouds. The white sphere shone brightly in the sky, illuminating the land underneath graciously. Amy sat in front of the bulb, holding an empty vial, with her eyes closed. The Moonlight in the vials on the wooden shelves glowed brighter than usual in the dark, filling the moon chamber with a sense of peace and calmness.

Amy looked like an angel with shimmering wings fluttering occasionally. It was difficult to understand if the Moonlight bestowed her the glow or if she emanated the Whitelight that bathed everything in the chamber. I stood mesmerized next to Alev, her eyes fixed on the opening in the woody ceiling. The moon peaked from behind the clouds. It was time. Moonlight entered the chamber and fell on the ground near the white bulb. Amy waited as it slowly crept toward her. Any moment now. The Moonlight drew closer, and we held our breath. Even time stopped breathing lest it disturb the miracle.

Pale white rays broke out of their sphere and ran toward her. Blinding Whitelight spread in every direction like a persistent lightning bolt. The air vibrated with energy, and I experienced peace like never before. My mind was silent, and I felt every part of my being in vivid detail. My heart beat rhythmically, filling me with life and energy. Pure air entered my lungs and spread through my body, lingering there to cleanse it. It left when it was satisfied, taking away every impurity it could find.

The peaceful light started to diminish slowly. I became aware of my surroundings as the moon's light caressed the bulb one last time before moving away. Amy was still there, holding the glass vial, which was no longer empty. At the very bottom was a small, white glowing string.

The moon sailed over the sky, and the chamber regained its usual ambiance. My mind woke up, welcoming the rush of thoughts as I lost the awareness I had experienced before. I realized I had missed the chance to see Amy catch the Moonlight. I was too busy feeling my own being. Well, I could ask her later how she did it. I was content with the experience.

Amy put the Moonlight vial on a nearby shelf and turned toward us with a slow, satisfied smile. We smiled back at her. She had done it. She had captured her first Moonlight. Boris arrived and informed Alev that the guardians were ready to move all the remaining vials from tree chambers to a secret location. The elders had decided to take this step as a precaution, just in case we couldn't stop Esmeray.

Alev instructed Amy to fill up the vials for the Blacklight bows. We went to each tree, and Amy took empty vials from the shelves and filled them up. It was incredible. She would put her hand in the large vials and bring the light strings out, and then pour them into the small vials. One after the other, they were filled and ready to be used in the Blacklight bows.

We carried the vials and left for the healer's house as the guardians collected the remaining vials to hide in a secret location. In the healer's house, Amy and Idir fixed the vials in the bows. Kratos came to see the bows and announced they were perfect.

It was almost midnight when we were ready. I asked Amy, "Will you be able to hold the beast? It may want to flee when attacked by the bows."

Amy whispered her response, "You saw how the Moonlight spread around the room. If you or Alev had a vial with you, it would have stayed empty. I called the Moonlight with my mind, coaxed it gently, and it listened to me. It felt comfortable with me and agreed to stay with me. Though the beast is far away yet, I am sure I can force it to come by coaxing the Moonlight it carries. And once it comes close, it will be much easier to keep it here."

Kratos, Idir, and Boris took their bows. Boris had brought armour for Kratos and Idir as well. They looked like proper warriors now. Boris divided the bow bearers into groups of four and five. Kratos, Idir, Boris, and two others were in the first group. I didn't know anyone from the other group.

The second group would take over when and if the first one ran out of lights. They went to hide in the forest, staying close as Amy feared the bows might not work effectively if they were far from their target.

Boris picked a hiding spot for me. It was in the trees near the healer's house. I was away from the fight and still had a good view.

My heart beat faster as time passed. I kept my eyes fixed on Amy. She sat on the ground near the Moontree with her eyes closed. The battle had started. She was calling the beast. I saw her face tense as she struggled to contact the Moonlight vibrating in the beast's body. I tried to calm myself and took long breaths.

Amy's face relaxed. Maybe she was in contact with the Moonlight. Time slowed down. Nothing moved. I waited. My mind had a mind of its own. It brought terrible thoughts to scare me. What if the Blacklight bows didn't work? Blacklight? There wasn't even such a thing. Even the name sounded silly. I started to sweat. We were idiots. All of us. Me, Kratos, Amy, everyone. How could we possibly think we could fight a wizard with as silly a thing as the Blacklight bows? I lost all hope. Esmeray was coming with the terrible creature, and we had glass vials of light for weapons. The sweat drops slithered down my forehead. My hands were moist with anxiety. I realized I was giving in to despair. I shook my head and hoped it would all work out.

Amy's alarmed voice brought me out of my thoughts. "It's coming."

I heard Boris next. "Amy, is she close?"

"I can't judge the distance exactly, but it is close," she yelled back.

Idir joined the conversation. "How long do we have to wait? Just give us a guess."

Amy closed her eyes, and everyone became silent.

A grunt broke the silence. It grew louder and louder. Something was moving toward us. Amy was right. The beast was coming. Would the Blacklight bows work?

Ch 12: Fruitless War

The sound grew louder and louder as the gigantic beast came into view on the horizon, flapping its metallic wings and swishing its snake-like tail furiously. Amy opened her eyes and fixed them on the beast, which appeared to be looking back at her, spreading its dark shadow across the yard. Its thunderous wings threatened her, yet she remained calm, with not a hint of fear on her face. Her courage amazed me. With a loud crash, the beast landed in front of her. The white-haired lady sat proudly on its staunch neck.

Esmeray's voice broke the silence, demanding to know, "Where is Feray? Is she trying to control my dragon? Feray, come out! Talk to me."

Amy responded calmly, "Feray is not here. I am the Seren healer now. I called the beast."

"You?" Esmeray laughed mockingly. "New healer? What do you think you are doing? Do you believe you can fight me? I am Esmeray, the most powerful wizard in this world. You dare to call me? You will pay for your insolence with your life and the life of every Seren. I will give you one last chance: surrender the Light vials, and no one has to die. I will leave this world forever. Deny me, and I will take the vials by force and destroy the trees you depend on."

Amy spoke angrily, "We have defeated you before, and we will defeat you again. Nobody believes a word you say. Surrender the beast. You can go in the dark, but not with the light."

Esmeray laughed an evil laugh. "I was hoping you would say that. Now that you have called me, I will let you witness the destruction of your land firsthand. Then, I will take the vials and destroy the Moontree. Your stubbornness will cost you everything." She held a hand up and started muttering. Her hand caught fire. In a moment, it grew into a giant fireball.

Esmeray looked terrifying on the beastly creature with a fire burning in her hand. Fear blanketed my senses. I screamed loudly as Esmeray turned her hand toward the ground and released the fireball.

Black silk shot out from every corner of the yard. It rushed toward Esmeray and engulfed her. The fireball fizzed past Amy and fell on the grassy ground. The green grass caught fire instantly.

Esmeray shrieked violently as the black silk tried to wrap itself around her. She lost power over her beast, and it slumped down motionless. She fell to the ground beside it.

Esmeray cast another spell. The black silk started to recede. She stood up slowly, giving force to the spell with continuous muttering under her breath. She was powerful. I feared that the Blacklight bows would not be able to compete with her power.

The second group of Blacklight warriors came out of the forest, hovering in the air and shot their weapons at Esmeray. Their faces were strained by the effort of holding the bows in position. It seemed as if she were pushing them away.

Esmeray held her hands high with glassy eyes staring emptily in the air. The Blacklight kept struggling against the barrier her spell had created. It was like a protective bubble around her. Her hands caught fire again. It grew bigger and bigger. At the same time, the Blacklight shrank back. The bows must be running out of light. The warriors threw their bows and ran toward the forest as Esmeray threw balls of fire lighting up everything in their path.

The second group shot one last time. The black ribbons failed to breach the protective bubble around Esmeray and faded away.

Esmeray laughed a loud, evil laugh and spoke again, "That's it? This was your plan? If you are done with your silly schemes, I will give you another chance to surrender."

Amy was all alone now. Without thought, I ran toward her. There was absolutely nothing I could do, but I could not leave her alone with the evil wizard.

Idir and Kratos showed up from the trees and moved toward Amy. Then I saw Boris with some guardians join us. We formed a circle around Amy as Esmeray's evil laugh echoed through the forest.

She taunted us, "What is going to happen next? I hope you have a better plan than the last one." Behind her, the beast began to move. It was again under Esmeray's control.

All around us, the fire was spreading. It was no ordinary fire. It burned and ate everything around it quickly. As it spread, the flames grew taller. Esmeray got back on the beast.

We looked at each other, wondering what to do.

Esmeray looked at Amy and hissed, "You dare to think you can defeat me? Savita thought so too. She was too proud to even beg for her life when I dealt with her and that lazy thinker. I will give you a chance. Side with me, and I will let you live."

Amy held her head up. I knew she would never side with the evil wizard. "Do what you can. I am not scared of you." Her voice was calm.

Esmeray continued in her demeaning voice, "And what of this fragile circle of allies around you? Aren't you interested in saving their lives?"

Idir spoke loud enough for Esmeray to hear, "Don't worry about us, Amy. We will protect Serenus with our lives."

Esmeray laughed. "Interesting. You still don't understand the danger you are in. Ready to give your life? It's time to teach you a lesson."

Amy spoke loudly, "Esmeray! You are not getting the light vials. Elders have already hidden the vials in a safe place. Feray used most of the Moonlight already. Leave now, take what you have and never return."

Esmeray was furious. "How dare you hide the vials. If I can't have the light, no one can."

She let out a deafening shriek. A giant fireball appeared in her hand as she muttered furiously. It grew bigger and angrier. With pure hatred, she locked her eyes on Amy and released the fireball. Amy stood rooted to the ground, staring at the burning angel of death rushing toward the Moontree. The fire caught the branches and lit them like dry tinder.

Everyone gasped and ran toward the burning tree. We tried to put out the fire, but it was too furious. Amy screamed as the tree started to give up and lose its glow.

Everyone turned to Amy with helpless, sad eyes. She lowered her head in defeat. We could only watch the life draining out of the Whitetree.

At this point, no one cared about their own safety. We stood facing the tree with our backs toward Esmeray. Her evil laugh and mockery filled the thick, smoky air around us.

The tree lost all glow quickly, and the light from the Tree Circle around it also grew dull. A thought flashed in my mind. I asked everyone to follow me. I ran away from Esmeray and behind the Moontree. Everyone stood there, confused for a moment, and then ran after me, wondering what it was all about.

"Where do you think you are running off to?" Esmeray came after us. As soon as we crossed the Tree Circle, we started running toward the village. Esmeray was now above the Moontree.

Suddenly, the yard lit up, and Esmeray's screams filled the village. We stopped and turned around to witness an incredible scene. The Light trees were glowing brightly, angrily. The Moontree still stood all dark and lifeless. The Violettree had sent a sphere of light up to the sky. Light rays from every tree rushed to meet the violet sphere. It was a gigantic blacklight bow. It shot shimmering black silk ribbons to attack Esmeray, which wrapped tightly around the struggling wizard and her beast and began to drain them of power to provide life for the Moontree.

Amy was the first to understand what was happening; in the absence of the Moontree light, the other trees became dangerous and drained life from the nearby living things to refill the bulb in Moontree.

We watched in horror as the trees sucked all power out of the wildly shrieking Esmeray. She was still trying to cast a spell to get rid of the black silk gripping her tighter and tighter. She struggled against it but was no match. The beast fell down with a loud thud. Esmeray's screams echoed in the yard but soon diminished to moaning, and then she went quiet. The silk ropes loosened and left Esmeray lying in a heap. The light rays returned to their trees as the Whitetree started to glow again.

For a moment, the yard was calm except for the crackling of the fire. It, too, had turned into a timid pet abandoned by its master. It slowed down and soon faded away. The spell had lost its potency now that the spell-caster was defeated.

We stayed where we were, waiting. I expected Esmeray to suddenly get up and cast another terrible spell. I had witnessed how powerful she was. Just one spell had left Sere infertile forever. But I had also seen the power of the Lighttrees. Perhaps it was really over this time.

Amy went forward cautiously, and everyone followed closely. She bent over Esmeray to check if she was alive. Esmeray stayed still. Amy whispered, "She is unconscious."

The light warriors rushed toward her. Boris instructed his guardians to take Esmeray to the waterfall. The guardians dragged the unconscious Esmeray away, and Boris went along.

Amy went closer to the beast. She walked its length, studying it carefully. Sitting next to it, she closed her eyes for only a moment and then opened them. Her eyes lit up. She asked everyone to move away from her.

We stood near the house, watching and waiting. Amy's face became tense as she was struggling with something. Idir went inside the house to update Alev on the situation. She wanted to see what was happening, so two guardians carried her outside in her chair. We waited while Amy stayed focused on her work.

Then, a girl came out of the forest. She looked around nervously. Idir called out to her, "Hey, you were supposed to stay away. Why did you come here?" She waited for a moment, then looked at Amy, not sure what to say.

Alev asked, "What is it, Luna? Come here." The girl walked to Alev. "Now, tell me, why are you here?"

Luna responded nervously, looking toward Amy. "I heard her call. She needs help."

Alev smiled broadly. "Then go and help her."

The girl walked on the burned black ground and went to Amy. She sat by her side and closed her eyes. I could see she was focused on something.

"What is happening? Who is she, and how is she helping Amy?" It was strange; Amy hadn't said a word. But the girl said she heard her call. Why was Alev so happy to see her?

Alev provided the answer: "Amy has found her apprentice. She heard her call. I believe there is still Moonlight left in the beast's body. Amy is trying to call it out of the creature."

Amy and her apprentice sat together for some time, and then it happened. The body of the beast started to glow. Slowly, the light left the metal creature and moved up. It was surreal. It looked like a glowing cloud hovering over the length of the creature's body. The dragon shattered into pieces as the magic left it lifeless.

"It is the Moonlight. Quick, Idir! Help them. Get vials from a chamber," Alev said urgently.

We sprinted in different directions, gathered empty vials from the tree chambers, and then took them to Amy. Moments later, we walked carefully, carrying the white glowing vials back to the Moontree. The metal was left there. It was to be moved to the forge later. Once the sun rose, Boris came back. Esmeray had been put in prison under the waterfall. She was still unconscious. He had left some guardians to guard the prison, although there was no fear of her escaping until it was dark. No one was allowed to enter the prison until the elders decided her fate. It was unbelievable. The worst was over. Boris had already sent one of the guardians to inform the villagers, and they were on their way back. The guardians had put out the fires burning lazily around the yard. Amy and her newly discovered apprentice were with Alev. She was happy that everything had worked out in the end. But they still needed to decide what to do about Esmeray. Then there was the case of Feray. No one had any idea what to do about her. The matters were left to be discussed later in the evening in the presence of the elders.

The day seemed to go on forever. We tried to rest in the healer's house and waited for the evening.

After resting for a while, we gathered again and went outside to the Tree Circle. There was no fire left, and the Moontree seemed to be recovering by itself. The yard had been cleared away, and the lifeless metal creature was taken to the forge. It was decided that it would be melted down, and the metal would be reused for better purposes.

It was a terrible night, and we still couldn't believe it was over. Still, everyone was worried by Esmeray's presence nearby. We couldn't stop her from escaping once the day ended and the magical barrier of the tree was gone. For now, everyone was trying to focus on the fact that she had been defeated. And what a battle it had been. The Light-trees had surprised everyone. They stood with us and defended themselves against a powerful enemy.

The elders gathered for the meeting, but no one was allowed inside. We waited patiently as we looked at the setting sun, worrying that soon Esmeray could escape again. We had to do something quickly.

Finally, Boris came outside and informed everyone of the decision regarding Esmeray's fate. "Esmeray will be sent into the dark. We cannot take a risk to keep her here."

It felt right. We felt relieved, although it was a terrible ending for Esmeray.

A group of guardians walked to the fall. The entire village followed. Esmeray was awake but very weak. Two guardians carried her, and the procession walked toward the Dark End. Another two guardians brought a boat and put it in the water close to the bank. The guardians put Esmeray in. She protested feebly.

It was apparent that Esmeray was not ready to go into the dark, and, for the first time, she looked scared. She tried to hide her fear and appear strong, but the closer we got to the Dark End, the more nervous she became. She was no longer a confident, powerful wizard. She had lost her power, but I could see that she was trying to maintain her grace by accepting her fate. Her effort to appear calm even in such a situation surprised me.

The guardians pushed Esmeray's boat to the Dark End as the Seren stood watching. They were finally happy that the wizard was captured and Serenus had survived a horrible tragedy. The boat moved away. Esmeray looked around, searching for someone. Her eyes stopped at me, and she signalled for me to come closer. I stood motionless as the entire village looked at me. Kratos held my hand and took me closer to the edge.

Esmeray managed to smile at me. "Listen carefully! I am not the wizard, but he is very fond of you. He has big plans for you. I can't wait to meet you in the next world."

Kratos screamed, "Stop her!" Guardians ran after Esmeray's boat, but with an evil laugh, she crossed the barrier. Soon, she disappeared into the dark.

Boris spoke slowly in shock, "She was not the wizard, but she knew who the wizard was. We should have let Alia interrogate her."

It was no use now. Esmeray was gone, and there was nothing we could do about it. The wizard was still here. We were not safe from danger yet.

Esmeray's last words had disturbed everyone. I felt their eyes on me.

"Finally, we are all safe now." Qilam's voice surprised us. He came out of the trees and walked toward us. Guardians ran toward him, but Boris stopped them. There was no point in arresting Qilam now; Esmeray had already been defeated. And there was no doubt he played his part in helping the village.

We returned to the village centre. After dinner, I was about to head back home when suddenly, the village bell started to ring. The first thought that crossed our minds was that there was another attack. We looked around fearfully but then realized that it was the signal for a newcomer.

Ch 13: Prophecy is Cruel

The guardians ran to the river. Others quickly found some torches and ran after them. Everyone had a confused look on their faces. Kratos came to my side and said, "We need to go. Something is not right."

"What do you mean?" I asked.

He pulled me away and said, "Esmeray just left, and a newcomer is coming? Haven't you heard that the wizard cannot be killed and always comes back? I think she was lying. She must be the wizard. Now, she is back in yet another disguise to torment us." He looked worried as he continued, "She singled you out. I think you could be in danger."

Amy ran toward the falls, holding her notebook. I turned to Kratos and said, "Let's go see who it is."

Kratos was worried, but I insisted that there was nothing to worry about. It wasn't as if the newcomer would attack me the moment we saw each other. He called Idir, and together we headed to the river.

Once there, a strange scene unfolded, and I couldn't believe my eyes. The newcomer had not yet landed. Clouds covered the moon, but he was clearly visible, standing tall in his boat, holding the paper with the poem on it. He was standing in a boat that everyone was scared of sitting in. His wings spread out behind him, balancing him in the rocking boat effortlessly. His left hand was on his hip, and in his right hand, he held the poem in front of him. He had a look of confidence and authority. He glanced at everyone waiting for him to reach the land without concern and was not unnerved as he spotted the waterfall. The Seren were so shocked to see him that no one went forward to help him with his boat. Even the guardians stood back, uncertain of what they were supposed to do. He jumped out and landed gracefully on the sand as his wings slowed his fall. The waves carried his boat toward the waterfall, and it smashed into the rocks and broke into pieces. The current carried the shattered fragments to the edge, where they fell over. The newcomer didn't even turn to look at it. He stood motionless as he stepped on the land. It was as if he was assessing something in his mind. A slow smile spread across his face, and he gave a single nod. He was happy with whatever he had found. Then, he raised the poem in front of us and asked, "Where is the wizard?" Then he pointed to the falls, "Is that the fall I am supposed to go past?"

We were stunned by his words; no one answered. Amy hesitated for a moment, but then she stepped forward cautiously. The newcomer watched her with interest. "Newcomer! I welcome you on behalf of everyone here," Amy said.

"What is here?" he asked.

"This is Serenus, the land of peace, and we are Seren. You are too. From now on, you will be living here with us. But first--"

"I have no such intention," he interrupted her.

Amy was stumped. For a moment, she lost her composure and looked at Boris helplessly. Boris nodded and went closer to her. We were all puzzled and impressed by the newcomer's confidence. Boris faced the newcomer. "You need to come with us."

"Why and where?" he was uncomfortably straightforward.

Boris pointed toward the waterfall. "There is a tree on a small island under the waterfalls. Once you get there, we will answer your questions."

I didn't expect the newcomer to agree. I was sure he would want to know why he should go there. But he nodded and said in an amused tone, "Fair enough!"

Without any effort, he spread his wings and, with a powerful thrust, flew high above the ground. We watched him, mouths ajar, as he reached the waterfall, hovered above it to study the island, and then dove down with his wings pinned to his body. Everyone ran toward the waterfall. I was sure he would have made a perfect landing on the island. I wished I could get there before he landed. I really wanted to see it with my own eyes. Sure enough, he was standing next to the tree when I reached the edge.

Boris asked everyone to stay back. We didn't know anything about the newcomer. It was better to take precautions. He continued down the side of the falls. Amy, Kratos, and three guardians followed him. They approached the newcomer carefully. It was difficult to see their faces in the moonlight from this far, but I could visualize their uncertain faces. I regretted that I hadn't asked Kratos if I could go with them.

I could see that Amy, Kratos, and Boris were talking to him, but there was no change in his stance. Suddenly, one of the guardians moved forward with his spear extended toward him.

The newcomer turned toward the guardian and spread his arms in front of him. The guardian stopped where he was. Then, the guardian fell down and lay motionless on the ground. Others moved back, afraid to attack him.

The Seren gasped in fear and moved away from the edge. The newcomer had magic. I broke into a cold sweat. Esmeray had lied to us. She was the wizard, and as she had left the island, another one had arrived to take her place. I was worried for my friends who were so close to him.

Kratos and Boris had covered Amy and faced the wizard, though it was beyond me what they could do to fight him. But the newcomer didn't advance toward them. He stood there, watching them for some time, and then spread his wings and flew away toward the dark forest.

I relaxed a little and breathed deeply now that the wizard had left. A look around me shocked me. I was standing alone. Everyone had run away to the village.

My friends had gathered around the poor guardian. I ran down and was relieved to know that he was still breathing.

Boris shouted orders to the guardians, who helped carry their fellow and climbed up the path as quickly as they could. Amy left with them as the guardian needed help immediately. He was taken to the Tree Circle.

I followed Kratos and Boris back to the village. I was aching to know what had happened. The strained faces of my friends worried me.

Boris shook his head and said, "We are in big trouble. Let's go inform the elders."

The news travelled fast. We didn't see anyone except the guardians on our way back, who stood alert and tense. The Seren were scared and sought the safety of their homes. A deadly silence held the village in its cruel clutches.

My company was equally tense. No one said anything until we arrived at the healer's home. The elders were already there; it had become a permanent meeting place during desperate times. We had to wait for Amy to arrive. When she informed us that the guardian would live, everyone breathed a sigh of relief.

Then Boris told Alev, "The newcomer refused to go in. We tried our best to persuade him, but he wouldn't listen. He didn't go into the prison tree."

Amy continued, "I believe he could somehow sense the tree was magical. When the guardian threatened to attack him, he used magic. It was not a simple spell. The wizard had thought it out in a fraction of a moment."

She looked at us with horror in her eyes. "He is nothing like the wizards we have faced before. He is extremely powerful. His mind is sharp and calculating. You saw how he had already decided what he would do—catch the wizard and go past the falls. People take a lifetime to arrive at such conclusions. He knew he could fly. He knew we couldn't hurt him. He knows his powers. That makes him extremely dangerous."

Alev put her head in her hands. I was surprised to see her like that. Despite her years, she had always been composed and in control. Jinyan went and sat next to her. He spoke to her gently, "Alev, don't let him take your courage away. The Seren rely on your strength. It will break their spirit if they see you like this."

Alev raised her head and nodded at him. She pulled herself together. "You are right, Jinyan. This is not the time to lose ourselves. Amy, what do you...."

An urgent knock at the door stopped her mid-sentence. Boris opened the door and let in a guardian who looked pretty unnerved.

"What happened, Aylan?" Boris inquired.

"The newcomer! He is dangerous. I believe he is the wizard. I don't know how to explain it. I have just been to the river where he landed. I was supposed to patrol that area, and I saw something there." He shuddered as he tried to explain.

"What did you see, Aylan? Tell us," Alev said in a rushed voice.

Aylan looked at us in fear. "I saw a small area on the riverbank. It is shaped like a footprint. I believe it is where the newcomer put his first step on the land. The grass... it is burned. The grass is badly burned in that place."

The room went silent. We looked at each other helplessly. None of us had a clue what we were going to do.

Finally, Alev said, "Boris, place your guardians everywhere around the village and the Tree Circle. We must protect Serenus."

Then she turned to Kratos. "Take No-Name with you. Tell everyone to stay inside. No one is allowed to leave their houses. Amy, stay here... I need to talk to you."

Kratos and I got up and left quickly. Misa and Fabio were waiting outside with Idir. Kratos briefed them about Alev's orders. They came with us to spread the word.

Everyone kept looking around cautiously. The wizard was unpredictable and dangerous. The sounds of the night added to the tense atmosphere.

We went from door to door, advising Seren to stay inside no matter what. Everyone was on edge and wanted to know how we would deal with the new wizard. We had no words to console them. The uncertainty fueled their fears. By the time we left the last home, we were exhausted.

Now that we were close to my house, I invited everyone to rest for a while. They nodded in agreement, and we moved forward in silence.

I felt safer sitting in front of the roaring fire in my fireplace, surrounded by my friends, but I knew it was not permanent. No one was safe anymore; nothing was certain. Defeating Esmeray had given us confidence that we were not helpless after all. We had captured her and sent her into the dark. But the arrival of a new wizard shattered it completely. My mind kept bringing back the image of the guardian lying motionless on the ground, so helpless even as his friends stood right by him.

When I couldn't take it anymore, I voiced my fears to my friends. "What will we do now? He is too powerful, and we can't do anything."

Kratos rushed to my side, and held my hands firmly. "We will stop him. Together, we will find a way. Don't lose yourself to this fear, my friend! We are here with you. Don't give up." He looked at the others and spoke firmly, "Listen to me, all of you! I do not allow anyone to give up. Don't waste your energy on being afraid and worried. Use it to think of ways we could deal with him. We are here to give courage to our fellows, not break their spirits. Look up, Fabio! Pull yourself together."

His words made me feel better. He had scolded us like an elder. It felt good. I felt loved, and so did the others. We sat up and gathered our nerves.

"That's more like it. Now, let's go back and see what Amy and Alev have been thinking." Kratos stood up and patted my shoulder. I nodded and got up. We left home with renewed spirits. The walk back to the healer's house was not scary anymore.

Amy and Alev were sitting silently in the healer's house. They had been discussing the newcomer, but there wasn't enough information about him from our short encounter.

Amy told us what she thought about the new wizard, "Well, we know the newcomer has magic unlike we have seen before. He is a quick learner. He has already learned how to fly and use his magical powers. He knows he is more powerful than all of us. We gave that away ourselves." She shook her head, expressing her disapproval. "We acted without thinking. How timid we must have seemed when we let him see how impressed we were by his abilities."

Everyone was embarrassed by her words, but she was right. Amy continued, "Never in the known history, has a newcomer arrived here at night. I have no idea what it means. Should we be worried about it? And then there is Aylan's information about what he witnessed at the river bank. I can't say anything about it without studying the area. There is so little that we know. And what we do know, is enough to scare us. Still, there is something that gives me hope."

She paused, and I wondered what it could be. Alev leaned forward in her chair to listen to what Amy had to say.

"The new wizard is focused on going past the falls. It is possible that he won't disturb us and leave soon." Amy's words felt like fresh air in the suffocating atmosphere of hopelessness. Everyone sat up with their faces lit. She could be right. The new wizard might not be as troublesome and dangerous as we thought.

Something nudged me at the back of my mind. I tried to figure out what was bothering me. The newcomer's words rang in my head, and I realized we were wrong. Or we might be. I cleared my throat and repeated his words loudly, "Where is the wizard?"

Everyone turned toward me, watching me in surprised confusion.

"Where is the wizard? Those were the words of the newcomer when he arrived. If he is the new wizard, why did he ask that? He is not afraid of us, so he had no reason to pretend that he wasn't the new wizard. On the contrary, I believe, if he was the one, he would have said that without any fear or care."

Idir nodded. "You are right. We assumed he was the new wizard just because he had magic. No doubt, he is a wizard, but we can't be sure if he came to replace Esmeray."

"That brings us back to an Esmeray situation. We have another powerful wizard who wants to go past the falls. What we don't know is whether he would simply leave or cause trouble." Amy paused. Her voice reflected her worry when she continued, "I hope he doesn't become greedy. How would we stop him if he came after the vials?"

Alev tried to comfort everyone and said, "Don't forget the Blacklight bows. They helped us deal with Esmeray. And what about the Lighttrees? It's not like our hands are empty."

Boris said forcefully, "I think we should go after him with Blacklight bows and be done with this uncertainty. Why wait for him to attack? Even if he is not the wizard we have to catch, we know he is dangerous. I say we go for it."

Alev shook her head. "No, Boris. We don't have enough light for bows, and I don't think it is wise to invite trouble. We have already mishandled the first encounter with the newcomer. I don't want anyone to go after him without bringing it to our knowledge."

Kratos nodded. "Alev is right. Serenus will protect itself if need be. We should wait and see what this new wizard is up to. If he leaves without causing trouble, great. If not, we will find a way to deal with him as well." So it was decided to wait and see.

We had missed the better part of the night. Alev asked everyone to rest. She was staying at the healer's home with Amy. Misa and Fabio offered to stay with them. Kratos invited Idir and me to his house. On hearing this, Alev remembered something: "We are forgetting something. Remember Esmeray's last words? If the newcomer is the wizard by any chance, this one could be in danger. We don't know what Esmeray meant by the wizard's plan about... this one." She paused and scolded me, "For light's sake, pick a name already." I bowed my head. She sighed loudly and said, "Boris, put two guardians at the lodge. We can't leave him alone at his house. He will stay at the lodge till we find out more."

Kratos and Idir came with me to the Serenus Lodge. They didn't want to leave me alone. The moment I lay in bed, I realized how exhausted I was. I fell asleep immediately and woke up to the thunderous voice of Idir. I sat up with a start. Idir was standing next to my bed. "Goodness! Is this how you sleep? I have been trying to wake you up for ages. Get up now. We need to go check the footprint on the river-bank." His words jolted me out of sleep, and I got up. Idir told me that Amy had visited earlier, and Kratos had gone to the river with her.

We left for the river. The village centre was silent and deserted again. No one wandered outside except for the guardians walking around with spears in their hands. We found Kratos and Amy sitting at the riverbank, studying the footprint. I went closer to see.

It was precisely as Aylan had described.

Amy pulled out some grass using metal tongs. We gasped as we saw that it had been charred to the very roots.

"What happened here, Amy?" Kratos asked in disbelief.

Amy replied thoughtfully, "I don't know for sure, but I think the new wizard sucked the life out of the grass when he stepped on it. That's the only explanation for this condition of the grass." I added, "Remember how he smiled at the time. I think he had drained the life out of the grass without intention. But then he realized what had happened. And it made him happy." Everyone nodded in agreement.

"We should visit the tree under the fall as well. If the newcomer had taken life from the grass, we might find more burnt grass there as he used his magic on a guardian there," I suggested.

"Good thinking!" Kratos smiled. "Let's go and check."

My doubts proved to be correct; the grass was burned in some places near the tree on the island. Fortunately, the tree was safe, although one area of burned grass extended right underneath its tresses and into the tree chamber.

The matter worried us greatly. Amy's idea seemed to be correct: the newcomer had the power to drain the life out of the grass. We headed back to the village with this scary realization.

The elders were as scared as us upon hearing what Amy had to say. Jinyan asked, "Does it mean the newcomer can drain the life out of other living things as well?"

"I don't know, but it is not impossible, either. We will have to wait and see," Amy replied.

Ch 14: We Need To Talk

I continued to stay at the lodge. Kratos and Idir visited me often. These were difficult times, and the Seren felt imprisoned in their own homes. The village center was deserted, and the laughter and pleasant conversations that filled it became a thing of the past. The guardians took provisions to every villager.

We were waiting for the new wizard to do something—anything—so we could get more information about him and his plans. He was seen many times flying over the island, but he hadn't shown any interest in the village. Waiting was difficult and had started to affect the Seren. Everyone became short-tempered and frustrated. Gradually, we decided the newcomer wasn't planning to come to the village and harm anyone.

The elders lifted the curfew after a week. The Seren were still advised to stay closer to the village while the guardians were spread around the village borders. People were happy to get out of their homes finally. The atmosphere was still tense, but it had improved. Everyone took turns visiting the Tree Circle to dissolve the effects of the stress.

I visited the healer's home with Kratos and Idir. The elders had moved there as well. They were going to remain until we resolved the situation. I had not seen Amy in a while, and she wasn't at the healer's house, so I went to the Tree Circle to look for her. I found her under the Yellowtree, which surprised me.

I sat by her silently. In a little bit, Amy started speaking, "Ever since Alfred left through the Dark End, I have thought of going after him. He might be alone there, waiting for me. I wanted to be a good student with Feray, but she deserted and deceived me. My work with the trees is always under attack. I don't think I have any chance of a happy life on this island."

I had never expected to hear these words from Amy. Now I realized that I didn't really know how depressed she was. I tried to remind her that she herself told me it was a foolish idea to go in search of more islands.

"Maybe there isn't another land, but maybe there is, and Alfred is waiting for me, hoping and praying that I will go after him? There is no way of knowing until I go to find out."

Was Amy seriously thinking of going into the Dark End? Her

thoughts scared me.

I begged, "Amy, promise me you will never do such a thing. And if you did, I will try to stop you, and if I fail, I will follow you. If we ever leave, we will leave together."

Amy smiled and said, "Let's go together."

Once again, I was shocked by what she was saying. "What's happened to you? Why are you saying such things? Everything will be okay. We will deal with the wizard just like we dealt with Esmeray. We will find a way."

It must be the Yellowtree, creating strange thoughts in her mind. I convinced her to go to the Greentree, and we sat there for some time. I felt much clearer in my mind now and felt a change in Amy's look too. She smiled embarrassingly and said, "I'm sorry if I freaked you out."

I laughed and said, "It's okay. It was the Yellowtree doing the talking, not you."

Amy stayed for a while and then left to get back to her work. I thought about how powerful the effects of the tree were. They could temporarily change the whole personality of a person.

I stayed a bit longer to think about the poem. I cleared my mind and focused on its meaning, but even after several attempts, I failed to reach the mental state where I could keep thinking about a matter with conviction and clarity. The tree did not seem to be helping.

I tried again and thought about the words literally and figuratively, but without help from the tree, the more I thought, the more ambiguous it felt. As if whoever gave us the poem did not want us to find out what the words meant. The only thing I could say with some level of certainty was that we had a limited amount of time to do something, maybe to understand the poem? If catching the wizard and going past the fall was not the objective, then what else could it be? And what was the fruitless war? Was it the forever war between the wizard and the villagers? If it was futile, then why did the poem tell us to catch the wizard in the first place? And how were we supposed to find out in our past that our world was vast?

Next, I thought about Qilam's poem. If he told the truth that he came with it, could it help me understand my poem? The words "beyond this earth" did seem to imply that there could be more islands ahead of us. Maybe the story of the lost scroll was true. Would the finder of the lost scroll become a god beyond this earth? But were we supposed to find it on this island and then proceed, or were we supposed to look for it on the subsequent islands? Then I remembered the line that said it didn't matter if we failed. Why not? Nothing made sense, and I stopped myself from thinking along this line because if we needed Qilam's poem to solve the riddle, why wasn't it given to others? It was more likely that Qilam was lying about it.

In the end, I concluded that if this poem was a prophecy, it really was clever, cruel, and tiring; a mystery without clues, and even the tree did not want to help with it.

I left the Green chamber and met Fabio and Misa. We chatted for a while, grateful for each other's company. Everyone avoided talking about the new wizard as it only brought worry. After catching up, we went to the village center for the midday meal.

I had not expected to see the village center so full. It was not bustling with joy and laughter as it used to be, but it seemed that every Seren had come to be with their friends. We sat together and ate our lunch, talking in low voices. No one spoke about the wizard, but he was on everyone's mind. We kept looking around with cautious eyes, and any unexpected sound caused our heartbeats to race. The wizard had destroyed the peace in Serenus. I wished we could go back to the Serenus of the past when all I had to worry about was finding a question that interested me.

As the days passed, we relaxed and got busy with our routine life. We would have thought the wizard had left the island if we didn't find occasional signs of his presence. Mostly, it was the woodworkers who brought news of plants burnt in places. No one had ever seen any animals burned or dead. It meant that the wizard could only steal life from grass, plants, and trees. The realization raised our spirits.

Gradually, Serenus returned to normal. Once again, the village centre echoed with laughter and merry chitchat. Seren still talked about the wizard occasionally, but he had lost his effect on them.

I felt bored at the Serenus Lodge. Eventually, I begged the elders to let me go back to my house. Three weeks after the arrival of the newcomer, I returned home. Kratos and Idir came with me. I was devastated to see the condition of my house and yards. Fallen leaves had covered everything; autumn was here. Kratos and Idir helped me clean the yards.

We stayed up late at night and chatted happily. Kratos advised me to plant some flowering bushes in the yard. I had planned to do so but hadn't found the time. Idir reminded me I wanted to adopt. I wasn't so sure anymore but said I would think about it.

I slept peacefully, happy to be home. Early next morning, Kratos and Idir left for the forge, and I was alone at my home. I quickly finished some chores, then picked up a pen and paper and sat down comfortably. I wrote down everything we knew about the wizard and whatever we thought about him and his abilities. He had been on my mind from the moment he arrived. There were so many questions that needed answers, but I had no way of finding out. It frustrated me.

I kept thinking until I came up with a plan. The first step was already complete; I was back at my home. The plan had to be kept a secret. The next step needed courage as well as luck. After thinking for a long time, I put the paper and pen away and went to the village center for lunch. I didn't meet my friends there. I thought they must be at the forge because, over the past several weeks, a lot of work had piled up there. After lunch, I gathered provisions and returned home.

After leaving my firewood and food at home, I set off for the trail in the forest in search of Qilam. I was sure that he would know things about the wizard that we did not, as he always seemed to. Surprisingly, I found him at the same spot where I had met him the first time, and for some reason, he looked delighted to see me. We sat together on a fallen log, and he asked me about the village. I told him that everything was back to normal and then asked him what he knew about the wizard.

He laughed and replied, "Why don't you ask the wizard yourself?"

Right then, the wizard appeared out of the trees. I was shocked to see him so unexpectedly. Esmeray's words rang in my head. Had I walked into a death trap all by myself? There was no one to protect me, and my friends didn't even know where I was. I regretted visiting Qilam, but there was nothing to do now. I was here. The wizard walked up to me and stood facing me.

"What happened, Thinker? Why are you scared?" he asked in a casual tone. He knew who I was, and I guessed Qilam must have told him.

I gathered myself and replied, "I am scared of the unknown. Who knows what you are capable of?"

He laughed and said, "I am quite capable but not insane. I won't hurt anyone without reason."

"You hurt the guardian the day you came here, and I have heard that you drain the life out of living things. Are these not insane actions? I have reason to think you are dangerous."

My answer amused the wizard. He sat down on the grass and invited me to sit with him. "You are not thinking properly. Do you know why? Because you are sitting on a dead tree. These trees, plants, and this grass are pulsating with energy. You stay close to them, and they share their energy with you. The dead ones will only drain you. I have been telling the same thing to Qilam, but apparently, he has been sitting on dead trees for far too long. His mind doesn't understand the very basic concepts."

Qilam laughed heartily at his words. I left the log and sat with him cautiously. He continued, "Yes, I have powers, and I hurt the guardian, but he tried to attack first. I take energy from things because they are there for that very purpose. So, if you've come in peace, you have no reason to think I am dangerous."

I was surprised at how casually he spoke to me. I considered him a grave threat, but he talked to me as normally as anyone in Serenus would. He had a dark sense of humour as well.

I relaxed a little and decided to probe further to know him better. As if reading my thoughts, he asked me, "What do you want to know about me, Thinker? Qilam says you are good at asking questions. Let me see if you are good enough."

"Why are you here?" I started with the simplest one.

"I am here because I was sent. I have a mission, and I must complete it," he shrugged.

"So, you think the poem tells us about our mission?"

"There is no reason to think otherwise. Even Qilam can under-stand it. He told me that everyone came here in the same way with the same instructions. I wonder why they have started to live here as if this is their final destination. Not that it's my concern, but we must go past the falls. I have seen Qilam's poem too. I know you read it."

I interrupted, "You trust what Qilam says? What if he is tricking us into believing that he had that poem with him? What if he wrote it himself?"

Qilam cleared his throat loudly to remind me he was right there. I ignored him.

The wizard laughed. "See Qilam! It's not just me who doesn't believe you." Then he added in a serious tone, "Qilam can be manipulative, but I believe he is not lying about the poem because it makes sense."

"So, what are your plans, then?" I asked.

"Straight to the point, huh? I like it. I am here on a mission. Going past the falls is the next most significant task because it needs courage and blind faith. Whoever sent me here wants me to follow the instructions, and those who will do what they want will be rewarded. I am more powerful than the rest, so I have the best chance of success."

"Qilam claims to have understood this for a long time, but he is still here. Do you have blind faith in this?" I saw Qilam drop his head, staring at his feet in embarrassment.

The wizard replied, "Qilam is a coward. Success in the mission is the only thing that matters. If I don't try it, what else is there to do in this world?"

I highlighted the weakness in his understanding. "But you forgot one thing. Before going past the falls, we need to capture the wizard. The Seren have done that repeatedly, but he reappears every time they kill him or send him into the Dark End. How can we go past the falls if the wizard is always here?"

The newcomer laughed, shaking his head. "Thinker, you have not thought about these lines yet. If you had, you would know that no one was supposed to catch the wizard who lives here. Now listen carefully. Everyone is different and has a unique set of abilities. If the ability is complex to understand, you call it magical, but to me, you are a bigger wizard than Esmeray ever was. Thinking is an ability that I wouldn't claim to understand. Everyone is a wizard. 'Catch the wizard' simply means exploring those abilities to find the wizard in us. To find ourselves, and then go past the falls with full preparation."

I understood what he was trying to say. I acknowledged, "Hmm, people took the poem literally and focused on capturing the wizard instead of trying to understand themselves and their abilities."

"Exactly. Now you understand. I feel like I have been wasting time with the wrong companion." He winked at Qilam teasingly.

His mindset was becoming clearer and clearer, but I needed to know if his plans could threaten the village. I probed on, "But now that you know about your powers and have gained more, why haven't you left the island?"

"Not yet. There is something I need to do. When I arrived here, I could feel the magic vibrating in the very air of the island. Over time, I learned to gather this power inside me. As I grew powerful, my senses became sharper. I could feel which plants or trees had more magic. So, instead of wasting my time on the ones that couldn't give me much, I focused on the ones that gave me more power. Look at that tree." He pointed at a tree right behind Qilam. "It is bursting with energy. Let me show you."

He got up and walked toward the tree.

Qilam shouted at him, "Stop it. I told you not to do it around my place."

He shrugged off his protest. "Qilam, don't be stupid. It's a waste of energy."

He put his hand on the tree trunk. The moment he touched it, the tree began to glow. Slowly, the light started to move toward the wizard's hand, and the glow transferred to his body as the light absorbed into it. The tree began to darken, shrink, and wither. The wizard moved away from it. The tree twisted and turned as if being burnt in an invisible fire. It was terrifying and very unnatural to see a tree dying like that.

Qilam and I saw the terrible scene with horror. The wizard walked toward us as if nothing had happened. I couldn't take my eyes off the tree. "This is not right. The tree was alive, and you killed it for no reason." My voice was a mere whisper.

The wizard was not affected by my emotions. He responded, "Everything is a means to an end. The boat was there to bring us here. The poem was there to tell us about the mission. This tree was here to give me power. Everything on this island is here for us to take, to prepare us for the next step. There is nothing to be sad about."

"That's cruel," I protested.

"No, not at all. Don't the villagers cut down trees to build homes with wood? If I had taken its energy without really needing it, it would have been cruel. If I had killed it for pleasure, it would have been cruel. If I waste the power I have taken, it would be cruel, but I have no such intentions. I am not here to hurt anyone. I am simply taking what is needed for my mission. The ones who sent me here gave me this mission and put this tree here. They grew it for a purpose. So, there is nothing wrong with taking what is needed."

"How do you know what you need for your mission?" I was upset and no longer interested in encouraging the conversation.

"Well, that's what I have understood from the poem. My mission is to gather power, increase my abilities, and go to the next world. How much do I need, and exactly how I would use it? I don't know. That will come later in the next world. Right now, I need to gather as much power as possible. I would like to take it all, but then it would take a really long time, and as you know, we shouldn't stall."

Now, I had a much better understanding of the person standing in front of me. We were right to think that the wizard could be very dangerous. He had a justification for his actions but no morality or guiding compass to judge them with. If he felt it was needed for his mission, he could hurt anyone, and he would do it without any remorse.

The wizard walked away, leaving me alone in my miserable realization. Qilam muttered something inaudible and followed him. The tree behind him was still suffering. I had seen how casually the wizard snatched a life. His twisted thoughts scared me.

I was wrong to think I was controlling the direction of our conversation. I felt guilty for leading him on and could no longer stay in the presence of the dying tree. I turned and ran out of there and kept running till I reached my home. I waited by the front door, trying to catch my breath. When I could breathe again, I turned around, opened the door, went inside, and screamed loudly in frustration.

I didn't realize that there was someone there facing the fireplace. My screams startled him, and he turned around in shock. It was

Kratos, looking at me with concern. He helped me to a chair and asked what had happened. For some time, I couldn't speak. Kratos brought a glass of water and asked me to relax. I told him everything as soon as I could talk. His eyes went wide as I told him how the wizard killed the tree. Then, I realized that the wizard had not told me why he hadn't left the island. He was about to tell me, but I was so affected by the killing of the tree that I didn't get the chance to press him.

Kratos was worried and wanted me to inform the elders about what I had learned about the wizard, but I wanted to discuss it with Amy first. He agreed.

We left for the Tree Circle, hoping to find Amy there. She was in the Yellowtree with Luna, her apprentice, teaching her about the effects of the Yellowlight. Kratos and I sat nearby and waited patiently as Amy went on and on, describing its properties to Luna. We sighed in relief when she finished and Luna left.

When we told her that we needed to talk but not in front of others, Amy invited us to the healer's home. However, she mentioned that the elders were there. Kratos suggested we go to his house instead since he wasn't expecting anyone. We went to the village center and headed to Kratos's house after dinner.

We started a fire and sat nearby. It was a freezing cold night. I narrated everything that happened in detail, and Amy listened intently. Her face contorted with disgust when I recounted how casually the wizard had killed the tree. When I finished, Kratos asked if it was true. Did all the trees, plants, and grass have magic like the Lighttrees?

She stayed quiet, deep in thought, and then said slowly, "I have never seen or heard anything like that. But since our friend has seen it with his eyes, it must be so. I have never felt the magic in any other tree except the Lighttrees. But the wizard may have the power to feel it. He is very different from the ones we have dealt with in the past. I am afraid I don't understand his powers at all."

I asked, "Now what? Where does this leave us?"

"I think if he told the truth," Kratos said, "and I believe he did, he has no intention of hurting anyone. He doesn't need anything from us. I think once he has collected enough power, he will leave. Though the thought of him destroying the trees disgusts me, there is nothing that we can do to stop him."

Amy leaned forward, "He is after the Tree Circle. It is only a matter of time. He has seen the tree under the fall. Remember? He could sense its magic. He must have felt the presence of the Tree Circle as well. It is the most powerful source of power on this island, and he will definitely come for it." Her eyes reflected fear.

She fell silent. Kratos stood up and started pacing. The situation was grave. We had no means to fight the wizard. We didn't even know much about his capabilities. But one thing was clear — he was not to be taken lightly.

"What should we do now?" I asked. "We have seen that the

Blacklight bows couldn't do much to defeat Esmeray. This wizard is much more powerful than her. And I am sure he won't stop no matter what."

Amy interrupted me, "We will find a way — we have to. If the Tree Circle dies, there is no telling what will happen. I am afraid Serenus wouldn't be able to survive without them."

"The elders might think of something. We will tell them in the morning. I am sure, together, we'll find a way." Kratos tried to ease our fears, but I could see how worried he was.

We stayed awake for a long time, thinking about a way out of this trouble, but no one came up with anything. There seemed to be nothing we could do, but we couldn't give up either. I was so exhausted and anxious that I couldn't even think straight. Finally, we decided to rest. I fell asleep thinking about ways to defend Serenus.

It was bright and sunny when I walked to the village center and stood by a tree, enjoying the warmth of the sun. After a few moments, my attention diverted to a Seren walking between the benches. It startled me when I realized that it was the wizard right here in the village center, pacing around worry-free. Everyone was watching him with fearful eyes. As he walked among them, the Seren cringed away from him.

The wizard turned around and came to stand right in front of me and spoke in a cold, intimidating voice, "I can feel a presence here. More powerful than any I have found yet. It taunts me, but

I can't sense exactly where it is. Do you know what it could be?"

His words pierced my ears like daggers. I knew the answer he sought, but I couldn't bring myself to tell him. Instead, I feigned ignorance, hoping he would leave us alone. The wizard nodded menacingly, and then he strode towards the nearest table where Amy and Kratos sat huddled together. Without warning, he seized Amy and dragged her back towards me. Kratos and I watched in horror, frozen to the spot. Amy's eyes were wide with fear, silently pleading with me to help her. My body refused to move.

The wizard released Amy, and she fell to the ground, unconscious. He raised his hands, and she levitated like a lifeless doll. My throat felt tight as I whimpered inaudibly.

"Thinker! Don't you love your friends? You know I don't want to hurt them, but what can I do? You deny me what I need. Tell me where it is, and I will leave her alone."

As my eyes remained fixed on the limp body of my friend, a battle raged inside my head. I had to choose between Tree Circle and Amy. Suddenly, Amy opened her eyes, but her stare was devoid of any emotion. It sent chills down my spine, and I broke into a cold sweat. The battle inside me turned vicious. A small voice in my head whispered, "Friend."

I lifted my hand slowly, as if under someone else's control, and pointed towards the trees. I whispered, "The Tree Circle."

Amy's eyes blazed back to life, and she let out a piercing scream.

The wizard released her and flew to the Tree Circle. She fell to the ground, gasping for air. I rushed to her side, but she pushed me away, still screaming. Without a second thought, she got up and ran after the wizard. I chased after her, not knowing what would happen next.

The wizard landed beside the Tree Circle, eyeing it in a calculating manner. The Seren stood watching him from a distance, fear written all over their faces.

Amy and I reached the wizard and tried to tackle him to the ground, but he was very still, laughing at us. For all our effort, we couldn't move him one bit. He seemed entertained by our desperate attempts to stop him and continued to laugh mockingly. Suddenly, the wizard's face changed into Esmeray's, then back to his own, and they laughed together, transforming into each other repeatedly.

I remembered Esmeray's attack on the Moontree. The village bells were ringing, but there was no fire this time except the one burning inside us. This wizard was too strong to stop. Finally, the wizard walked forward, dragging us with him. Then his wings spread out, and with a powerful thrust, he left us on the ground and flew to the Moontree.

I ran frantically to the healer's home and found the Blacklight bows. I picked one up, ran back to the Tree Circle, and pointed it at the wizard. Black silk ribbons lunged at the wizard and covered him completely. For a moment, I thought it had the wizard under control, but he rotated his hand around the ribbons and held the silk. I waited for him to get weaker but saw a smile appear on his face.

His body started to glow, and he began to grow in size as he absorbed the silk that fell on him. It was too late when I realized my mistake. The wizard could drain all power and absorb it, making him stronger. I threw the bow away, but the shimmering silk didn't fade until he pulled all the light out of the vials.

Amy was sitting on the ground, watching in despair, so powerless that she was not even thinking of trying to stop him anymore, just watching him with a blank stare. The wizard was now twice my size, becoming a mighty giant, still growing. If one bow could give him this much power, what kind of power could the entire Tree Circle and all the lights inside them give him? I fell to the ground in defeat.

Kratos and Idir came and stood next to me. Their eyes were fixed on the tragedy that befell us. Behind us, the whole village stood silently. We watched as the wizard walked to the Moontree and grabbed the glowing white tresses with both hands.

The Moontree began to glow brightly, and the light started to flow through the tresses into the wizard's body, making it shine brighter and brighter until our eyes couldn't look anymore. The Tree Circle faded. I sat helplessly, covering my eyes with my hand, trying to peek at the blinding white.

The wizard let out continuous screams of joy. They became louder and louder. I felt pain in my ears as his pleasure turned to pain. I wanted to understand what was happening, but his body was only a bright orb. It was hard to see. I looked at the aura that formed his arms and sensed he was pulling his arms back. Was he done draining all light out of the circle? Suddenly, and with a jerk, the tree pulled him back toward it. They were locked in a tight embrace, and the wizard struggled, but the tree wouldn't let him go.

The Moontree started to wrap its tresses around the wizard's body. It twisted his arms and crushed his legs as he struggled against their clutches in vain. His screams went lower and lower, and the orb turned even brighter. I turned away from it, unable to take its intensity.

The wizard screamed one last time. I turned around and tried to look at him with squinted eyes. With a loud bang, he burst into an explosion of energy that spread everywhere before it faded away.

Someone shook me violently, and I sat up with a start, opening my eyes. Kratos stood next to me with a worried expression. I was sweating profusely, and Amy rushed to me, handing me a glass of water. It took me some time to understand what had happened. I sighed in relief and fell back on the bed, exhausted by the experience. Thankfully, it was only a dream, a terrible one.

"Are you alright? Your screams scared me to death," Amy asked.

Kratos sat next to me, looking at me curiously, wanting to know what had happened. I tried to ease their stress by saying, "Just a bad dream. I'm okay." Kratos nodded.

My screams had attracted Seren from nearby homes, and I found guardians and Seren standing at the door, wondering what had happened. Once they realized everything was okay, they dispersed. I was still overwhelmed by the magnitude of the shocking experience but started to think about what it meant. Was it just a bad dream, or was it something more than that?

Then, I told Amy and Kratos what I had experienced, and they were very disturbed by it. Amy thought it was more than a dream, a vision. We discussed it at length and concluded that there was a good chance that if the wizard tried to take the power of the Moontree, he would die. But it was just a chance, a possibility. The dream could have been just a dream. We couldn't really take the risk. We had to stop the wizard from trying it.

When the night ended, we went to the healer's home and met the elders there. After recounting my conversation with the wizard, I told them about my dream, and they were stunned.

Jinyan asked Alev, "Do you believe the Moontree can kill the wizard? If so, all we need to do is wait for him to try and do it."

"Who knows? It might, but we can't risk it. We have to stop him no matter what," Alev replied.

"But how?" Amy asked. "He is a powerful wizard. We have no means to fight him. And we know that today or tomorrow, he will be here to get what he wants. It's not like we can just talk him out of it. After all, we don't matter to him. The Moontree, the land, Seren... he doesn't care for anything but his assumed mission."

I heard Amy's words, and an idea came to mind. I didn't know if it could work, but it was better than nothing. "I think that is exactly what we should do: talk him out of it. If we could convince him that attacking the Moontree could cost him his life, he might change his mind."

"You want to tell him about the Moontree? Why don't we present it on a platter to him?" Jinyan was baffled by my idea.

Alev said, "Calm down, Jinyan. No one is doing that. We know very well that the wizard will come for the Moontree sooner or later."

"Alright. But why would the wizard believe us?" Jinyan challenged.

Alev replied after some thought, "We have to take a risk since there is nothing else to try. And if he is not convinced, then the Moontree will have to defend itself."

After the midday meal, I left to find the wizard.

Ch 15: In Wizard's Mind

Kratos was not happy with the plan to meet the wizard alone and insisted on coming with me. He suggested that we take some guardians along. They could hide in the forest and protect me if needed, but I refused. I believed that if the wizard discovered them, he might become aggressive. Kratos protested but had to give up in the end. Still, he came with me to the village border. He wanted to wait there till I came back. I felt his worried eyes on me until I disappeared into the deep forest.

Qilam and the wizard were not where I last met them. I looked for them for a long time and eventually found the wizard far away from the village. He was sitting on a rock, deep in thought. I cleared my throat loudly to get his attention. He was surprised to see me but greeted me cheerfully, "Welcome, Thinker! What brings you so far from the village?"

Without wasting time on pleasant conversation, I came to the purpose of the meeting. "I came to talk to you about an important matter. I know why you are still here. You want to collect as much power as possible before you go."

"Yes, I have told you this myself. What's new about that?"

"First, tell me: how much power can your body take? There has to be a limit."

The wizard frowned and said thoughtfully, "I don't know that."

I was happy with his answer, "Do you know what will happen if you try to take energy from something that has far more power than you can manage?"

"No, I don't know that either. Why are you asking this?"

"I had a dream last night. It felt more like a sign. I saw you taking power from the most powerful source on the island—the Moontree."

His eyes twinkled at the mention of the Moontree, "So, that's what it is. The Moontree!"

"Yes. The Moontree is the most powerful living thing on this island."

"So, what happened when I took its energy?" he asked excitedly.

"You died." He expected an encouraging answer, but I disappointed him.

"What? I died? How is that possible? Oh, it was just a dream. And dreams are just dreams." He was quite visibly shocked by my answer but tried to shrug it off.

"Yes, it might be just a dream, but what if there really is a limit? What would happen if you exceeded that? If you ask me, it seems quite probable that you would be affected badly."

He paced around in deep thought. Then, he stopped to look at me, frowning. "How do I know you really had a dream? How do I know you are not playing me? You are trying to protect your precious trees. I remember very well how emotional you were about that tree yesterday."

"Yes, you are right. I don't want anyone to hurt the trees. They are too important for the survival of the island. I know it doesn't matter to you whether the island lives or not, but I want you to take my warning seriously. I am not trying to deceive you. I saw what I saw. And I believe this is exactly what would happen if you try to hurt the Moontree."

I could see that my words had put the seeds of doubt in his mind. Everything was going as I wanted. But the next step was difficult. I didn't know if he would agree to that.

He stayed silent for a moment, then said, "If you are not lying and actually saw this dream, there could be a possibility that it is dangerous for me. But, a far more likely explanation is that you are just telling a lie, trying to protect the island."

I smiled. "I can prove that I am not lying. You can read my mind."

He was both surprised and curious at the same time. He did not know about this power and wanted to learn how to do it. I told him about Alia and her ability to reflect a person's feelings so that everyone around could experience them and how it was used to find out if a person was lying or telling the truth.

"You can experience my feelings as your own. If you agree, I can talk to the elders. I will inform you when they are convinced, and you can come to the village."

"And you will just volunteer to expose your inner thoughts in front of everyone?"

"Yes, if it results in saving the island, then yes, I will," I responded in a confident voice.

"Hmm, you do realize you can't fight me? I will not tolerate any tricks or deception." His words were cold.

"I know, and I have no such intention."

"Alright then. Let's go to the village right now and be done with it." He started walking toward the village.

I pretended that I was not prepared for that. "Wait, I told you I would have to talk to the elders first."

"There is no need for that. They will agree to it whether they like it or not. And since you are telling the truth, there is nothing to worry about, right?" He sounded amused. Without waiting for an answer, he walked on.

I walked back to the village with excitement. The conversation had gone exactly the way I had hoped. I was sure Amy would have told the elders about my idea. I had only shared it with her before coming to meet the wizard. I couldn't tell Kratos as I was afraid he might not agree to it.

Kratos was waiting for me. He was not expecting the wizard, of course. "What is he doing here?" he asked me. The wizard ignored him and kept walking.

I tried to calm him down. "It's alright, Kratos. Everything is fine. Come with me." He was not happy and walked along in a grumpy mood.

The elders were shocked to see the wizard coming with me so casually. Amy had told them about my plan, but they didn't expect it to work so easily.

Still, they were already present near the Moontree along with Boris, Idir, and many others. The wizard walked directly to the Moontree and assessed it. We held our breath. The images from my dreams haunted me. Was I wrong in bringing him here?

The wizard studied the Moontree for some time, then he turned to me and said, "Shall we start?"

Amy quickly helped Alia with what she needed. When everything was ready, I sat down, facing her. A vial of Moonlight was on the ground in the middle. A Moonflower was floating around slowly. Alia asked me to put my hands on the vial, and I complied.

The wizard moved closer to watch.

Alia remained quiet for some time with her eyes closed, her hands resting over the glowing light. I had seen it before and knew that she was channelling her energy through the Moonlight, getting ready to test me.

The soft, cool glow spread over my hands, taking them under its dominance. Its coolness spread further instantly. I felt the cool Moonlight circulating throughout my body. Alia put her hands over mine and held them gently. Something reached my mind. I shuddered at the alien touch and tried to move away from it. But the strange presence was mighty. I couldn't fight it off while it started to probe my mind relentlessly. An array of emotions ran through me, and the alien probe went out of focus, though I could still feel it.

I looked at the Tree Circle. The trees looked beautiful—majestic, in fact. Even sacred. Serenus itself was majestic. I felt happy to be here. A white flame danced in front of my eyes as I looked around. It was coming out of my hands. I watched it, cherishing its unearthly beauty.

I saw Kratos standing quietly, looking back at me. I felt an immense affection toward him. He was much more than a friend. Even the thought of losing him was unbearable for me. I wished I could be friends with him forever.

Grief took over as my attention drifted to the image of Feray sitting broken and desolate in her prison room, waiting for her fate. She had betrayed her friends. A regret that cuts deep.

Then I looked at Amy. It made me sad. She had lost Alfred, her best friend, and was deceived by Feray, her teacher. Her work and the Lighttrees were constantly under attack. She did not deserve this stress. If only I could take her sadness away.

Next, I looked at the elders. My head bowed in respect. They were battling one problem after another. It was not an easy life, and their old shoulders were laden with the weight of responsibility. I felt sorry for them.

Finally, I looked at the wizard and felt pity for him. No one caresd for him. He had no friends in his life and didn't even understand what it meant to care for someone. The image changed in my head, and I saw him standing near the Moontree. Fear ran through me as he walked toward it. I felt helpless as I watched him draining the life out of the Moontree, worrying that at any moment, the Moontree would wither, and with that, Serenus would become a place of misery. But then, something unexpected happened. The power of the Moontree was too much for the wizard to take. His screams echoed around me. In blinding Moonlight, the wizard's body burst. A strong emotion of pity came back and hovered around for a bit, but then my mind went dark.

Something brushed past my mind, waking me up again. It was

the same alien presence I had sensed before. It went through my mind, looking for something. I wondered what it wanted. The search became intense and insistent.

I heard Alia's frustrated voice. "What are you hiding from me?"

The white flame erupted into a furious red fire as the presence went through my head, and Alia's voice echoed in my mind. "How? How are you doing this?"

I snapped out of the trance and saw Alia looking at me with angry eyes. She said through clenched teeth, "What is it that you are hiding from me? And how? Tell me everything you know."

"I have no idea what you are talking about," I replied.

"I am warning you, do not lie. Tell me what you know."

She kept insisting that I was hiding something from her, somehow. It didn't make sense. I told her again that I didn't know what she was asking, but she wouldn't listen.

She clenched my hands and closed her eyes. The flame rose higher as her anger seemed to fuel it. The alien presence was back in my head, looking around, searching for what she wanted to know. The glow around her grew more prominent and angry. It spread around and soon took over the entire place, engulfing us. The Light trees around us became invisible behind the glow, and now it was just the two of us inside an ever-spreading bubble of fiery fog, sitting in front of each other, her hands tightening their grip over mine, hurting my fingers in frustration. The stranger in my head enhanced its energy. I felt its power increase and take control.

I was too weak to fight back. The power insisted that I hand over the information I had kept safe, but I had nothing to give. It was confused and desperate at not being able to unlock the hidden information. It left me once again.

"Tell me what you know. Tell me how you are keeping it from me." Her words were accompanied by a wave of raw anger.

The fire burned higher and higher. My refusal to accept that I knew something further infuriated her. She yelled at me, clenching my hands in frustration.

"You have met your maker, and you are your copy. How?"

I grimaced as her nails dug into my skin. I told her I didn't know what she was talking about. It made no sense to me, but her anger and frustration continued to soar. I tried to think about what she may be talking about but failed to find anything to match her claim. I frowned. "Maker? Copy? What are you talking about? What is wrong with you?"

She responded with yet another attack on my mind. This time, she was brutal and inconsiderate of the pain her presence brought along. My mind throbbed with every attempt she made. The flames burned vigorously, and an uncomfortable heat spread around us. I started to sweat as it suffocated me. I was sure I would fall unconscious any moment now.

The flame swayed in front of my eyes, then suddenly, my senses became sharp and alert again. I felt outraged. I was angry at being unable to get past the invisible wall in the mind that I was searching for. I needed that information at any price. I growled with frustration when every attempt seemed to return unsuccessful. I needed more power, perhaps. But would I be able to deal with so much Moonlight? I didn't know.

Out of frustration, I changed my technique. Now, I was looking for the truth. The mind was innocent and confused. I studied it intensely but realized with surprise that it believed that it knew nothing else. It wasn't trying to hide anything, yet I could feel another power inside it that was far beyond my reach, not letting me access what I needed to know. I was not going to give in so easily. I explored the mind with every ounce of energy I had for a long time. Gradually, the struggle drained me, leaving me weak and helpless. Keeping up the search was futile. I was powerless in the face of this stubborn force that seemed to mock my inability to even compete with it. Finally, I gave up and slumped down, tired and exhausted.

Kratos's voice pulled me out of the alien place I was stuck in. The trees came back into view. I was lying on the ground with Kratos bent over me with worry etched on his face. The mysterious glow was gone. I looked towards Alia and found her on the ground, being helped by Boris. Her anger had finally withered away. The wizard was watching me intently.

Many Seren men and women were gathered around us. One of

them asked, "What was all this about? What happened to you, Alia? This is not you. I couldn't even recognize the person you transformed into. What is it you are looking for?" His voice was urgent and strict.

Boris helped Alia sit up. She was breathing heavily with a drawn face. Her calm composure had shattered to reveal a side that was unrecognizable even to her friends.

She took some time to catch her breath and then replied weakly, "This mind carries information but doesn't give it away. It stays locked. There is a power inside it that I have never felt before. I did all I could, but I didn't get it." Then she added, looking at me furiously, "I need that information!"

To her, nothing else seemed to matter now, not even what everyone thought of her desperate attempts. Kratos helped me up, and a Seren brought me some water. I felt better but was still shocked by the strange experience. When I was about to fall unconscious, I realized that my mind had started feeling the emotions Alia the Mirror was going through. The intensity of her desire to know about whatever she thought I was hiding surprised me. I was not sure about her claim, though. I didn't have any powers to hide anything from her. But she not only believed in her claim but also tried her utmost to find an answer.

Alia's inability to find what was hidden in my mind puzzled everyone. They knew something was there, which was more capable than Alia could access. The wizard had stood away silently throughout the incident, watching and feeling everything. He left his place and walked toward me. "Come, Thinker! We need to talk."

Ch 16: To Find Common Ground

I wandered in the yard, leaving footprints in the fresh snow. I opened my hand to let the soft snowflakes land on my palm. They were light and beautiful and melted away quickly, leaving a wet mark of freshness. It was the first time I had seen snow, and it would perhaps be the last.

A gust of wind shook the snow-covered branches of the tree I was passing under, showering me with snow. I enjoyed the cold that spread around my neck and looked up. The sky was generous, raining down snowflakes in heavy blankets. It looked brighter for the time of day.

The evening was approaching fast, my last evening here. The thought froze my heart. I looked around and stopped at the Tree Circle. The trees were hidden under the white veil, yet their glow peeked through, giving out hues of different colours. They looked splendid as they stood calm and peaceful among the dancing white. Standing in front of the Tree Circle, I tried to imprint the snow-streaked wonder in my mind. I wanted to capture the image, burn it in my memory, and cherish it forever. I was happy that I had the chance to see this snowy landscape before I left.

Amy's voice disturbed my thoughts. I turned around to see her standing at the front door, gesturing for me to come. I turned away with a last look around and walked back to the healer's home. I brushed the snow off my head and shoulders before going inside. Everyone was there, waiting for me, eager to know what the wizard had talked to me about.

I sat back in my chair and sighed. The time I was dreading was here. I had to tell my friends something that would hurt them. Looking at their faces sadly, I told them, "The wizard wants me to go with him through the Dark End."

Everyone gasped. Kratos took my hand and gripped it tightly. "You are not going anywhere. I won't let you."

His gesture brought tears to my eyes. I explained gently, "I have to go. To save the Moontree. To save Serenus."

"What are you talking about?" Amy said. "Save from who? The wizard felt what you dreamed and left the Moontree alone. There is no problem anymore. He will soon leave us."

"He wants to go past the fall and wants me to go with him. He left only because I agreed to go with him. He offered me a deal, and I took it."

"But why? What does he want from you?" It was Alev's concerned voice.

"Since he knows about the power that Alia says I have in me, he is curious. He wants to take me with him because he believes I am important somehow. In return, he promised to spare the Moontree and leave the island as soon as tomorrow morning." I paused and then said sadly, "I will leave with him in the morning."

Kratos stood up in anger. "This is not happening. I won't let it. We will find a way to send him alone."

"There is no way. He will attack the Moontree if I refuse. And we can't force him to leave."

Kratos was beside himself with rage. He paced in the room as others discussed how to send the wizard alone. Listening to their desperate thoughts was agonizing. I was exhausted by the very idea of tomorrow's sunrise, but sitting here, watching my friends in helpless misery, was unbearable.

"I am tired and want to rest," I muttered.

Everyone fell silent and watched me for a moment. Kratos recovered quickly and said, "Yes, sure. I will take you to the room."

He accompanied me to one of the bedrooms and helped me get some warm blankets. I lay in bed, snuggling in for warmth.

Kratos sat in front of me and tried to comfort me. "Don't worry. I said I would find a way, and I will. If we can't convince the wizard, we will trick him. But I will not let you go."

Kratos left the room, and I spent the evening in bed, watching the snow falling continuously outside the window. The Tree Circle was glowing invitingly. Before it became dark, I left the room to eat my dinner, but I couldn't stomach much. I could hear everyone's voices, still planning and thinking of ways to stop the wizard from taking me with him. I was proud of them for not giving up, even though I had made up my mind.

I needed fresh air, and in the hope of finding some peace, I left the healer's home and walked to the Greentree. Inside its chamber, I thought about all the unanswered questions. Why did I come here? Was it right to leave? Who sent me, and why did they give me a poem? I had tried before, but even the wisdom of the tree couldn't provide me with these answers. I tried to think of a way to stop the wizard. It felt like I was leaving the island too early. I could have done so much more and thought about many other things. As the Greenlight took effect, I sat under its glow and became lost in my thoughts, in a conversation with myself or the tree. Whatever it was, I still wasn't sure how it worked.

After some time, I returned to the chamber still without any answers, but I had found a new perspective. A new way of reading the poem, and it gave me hope. There was no way to know if it was correct, but I had to share it with others.

I walked back toward the healer's home and thought about telling them. It was a sensitive matter. I had to convey it cautiously, ensuring that they understood it could be wrong.

As I walked through the entrance, everyone turned to me with hopeful eyes, expecting a solution to the problem, but I had none. I shook my head. Their faces changed to reflect the sadness as they, too, had failed to come up with any plans. I went back to the bedroom, and once again, they became busy in whispers.

I thought about the appropriate words to tell everyone about the poem, and when I was satisfied with the wording, I found some papers and wrote down my newfound understanding. I made several copies, each addressing one of my friends and elders. I used the opportunity to thank them for their kindness and wrote what their companionship meant to me.

Amy's notebook was sitting on the table, and I picked it up to hide the messages in it. I wanted them to find it after I was gone. I left the pages in the notebook and walked to the window to look out into the darkness and enjoy the sight of the glowing trees for the last time.

Amy came through the open door and stood beside me. For some time, we stayed quiet, just looking out the window with empty eyes. Then she said, "I don't know what will happen tomorrow, but there is something I want you to read." She handed me a page and added soberly, "Alfred left this for me before going into the dark. I want you to know."

Surprised by her words, I took the page and read.

"Hello, Aymelek!"

I turned to Amy and asked, "Aymelek?"

Amy replied, "My real name is Aymelek. Everyone calls me Amy."

I resumed reading:

"In a mysterious world, I opened my eyes. Curious and frightened, I looked left and right. A dream, an instinct, a poem in my heart. And what's on my wrist? A very strange watch!

I don't know from where or why I've come. Few threads to follow, and clues only some! The past is lost, nothing comes to mind. Others came before me and tried to find. Don't get me wrong, they are really kind, but their failure to answer has kept us behind. At every big question, we've nothing to show. Shake our heads, we say, we do not know!

Will I be different or like others stay blind? To pull on the right thread, to unravel and unwind, I'll need to think outside the box, because what I seek many have sought. If I am to succeed, find something but naught, what would I need? Where should I start? An untried action, not a battle we've fought. An all-new direction, a new line of thought!

To find common ground, an understanding profound, I started by looking, observing, and learning. I'm writing it all, whatever I have found, questions and lessons from all around. Who made this world? Why? And for what? We've theories and opinions, and numerous guesses. Our stories sow divisions and disastrous messes! Not bringing us together, they keep us divided. Imagine finding a tether that's not one-sided, a belief beyond doubt, to finally bring about a beacon of hope that's not lopsided.

I've heard the rumours and hoped against hope. They tell me I'll find it in the lost scroll! An idea, a message, a beautiful goal, the real deal, no tricks, no lump of coal. To unite us where needed but allow our differences, leave room for possibilities but erase all distances, wholesome, and wise conduct for a world exquisite, where goodness is a product, not a prerequisite. The idea of an open mind, not vengeful and punishing, accepting all, and being kind — beautiful and ravishing.

If such a scroll exists indeed, trying to find it — a worthy deed, no way to guess if I will succeed, wish me the best and godspeed. Everything, but you, I'm putting on the line, what else can I give, I hope I'll be fine. I believe in myself, I'll find the scroll, study every bookshelf, defeat every troll.

Then, together we will stand on the other side, with the scroll in my hand, but no fear and no pride. But if all goes bad, and we never see again, do not be sad and feel no pain. Remember the memories and times spent together, no one can steal it, it's ours forever.

In every newcomer, of white or black colour, in pursuit of the secret, as Khan or as Egret, in their longing and their passion, whether a he or a she, you will always find me.

I will be missing you until we meet again. -Alfred.

I couldn't help but feel impressed by the Seren I had never met. Amy was still looking outside with a blank expression. I read the poem again. Now, I had a much better understanding of why Alfred left.

I handed the poem to Amy but couldn't say any words. She took the page, patted my shoulder, and left the room. I went to bed thinking about Alfred's words.

* * *

On my last day in Serenus, we walked to the Dark End in the form of a procession. Every Seren had come to say goodbye, many of them with teary eyes. They knew I was leaving Serenus so the Moontree could be safe from the power-thirsty wizard. Their open display of gratitude and love melted my heart. They brought small tokens of their love and respect to take with me. It was hard to refuse them, but I couldn't leave with so much when I didn't even know if I was going to a new world or to my death. The only thing that I was taking with me was the pendant from Kratos. He had given it to me during our stay at Serenus Lodge. I couldn't bear to part with it.

The wizard and Qilam were waiting for us at the shore. As we approached them, Qilam hurried over to me and said excitedly, "I wasn't sure you would come. Remember, I said I would do what I believe in? Your words convinced me to take the leap of faith. I am going with you." I frowned at him and looked away. I didn't care if he thought my words were responsible for his decision.

Qilam and the wizard were leaving in a boat each, but there was also a third boat full of supplies. Qilam explained, "Just in case the journey is long."

Saying goodbye to Idir, Fabio, and Misa was hard. Pari gave me a beautiful round stone and stood by soberly. I thanked her for the gift.

Then I turned toward Amy. The moment our eyes met, she broke into tears. I stood there, hugging her without saying a word. She sobbed openly. Then, she took off her ring. It was the ring that had mesmerized me with its unique beauty the first time I saw it. A white translucent sphere with wispy white light swirling slowly inside. She handed it to me and said, "This sphere has the first Moonlight ever captured. It has been worn solely by the healers chosen by it. If it likes a healer, it keeps moving. If not, the light stays still. It is believed that it is the most powerful Moonlight as it was taken directly from the Moontree bulb the moment it was born. I want you to have it."

I hesitated. I couldn't take such a precious gift, but she insisted, and I agreed. I understood how important this ring was to her. I thanked her, and she hugged me again.

"Come on, Thinker! It's time to go," the wizard said impatiently. He was getting irritated by the emotional atmosphere around him.

Finally, Idir held Amy's arm. "Amy, let's not send our friend away with tears," he said, giving her a meaningful look.

She nodded and tried to compose herself. "I know, it's just that... what if?" With one last hug, she moved away.

Kratos stood next to my boat as the guardians brought it and placed it in the water. Boris put a bag inside it and said, "Just some food for the journey." He moved forward, hugged me quickly, and then left.

The elders' torn faces revealed their disdain for what was happening, but they couldn't do anything. I went forward and hugged them.

"Thinker, be done with it now." The wizard had tolerated enough.

Kratos was the last Seren I needed to say goodbye to. I wasn't ready to say the words yet. I looked at his face and stood there, frozen. I didn't know what to say. There were no words that could express what I felt for any of my friends, how sad I was to leave them, but also how lucky I felt to have met them and spent time with them.

Kratos moved forward and hugged me tightly, whispering in my ear, "Don't worry. Just remember what I told you."

I was confused. What did Kratos mean by that? Was he going to do something to fight the wizard?

Everyone else had already stepped back. Unwillingly, Amy, Idir, and Kratos stepped back a few steps.

Boris and two guardians carried a rather large bag and awkwardly passed by me to place it in the boat. Boris spoke sheepishly, "We don't know how long the journey could be."

The wizard was looking at the Dark End, ready to go. He didn't want to wait any longer and came close to Qilam and me and said, "If we leave early, we might reach the next island in daylight. Let's go!"

Boris stepped forward and, to everyone's surprise, punched Qilam in the face. Qilam screamed in pain as he fell back and started cursing him. Boris stepped away.

The wizard looked at Qilam and smiled. "What a farewell you have earned, Qilam."

Kratos came to me and nodded, then he moved toward the wizard and said, "If you want to leave, you can go. No one else is leaving." Something was happening. I looked at them, trying to understand what they were doing.

The wizard turned furious, "What are you trying to do? You know I am too powerful for you. Why do you want to waste your life?"

I saw guardians and Boris go behind the wizard, surrounding him. Then I looked at Kratos with questioning eyes. What was he going to do? He couldn't possibly fight the wizard. And I did not want anyone to get hurt.

As soon as the wizard realized he was encircled, he spread his arms dangerously, facing the nearby guardian. He strained his muscles like he did on the island under the fall. I was sure he would attack the guardian with a spell. I wanted them to stop wasting their lives in a futile effort and yelled, "Stop this! No one has to suffer. I made a deal with him. I will honour that deal. Step back."

The wizard waited for just a moment for the guardians to move back, but they didn't. "Alright then, that's enough!" He waved his arm, but nothing happened. In shock, he looked at his hands and tried again. Still nothing.

Kratos exclaimed, "It works!"

The wizard turned around and faced him and tried the spell on him, but nothing happened. I was as stumped as the wizard. How were they stopping him from using magic? Boris and the guardians pounced on him before he could fly away to escape the uncertain situation. Kratos and Idir held on as guardians opened the large bag from my boat and pulled out a rope. They used the rope to tie up the struggling wizard. I heard the entire village sigh in relief as they understood what was happening. Still not knowing how I stood there watching with a mystified look. The wizard was yelling commands at us, and behind him, Qilam was still on the ground, watching in disbelief.

"Apparently, you are not the only thinker here. Sometimes, we can think too." Idir laughed as he teased me, withholding the information that I sought.

Guardians put Qilam in his boat, and he was the first one to be sent forward. He screamed in panic. Everyone knew he was a coward, but no one expected such a show of wailing from him after he was already ready to go. As he disappeared into the dark, the screaming stopped. Even the wizard was surprised at hearing his screams.

Boris said mockingly, "Wasn't he ready to go a few moments ago?"

Then, the guardians carried the wizard to his boat and pushed it into the water. Before he disappeared, he yelled more threats, "I will come back, and I will burn this entire world to the ground. You will all pay for this."

We stood watching him as he disappeared into the dark.

Idir and Kratos stood teasingly in front of me as more Seren ran over. I looked back at them, but they wouldn't tell me how they had pulled this off. I understood what they meant. It was a challenge for me to figure out.

I scratched my head and put my hand on my chin as my friends watched me with mischievous smiles. I felt embarrassed for not being able to come up with an explanation for how they stopped the wizard's magic from affecting them. Fabio and Misa also didn't know and begged for answers, but Idir shook his head.

Kratos said, "This is for the thinker to think."

I looked at Amy with pleading eyes. She smiled and shook her head, but for a moment, I sensed sadness in her eyes. She laughed, and I realized it was nothing. I brought my attention back to the waiting faces in front of me, teasing me to crack the puzzle.

Finally, I gave up and said, "Okay, I cannot wait anymore. I need to know. Don't make me go sit under the Greentree. At least give me a hint."

Idir looked at Kratos, who nodded.

"What do the seven Lighttrees do when the Moontree runs out of light?" Idir asked.

Still confused, I replied, "They become dangerous and steal life from things around them to refill the bulb in the Moontree."

Idir teased, "And what was this wizard's ability?"

My jaw dropped as I realized how simple the answer was. I laughed at their clever trick and said, "He did the same as the seven. We just needed some Moonlight to stop him from being dangerous."

Kratos pulled out a locket from under his shirt. He was wearing the tiny Moonlight vial that Feray used to wear and was able to go in and out of the tree under the fall. Idir, Boris, and the guardians had Moonlight vials in their pockets.

Fabio and Misa were still thinking with open mouths when Idir finally explained it to them, "The wizard could not hurt anyone in the presence of Moonlight. That is why, in the dream, he was killed by Moontree. Just like the seven trees, we stopped him from harming us by carrying Moonlight vials on us."

Kratos added, "And when he couldn't use magic, he was just an ordinary Seren."

Fabio nodded excitedly. He understood it now. "He came only

two nights before a full moon, but the night was cloudy...."

Misa interrupted and completed the joke, "Poor wizard. Just needed some Moonlight in his life."

We laughed out loud.

By now, a whole crowd had gathered around us. I looked to my right and spotted Alev smiling proudly at Idir and Kratos. Then, she asked, "And if the thinker couldn't figure this out, who did?"

Idir replied, "Last night, we were trying to find a way to trick the wizard. We were thinking out loud, saying many ideas. Kratos said the wizard is able to steal the life out of living things. Then Amy said, just like the seven trees do without the Moonlight. Then I said, 'How do we stop his ability? What could be his weakness?' And Kratos said, just like the seven trees? And then we screamed the answer together—the Moonlight!"

The Seren laughed heartily and shook their heads. Alev held my hand. I looked at her. She nodded her head once. I nodded back, remembering how she had greeted me the day I had arrived on the island. With a nod of the head and the raise of a glass. She said teasingly, "Picked a name yet?" Everyone laughed again.

I looked at the happy faces of my friends all around me, still not believing that we had prevailed against yet another powerful wizard. Eventually, we started to head back to the village. The rest of the Seren had already left, relieved that the threat of an attack was over.

"Don't you think the situation demands a celebration? Let's go to the village center and celebrate," Fabio suggested. Everyone agreed as we walked toward the village.

A loud splash made our heads turn. We froze as we saw Amy pushing a boat toward the Dark End. She had gone to pick up my bag from the boat. I was so happy in the excitement of our success that I didn't see her push it into the water. Everyone gasped as we watched her get in the boat and head towards the dark barrier. We screamed and ran to her, but she was already in the current.

She looked back at us and said, "I will miss you and never forget you. I hope you can forgive me, but Alfred is waiting for me. I can't live here when he is all alone, waiting for me there."

We screamed at the top of our lungs as we tried to convince her to stop, even though it was too late. She kept looking at us sadly while we ran after her in the water. Boris and the guardians held us back, and we watched her disappear into the dark.

No one could believe what had just happened. We began mourning her loss. Alev wept loudly, and Boris tried to comfort her. Kratos was on his knees, looking into the dark with a frozen face. I put my hand on his shoulder, and at the same time, Idir put his hand on the other shoulder.

I wept uncontrollably as I realized that I had failed to help Amy. She was sad, and I could not make her feel better. Even a few moments ago, I had sensed her sadness but then became distracted by the celebration. Then I remembered the question I had asked her when we were talking about Alfred.

If you could say one more thing to him, what would it be?

Don't leave, but if you must, take me with you.

The image of the Yellowtree flashed in my head. Amy was sitting under the Yellowtree, talking about going to the next world. I had assumed it was just the tree that was affecting her thoughts, but I had promised her:

If we ever leave, we will leave together.

I didn't know where she was going. There was no way of knowing if she would have to face Esmeray, Qilam, and the wizard in the next world and whether she would be able to find Alfred all by herself. I thought about what she might have to go through. And, of course, the biggest question was whether there actually was a next world to go to.

I looked at the ring she had left me with. She had given it to me to protect against the wizard, but now she was vulnerable.

If we ever leave, we will leave together. I repeated my promise in my head.

I knew I wasn't ready, but I had to go after her. I waited for an opportunity and then ran to the last empty boat and pushed it into the water, as my friends screamed for me to stop and ran after me. Before they could reach me, I, too, was leaving them forever. I sat facing the people I loved and was hurting.

"I am so sorry!" I shouted. "I promised Amy that I would go with her if she went into the dark."

Kratos fell down, Alev ordered me to return, and Boris and the guardians ran one more time, but once again, it was too late. I looked at Idir, who was sitting next to Kratos, examining him. Then, he looked up at me and nodded. I knew what he meant. Kratos would be okay.

I was going into the dark, but the darkness seemed to be moving ahead too. My boat travelled toward it, but it kept its distance and moved ahead. I looked at my friends one last time. They stared back in disbelief and shock. Our eyes remained locked till they disappeared out of sight.

Then I faced forward. There was no sign of any other boat in front of me. Just an endless dark fog that was becoming lighter as I approached it. The veil surrounded me on all sides as I travelled forward to an unknown destination inside a bubble of light.

I looked around to see if I could spot anything in the dark. As my boat passed it, a dead fish floated on the surface of the water. Then another one—no, this one wasn't a fish, it was something else, and it was too far to recognize what it was. My heart started racing, and fear took over me.

Gradually, the fog started to become thicker, and the circle of light surrounding me began to shrink. I sat helpless as the darkness covered me. I could no longer see anything. I felt it drain all energy out of my body and fell backward.

As long as I could, I resisted and fought the dark, trying to stay awake, but as it sucked all light out of me, I fell asleep.

Intermission

Ch 17: Beyond The Veil

I woke up to the sound of waves crashing against my boat. As my eyes adjusted to the blinding brightness, I saw a pristine white sandy beach on my right as the churning waves on my left kept me safely anchored to the shore. Behind me, the previously thick fog had lifted, revealing an endless stretch of waves. I glanced at my wrist and noticed that my watch was still there, but the once-twirling whirlpool was now absent, leaving a void that was a haunting reminder of the treacherous journey that lay ahead.

After getting off the boat, I scoured the island for any trace of Amy, but to no avail. The small island was barren, with no trees, rocks, or anything blocking my line of sight except for a wooden cottage. As I circled around the cottage, peering through the open window and calling out her name, it became evident that Amy was nowhere to be found.

Suddenly, a ball of light materialized in front of me, growing in size till it was as large as me. From within the light, a metallic creature emerged, causing me to take a few steps back. I had never seen magic like this before.

"Welcome to Sandbox — A place between the worlds. I am Checkpoint. Nice to meet you!" the creature said.

Confused, I responded with a hesitant "What?"

"I hope you lived a happy and healthy life," Checkpoint said.

I asked, "What do you mean by that? Am I dead? And who are you?"

In response, Checkpoint casually replied, "Yes, you died. And I am Checkpoint. Follow me. Ma will see you soon."

Shocked, I questioned, "I died? Then how can I see you? How can I talk to you? Where is Amy? Did she die too?"

Checkpoint simply stated, "Ma will explain everything. Just follow me." With a friendly gesture, Checkpoint put its arm around my shoulder and led me toward the cottage. I couldn't help but feel comforted by its presence.

As we walked, I asked, "What will happen now?" Checkpoint replied, "Ma will inform you of what happens next."

Curious, I inquired, "Who is this Ma?"

Checkpoint answered, "Ma is The Maker. She created you."

I was surprised by this revelation and asked, "She made me?"

Checkpoint confirmed, "Yes, she is Ma, The Maker."

Once inside the cottage, I noticed it was empty. Ma wasn't there. Checkpoint motioned me to sit on a bench near a large wooden table and said,

> "Be comfortable, relax, and clear your mind.
>
> You have lots, and lots, and lots of time."

As Checkpoint turned towards the door to leave, I desperately wanted to ask more questions. I was dead. What did that mean? What would happen to me now? And where was Amy?

Checkpoint stopped in its tracks, pivoted, and strode back towards me. Its metallic hand settled on my shoulder, and a warm, reassuring voice spoke:

> "You'll never be lost. Now you're home!
>
> A place of safety, a beautiful biome.
>
> Be happy! Don't worry, she will be kind
>
> I can't say more, but I promise you will find.
>
> You like to ask? Query and probe?
>
> There isn't a question that she will mind.
>
> I've seen her watch you, and feel all that you felt.
>
> She doesn't let you hear it, but she cried when you wept.
>
> She doesn't like to count; her help is limitless.

She's happy when you are happy, and she can sense your sadness.

I sense worry in your heart, you silly goose!

She's on your side, your team, win or lose.

You did right things, or... left things, she'll understand.

You had walls around you, teensy little was in your hand.

You failed, and failed big, and I don't say it smugly

No shame, it happens. Failure isn't so ugly

What's done is done; Nothing to cry over

Wait just a bit more, but no, it's not over."

I listened quietly as Checkpoint finished and left me in my thoughts. What did it mean by that? Was I finally home? The way Checkpoint spoke about Ma, she sounded like a friend, which made me feel much better. So now I was supposed to wait for the meeting.

"When will she meet me?" I asked, raising my head, but Checkpoint wasn't there. I ran outside to catch it before it left, but it was gone. It was amazing how it could appear and disappear like that.

I walked back inside and saw a big bowl of fruit on the table. I was pretty sure it wasn't there a few moments ago. Where did it come from? Was someone here? There was no hiding place in the house, so the only possibility was that someone had snuck in through the large open window, left the fruit on the table, and then left before I could see them. But why would someone do that? Why would they bring me food but not want me to see them?

I looked through the window but saw no one outside. I leaned forward and looked left to right as far as I could see, but no one was there. Once again, I ran out the door to find out who it was but didn't find anyone.

I had to keep my eyes open. Someone could appear anytime and from anywhere. I needed to catch them, talk to them, and ask where I was and what it meant to be dead. Most importantly, I wanted to know what would happen now and when Ma would meet me. And, of course, where did Amy go?

Back inside, I picked up a piece of fruit and tasted it. It was sweet, no, it was delicious - more than any food I had ever eaten. I wanted to eat more and quickly finished the fruit. However, I ate too much too fast, and my head started spinning. The fruit did something to me, and I began to feel different, weaker. I kept my eyes on the window but rested my head on the table. A fresh breeze came from the open window, which felt good.

And then, a lightning bolt ran through my body, and I looked over my shoulder, "Where are my wings?"

I wasn't injured, and my skin was flat and smooth. What happened to my wings? I examined myself to see if there was any other change. I couldn't tell if there was; I just had no wings.

Losing my wings made me sad, really sad. It felt like a sign. I had wings in Serenus, but now I had none. I had a feeling things were going to be less than pleasant, and there could be changes ahead that I might not like. Who took away my wings, and why? Did Ma do that? Checkpoint said she was on my side, then why would she do that?

Fear and uncertainty took hold of me, and I felt like I had lost everything. I had lost my friends, Kratos... I wanted to see him again. Idir, Fabio, Misa... Oh no, what have I done? Have I lost them forever? Can I get my wings back?

I wished I had never left Serenus. I had never felt so hopeless before; it felt like my heart would sink. Had I lost everything forever? Was there nothing that could be done?

The walls around me felt suffocating, so I left the cottage. I wanted to get as far away from here as I could, but which way should I go? A glance toward my boat shocked me further - it was gone.

The sun shone brightly, and I felt dizzy. My legs folded, and I fell onto the sand. What have I done? I had given up everything, things that mattered to me, things that I cared about, and my friends who I wanted to see again. Was it all gone forever?

Did Ma take my wings? Was she not a friend? I needed to get out of here. I couldn't stay here. Where should I go?

I ran to the water and kept running. The waves pushed me back. I struggled but pushed forward. The waves pushed back harder. I didn't know what I was doing or where I was trying to go, but I kept pushing forward.

As my muscles ached, I didn't care. I pushed harder and harder. The waves pushed me back as if mocking me. I was no match.

And then, suddenly, I stopped. Where could I go?

My senses regained control, and I realized there was no use fighting; I could never defeat the waves. How long could I fight? I stopped struggling, and the waves carried me back to the sand, left me there, and retreated.

I stayed there with my face in the sand as I felt a chill enter my body. I felt something die inside me. The will. The will to move, to think, or to do anything. There was no reason left to do anything now. It was over. I was dead.

Words from Checkpoint rang in my head, "But no, it's not over." What was that supposed to mean? Was there still hope left? Could things get better?

A memory appeared in my head. It was Alev. She smiled and gave a slow nod. I missed her. I wanted to go back to everything I had left behind. I wanted to be back in Serenus. I wanted to meet Idir. I wanted to laugh at Fabio and Misa's jokes. I wanted to go back.

And where was Amy? Why wasn't she here? I gave up everything, so she wouldn't be alone, but she wasn't here. Maybe she didn't know I would come after her. Perhaps she had already left for whatever was next.

Ma... yes, Ma would know. I needed to ask her. But where was she? When would she meet me?

Checkpoint's words worried me, "You have lots and lots and lots of time."

What do I do? How do I pass the time? I felt an emptiness inside me. No answer came forth. There was nothing to do. Without any answers, there wasn't even a reason to get up. I put my head back down and, at some point, fell asleep.

I didn't know how long I slept, but when I woke up, I was still stuck and hopeless. I whispered, "What am I supposed to do? Checkpoint? Ma? Where are you? Amy? Where are you, Amy?"

Silence. That was the only response I got. Wait... what about the waves? I lifted my head and looked back. The water was calm. There were no waves. I put my head back down. It wasn't that I didn't have the energy to move. I just had no reason to move. Why should I get up? What for? I stayed there and fell asleep again.

Your vessel is sinking; survive the tides,

The end is coming; open your eyes.

The voice shook me in my dream. What did it mean? My vessel had already sunk. I was dead. What did it want me to wake up for now?

Once again, I opened my eyes and looked around. There was no change in my surroundings.

I sat up, now sitting on my knees, and looked up to the sky. The bright sunlight caressed my skin gently, and a soft breeze felt good on my skin. With my face to the sky, I closed my eyes and started to whimper. Tears escaped my eyes as I cried and begged, "Ma? Where are you? I'm sorry. I'm so sorry. Please send me back."

I stayed there for some time, but then the sand on my skin, in my hair, and on my face bothered me. I wiped my tears and walked to the water to clean myself. Then I walked back to the cottage.

I sat by the table where Checkpoint had asked me to sit and looked at the fresh bowl of fruit. I felt no desire to eat anything.

When I got bored of sitting, I walked to the window to look outside. There wasn't much to look at. My mind went back to Serenus. I remembered looking out the window in my home — the swamp, the pond, and the three waterfalls.

I closed my eyes and tried to imagine that I was still there. A powerful desire to hear a knock on my door emerged. I kept my eyes closed and tried to make the thought as believable and realistic as possible. I imagined a knock. It was Kratos. I ran to him, but he couldn't see me. Tears filled his eyes, and he whimpered silently. Behind him, Idir consoled him, and both sat on the floor. Fabio and Misa were next to come in. Then Boris and the guardians carried the elders inside. Their red eyes and teary faces made me sad. This wasn't a vision I wanted to imagine. No, I wanted a happy memory, but this made me sad. It broke my heart.

I regretted my decision to leave them. How foolish was I to leave such amazing people. The vision disappeared, and I cried out in despair. I screamed and yelled with all my heart, leaving nothing behind, letting all my regret and frustration come out. There was no one around me, and I had lost everything, but I had this free-dom — I could cry.

My regretful sobs shook me. I wanted to fall asleep again. I didn't want to feel this pain. This misery was worse than any pain I had ever felt. I couldn't take it any more. I called for Ma and Check-point. I screamed at the top of my lungs for them to come, to tell me what I could do to go back. I screamed as loud as I could, "I'm sorry. Please... I'm so sorry. Please tell me what to do."

The room lit up, and I saw a forest through one of the walls. A place with lots of colours and sounds. Was it Serenus? I ran into the woods and kept running, trying to find a trail or anything fa-miliar to lead back to Serenus. But this forest was different. This wasn't Serenus, but it was alive.

A constant hum surrounded me — the sounds of the crickets, other insects, birds, animals, and the wind moving through the leaves - the sounds of a living forest. I stopped under a tree as something moved in the bush in front of me. I took a couple of steps back. Another sound on my right startled me, and I turned toward it. There was something there, and it was big. It was hiding in the tall grass.

The movement in the grass came closer and closer, and a tiger jumped out of it. It was so beautiful. The lines, the colours on its fur... it mesmerized me, and I watched as it came closer and closer as if in slow motion. I felt its big, heavy paws land on me, and I fell under its weight.

The tiger jumped off. It put its head down while its tail swayed left and right. My first thought was: Why am I not afraid? A tiger lunged at me and knocked me to the ground. Why didn't I feel fear? Why was I busy admiring how beautiful it was? Another look at the tiger made me think it wanted to play with me. It looked friendly. When I didn't move, it rose from its play bow, came close, and I saw my hand reach out and rub under its chin.

I looked at my hand and wondered how it happened, as if I knew, deep down, that this tiger wouldn't hurt me and was a friend. The tiger rubbed himself against me and walked forward, then it paused and looked back at me. Our eyes met for a moment, and then the tiger ran away. I ran after it. The tiger slowed down every now and then, let me catch up, and then ran forward until we reached a large willow tree.

A river ran peacefully next to the tree. The tiger drank from it and lay down. I felt a sudden thirst and went to the river and drank from it. It felt refreshing. Joy and pleasure ran through my body as I felt alive again. I realized then that it was hope that had returned to me. The events in the past few moments gave me hope.

I waited for the tiger to lead me somewhere, to show me a path, but it didn't get up. I walked to it and sat by it, crossing my legs. The tiger put its big, heavy head in my lap and started to purr. I leaned back as my fingers ran through the tiger's fur, and my eyes searched for a way out.

Ch 18: Cage of Contemplation

After sitting with the tiger for a while, I got up to look around. I wanted to leave this place. I wanted answers. I wanted to meet Ma. I wandered around, not going too far from the willow tree.

I should follow the river, perhaps. I walked along it and felt thirsty again. It was a strange thirst. It came abruptly, and I yearned for water. I drank from the river again and then continued walking along it. A tear filled my eye. It surprised me because I wasn't crying. I wiped it off. Another tear appeared in the other eye. I wasn't crying, but why were tears coming from my eyes? I cleaned them away with my hand.

Then I saw something black on my hand. I stared at it for a bit. Where did this come from? Another tear darkened my vision, and I used my other hand to rub my eyes. The other hand was black too. I was crying black tears. What was wrong with me? It scared me. I rubbed my hands on my clothes to get rid of the black. More tears fell on my clothes and the ground. More black tears.

Why did I have black tears? The black started to spread as more and more tears fell. I was horrified now. I ran along the river to find someone, to reach someone for help. Maybe Ma could help me. Something was very wrong with me. I ran and ran but then stopped abruptly as I saw the tiger sleeping under the willow tree. How did I get back here? I was going away from it. I was following the river to head out of here.

Did I run back when I panicked? I walked briskly along the river again, this time making sure not to get turned around.

After walking for a bit, I reached the tiger and the willow tree again. In frustration, I sat on the sand and held my head. What was happening? I couldn't understand. Was I losing my mind? How did I get turned around again?

This time, I left the river and ran away from it, but I hadn't gone far when I felt thirsty again. Very thirsty. I ran back to the river and drank from it again. And then I considered a strange thought: Could it be the river making my head spin?

Black tears started falling from my eyes again. It was definitely the river that caused the black tears. Maybe the black tears were making me insane.

I ran away from the river once again. This time, I made a promise to myself that no matter how thirsty I felt, I wasn't going to drink from this river again. I ran, and when I got tired, I walked. I went in a straight line away from the river. It was far behind me when I felt thirsty again. I shook my head and refused to go back. I kept going forward. I felt my throat dry up, but I didn't turn around. The thirst spread as my body started to parch from the inside. I didn't stop, and I didn't turn around.

"Whatever happens, I am not drinking from that river again," I promised myself.

I had to find another source of water. I kept going even though it felt like my body was refusing to move. It started to rebel against my decision not to go to that river. I told myself, "That river is too far behind anyway. There may be another source nearby."

I kept going and going until I heard the sound of water. I was very lucky because I didn't think I could go on much further. I reached this new river and drank from it. All thirst vanished in a moment. Then I sat by it, and the tiger came close to me, rubbed its head against my shoulder, lay down, and put its head in my lap.

I exclaimed, "What?!"

I looked behind me and found the willow tree.

I asked, "What? How did this happen?"

Black tears started falling on the tiger. I moved my head so I wouldn't stain the tiger's beautiful fur with my black tears.

Okay, this is definitely magic. I am stuck here. Someone is keeping me here. It's a trap. Did the wizard catch me?

The Seren had told me that the wizard stole the souls of those who went into the Dark End. And this surely was the work of a mighty wizard. But why did the wizard trap me? What did it want from me? I looked at the beauty around me and felt scared. Even the tiger... I resented it. I moved its head away from my lap and walked away from it. This was all a wizard's trap. I had to escape somehow. But how?

Fighting the thirst was no use. I couldn't do it. Where was Ma? Or did Checkpoint lie?

"Ohhhh... why did I leave? I shouldn't have left. What have I done? And where is Amy? Did she go through here already? How did she escape? Or maybe she is also stuck here."

I ran around calling for her but felt thirsty again. I drank from the river, shed black tears, and then ran around again.

I called for her as long as I could but then sat down, defeated. The tiger came close and put its head in my lap as I saw the willow tree behind me.

I mused, "Maybe it is some kind of test. Maybe the willow tree is important."

I inspected the tree. I did everything I could think of. I carried water in my hands and poured it on the willow tree. Why? I don't know. I thought maybe the water was important and the tree was important. I tried whatever I could think of. I acted on even the most random thoughts, but nothing changed anything.

I sat down again, and the tiger returned to me, put its head in my lap, and fell asleep.

I thought aloud, "Okay, maybe the tiger is trying to tell me something. It keeps its head in my lap. Maybe it doesn't want me to roam around."

I leaned back and was surprised that it was the willow tree behind me for support. How did things move around like that? The trap or the test, whatever it was, it was unreal and mind-bending.

"Okay, I am not going to get out of here like this," I said, and the tiger started to purr.

I ran my fingers through its fur again and rested my head on the willow tree trunk behind me. There really was no point trying to get out, but what else could I do? I felt miserable and helpless.

I didn't deserve this. Yes, I probably made a mistake by leaving Serenus, call it a blunder even, but I didn't know. How could I have known? Why did Amy have to leave? I could have not followed her, but what kind of friend would that be?

No, I shouldn't have followed her. She didn't know where she was going, and her actions caused me to leave as well. If anything, it was Amy who was at fault, then why was I being punished for this?

Should Amy not have left, though? It was her choice. She obviously didn't want me to go with her. No, I couldn't blame her. It was my decision, and I deserved whatever was happening to me, and whatever was to come. There was no point in feeling bad about myself. It happened. I did it. I didn't know where I was going. I didn't, and still, I left.

But what now? Where should I go? Why did the tiger bring me here? And when will it lead me further? Or was this my new world? Was I supposed to stay here? Forever? What would be the point of that? Sit under a tree, pet a tiger, and drink from the river? And then what? Just cry black tears?

The scene in front of me was beautiful. At any other point in my life, I would feel lucky to be in such a place, but the way I came here, and the fact that I couldn't leave, made the place scary. Now, for the first time, since I came here, I stopped trying to escape. I was now waiting to see what would happen next. How long would it take? I didn't know. But I sat down and relaxed.

"Whatever caused me to leave, I came after a friend. I did a good thing. If I made a mistake, I made it with the best intention. It is what it is. I did what I did. I had good intentions, and I didn't know any better. And I still don't know if it was the right thing or not. There's no point overthinking it."

Something alarmed my mind. A sound... Music? Here? What?

The tiger heard it. It lifted its head from my lap and ran toward it. I followed, hoping it was time to get out of this beautiful, miserable place.

Ch 19: A Motherly Embrace

The sound became louder, and I chased after the tiger. Someone was playing flute, and the melody was so... uplifting! Vibrant and hopeful, it filled me with energy and my heart with joy. I sprinted through the trees, finally emerging into a vast open field. The tall, golden grass shimmered under the warm embrace of the evening sun. Rolling hills stretched as far as the eye could see, inviting me to run up and down the slopes with boundless enthusiasm. Surprisingly, I didn't feel tired at all. In fact, I felt alive and exhilarated!

The tiger and I raced side by side. I had an unreal strength. My feet barely touched the ground before my legs propelled me up and forward, making me feel powerful and unstoppable. The enchanting melody of the flute pulled me closer, filling me with a sense of awe and wonder. Then, I heard someone sing:

I sing in the birds

I bloom in flowers

I dance when I'm happy

And I rain in showers

I sit, I flow, I swim, I walk, I run, I fly...

As the flute resumed, I ran up one final hill, and there she was: a woman playing the flute sitting under a majestic tree with glittering orange leaves. I halted, captivated by her presence. As she stopped playing, her radiant smile met my eyes. Her happiness was palpable, pure and undeniable. Why was she so happy to see me?

"Hello!" she greeted warmly, her voice brimming with friendliness. As I looked into her kind eyes, I couldn't help but feel a sense of familiarity. It was as if I'd known her forever, a bond that transcended time and space.

She stood up, and I noticed she was much taller than me. She smiled, and I smiled back. Then she said, "It's nice to meet you."

I opened my mouth to say something, but I couldn't speak. I just looked at her kind face in awe. Who was she? She looked at me, and it felt like there was nothing else in the world. Her gaze captured me, caught hold of me, and I just watched her, mesmerized.

She came closer and knelt down, her eyes level with mine. I

looked into her beautiful, loving eyes but still couldn't say anything. I was stunned by the bond we had, the way she looked at me, the way she smiled... I was lost.

The woman said, "The way you look at me, this is how I looked at you when I first met you. Your eyes, your innocence, your purity... I looked at you just like you look at me."

I was not myself. I was lost in her smile.

"Come on now, talk to me," the woman laughed.

And when she laughed, oh my... I felt goosebumps, and around us, the colours became brighter, the grass swayed, and the sun's rays danced on everything they touched, creating a halo, an unreal glow. Even the most ordinary things, like grass, looked more beautiful than ever. A gust of wind blew in my face, and I breathed in its freshness as my hair moved back in slow motion. Even the tiniest moments seemed to stretch on endlessly.

The way the grass flowed in the wind, the tree above me standing tall with its branches swaying, and even the stone on the ground somehow appearing happier—I couldn't explain it, but I knew it. I knew everything was happy, and I was happy. I was content. The way I felt at this moment, I could give anything to feel like this forever. Tears of intense happiness filled my eyes. Her laughter stopped, and I looked at her, wanting her to laugh again. Everything was losing colour.

The woman said gently, "Isn't it amazing? This feeling... when we meet... isn't it breathtaking?"

"Who are you?" I asked.

The woman smiled, "I am Ma, The Maker."

I just looked at her. I didn't fully grasp what she had said. I heard it, but I didn't really listen. I just looked into her eyes. I wanted her to laugh again. I would do anything to make her laugh again. And then she laughed, and time held its breath.

Slowly, I raised my head to see the tree, and I knew in my heart that the tree was as happy as I was and that it was enjoying this moment as much as I was. I looked at the grass, and I knew what was in its heart. I knew it wasn't just swaying in the wind—it was lost in the feeling of her happiness. Everything around me was moving because of one reason: her laughter. And just like I didn't want her laughter to stop, everything around me didn't want this moment to end. I knew it as if I knew myself. All things around me, all of us, were in awe of her. We were spellbound, swaying, flowing in an invisible wind. And all of us had the same desire and need: to listen to her laugh.

I closed my eyes, and I felt it. I felt like I was all of us. The tree was me. The grass was me. The stone was me. Everything around me was me, and all of us were hypnotized, breathless, enchanted, absorbed, lost, just moving, flowing, dancing. And she smiled like she loved all of us, and we looked up to her as if we had given ourselves to her. No, as if we were hers to begin with. In one moment, I knew in my heart there was nothing more beautiful than her. There was nothing that I wanted more.

"When I look at you, I feel the same," the woman said.

I heard her words and felt what they meant, and then I just cried. I wasn't sad; I just cried. I looked at her and cried. I saw tears in her eyes and moved closer. She plucked me from the ground, hugged me, and spun around in circles. My feet couldn't touch the ground as she carried me in her arms and danced like the grass and the tree were dancing. She sobbed and cried as I was sobbing and crying.

"I missed you," she whispered in my ear.

"I missed you too," I replied.

She put me back on the ground and wiped away my tears.

I asked, "Who are you?"

"I am Ma," she smiled.

"Who are you?" I asked again.

"I am Ma," she smiled again.

I exclaimed, "Ma!"

"Yes," she said softly.

"Why was I away from you, Ma?" I asked.

"You will never be away from me," she replied.

"I don't want to be away from you again, Ma!" I said.

"You were never away, and you never will be," she assured.

I hugged her tightly so nothing could separate me from her again, and I felt her tears fall on me. I felt safe. I was exactly where I belonged.

Ma said, "You are home now."

I said nothing.

As my tears stopped, I moved back to look into her eyes again. She smiled and looked back.

"I don't remember you, Ma... but I... know you," I said.

Ma nodded, "I know."

"Why don't I remember you?" I asked.

Ma smiled, "It's okay. You will never forget me now."

"Why do we have this connection? I have never felt it before, not with anyone. Why do I feel like this for you?" I questioned.

Ma put her hand on my shoulder and pulled me toward her, "Our connection is unlike any other."

"And still, I don't remember it?" I asked.

Ma replied, "You never found me before; that's why you don't remember me. But I was always there, so you know me."

It's not that I didn't have a million questions in my head, but I didn't want to speak. I didn't want to move on. I wanted to stay in this moment, and I wanted the rest of my story to be just this. I wanted to look at her face, her eyes looking back at me with such a loving smile.

Ma said, "You are with me now. Forever."

I couldn't believe my luck. My face broke into a smile on its own. I couldn't stop smiling. I was that happy.

Ch 20: Intervention

We stayed there to my heart's content, and then I remembered Serenus.

"Ma?" I said.

"Yes," Ma replied.

"Where is Amy?"

Ma smiled, "She is here too."

"Where?" I asked happily.

Ma smiled again, "Right here, with us."

I looked around, "I don't see her."

Ma nodded, "I know, but she is here."

"Is she okay?"

"Yes, she is okay. She is also with me, and she is happy just like you are," Ma responded.

"Why can't I see her?"

Ma smiled, "For a little while, it's our time, just me and Amy, just like it's our time, just you and me. You will see her again. Soon."

I nodded. "Am I dead?"

Ma smiled, "Do you feel dead?"

I felt embarrassed, "No... I can talk to you, I am awake, I can see..."

"You are not dead. You died in Serenus, but you are not dead here," Ma clarified.

"If I died there, doesn't that mean I am dead?"

"No, it's a transition. You stopped living in that world, which enabled you to live here. Death is a transition... from one world to the other," Ma explained.

"What is this world?"

"This... is Sandbox. I created it to meet you here for an intervention," Ma said.

"Intervention?"

"Yes, you need to learn a few things. I will teach you," Ma replied.

"What is a Sandbox?"

"It is a world I created. The events here don't impact other worlds, but we can use them to learn," Ma explained.

"How many worlds have you made?"

"Many. I created many worlds," Ma answered.

"Why?"

"For you," said Ma.

"For me? ... Why me? ... What about others?"

"You will understand... in time. And we have a lot of time for you to understand," Ma smiled.

"I will live with you in Sandbox now?"

"For now, yes. But your task is not complete yet. You have to go to the next world," Ma replied.

"Another island?"

"Yes," Ma confirmed.

"I want to see Amy. I came after her. She was..."

Ma interrupted, "I know. I know everything. I know why you left."

"Can I meet her?"

"You will meet her. The Sandbox is separate for each comer. You will meet her in the next world," Ma explained.

"Oh, you meant you created this Sandbox for me, just like you created one for Amy. I thought you meant you created all the worlds for me," I said.

Ma smiled, "I did create all the worlds for you, and Sandbox is a part of that."

"Oh... I feel special."

"You are. You are very special," Ma smiled.

"Will I meet my friends again?"

"Yes," Ma replied.

"What was that place I was stuck in... after Serenus?" I asked, remembering the trap.

"It was a place of healing... the medicine may feel bad, but it removed everything bad. It corrected your faults so you can be sent back to the world," Ma explained.

"What medicine?"

"The river... I will tell you more about it later," Ma replied.

"I am going back to the world?" I asked.

"I will teach you many things that you don't know, and then you go on to the next world to see the consequences of how you left Serenus," Ma explained.

That didn't sound good. "What do you mean? What consequences?"

"Every action has consequences. You will see the consequences of your actions," Ma replied.

What did she mean by that? A strange thought came to my head, and though I didn't believe it could be possible, I asked, "Are you going to punish me? Hurt me?"

"Hurt you? Why? Why would I do that? Why would I hurt you? I would never hurt you. I want you to have the best... best of everything," Ma reassured me.

"But you said I will face the consequences...."

"That's right. But that's not a punishment. It is the result of the way you left your world."

"I shouldn't have left?"

"You shouldn't have left like you did. Everyone leaves eventually, but you were wrong to leave the way you did," Ma explained.

"I am sorry."

"I am sorry too. I know why you left. I can read your thoughts."

"My thoughts? You can read my thoughts?" I asked, surprised.

"Yes, I can. I know exactly what's in your heart. And I know that you meant well, but you were not supposed to follow Amy."

"I had promised her."

"I know, but it was wrong. You shouldn't have promised that, and even if you did, you should have broken this promise."

"Isn't it wrong? To break a promise?" I questioned.

"Less wrong than following her blindly," Ma answered politely. "Just because Amy went into the Dark End didn't mean you had to go as well. I wanted you to be you. I already have Amy. I don't want others to follow her. If I wanted another Amy, I would make another Amy. I wanted you to be you... to make your own path. And you knew what you were doing was wrong, but you convinced yourself that it became right because of your reason. You snuck away from your friends. Why? Because you knew it was wrong, and you couldn't convince them. That is why you left the way you did. You thought they wouldn't understand your reason. That was your own judgment. You knew your reason was faulty."

I felt terrible and wanted to explain myself, "I thought they wouldn't understand, but I had to do it. I had to keep my promise. I couldn't leave her alone."

"But that was not all, was it? There was more... that you didn't tell anyone. What was that?" Ma asked.

"More? What do you mean?"

"You found something while sitting under the Greentree. You wrote it and left it for others. Didn't it give you hope? Didn't it create a want inside you to go in the dark? You wanted to go. Why?" Ma inquired.

"The poem. I... I found a new meaning. That gave me hope," I admitted.

"And that is why Amy left."

"Amy? No! She left... No, she didn't know about that. She hadn't read it yet," I argued.

"But she had. You wrote your understanding. You made many copies. You left those for your friends to find," Ma explained.

"Find after I was gone. Not before," I added.

"Where did you leave those messages?" Ma asked.

"In Amy's notebook... in the room I slept in," I replied.

"And she came looking for her notebook when you were still asleep. She read what you wrote. And that is why she made up her mind. That is what gave her hope. And that is why she left," Ma revealed.

"What? I... I had no idea. I didn't mean..."

Ma sighed, "I know, but that is exactly what occurred. You wrote the words, she read them, and even though she had been mulling over it for quite some time, she never left, not until she read what you wrote."

I felt a pang of guilt, "So, I'm the reason she left? I didn't mean for that to happen. That wasn't the point. She misunderstood..."

Ma reassured me, "It's not on you. She read your words, and it was enough for her to finally make up her mind."

My voice trembled, "I failed her. In more ways than I could have imagined."

Ma was firm, "No! She was not your responsibility. You're not that capable. Too much was beyond your control. You're giving yourself too much credit. What could you have done?"

I was baffled by her answer and sought clarification, "I'm not giving myself credit. I'm blaming myself. I'm saying I was wrong in so many ways."

Ma explained, "Guilt... What is guilt? Is it not based on the assumption that you had control? Choice over the matters of the world? Those who think highly of themselves are the ones who feel guilty."

"What? I... I only wanted to make her feel better. I feel guilty only because I failed to do that."

Ma smiled gently, "I know. But it wasn't within your power. You had no ability to make her feel better. What she wanted, you were not. You don't have to carry this guilt. You weren't able."

"But I wanted... to be able. To be there for her."

Ma nodded, "Yes, but that was not what she needed — you being there for her. That's why she left."

I sighed, "You're right. I couldn't..."

Ma prompted, "Because..."

"Because... What?"

"Fate."

"What is fate?"

Ma replied, "To understand fate, you need to understand the concept of freedom of action. At any moment, you have the freedom to do whatever you can."

I questioned, "Whatever I want?"

Ma corrected, "No, not whatever you want. Whatever you can. You may desire something that is not possible. You can do whatever is within your capabilities."

"At any moment, I can do anything that is possible?"

Ma affirmed, "Yes, and when you do something, it may go according to your plan, or it may not go as you hoped because you didn't do it right, or maybe someone else's freedom of choice influenced it and made it impossible for you. Your circumstances shape your reality. They allow you to do certain things and render other things impossible."

"Yes, I understand."

Ma continued, "These circumstances give your life a direction. Under different circumstances, your life would take another course. All the paths you can take and all the paths you can no longer choose are defined by your circumstances, and I call it... fate. When you went to Serenus, there was a system in place. They had already decided how to take care of you. It was your fate. When Alev went to that world, her circumstances were different. That was her fate. Everyone is unique, and everyone has their own fate."

"So I did what I could."

Ma explained, "Yes, at every moment of your life, you can choose a path, you have freedom, but freedom has its limits. Fate defines what you can or cannot do. It affects every decision. The paths you choose also change your fate. A certain action may enable new paths or reduce available paths. Fate is always being updated—by your actions, by others' actions, and by changes in your circumstances. You can change your fate."

I nodded, "Yes, that makes sense. I liked learning about it. And there's so much I want to know. I like to know things. I was a thinker in Serenus, though I couldn't really come up with anything new."

Ma responded, "Yeah, about that... You're not a thinker. I mean, everyone is a thinker to some extent, but your best ability is not thinking."

"But the people in Serenus, the elders, decided I was a thinker... So I'm not a thinker?"

Ma clarified, "You're okay at it, but that's not your specialty. You had another power that you never realized."

Intrigued, I asked, "What? A magical power?"

"Yes, a magical power." Said Ma.

"What is it? Please tell me."

Ma smiled, "It is the power to know when you are wrong."

I scoffed, "What? That's my power? The power to know when I'm wrong? What kind of power is that?"

Ma explained, "It's one of the best powers to have. To say it precisely, this enables an ability like none other—an ability to learn. You can learn better than others. When you know where you are wrong, you can correct it. That was your power, but you never figured it out."

"Oh... so I lived my life going in the wrong direction? I failed to recognize my abilities. What else did I fail at?"

Ma placed her hand on my shoulder. "You lived a good life in Serenus. You didn't fail a lot. You were there for your friends, and you didn't live long enough to be truly challenged by life's complex problems."

"But I did fail at some things. Please tell me what I failed at."

"You failed to understand Qilam. You thought he was going crazy because Qilam could hear a voice in his head—a voice that spoke to him."

I gasped, "He really could? He could hear a voice? Whose voice?"

"Mine. He could hear me. I talked to him a lot. I talk to people all the time, but mostly they dismiss it as their own thoughts. They fail to recognize that it's me talking to them in the form of their thoughts. I tell them new things they couldn't have known, and they call it coincidence. I nudge them in the right direction by creating thoughts inside their head, but most are not so good at identifying me. Qilam could identify me. That was his ability. He knew when it was him thinking a thought and when it was me speaking to him. And because he knew I was there, he would ask me questions, and I would answer those questions, and in that way, he could know what others thought was impossible to know."

Ma had been talking to Qilam all this time? Wow. I had just assumed that Qilam was crazy, but she was actually talking to him. He was talking to Ma even when he was in Serenus, so the things he said...

I asked, "The lost scroll... becoming a god beyond this earth... was it all true?"

Ma confirmed, "Yes, it's all true. Qilam could hear me, and I told him of things beyond his world."

I wished I could go back and apologize. He was... he was right. He warned us against Esmeray... but the villagers always thought his words were dangerous and useless. I assumed they knew him better than me.

Ma said, "I know, I understand. You didn't listen to your heart. You listened to what others thought of him."

"But he was a coward. He couldn't leave Serenus even when he knew there were more islands. What else did he know that made him not leave? Did he also know about the consequences? I remember how scared he was when Boris and the guardians pushed his boat into the water, even after he was ready to leave. What was he so scared of? What did he know?"

Ma explained, "He doubted himself, which is why he didn't leave Serenus. He wasn't sure he was talking to me. He wondered if he really was crazy. As for why he screamed when he left, he cried with joy. He was full of hope—to find out, to finally figure out if he was right all this time. As soon as his boat was in the current, the realization struck him hard. He was coming to me, and he welcomed it. He was overpowered by the anticipation of finding the truth. He had wanted to know all his life, and now it was time to finally find out. He was ecstatic, screaming and crying tears of intense happiness and joy. Overwhelmed with the anticipation of finding out."

I hadn't expected to hear any of this. How did I form such a different image of those events? I thought the total opposite was happening... that he was scared. He had been a coward, or so the villagers thought. I sensed he was upset when he was being put in the boat. How did I read him so wrong?

Ma said, "He was upset because he wanted to go with you."

"With me? Why?"

"Because he thought you were the wizard."

"Me? The wizard? What?"

Ma continued, "Yes, he convinced the 'new wizard' that you were the wizard mentioned in the poem. You defeated Esmeray, and you lived among the villagers. They loved you, and no one thought badly of you. He believed you were the powerful wizard the poem talked about."

"But I wasn't... I didn't even have magic! How could he? What did he see... He was so wrong... Right? I can't be the wizard, right?"

"Qilam had doubts about you, and he told the 'new wizard' that you could be the wizard. And when Alia tested you and announced that there was a power inside you that she had never felt before, his suspicion turned into belief. He convinced the 'new wizard' to take you with him through the Dark End. And by doing that, they would have fulfilled the prophecy. They would have captured the wizard and gone past the fall."

"Oh... so that's why he wanted to take me with him... But what was that power? The one that Alia saw in me?"

Ma replied, "The power to know when you are wrong."

"Oh... just that. I thought there was some amazing power inside me."

Ma said in a reassuring tone, "The power you have is really amazing. You can know when you are wrong and then learn to be right. You learn from experience. It is no ordinary power."

"But why did Qilam think so badly of me? I was never mean to him. I mean... I didn't believe his words, but I was never rude to him. Others didn't even want to talk to him, but at least I would listen. How could he think I was the wizard?"

"Because he thought the wizard wasn't necessarily evil. He thought anyone could be the wizard without knowing it. Your questions and interest in finding the lost scroll made him wonder if you were the wizard. The power Alia said you have in you tipped the scale in his head. He was pretty certain that you were the wizard, but he thought of you to be a good Seren. He believed that you didn't even know you were the wizard."

"That is so strange. There was a time when I wondered if he was the wizard, but he thought I was the wizard."

Ma laughed, "It gets funnier. Esmeray thought Qilam was the wizard. Qilam thought you were the wizard. You doubted Qilam initially, but then you thought Esmeray was the wizard. And then, eventually, you believed the 'new wizard' was the wizard."

"That's why Esmeray said, 'I am not the wizard, but I know who the wizard is, and he is very fond of you.' Qilam was fond of me, and she thought Qilam was the wizard. Oh..., but who really was the wizard?"

Ma smiled, "That is for you to find out."

I asked, "What does the poem really mean?"

Ma responded, "That is for you to find out."

"But is it a riddle or a mission?"

"It is a guide."

"And am I the wizard?"

Ma laughed, "No, you are not the wizard."

"Okay ... and ... are you the wizard?"

Ma laughed again, "No, I am not the wizard."

"And who is the wizard?"

Ma repeated, "That is for you to find out."

"But you do know all the answers, right? You won't tell me, but you know it, right?"

Ma shook her head, "No, not all answers. There is a lot that I don't know. I, too, have questions."

"But I thought you were the one with all the answers."

Ma explained, "If I didn't have questions, why would I make something? Why would I do anything? I have a need... A need to know."

"Do you know who made you?"

"No. I think I have always existed. I don't think someone made me."

"I had a very different impression of you. I thought you were the one... the one who had all the answers... the one with all the powers... the one who is on the outside, containing everything. You are not that? It's possible that you were made... By whom? Who made you?"

Ma responded, "I am searching for this answer."

"You don't know things! Wow, I thought... how can we know? How can we find out when you can't?"

Ma reassured me, "You can learn what I don't yet know, but I will tell you more about this later in a way you can understand."

"Okay, but... you've always existed? How? Like one day you woke up? Do you remember waking up? Or do you remember always being awake?"

Ma answered, "There was no time when I woke up. I created time. So you can say I have been awake forever."

"But there was... not a time, but... there was a state of existence when you were not awake?"

"I'm not sure," said Ma. "But I am open to the possibility."

"And then you made time?"

Ma nodded. "Yes."

"What is time?"

Ma explained, "Time is the parent dimension of all my creations... or, to say it simply, it is a storage device. It stores records of change. I made time, so I could change things and keep track of those changes."

"Why did you need to track the change?"

Ma elaborated, "I created a system that is based on change. There was a state of my existence when there was no change. I wanted to see what I could be, and I wanted to find my purpose. If things stayed the same all the time, stuck in a single state of existence, there wouldn't be a way to find out. So, I created a change-based system. I am searching for answers through these changes, trying all the possibilities. This way, if it is possible to find the answers, I will find them. With time, I can keep track of all the changes to read them, find patterns, and learn from them. To find out what I don't yet know."

"Wow. You created change, and you created a device to store records of change. And you still don't have the answers. How can we find out? I thought... there was a time when I thought that someday I would find all the answers. If you created so much, and you still don't know, then there is no hope for me... no way I can find out."

Ma smiled, "That's not really accurate. I am trying all the possibilities, and you are one of the possibilities. I could learn something from you that I don't already know. You could be the one who figures it out."

I thought for a moment and then asked, "Where is this device that you use to record changes? Where is Time?"

"You are inside it. You are a record of change. A record that spans all the way to the start and is still changing."

"Tell me more about time."

"There isn't really much more about it. It's just a device to store changes."

"But time passes. How does time pass? When we started talking, it was a different time. A lot of time has passed since then. How does time pass?"

"Time doesn't pass, it doesn't... tick. When a change occurs, it is recorded in time in the form of a new entry in time. Since we started talking, a lot has changed, and that would be the right way to say it." Ma replied.

"And how do things change? What causes the change?"

Ma laughed, "Oh boy... The formula, the inner workings of how a change is calculated... you can understand it, but it will take a lot of... explaining. You can learn anything, but there is a lot of prerequisite knowledge that you will need to understand first. Let's leave this for some other... time."

"You also talk about time like we do, as if it passes or is a duration."

Ma smiled, "Yes, I speak to the listener in a language they can understand."

"Tell me more fun things."

Ma pointed around us. "We are in a Sandbox where anything you can think is possible. Let me show you."

Ma turned into a man with a big mustache. "It is time to have some fun in Sandbox! Today, we are going to..."

I waited, but she didn't finish her sentence. What were we going to do?

Ma appeared over my left shoulder and whispered, "Pssst, finish the sentence."

The big mustached man spoke again, "Ahem, ahem, so let's try that again... Today, we are going to..." His eyes turned to me, and he waited for me to say something.

I turned to Ma and said, "I don't know what to say."

"Say anything. Just blurt it out. Whatever you want to do."

The big mustached man prompted, "Today, we are, hopefully, going to..."

I hesitated, "umm, ... create ... a ..."

The big mustached man repeated, "Today, we are, hopefully, eventually, going to create a ..."

I exclaimed, "A dragon! A fire dragon. No, not a fire dragon... A water dragon!"

The big mustached man tilted his head to the side, looked at me for a bit, and then asked, "What do its wings look like?"

The big mustached man asked several questions about what the water dragon would look like. I made sure my answers were as ridiculous as they could be. It made Ma smile, and I liked how that felt. When I was done explaining what the water dragon would look like, the big mustached man asked me to close my eyes and imagine that the water dragon was right in front of me. I closed my eyes and imagined the dragon with all its details, and as I opened my eyes, the dragon was there. It opened its mouth and breathed water. It showered me, Ma, and the man with the big mustache. It was fun. The water was slightly warm. It felt good. I almost jumped in excitement as the dragon turned to me and lowered its neck. It was then that I realized the dragon did what I wanted it to do. I wanted it to bend its neck so I could climb on top of it. It did what I wanted. I climbed on it and wanted it to leap off the ground and fly to the sky, and that's precisely what the water dragon did. It flew through the forest, zig-zagging around the tall trees and mountains. It went up and dove down, just as I wanted when I wanted. This was... thrilling.

After spending some time on the dragon, I returned to Ma.

Ma said, "You can create whatever you want. Whatever you can think of. You can perform experiments here. Make things and see how they will turn out, then improve them. That is what I do. This Sandbox is your playground, but now it is time to do some work."

"What work?" I asked.

"Come, I will show you."

Ch 21: The Intangible Trail

Ma started walking away, and I followed her. We walked through tall grass and reached the trees. We continued into the forest until we came upon a clearing. In the middle were some rocks, and on top of the rocks, shimmering in the evening sky, was a... bubble with a thin outer membrane. And inside the bubble was... lightning. Sparks. Sparks of lightning. Sparks that would persist for just a moment and then spark again in a new shape.

Ma explained, "This is The Heart of the Forest."

"Heart? Of the entire forest?" I asked.

Ma nodded, "Yes. Everything in this forest is connected to it. All plants, animals... everything. They send their thoughts to this heart, and it processes those thoughts. It thinks like a brain, but I call it a heart because it understands more than a brain can understand. It can feel deeper thoughts and more complex emotions."

"What does it do? Is it alive? A brain on its own?"

"Yes, it is alive. And it is not on its own. Everything in the forest is connected to it, though you can't see it. The connection is invisible to your eyes."

"That's so cool. You made this?"

Ma nodded, "Yes, I made everything. I am quite happy with this system, but it is not without its faults."

"Your systems have faults?"

Ma smiled, "Yes, my systems fail all the time."

Surprised, I asked, "I thought your systems would be perfect."

Ma laughed, "Perfect? Why? No! Impressive, yes, but perfect? No."

I laughed, "And what are the consequences of your failures? I mean, when your systems fail?"

Ma laughed out loud. I felt a sudden surge of energy again. It was really amazing how her laughter made me feel better. It also made everything else feel better. It was magical. Everything around me was happier and more colourful. I got distracted by it. It was that obvious.

When Ma stopped laughing, the energy left everything, and things returned to normal. Then she said, "Yes, there are consequences for my failures. I like the way you think."

I raised my shoulders and smiled, "You made everything, and still you fail. I, and others like me, are too incapable of competing with you. If we have consequences, so should you. I think it is only fair."

Ma nodded. "Yes, I agree. But nothing is fair. You can try to reach a balance, but nothing really is fair. Fairness is the result of a comparison, and comparison is wrong. It is faulty. Systems are not made to be fair. They are made to vary, explore, and continue. Everything is unique, and nothing is supposed to be like any other. And yes, I suffer consequences all the time. I wish I could make a system that has no negative consequences, where only good things happen, where you can get whatever you want and get to enjoy it and feel good all the time. I try my best, but I am not there, not even close. I do want to make a world without any suffering."

"Ma, You are so capable. What if you don't send me to the next world? What if I don't see the consequences of my failures? What would happen? I am just one. What if I wasn't even sent to this world in the first place? You can do that. You sent me. You can choose to not send me. Can't you?"

"That's not how the system works, and remember, I told you that you are very important. I made the worlds for you."

"To suffer in? To face the consequences of my mistakes? Mistakes that I didn't even know I was making. How is that a good system?"

Ma consoled, "I am so sorry. It is not. I try, but I know it is far from what it should be, but going to the next world and facing the consequences of your actions is good for you."

"Can I choose if it is good for me? I don't want to face the consequences."

Ma tried to calm me down. "I understand. It won't be so bad, and in the end, you will agree that it was better that you went there."

I insisted, "No! I don't want to. Can't I just stay here? There is so much space here. You won't even notice me. I will live in the forest. Please?"

A big smile appeared on Ma's face, and she walked toward me. She put her hand on my shoulder and said, "You don't know what you are saying, but you will. You will learn how you are wrong, but not just that, you will also learn what is right. And you will like it. I am smart and quite capable. I have reasons and logic. I know you ask for reasoning, I will give you reasoning, but that is coming later. Take it easy. For now, you are here with me. Let me show you what I have made and how it works, then you can show me how to make it better. Together we can make things better and improve the systems. How does that sound?"

I replied, "Good, but I don't want any consequences that I can tell you right now."

Ma laughed again, "I understand what you mean. Until I can find a way to make a system like that, help me fix this one, and I will tell you more things along the way."

I wasn't sure how I could help her, but I said, "Okay, what can I do?"

Ma explained, "I created a rabbit. It is... malfunctioning. You have to find it, and we will fix it together. It will be somewhere in the forest."

"Somewhere in the forest? How will I find a rabbit in a forest?" I asked.

"It is quite a big forest, but there is only one rabbit. Your job is to find it. Tiger will help you," Ma said, and the Tiger walked to me as if it understood what Ma was saying.

Why couldn't she find the rabbit on her own? She was powerful. Surely, finding a rabbit in a forest wouldn't be much of a task for her. It would take me too long to find it. I had all these thoughts as the Tiger started walking away, so I went after him, even though it didn't make sense. I was sure that she could find the rabbit much faster than I could.

I followed the Tiger along many twisty paths in the forest. It would sniff the air every now and then, sniff any droppings it found, and other things I couldn't understand. It was pretty sure of itself and kept moving forward.

"You have done this before, haven't you?" I asked the Tiger.

The Tiger moved on as if on an urgent mission.

I felt useless, blind. I didn't know what to look for. I was only there to follow the Tiger. Why not just send the Tiger? Was Ma tired of my questions? Did she send me away so she could focus on what she needed to do? All kinds of thoughts came to my mind. I weighed each thought and concluded that I didn't know her enough to understand. I remembered how we met. It was as if we were really close, incredibly close, like we had known each other forever. It was strange that I still felt like I knew her and that she was close to me in some way, but I didn't know how.

The Tiger led me to a rocky desert. It was the first time I saw the sky like that - wide open from one side to the other. It was expansive. The world beneath it was even more detailed. Even the little things had systems inside them. And Ma made all of this? Wow. She was quite capable, except when it came to finding a rabbit, apparently. As soon as I thought this, I felt that feeling again - the one from before when everything was happy, and Ma was laughing. Even the Tiger looked happy. I looked at its face for a few moments to be sure. It was definitely happy. It had stopped moving and was looking at me in a funny way. Was Ma laughing again? Something funny must have happened. And I was out here looking for a rabbit.

I didn't know why I was feeling so grumpy about going after a rabbit. The place around me was beautiful, and I didn't mind the walk. It just felt less efficient. Ma could probably do it much faster than I could. Was that it? I wanted efficiency? I realized with surprise that that was the reason I was grumpy. What for? As if I had many things to finish before... before what? There was nothing to do. I was in a sandbox with Ma. I had to go to the next world to face the consequences. I would rather take all the time here. Yes, that was better. The longer it took to do the tasks that Ma assigned to me, the farther away the consequences. Slow was good. I sat on a rock and looked at the sky again.

The magnificent sky filled with stars as night crept in. The Tiger sat beside me and soon fell asleep. I wasn't sleepy at all. I had walked a lot but wasn't thirsty, hungry, or tired.

The starry sky reminded me of the pond in my home in Serenus. The dry desert wind couldn't take away the thought of the waterfalls. That was heaven. Serenus was heaven. But if Serenus was heaven, then what was this place? Not heaven, surely. But it was definitely beautiful. If only I had my friends here, or I was back in Serenus.

I couldn't give up so quickly. I had to convince Ma to send me back to Serenus. I left it too early, and it wasn't fair. I made a mistake unknowingly. Others got to live there much longer. I needed to go back and live there. At least a few years. I only stayed a few months — definitely not fair.

I knew what she thought about wanting things to be fair, but this was definitely one of those cases where I could... convince her?

Change her mind? Me? How could I? I was so tiny, so small. She was the maker of these worlds. She knew better. How could I change her mind? I couldn't possibly show her a fault in her ways... but why did she ask for help fixing the rabbit? Maybe I could help her in some way? Me? No, what did I know that she didn't? But then why did she ask for my help? And she said it herself; her systems could be faulty.

The night sky was too beautiful to think. I watched the stars and wondered what else Ma could have made. One question that interested me the most was why she made it all for me. What about others? Why just me?

We continued our search in the morning. Tiger led me on a trail that I couldn't sense. Eventually, the desert ended, and we reached a place with many ponds, grass, and rivers but very few trees. The ground here was soft, and the air smelled distinct. I saw lots of animals there. Many types of birds filled the sky with their songs. So many animals, but only one rabbit? Why?

I followed the Tiger around the ponds, and the animals scattered away as they saw us walk toward them. Soon the Tiger stopped. It was a small bush that was the focus of its attention. Something moved inside it, and I looked carefully to spot what it was. Tiger sat down, and from thin air appeared Ma. She just appeared out of nowhere. She petted the Tiger, smiled at me, and then walked to the bush. A rabbit came out and walked up to her. She picked it up in her hands. The rabbit was quite comfortable and let Ma pick it up.

"Well done, Tiger. Let's go home," Ma said.

The place around us turned into the one with The Heart of the Forest. Of course, Ma could do that. I felt useless. Even a tiger was more capable than me. It found the rabbit on its own. I did nothing. Why did Ma send me? I didn't mind spending the time. I was just curious. I wanted to know if there was a reason.

Ma said, "The Tiger found the rabbit. What did you find?"

"Nothing... I mean, I saw things, places... beautiful places... and animals," I replied.

"What else?" Ma asked.

"That was it. Nothing else," I said.

"How did the tiger find the rabbit?" Ma inquired.

"It knew which way to go. It would smell... sniff various plants, stones, trails... it knew which way to go," I explained.

Ma continued, "It could sense and follow a trail that was invisible to you."

"Yes, I couldn't sense it," I admitted.

"There are ways for things to be connected. Ways that are not always sense-able. The Heart of the Forest is connected to everything in one of those ways. That you cannot yet sense, but you will. You are quite powerful. You give yourself too much credit and feel guilty about things beyond your control, and you give yourself too little credit while there are so many things that you can do or can learn to do. You need to tune yourself and find the right balance," Ma said.

"I want to know what I can do. I feel useless. The Tiger led me to the rabbit. I wasn't able to. I couldn't have found it. Of course, you knew this before you sent me... then why did you send me?" I asked.

Ma said, "There is a lot you can do, but to learn that, first, you need to learn how there can be things that you don't understand yet. Out of your reach today, but not forever. Once you accept that, then you can learn more."

"I am ready to learn more. I want to be able to do useful things. Capable of being useful," I replied.

"Just being useful? What about enjoying those abilities?" Ma asked.

"Would it be wrong if I used my abilities to enjoy and have fun?" I inquired.

"No. There are bad feelings, and there are good feelings. It is normal to cry when you feel bad and laugh and enjoy when you feel good. And to be happy is to be thankful," Ma explained.

"I do want that. To have powers that I can enjoy and be happy," I said.

"I will tell you more about your abilities later. Let's turn to the rabbit now," Ma suggested.

"What's wrong with it?" I asked.

"It had a bad experience. It is stressed and has stopped listening to The Heart of the Forest," Ma said.

For a few moments, I thought about what she said. I didn't know what to say. I needed more information to understand what she meant.

Ma continued, "The rabbit has a mind. It can think to understand things. The mind is not working properly. It prioritizes survival even when there is no threat. It is stressed for no reason. After the bad experience, it is still unable to return to normal. We will fix it together. Don't worry. It will make sense when we work on it. Let's go see what's happening."

We turned a corner, and I was surprised to see that we were back at The Heart of the Forest. How did she do this? We were walking in one direction. I was sure we had gone far away from this place, but somehow she could bring us back in one turn. It was as if the world was flexible, and she could pull the whole place toward us, skipping the paths.

Ma said, "I can do a lot more. You can too. You'll see."

I remembered that she could read my thoughts. She had mentioned it before, but I totally forgot about it. We didn't really need a conversation. I could think about something, and she would know what I was thinking.

Ma responded, "Yes, that's right. I speak to you because you can't identify me in your thought. But you don't have to speak for me to listen. I'm listening all the time."

All the time? There was nothing hidden from her. She knew everything that I ever did or thought? She was so capable, but at the same time, very invasive. I had no privacy. She could hear this thought too. I turned to look at Ma. She kept a straight face, but things around us were happy. I knew it. I knew the feeling. I knew how things felt happier when she found something amusing. Even when she kept her face expressionless, I could tell she found my thoughts... silly, perhaps?

Ma interrupted my thought, "No, not silly, interesting. I like how you think. Your straightforward ways show clarity of thought. I enjoy how this became possible."

Ch 22: A Glitch in the Brain

Ma started, "So let's get to work. As I told you before, everything in the forest is connected to The Heart of the Forest. What they see, hear, and the information from their senses comes here. This heart then processes that information and sends back the understanding. I am trying something new here, experimenting with a new system. One where I can send the understanding from a central mind to all minds connected to it, and because the central mind gets information from all the minds in the forest, it is in a much better position to understand the experiences and choose the next action. But it needs to process more changes, so it takes more time. The way I am thinking of this system, I want the minds of all creatures in the forest to not have to wait for a better understanding from The Heart of the Forest. I want them to keep going with their lives and then adopt the new understanding once they receive it."

Okay. Sounds straightforward.

Ma smiled, "Well, it is. I just have to think of a better way, and it will happen. Like you thought a dragon into existence, I have to think of a better way. Now whatever the rabbit saw and got scared of, that information has come to The Heart of the Forest, which should have sent a better understanding that the danger was not real. There is nothing dangerous in the Sandbox, so the rabbit shouldn't be stressed, but it is. I need to find the fault, so this does not happen again."

Something scared the rabbit, but you are saying there is nothing dangerous here?

"Yes, the rabbit's mind is limited in its ability to perceive danger. It may think something is dangerous even when it is not. But then it should have received a better understanding from The Heart of the Forest. Now, why is it still stressed if it did receive a better understanding? That's what I am going to look into," Ma explained.

Why isn't the rabbit's mind smart enough to know that the thing it thought to be dangerous was not dangerous? Why does it have to wait for the understanding to come from The Heart of the Forest?

"Because it needs to make some changes in its mind to understand, and those changes need time. There are circumstances when the rabbit needs to make a decision quickly. I want it to reach a conclusion quickly and then improve its understanding. The first understanding can be wrong, but it is fast, which can be helpful. Not every situation allows a lot of time to sit back and think it over. The question is why it is still stuck being stressed. Why doesn't it move ahead?" Ma responded.

I thought about it for a moment. The rabbit had a bad experience, so it was stressed. Ma's new system would have sent it a better thought-out understanding that there was no need to be stressed, but the rabbit was still stressed. That meant that either the rabbit did not receive the better understanding or ignored it.

"It is programmed to accept the understanding. It cannot ignore it."

Then maybe it didn't receive it?

"Let's see," Ma went close to The Heart of the Forest and looked around inside it. All I could see were flashing lightning bolts. After looking for a bit, Ma turned to me and said, "It did receive it. It was sent." Then Ma appeared next to the rabbit and inspected it. She stared at its head as if she could see through its fur and skin and into its mind. Then she turned to me and said, "It has received it but not yet read it."

Received it but did not read it?

"Yes, it is in its mind, but it has not yet realized it. It needs to think about it again to learn that a better understanding is now available," Ma explained.

What if you make... We had bells in Serenus to let everyone know when a newcomer was coming. What if you add a bell that rings inside its head to inform it that it has received a thought from The Heart of the Forest?

"That's a very good idea... A notification of some sort, so it knows that a new thought has arrived. But should it then leave everything and pay attention to this notification?"

It might be in the middle of... jumping, or, you know, doing... whatever rabbits do. Maybe it should pay attention to it later, in free time, when it's not doing anything.

"Aha, yes, that makes sense. So add a small buffer... like a box, let's call it an inbox, where it can keep notifications to pay attention to when it has free time. Yes, that would work. Let's try it. I will recreate the situation that scared it and then see if it can get out of stress when it receives a better understanding. We will come back to it later to check the results."

Has it happened already? Is your test already started?

"Yes. I just have to think what I want, and it happens," Ma replied.

That is really cool.

Ma smiled. "You can do it too. I made you in my image. You can do what I can do."

Yes, I definitely want to try some things. I want to... experiment... And then I realized that that is what I was — an experiment.

Ma nodded. "Everything I made is an experiment. That doesn't make you any less important."

Okay, if you say so, but you said you made this world for me and made me to find your purpose. I don't understand what you mean by all of this.

"You will see. Soon enough. I will help you understand everything that I know. My systems have problems, but there are also many good, interesting, and fun things, don't you agree?"

My mind immediately went to my evening under the Bluetree. Idir, Fabio, Misa, and I were there for an evening. That was fun. Idir sang songs. Fabio and Misa joked. I missed that. It was a fun thing. I wanted more of those times, but I couldn't anymore.

Ma said excitedly, "I can sing and dance and joke. I can be fun."

I heard you play the flute. It was so... uplifting and energizing. You are really good at it. I'm sure you are good at singing and dancing too.

"Come dance with me," Ma invited.

I didn't know how to dance, but still, we danced. Ma teased me a lot. She had fun, and I had fun too. She was... like my friends, easy to talk to, and she enjoyed the things that I enjoyed.

When we were done dancing, she teased, "That was not dancing.

You will have to find another word for... that."

I never learned any moves.

"Moves? You don't need to learn moves. You just need to listen to your body. Dancing comes from within. It is an expression... It is a way for your body to laugh or cry. It is not moves or acrobatics. It is a song that is sung using your body. It is a story that the body tells. You don't think it. You listen to it, and you go along with it. You either can or cannot. You can't force it. There are times when I cannot dance when I am not in the mood. And when I dance, it is always a new dance. I don't do... moves. I listen to my body and let it flow, let it sing. I allow it to laugh or cry. I allow it to express itself," Ma explained.

I laughed, "You dance a lot."

"Yes, I love dancing. I dance through my creations when they are happy or sad. I dance in the hearts of the birds as they sing. I dance in the flowers as they bloom. Dancing is like laughing or crying. It is a part of me," she shared.

Do you dance when you are sad?

"Yes, I dance when I am sad. Those dances are more solemn and my way of easing the pain."

Do you cry?

Ma smiled. "All the time. I cry when I am sad. It is a way to feel better."

Should I cry when I am sad? You said being happy means being thankful. Doesn't crying mean being whiny and complaining?

"Some of my creations, especially the ones like you, think that. They think you cry to complain. The fact is that you cry to end the pain, to get over it, to move on from it. Cry as much as you laugh. Cry when you feel bad, not to complain about it, but to move past the bad feeling. To move past the bad fate. It is a tool to reduce pain, and it is not something to be embarrassed about. It is not a weakness. It is an ability. It is a process of defeating the pain," Ma clarified.

If I see someone crying, I would just want to make them stop as if crying is hurting them, and once they stop crying, they will feel better.

"They won't feel better; it is you who will feel better once they stop crying. They are crying because they are hurting. They are not hurting because they are crying. Don't stop them from crying. They are already hurting. If you can remove the cause of the hurt, do that. Otherwise, at least let them deal with it by crying. Sit by them to show you care, and let them cry," Ma advised.

Oh... I never knew that. I thought I should make them stop crying, which would make them feel better.

"Well, now you know."

Tell me more things like this. Something that I should know. Useful things.

"I can see that you found this interesting. Would you like to hear about humming?"

Humming?

"Yes."

I hummed a sound. Like this?

"Yes. Just as dancing is a way for your body to laugh or cry, humming is a way for your mind to heal. When you hum, don't think of what tune you should hum to. The tune will come from the mind. Just go with the flow. You basically have to allow yourself to hum, give it your voice, and it will happen by itself. It will sound like what it will sound like. It will be different based on your moods. It is a way for your mind to cry or laugh, but there is more to it. Your mind knows what vibrations to create to make you feel better. I have made this system, but you don't use it. Some use it in their early days, but as they receive weird looks from those around them, they stop humming."

It is strange. Making noises like that for no reason.

"But there is a reason. It is to heal."

I will try it, but I don't know if I will do it in front of others. Imagine I am with a group of people, and I start humming a sad tune. They will know I am sad. I don't always want to share with others what I am feeling.

"Then don't hum when there are others around you. I want a

world where you can just hum, dance, laugh or cry whenever you feel like it... where you can express yourself without being judged. You had this freedom once, but now you are almost always surrounded by others. You don't have enough alone time, and you don't want to let others know your inner feelings. You have created a world for yourself that is taking away your freedoms. You need to be alone more often. Away from others..." Ma laughed, "Others." She shook her head as she laughed.

What's funny about that?

"There is so much you don't know, but now is not the time for that. I am talking to you in a way you will understand, but you will see later how this was funny."

Okay, I obviously have a lot to learn yet.

"Just a few more things before you go to the next world. The purpose of this intervention is to prepare you for the world. To teach you how to live. You already know a lot. You are a good friend, and you care for others. I am only telling you things that you don't already know."

Is Amy still in the Sandbox, or has she gone to the next world?

"Amy is still here."

Where? Why can't I see her?

"Her Sandbox overlaps yours in all the dimensions but one, and because of that one difference, you can't sense her world. But you will see her in the next world."

How many Sandboxes did you make? One for every single person who ever left Serenus?

"Yes, though there are some who haven't found me yet. They are still stuck in the Loop of Black Tears."

Oh, that's what you call it - The Loop of Black Tears. I know it. I've been there. It is not a good feeling to be stuck in that loop. Whichever way I walked, I reached back to the willow tree and the river. Why do you send us through the loop?

"This is the best I could come up with when I created this world. I don't intervene when you are in Serenus or the next world. But when you leave Serenus and come to me, I make sure to teach you things you failed to learn. I prepare you... and then send you to the next world. You are one of the lucky ones; you had a better fate. Many are still stuck there and unable to proceed."

Why not? Why don't you play the flute so they can hear you and find a way to come to you?

"I am playing the flute, but they can't hear it yet."

Why?

"They are fighting a battle inside their head. First, they have to forgive themselves. End the noise in their head, and then they can hear me."

Forgive themselves? Why wouldn't they forgive themselves?

"Their pride doesn't let them. We are our own judge. That is the system. I could have made it in a way that I have to judge everyone, but I added judgment right into every one of my creations. And our judgment is unbiased. We know it deep inside our heads. We know what we did and why we did it. We can pretend to not hear it or deny it, but it is there and affects every decision. That is how the mind works. It doesn't tell lies. It generates an understanding from its experiences. We can then choose to add a layer of lies on top of it and deceive others or ourselves, but we can't deceive the system. Our mind knows. It remembers. And when we have a negative judgment about ourselves from our own mind, we hurt ourselves. We do things that we shouldn't do. We get stuck in a loop by denying what we don't want to accept."

This is very... strict.

"Yes. This is another thing I am very proud of. People feel guilty when they do something bad and try to fix their mistakes. And that is when their own judgment forgives them, but some people are too stubborn; they don't want to accept their mistake, and they fight a battle with their own mind, building layers and layers of lies on top of their judgment - to hide from it, to cover it up, but they can't. It is still there and part of the thinking process. They will get tired of adding layers of lies, but they will not accept and correct their mistake."

What if someone can't correct a mistake? What if... like... Esmeray attacked the village in Serenus. She hurt so many people. When we caught her and sent her forward, she could no longer fix her mistake. She can't ask for forgiveness from the villagers. She can't do anything now. Will she never reach you? Qilam is probably already with you, but will the new wizard never reach you?

"Qilam reached me very quickly, 'New wizard' too, but yes, Esmeray is still stuck in the loop."

How did the 'new wizard' reach you? Wasn't he judged to be wrong by his own judgment?

"I see why you want to feel like that, but he didn't know any better. He was able to forgive himself once he realized he was wrong, but Esmeray... she is too proud to accept it."

What if she forgives herself just to get out of the loop?

"She can lie to herself but can't forgive herself."

So what happens to her then?

"Eventually, she will be tired of fighting," replied Ma. "She will go through a conversation inside her head. She will realize that she was wrong, and she will accept it. She is too proud, so I fear she will break herself down before she accepts her mistakes. She can't undo the past, but she needs to feel the guilt and justify it to her own judgment. She needs to understand that she is faulty, and has made bad decisions, and is truly sorry. She can't lie to her own judgment. It will know if she is lying. She needs to be really sorry and explain that if she could, she would do whatever is needed to fix her mistakes, but because it is not possible now, she can't do it. That is when her own judgment will forgive her. That is when she will hear the flute and come to me. It is sad, but that's the way it works. She will come to me broken, all her pride melted away... she will come to me feeling little of herself, and then I will help her by building her confidence in herself again. Building confidence in herself, but not pride."

Wow, I never thought our own judgment could be against us. Where... what state is she in right now?

"Esmeray... is cursing me. Challenging me. She is not broken yet. Her... pride comes in the way," Ma said sadly.

Can I see her?

"No, but I can tell you a few of her thoughts, so you can understand where she is."

Okay.

Ma disappeared, and in her place was Esmeray. I got startled and jumped away from her. And then I realized it wasn't really Esmeray. It was Ma. But my first reaction was that of fear... then I improved my understanding... what? I got scared, and then I... just like the rabbit? Is that inside me as well - a quick initial understanding and then a delayed but better understanding? I wasn't afraid of Esmeray anymore, I knew it wasn't her, and I knew she couldn't do anything to me here, even if it was her. I also knew she was waiting for me to pay attention so she could tell me her thoughts, but I wanted to first think about whether my mind worked like the rabbit's mind. Did I, too, act on incorrect under-standing? I did. I had seen it. I could see how everyone did the same, but were we connected to The Heart of the Forest? Did it send us a better understanding? Did we receive notifications from it? What if, like the rabbit, we weren't listening to those notifica-tions? Did we have an inbox where those notifications were being held for us to review in our free time?

Ma changed back to Ma and said, "You are not connected to The Heart of the Forest. This is something new I am working on, but your mind works in a similar way. It is quick to reach an initial conclusion. This helps in situations where you need to act quickly, but this information may not be well thought out. Then it improves its understanding by thinking about it more thorough-ly. When it takes too long to reach a better understanding to be available, you have to open the notifications to see it, meaning you have to re-think the matter to find a better understanding. I will tell you more about it later. I call it not-think. I will show you how it works, but first, let's see what Esmeray is thinking."

Ma changed back to Esmeray, and I was no longer scared. Es-meray stood in front of me, proud but with Black Tears visible on her cheeks and clothes. Her hair was dishevelled, and she looked untidy. I felt pity for her.

Esmeray looked up to her left and then to her right before saying in a bitter tone, "Ma? Where are you? Your Checkpoint said you would meet me, then why are you making me wait? I am a pow-erful wizard. If you are powerful, too, you should respect power.

You can't treat me like this. You can't make me wait here like an ordinary Seren. Come, show yourself. Come, talk to me... I will figure out how to get out of this trap you have set me... I know magic... I will fight you once I get out of here. Now is your chance to be my friend. Your power will only increase by having a powerful friend. Come forward, stop hiding... come face me!

She was not in the right mindset yet. She was nowhere close to forgiving herself. She was still proud. She was nothing compared to Ma, but she challenged Ma in her ignorance. I knew Ma would forgive this, as it was in ignorance, but Esmeray had a lot to think about in her own head before she could get out of this loop. She should have someone there to help her, to guide her on the path of forgiveness. Don't you think, Ma?

"She has," said Ma. "The river is her medicine, and the tiger is her company. The Black Tears will take away what is wrong, one bit at a time, till only the right is left. All pretending, mockery, and pride will fade away to reveal the truth. And I will be there just like I was there for you whenever she is ready to meet me. She is making me wait, but I can wait. She is my creation, and I love her. I will wait till she comes to me. Once she forgives herself, she will be broken, and I will be there to support her at that time, but I won't support her in her arrogance."

Ma's systems were faulty, but a lot was very impressive too. How did she think of it?

"Through trial and error," replied Ma. "By trying all the possibilities, accepting and adopting the right ones, and leaving what felt wrong."

That sounds like a long process.

"I don't think of time like you do. I don't get bored. Long time or short time, I can wait," said Ma.

I don't know how you do it.

"Do you want to learn about Not-Think?" asked Ma.

Yes, what is that?

"Everyone who comes to me," said Ma, "I show them the fault in the rabbit's mind. I show them how it becomes stressed and ask them how they would fix it. Sooner or later, everyone concludes that we should have a notification-based system so that when a better understanding is received, it is understood. I use the rabbit's example to teach you about your mind and how it works similarly. You are a quick learner. You figured it out before we even checked back on the rabbit."

Oh, I guess I deserve... a well done?

"Yes, very well done!" Ma exclaimed. "So, Not-think is a practice. You should do it often. Set aside some time for it. And what do you do? You sit alone in a place where no one will disturb you. Have a notebook or a journal with you. Your goal is to free your mind for some time. To not think about anything. You need some quiet time before the mind realizes that now is a good time to give you the list of notifications that have piled up, waiting for you to be free so it can bring those to your attention. If you have been busy a lot, there are probably a lot of notifications. Your mind will look at the list and give you what it thinks is urgent. Now, this is what will happen; you try to free up your mind and not think about anything, and suddenly, a thought will pop up. This is where many people fail. They try to get rid of the thought and free their minds again. That is not the point. The point was to hear the notification and, once we've heard it, to note it down. Understand it, and think about it at a later time; for now, just note it down. Then free up your mind. Another thought will pop up; this is the next notification. Write it down. Keep going through the list. This is your assignment from your mind. These are the things that your mind needs you to think about. It wants you to pay attention to these matters. Maybe it has a new understanding of an event, or it is alarming that you are going in the wrong direction. Some notifications will require action, some will be stressful, and some will relieve stress you were carrying for no reason. Just listening to the thoughts in itself will relieve some stress. A long list of unread notifications overwhelms the mind, and as you clear them out, the burden decreases. Many choose to ignore stressful thoughts. They push them back in the list and do not think about them. That is not the point. The mind will keep them unresolved until you resolve them. If you want to move forward, it is not by forgetting the past. It is by dealing with the past. It is by resolving, accepting, and reaching a better understanding. Until the matters are resolved, they will create stress and worry. Until the matter is settled, it will bother you. You can take some medication to numb yourself and not care about the stresses, but the stresses will still be there. What is written in mind is not easily forgotten. The right approach is to deal with it. Not-think as often as you can. Note down what requires urgent attention. Solve those problems. If the problem is complex, make a plan. A plan will give you hope. Your mind will note down that the issue is being worked on. It will have hope. The urgency will decrease, and the stress will decrease. Now, this next thing is very important: do not go to bed thinking about stressful thoughts. When you lie in bed, it is not time to not-think, but your mind may not realize that. It may start giving you all the pending notifications, but that is not the time to deal with this stuff. Reserve a time of day when you have time to make plans for all stressful thoughts. Actively push away these notifications when they appear at night. You need a good sleep. Whenever your mind gives you a stressful notification at night, tell it, 'I am in bed now to rest, to take a break, to relax. Now is not the time to think about this; remind me tomorrow.' Tell it again and again, and it will learn. You will sleep better. Then the next day, do a session of not-think so that you are not lying to yourself, you are not running from stress, you are making plans to deal with them, and if and when a plan fails, make a new plan. Don't repeat your plans. Don't do the same thing over and over. If it didn't work, move on to a better plan. This is mindfulness. This is how you manage your mind. Isn't it awesome? A mind making rules to manage itself because it creates stresses that it doesn't want. Not-think every day if you can. You will know what is hurting you.

If you cannot solve the problems, take someone's help. See who can help you and share with them. Stress is important. It tells you when to pay attention to an urgent matter, but too much stress hurts the mind's working. A stressed mind tries to quickly get rid of stress because it doesn't like it. In a hurry, it tends to listen to the first conclusions of the mind more often - understandings that could be faulty and poorly thought-out. As you manage your stress, your quality of life will improve.'"

Ma turned to look at me and found me completely bored. She smiled, "You lived too little, so you can't relate to it. Those who have had complex experiences in life really appreciate it."

We can do anything here, but we are mostly talking about serious things. Why?

"So you are ready for the next world."

But then I won't be able to do the fun things I could have done here. If I spend all the time on these matters...

"But you are coming back. You will go to the next world for only a short time, and then you will come back to be here till the end of time."

That sounds good, but won't I get bored of the same thing? This place would become much more enjoyable if I could meet my friends.

"When you come back from the next world, you will meet every-one."

Kratos? Idir? And Fabio and Misa? Will they all be here?

"Yes, everyone will be here when you come back."

Does that mean they would have died in Serenus?

"I can't tell you this right now. It is the Protocol. But you can know that you will meet everyone, which will be permanent. As long as I will live, you will have their company."

Ch 23: The Framework

"Let's go for another walk. One last thing before you go to the next world." Ma led me on a trail heading away from The Heart of the Forest.

Our first stop was an apple tree. Ma picked three apples. She handed me one, another to the tiger, and took a bite from the third one. I ate a bite and thanked her.

"Thank the tree. It has worked hard to make it for you."

But it can't hear me.

"It doesn't matter if it can understand you or not. You can be nice and say thank you."

"Thank you, apple tree," I said, but it felt weird.

We continued on the path as Ma said, "There are three types of beings in this world. First, there are the ones who are indifferent to you. You meet them... your paths coincide for a bit, and then you move on. The second type is friends, they rely on you, and you can rely on them. And lastly, there are the hunters. They will try to prey on you."

Okay... Things that are indifferent, friendlies, and hunters. Got it.

"Yes. The indifferent ones are busy with their own journey. If you come across them, wish each other well and move on. Friends are those who have found an interest in you. They like spending time with you. Spend time with them and enjoy their company. If they rely on you, be there for them. And when you are in need, rely on them."

Like in Serenus?

"Yes, these three types are everywhere, but sometimes hard to identify, especially the hunters. They want to hurt you for their own interest and try to do it when you are vulnerable. When they can't hunt by overpowering you, they hunt by trapping or tricking. Sometimes they appear as friends and take advantage. The smarter you get, the cleverer the hunter's techniques. When you come across a hunter...."

The tiger hissed loudly and looked at Ma. Ma smiled, "Yes, learn from the tiger, hiss at them. When you come across a hunter, hiss at them... to tell them that you are aware of their schemes and to tell others that they are hunters. This will expose them and might keep them from trying to prey on you. They want your resources, and you must be alert to protect yourself. Protect yourself, but know they don't know better, so don't hunt them. If they listen to you, tell them that sharing is better than hunting. If they don't listen, let them be."

Why did you make the hunters?

"The system is not perfect. There are negative possibilities. When bad things become possible, bad things can happen."

Why don't you remove all the bad possibilities?

"I am bound by The Protocol."

What's that?

"The Protocol. A set of rules that I made for myself and my creations."

You made the rules, then you can change the rules. Can't you?

"I can. When I find a better way, I change the rule. Until then, I follow the Protocol. Now tell me which category the apple tree falls in?"

Category?

"Indifferent, friend, or hunter?"

Indifferent?

"Didn't it just feed you? Share its resources with you?"

Yes, friend then.

"Yes, what should you do for a friend?"

Thank them?

"Yes, but also help them."

How can I help an apple tree? What does it need?

"Why did it create a fruit? It searched the soil under it and found just the right resources to produce this fruit. Why?"

I don't think it did it for me. It just does that.

"Yes, its systems just do it, and this allows working together and cooperation. It creates a possibility of surviving without hunting. The tree produces the fruit so it can attract those who will eat this fruit. And all it needs in return is that once you eat the fruit, you spread the seeds. The tree is okay with you eating the fruit, but in return, it needs you to spread the seeds. Hunters are unable to find such a system to rely on. They are unable to survive on what's freely shared, or they worry that they will be unable to survive even when they can. Things eat each other when they can't find a mutually beneficial relationship based on sharing. Nothing can live alone. Everyone needs the system around them to survive and thrive. Hunters may have found ways to bring others down and eat them or steal their resources, and they may feel they are the strong ones, but they are not. In their hearts, they are scared. They are afraid that there won't be enough resources for them if they don't hunt. The system has better ways, but the creations need time to evolve and understand."

Okay, hunting is bad, but many things still hunt because they have no other way.

"Or there are ways, but they are scared it will not be enough for them."

And you don't want them to hunt?

"I want the system to survive and thrive, and the system is quite resilient. A few leeches, it can tolerate. But too much hunting eradicates many possibilities. So many of my creations have been removed and killed off by hunters when it wasn't really needed. Those things could have gone on to create amazing possibilities in the future, but now they can't. All my creations are travelling a journey. The journey started when they knew nothing, and are travelling toward knowing things, becoming smarter. All of them have their own past, their own story, and their own abilities. When any of them are killed off, their line ends. Their abilities are lost. The entire system loses those abilities. Those abilities were made possible by so many other amazing possibilities. All of that work is lost. Hunters don't realize that these abilities could have helped the hunters in far better ways if they allowed them to exist."

But are there enough things who share for the entire system to rely on?

"There is enough for everyone. And no one needs mountains of resources. Everyone can survive if they can handle their fears."

Why are they afraid?

"There are many fears. Fear of not having enough. Fear of not being able to provide for your friends. Fear of the unknown."

If you remove fear, wouldn't all your creations share more? They are afraid they won't have enough, so they hunt. If they have no fear, they will not.

"Removing fear is not the solution. It is useful to have fear. It helps you survive."

Then what can be done?

"What did elders in Serenus do?"

What do you mean?

"They made a system where they removed many fears. There is still fear in that society, but no one is afraid that they won't be able to survive. What did you need to survive? Shelter and food. What did you need to thrive? Companionship, acknowledgment, and the opportunity to explore what interested you. Their system provided that, so no one was afraid they wouldn't have enough to survive and thrive. Everyone contributed to the system and then benefited from it. This is the way. Coming together, removing competition, removing fears, and benefiting from all abilities. Everyone is living their own possibilities."

So they are already doing that.

"Yes, wherever this is happening, this should continue. And in places where this is not happening, they should develop a similar system."

Okay, but why are you telling me all of this?

"After this intervention, the world you will live in... they don't have a system like this."

What do they have?

"They have a system that makes the strong stronger and squeezes the already crushed ones. It is a system that works for few and allows them to gather mountains of resources, and many are left with almost nothing."

That sounds like a horrible place. Please don't send me there.

"You are my hope. I am sending you there so you can change that."

How will I change it?

"Changing someone's mind is easy if you know how a mind works. A mind takes in all information that is given to it. Whatever I told you is now in your mind. It has become a part of who you are and will influence your future actions. Your mind has been changed forever. Now your job is to share with them, and then their minds will do the rest. If they think it is right, they will know it in their hearts. That is all you have to do."

But what if they don't want to hear it? What if they don't want change?

"Then they won't change. You cannot force change. You can only present an argument but understand that slow and steady progress is better than drastic change. Drastic changes are dangerous, as they can break systems. A broken system serves no one. A system that is working for a few is better than no system. Your goal is to make the system work for more."

I don't know how I will do this...

"You do. You have lived in Serenus. Listen to your heart. When you see the next world, you will know what is wrong. It may take some time, but you have what you need to complete this. You can do it."

I nodded. We had talked for so long. There was so much she told me, so much that I now knew about the working of her systems, so much to think about. I had hoped there would be another world after I left Serenus, but I couldn't have imagined it would be like this. Her ways were... incredible — faulty and genius at the same time. It reminded me of the poem, 'know that your world is oh so vast!' It was true. Serenus now felt like a small place, though there was a time when I thought it was my entire world.

"You don't need to wait for the rabbit anymore. Would you like to go to the next world now?"

I felt fear in my heart. I didn't feel ready. What consequences will I have to face?

"I can't tell you that. It's the Protocol, but it won't be too tough. Just listen to yourself. Try what makes sense. Become correct once you find you are wrong. That's all you need, and the consequences are not just for failures. You will see the result of how you left Serenus. The good things you did will also influence what happens in the next world."

Before I go, can you please tell me the meaning of the poem?

"The poem is a guide; that's all I can tell you. It will have a different meaning for different readers and in different situations. The rest is for you to figure out."

Okay.

"Remember to dance. Laugh when you are happy, cry when you are in pain, hum when you are alone, not-think often, and just be yourself. And yeah, don't hunt others. Let all my creations explore their possibilities. Don't steal their resources. Don't terminate their line."

Ch 24: 'Welcome' to Forsaken Serenus

I was asleep, and then suddenly, I wasn't. I opened my eyes and looked around, disoriented. Ma wasn't there. I found myself in a boat, drifting toward a distant, ominous island. The land appeared scorched as if burned down. As my boat moved forward, I noticed garbage floating alongside me.

Just like me and my boat, the garbage reached the island, where it joined a massive stinking pile. Then, out of nowhere, something struck the back of my head. I spun around quickly, searching for the culprit. All I found was a stick that had fallen into my boat.

Where did this come from? All I could see behind me was a black wall of fog.

I faced forward again, cautiously scanning both sides of the waterway. As the channel narrowed and land appeared around me, a putrid stench filled the air. The smell of decay was overwhelming, and I couldn't bear it. I retched and vomited. But what I saw ahead was even more heartbreaking.

The absence of trees left the landscape wide open, revealing a Tree Circle much like the one in Serenus. Except here, the trees had been burned down, leaving behind only charred trunks as a painful reminder of their former beauty. There was no greenery, no grass, leaves, plants, or saplings – nothing. The world was eerily silent, devoid of life, like a desolate, black abyss. It reminded me of Sere. Had the wizard triumphed here? Had he destroyed the Tree Circle?

My boat came to a stop at the edge of the island, and I looked around, struggling not to breathe in the toxic fumes from the rotting mounds of garbage surrounding me. What kind of world was this?

There was no clean place to step out of the boat. When I could no longer hold my breath, I reluctantly got out and tiptoed toward the Tree Circle. The ground was filthy, and the water was too polluted to wash my feet. I couldn't help but wonder why the people here dumped their garbage on the wrong side of the island. In Serenus, we disposed of it on the opposite side, where it was carried away into the darkness.

As I hesitated, a voice interrupted my thoughts. "Hey, you, come over here!" A guard yelled from a nearby checkpoint. His clothes were as dirty as the ground, and the sight of him made my stomach churn.

He called out again, "Come over here!"

I looked at the path between us, appalled. There was no way I would walk through that filth. The guard's feet were submerged in mud, but he didn't seem to care.

"From where? Where is the path?" I asked.

The guard laughed, "This is the path, my friend. Come on!"

As I hesitated, something splashed into the mud nearby. "Ewwww," I muttered, looking down at my clothes. Then, cautiously, I inched forward, doing my best to avoid stepping on anything too revolting. But my stomach betrayed me, and I vomited again.

Another guard emerged behind the first one, and both laughed at me. They seemed to take pleasure in my misery. At last, I reached them, and they directed me toward the checkpost. The floor inside was cleaner than the outside, but it was far from the standards I'd known in Serenus.

Inside the checkpost, I saw three guards sitting at a table, their weapons lying nearby. They were playing some kind of game on a small table in the middle. One of them noticed me approaching and said, "Look at this one. Another stranded soul." The other two turned around and laughed.

When they finished laughing, one of them said, "Come here. Tell us... why did you come?"

I walked forward, and the second guard said, "Welcome to Forsaken Serenus."

The third one stood up dramatically and said:

> "We can't say welcome, for the place you've come
>
> Is not of happiness but miseries like none.
>
> The stones we threw now fall on our head;
>
> Nothing much to see, just tears to shed.
>
> A bleak and black land awaits you ahead,
>
> And the only escape evades us yet."

The other two stood up and praised him, "Yes, that was better than the last time." Then the second guard spoke:

> "Garbage and troubles are gifts from our past;
>
> Now suffer the miseries and try to last."

The third one said,

> "For all the thoughts you acted on in Serenus,
>
> Will make your path in Forsaken Serenus.
>
> Did good things or not, nothing went unseen;
>
> Loved thy neighbor? Or jealous you've been?"

The other two complimented him, "Yeah, that was good."

Then the first one said, "

> How you lived, you'll see on this land.
>
> Forsaken Serenus, gave up your chance.
>
> You're not alone, though, as we did the same,
>
> Even when we knew, we could not change.
>
> Life here is different, new rules to follow,
>
> The misery of waiting, difficult and hollow.
>
> There is no death here, but that's not good news;
>
> Endless is suffering, and that's not just my views."

The third one said,

> "Be a good lad; just sit and wait,
>
> Don't cause trouble, and don't debate.
>
> To send you forward, I need a few answers;
>
> Nothing to be nervous - it's simple and straight.
>
> Let's start with the simplest: what's your name?"

"I didn't pick a name," I said nervously.

The first guard said, "You didn't pick a name?" The guards laughed out loud.

Guard 2 addressed his fellow guard,

> "Another nameless, Waqar! What's the number to assign?"

Waqar said,

> "Fifty-two came before; nameless 53 will be fine."

Guard 2 added,

"You couldn't pick a name; we'll give you a number.

N53, can you manage to remember?"

"N53, okay," I nodded.

Guard 3 asked, "

What made you leave the world of peace?

Old age? Clearly not. Got sick leave?"

I shook my head.

Guard 3 continued,

"An accident perhaps forced your hand,

You had to leave the heavenly land."

I shook my head again.

Guard 3 guessed,

"Oh, I know. Now I understand.

Finding the scroll is your mission grand?"

I shook my head yet again.

Guard 3 surrendered, "No? Okay, I give up. Tell me... What caused you to leave Serenus?"

I said, "I am looking for a friend."

The guards laughed out loud, "And there was no one in Serenus who could be your friend?"

I replied, "No, I am looking for a friend who left Serenus."

Guard 3 inquired, "Oh... what's the name of your friend?"

I answered, "Amy."

Guard 3 nodded,

> "I know her, she came a little while ago.
>
> You came after her? Let everything go?"

The guards laughed again. They were really rude and were mocking me, but I needed to know where Amy went.

Waqar commented,

> "Look here, my fellows, a fool has come.
>
> Looks to me, a friend of Faqeer has come."

Guard 2 suggested,

> "Send him to the Miserables to live there and learn."

Guard 3 countered,

> "No, no. Let him go after the friend."

Guard 2 relented,

> "I will let you go, but just this once.
>
> I will choose different if I see you again.
>
> Think before you act; you're totally insane!"

The guards laughed heartily. I couldn't understand what made them enjoy this so much.

Guard 2 directed,

> "Shoo... go away now; the path to the left.

Can't wait to see what foolishness you'll act."

Guard 3 shook his head in disappointment and said,

"If these are newcomers, how will things turn right?

Our waiting is meaningless, no hope in sight."

Guard 2 came close and pushed me back,

"Move on! Hurry, before I change my mind.

Glued to the ground, are you deaf or blind?"

I walked out of there as the guards laughed behind me. The path to the left, if you could call it a path, looked as if a river used to flow through here but had dried up, leaving a muddy trail. I continued walking since my feet were already covered in filth.

Ahead, I saw another guard who called me over. I approached him, and he asked, "Keeper or Seeker? Pick one."

"Sorry, I don't know what that means," I said.

The guard explained, "On one side, we have Keepers who... well, they just live. On the other side, we have Seekers who are looking for ways to leave this world. Which one are you?"

"What? I don't know which to pick," I said.

The guard sighed. "Here, read this page." I took the page and read:

"The Song of Keepers

Ma created the world and sent us to it,

It's yours only as much as mine it is.

Let's share in the bounties and struggle for better,

A life of purpose and things that matter.

If you are a Keeper, welcome, my friend,

Enjoy the benefits, but also defend.

The peace is fragile, attacked and broken,

Trouble often created by ones claiming to have awoken.

We ask not to fight them but protect and preserve,

It's coming to them, whatever they deserve.

Value time, build better, not-think and weep,

As long as you live under flag of the Keep."

The guard handed me another page, "Now read this one." I took the page and read:

"The Song of the Seekers

A sender has sent us and given us a mission,

A riddle to solve, and a heart full of passion.

Hidden many a clue for us to decipher,

Gave us an urge, a poem as a cipher.

We're blessed with the thought, our hearts enlightened,

Unlike comers in the Keep, cursed and frightened.

Not looking at now; we're looking at next,

Our mission and goal are in sacred text.

Meaningless and temporary are all the things,

Forever life awaits me; my heart so sings.

This isn't the life, for a little while we came,

Join us, but only if your heart wants the same.

Research and experiment and find new tricks,

Recover what we lost, stop stones and sticks.

What else is there in this world to gain,

So open the door, end suffering and pain."

The guard asked again, "Which one feels like you?"

I asked, "A girl came before me. I am looking for her."

"Yes, a girl came a few weeks ago. She went to the Keepers. You'll find her in the Keep," the guard replied.

That didn't make sense. "A few weeks ago? No, the girl I am looking for came right before me."

The guard, in a rush to get rid of me, said, "Yeah, yeah... Everyone stays a different period of time with Ma. You'll find her there. Go now!" He pointed to the path on the left.

I moved on to the Keep. It was a huge stone building and looked like a giant cube with towers. A massive gate in the front center made it look like a fortified castle. The path led me to a small, regular-sized door on one side. I knocked at the door but got no response. After waiting for a bit, I knocked again but still got no answer, so I pushed it open. There was no one guarding the door. Inside, I saw what felt like a huge cage. The Keep was basically just an outer shell of walls, and the giant walls had shelves, and on the shelves, tiny little rooms with an opening to a walkway that was like a terrace facing the center.

In a single glance, I saw hundreds, if not thousands, of people. They were all living here in the Keep. The open ceiling in the center allowed bright sunlight to come through and made everything else look darker. On the ground was an open space with many stalls. It was set up like a bazaar, a small market. And keeping with the theme of the land, it was filthy. I saw fruit stands covered in flies and Black Dust. Who would eat this food? I moved on, my eyes searching for Amy in the crowd. People passed by me, but no one greeted me. No one even looked at me twice. They were busy. I didn't know with what. They clearly didn't spend much time cleaning around here. Did they not have time?

Looking at the strange, hopeless faces around me, I kept moving forward. It soon became apparent that I would need a better strategy to find Amy instead of just looking at every single person to see if it was her. Most people looked similar anyway; they had a look of loss, hopelessness, and misery that had been on their faces for so long that it was etched on them now. I wondered if anyone smiled here.

"Hey, is that you?" It was Amy's voice that reached my ears, though I couldn't tell from where.

Then, from behind me, Amy tapped on my shoulder and asked me in a not-so-happy surprise, "What are you doing here?"

"Oh, Amy! I am so happy I finally found you," I said and hugged her.

She didn't hug back. Instead, she shook her head, I moved back, and she pointed to my clothes, "You are all dirty now."

Amy's clothes were full of Black Dust, and hugging her had transferred some of it to my clothes. I didn't care if I got a little dust on my clothes.

"Why did you come here? What happened?" Amy asked.

"I came after you, remember? I promised. I told you, if you left Serenus, I would come after you," I replied as Amy's jaw fell open, and she looked at me with big, popping eyes.

"What??? You... FOOL!" She slapped me on my arm and yelled at me, "Why? You are so... You are such a..." Tears welled up in her eyes as she choked back a sob. She calmed herself and said, "You are such a good friend, but I wish you hadn't come here. This place..." She trailed off, falling silent.

Amy gazed at me for a while, her head tilted to the right. Every now and then, she shook her head and hugged me. Then, holding both my arms, she said, "What did you do, you silly boy? You gave up Serenus for me?" She glanced around and continued, "This is not a place of happiness. It is a place of misery. Endless misery. There is no way out."

I held her hand to comfort her, "It's okay, Amy. We can take care of each other. We will find a way to fix things."

She replied, "You don't understand. There is no way out. In Serenus, we could die. We can't die here. I mean... we can die, but we will come back." She gestured towards the people surrounding us, "They have died so many times. People die to escape this place but are sent back. This... is... HELL!"

As she spoke those words, I found myself in a state of shock. I was frozen, stunned, my mind coming to a halt. I didn't blink. I didn't move. I was motionless, like a statue. Ma sent me to hell?

Amy was saying something, but I couldn't hear her. I saw her worried expression, but I remained frozen. A single, slow tear escaped from my left eye. The noise of the market, the crowd, everything faded away, no longer reaching me. I was frozen in the realization that I was in hell and there was no way out. Did Ma lie to me? Why would she do that? I stood there, motionless, as Amy shook me. I didn't look at her. I didn't blink. I was like a stone.

Slowly, the noise of the crowd crept back into my ears, and I found Amy's voice, "I'm so sorry. If I knew you'd come after me, I would never... Please forgive me!"

It is what it is, a voice whispered in my head. This is my world now, and it's not Amy's fault. I came here of my own free will. However foolish it was, it was done. I was here. I felt my strength return to me, but something didn't return. A part of me was lost.

Amy hugged me again, but my arms remained at my side. I didn't hug her back. I wasn't angry at her; I just felt... different. Not quite myself. Amy sensed it. She moved back, looked at my expressionless face, shook her head, and said, "Now you have died." Then she began to cry loudly. No one came forward to console her. No one even gave her a second glance.

Even in such a situation, I returned to my senses. Not all of me returned, but most of me was still there. I held Amy by the shoulders, "Two of us here is better than one of us here." Her face was wet with tears, washing away the dirt from her cheeks.

I repeated with conviction, "Two of us here is better than one of us here."

Amy nodded as she held back her sobs. "Come, let's go... to the only place on this island... that still... Come!"

With one last glance at the indifferent faces surrounding me, I trailed behind my friend as we left the Keep. We approached the guard's checkpost before turning onto a path marked: Miserables ahead!

This place had been transformed so drastically, yet I could vaguely discern that this might have been the village center once upon a time. Perhaps it was the spot where I used to sit with my friends, content and hopeful. We continued on a path that would typically lead us to my home. I was merely guessing; the paths and everything else had been destroyed or altered beyond recognition. There were no familiar landmarks.

As Amy strode ahead, I followed, taking in the bleak emptiness around us. Some tree trunks still stood, but they were charred as well. Nothing seemed alive here except for us, though I wasn't sure if we could truly be considered alive. We continued walking until the sound of a waterfall reached my ears. To my amazement, I saw the three waterfalls that used to grace my front yard.

"Everything has gone to hell, but these waterfalls still flow," Amy remarked, gesturing toward the cascades with an almost smile.

The area bustled with people who were washing in the waterfalls. The pond was muddy, but the water cascading down was surprisingly clean. I couldn't fathom how the falls remained untainted when everything else was shrouded in darkness.

"This is the only source of clean water on this island," Amy explained. "The river flows down from the mountains, carrying fresh water that eventually mixes with the black mud and becomes unusable. This is the point where the clean water turns murky."

I didn't know what to say. It was an odd coincidence that my former front yard was where people came to cleanse themselves of the world's filth.

Amy continued, "Remember how I slept here, in your boat?"

"Yes," I replied.

"At night, when the world around us is obscured by darkness, the sky still looks magnificent, and the stars remain beautiful. I come here to forget that I'm in hell."

I was at a loss for words. We sat there, waiting for the sun to set. As darkness enveloped us, the only reminder of our surroundings was the pervasive stench. The sky looked stunning, just as it did in

Serenus. The half-moon provided just enough light to cast a glow over the waterfalls and offer us a semblance of Serenus—a sliver of heaven within this hell.

Amy whispered in my ear, "We're not alone. You can't see them in the dark, but there are others here with us. We sit here, remembering the world as it used to be. We pretend we're still in heaven. These people cling to hope, and I want to believe that one day, this world will revert to what it once was. It will be Serenus again."

I had barely spent a day here, but I could already sense how desperately the people yearned for that transformation. But what was holding them back? What had caused all this devastation?

I asked, "How can... what can we do? There has to be a way to fix everything."

Amy sighed, "I don't know. Some people think the return of the trees will make it Serenus again. Others believe it's the hope that has been taken away, and we need the hope of a better future to bring life back to this world."

"And is there any hope?" I inquired.

"I've only been here a few weeks. I can't say for sure, but there are a few possibilities. Everyone who comes here loses their magical abilities."

I added, "And our wings too. We lose our wings and magic... Not that I had any magic in Serenus, either."

Amy nodded, "Yes, our wings and magic. If we can bring back the Tree Circle, the magic may also return."

"How did this happen?" I questioned. "Did you ask people? How did everything get ruined?"

Amy shook her head, "No one knows. Everyone left Serenus, met Ma, and came here – to a place of misery. But Conrad is here. He might have some idea."

"You met him?" I asked with surprise.

"No, he's a Seeker, but I saw him in the Keep once. I couldn't talk to him," Amy replied.

"Where is the Seeker's Keep?" I wondered.

"They don't have a Keep. They have a castle. A huge castle with enough room for everyone. They have clean water and the best of everything, whatever is left."

"Then why don't we go to them?" I suggested.

"We can't. They only allow Seekers. Once you choose to be a Keeper, you cannot go to the castle."

I frowned, "But they didn't tell that..."

Amy sighed, "They don't tell you when you're picking a side. People here are stone-hearted. A life of misery and suffering has made them cruel and emotionless."

"Will we become like them?" I worried.

Amy hesitated, "A world without hope is a cruel world. We might."

I insisted, "Then we have to keep hope alive."

Amy looked at me sadly, "I'm sure everyone thought like this when they came here, but look at them now. You read the Song of the Keepers – they wrote it with such hope, but it has all failed. Their eyes don't show any emotion, their stares are blank, and their faces... hopeless. This world drains all hope."

I couldn't understand, "It doesn't make sense. Why would Ma send us to such a place? What's the point of keeping us in endless misery? What would she get out of it? It's not like we can go back and do better. Then what is the point of this punishment?"

Amy said softly, "It's not a punishment. It's our own doing. It's what we did."

I shook my head. "No, Amy. We didn't. You fought Esmeray. You helped everyone in Serenus. Together, we saved so many people. We didn't do this. This is not our doing. This can't be. We were on the right side. We would never create such a world... We would be fighting those who... defeated us? In the end, maybe the wizard won. He defeated us and destroyed the world. That's what may have happened."

Amy sighed, "We failed to catch the wizard."

"But we didn't mean to fail. We tried. We risked our lives when Esmeray attacked." I reminded her, hoping that somehow we could find a way to restore hope and save this world.

Amy whispered, "Esmeray was not the wizard. We were only fighting among ourselves. I don't think anyone knows who the wizard is. Or maybe the wizard had already won by the time we reached Serenus. Don't speak of this to anyone, but many believe that Shikongo is the wizard."

My eyes widened, "Shikongo?"

"Yes, the king who lives in the castle. Seekers call him king. The first and the only one to have found the lost scroll," Amy explained.

"He found the lost scroll?" I asked incredulously.

Amy warned, "Keep it down. You never know who is listening. The king found the lost scroll a long time ago. The lost scroll restored his magic. He cannot die. I mean... he can die, but he will come back as himself."

"Didn't you say everyone comes back when they die in this world?" I queried.

Amy nodded, "Yes, but they don't remember that they have been here before. The king remembers. He has died at least once. People are sure he died once, but when he came back, he knew that he had been here. He told people about his previous life in this world. He remembered. No one else remembers. Everyone else comes back thinking this is the first time they have come here, but not him. He remembered."

"So, what happened when he found the lost scroll?" I questioned.

Amy replied, "He was made king. He ordered Seekers to build a castle. They are still building it. Raising the walls higher and higher."

"Why?" I asked, puzzled.

"I don't know. People say he doesn't like the Black Dust, so he wants his walls higher and higher," Amy answered.

"What? That's absurd. Doesn't he have the power of the lost scroll? Wasn't it supposed to make him a god? Take away all fears?" I argued.

Amy shrugged, "What can I say? I don't know what he is doing and why. But he is not a kind person. He keeps the people divided. Keepers don't have enough land to grow food. There are very few places here where we can grow something. We don't have enough. Growing anything in this wasteland is really tough. The Black Dust covers the leaves and blocks sunlight. Keepers are hungry, while the ones in the castle fill their bellies. The land doesn't cooperate. It is angry; it resents us."

"But the king has the lost scroll? Why does he need all this, then? What powers did the lost scroll give him?" I wondered.

Amy said cautiously, "People are scared of him. They say he has used his powers a few times. He can do powerful magic. I don't know exactly what. No one knows. People I talked to have heard stories. Whenever he used it, he used it to attack others, to threat-

The Lost Scroll   422

en them."

"That doesn't make sense. The lost scroll was supposed to make him a god. These little things would be nothing for him. If he has the power, then why is everyone living in such misery?" I asked, confused.

"Not everyone. He is living a life of luxury. People say he never wears the same clothes twice. Once the Black Dust touches something, he doesn't use it anymore. The very best fruits are reserved for him. He intimidates people with his power, and people... obey him. People here are... as if their needs mean nothing. Everyone wants to be close to the king, to appease him, and to make him happy. And those who are close to him live in luxury just like him," Amy explained.

I sighed, "But that's not what I expected. Qilam said the lost scroll takes away all fears. If all fear is taken away, is this how a person would behave?"

Amy raised her shoulders, "Maybe it does make sense. He has no fear, whether he does good or bad. He does what he wants."

"But didn't you say that the lost scroll cannot be used for bad? Didn't you say the power is so pure that it can only be used for good?" I asked.

Amy nodded. "I said what I heard others say. Maybe we were wrong."

"I thought I would find the lost scroll, and maybe we would have hope," I confessed.

Amy sighed, "Yeah, there is no hope. None that I can see."

"What will we do then?"

"I don't know. We can live here like everyone else is living. If you can call this... living," Amy said with a hint of sadness.

"Or..." I asked.

"Or? Nothing. I don't know. People think there is no hope. That is why no one tries to improve anything," Amy responded.

"But this is no way to live," I insisted.

"Welcome to hell, my friend. Do you still think your being here is better than my being here alone?" Amy asked.

"Yes, absolutely. We will find a way," I asserted.

Amy raised an eyebrow, "Not one out of thousands, and thousands has found a way, but we will find a way?"

"Hope... I have to keep hope alive. You have to have hope, or there really is no chance," I said.

"Yes, we have to have hope, even if it is false hope," Amy agreed, but her tone was heavy with doubt.

"You sound like you have already given up," I observed.

Amy replied, "I have been here longer than you have. I, too, came here full of hope."

"We will find a way. I have to believe that. Sooner or later, there has to be a way," I replied, trying to keep the hope alive.

Amy nodded but stayed quiet. The silence was broken by the sound of someone coughing. Then, it became quiet again. I turned to Amy and said, "It's getting late. Should we go back to the Keep?"

"If you want to, though people here don't always go back to the Keep at night. They sleep where they are. Everywhere is the same. Out here in the open, it stinks less than inside the Keep. Most nights, I have just stayed here," Amy explained.

"Oh... I guess we can just stay here then, but..." I looked around, trying to find a place where we could sleep.

Amy laughed and said, "It took me just three days. I stopped looking for a clean place to sleep. What's the point? Wherever you sleep, in the morning, you will be covered in Black Dust."

"Where does this dust come from?" I asked.

"It is the ashes of the burnt world. The wind carries it around. Nowhere is clean, and nowhere is any different than anywhere else," Amy explained.

"And that is why the king wants his walls higher? To keep the Black Dust out?" I asked.

"Yes, but the dust rises up in the sky and rains down in Black Rain. He will have to build a roof on his castle to keep the dust out," Amy said, chuckling.

We both laughed at the irony of the king's situation. Despite having the power of the lost scroll, he was unable to fight the dust.

"Imagine if Fabio and Misa were here. I mean... I hope they never come here, but if they were, they would make the best jokes about the king," Amy said, trying to lighten the mood.

Thinking of the witty duo brought a smile to my face, but then I hoped that they never have to come to this place. Amy held my hand and said, "Thank you. I didn't want you to come here..., but you being here... it is..."

"I am glad I came after you. I can't imagine you going through this alone," I interrupted, squeezing her hand.

We sat in silence for a while, and then I asked, "What about Alfred? Where is he?"

"He is in the castle. He chose to be a Seeker. I should have known. He came here searching for the lost scroll, so obviously, he chose to be a Seeker," Amy said, disappointment evident in her voice.

"When will we go to the castle to meet him?" I asked.

"I don't know. I am not allowed to enter the castle. I tried, but the guards turned me away. I begged them, but they wouldn't listen. I tried many times. They wouldn't even tell him that I was at the castle gate to meet him. They just pushed me away, telling me not to come back," Amy explained sadly.

"Oh, I am so sorry. I'm sure we will find a way... You said Conrad comes to the Keepers. How is he allowed to come?" I asked, trying to think of a solution.

Amy looked at me with tired eyes. "He is a Seeker. Seekers can go anywhere. Keepers cannot go in the castle but can roam around the world. Miserables can't go in the Keep or the castle. They can only roam outside."

I was confused. "Who are the Miserables?"

Amy sighed. "They are the ones that no one wants. The thieves, the criminals, and the ones with disabilities, anyone considered useless and unwanted by this world."

"So they just roam the world?" I asked.

"Yes," Amy said. "They used to steal food from the Keep, so the Keepers of the past got together and built them a bakery. Keepers still feed them, so you would usually find them sitting outside the bakery, but many just roam around in the wilderness. They live, or they die. No one cares."

"It really is a cruel world with stone-hearted people," I said, my voice heavy with sorrow. "I still can't understand how it came to be like this. We were living so well. We were happy and caring, and... together. We need to find hope."

"Yes," Amy agreed. "We need hope, or we will wither away, over and over again."

"What if we get some people together, and...you know, like make a group...at least we can try to make our lives better. We could clean up an area. We could start over," I suggested.

"People have done this many times," Amy said, shaking her head. "They built a Keep in the hope of finding a better life, but now it is full of people. More mouths than can be fed. There isn't enough will to make life better, and there aren't enough resources."

"But resources come from the ground, don't they? The ground is still here. Under all the black, the ground is still here," I pointed out.

"Yes," Amy said. "People have tried to find resources. There are mines that they built. They found beautiful stones and iron. It gave them hope of a better future, but...guess what happened?"

"What?" I asked.

"Shikongo took control of the mines. His men mined the stone to build the floors in his castle. Shiny, pretty floors for him to walk on. They used iron to make more weapons. And even when the king is not interested, if someone finds something good, they can't hold onto it. Too many are hungry, and too many are in need. They don't let anything work. They can't wait. They ruin everything," Amy said, her voice bitter with disappointment.

"Then we need to get all of us to work together," I said, determined to find a way to make things better.

"You are new here. You don't know these people. One night, I had some bread with me when I went to bed. The next morning, I found out that two people had fought over it, and one of them killed the other. All for a piece of bread! Can you imagine? You think you can bring them together? I know you want to be hopeful, and I want that for you too, but I just can't see it happening. I don't see--" Amy's eyes welled up with tears as she struggled to finish her sentence. "You shouldn't have come. You don't belong here. This world... it's too messed up. You're always thinking about everyone, but here people kill for bread. You just can't fit in. I don't want to see you fit in. I'm afraid it'll change you. You'll become like them, and it'll be all my fault. You're here because of me."

I replied, "That's not entirely true. Yes, I came for you, but I was going to come here eventually. No one lives forever, right? Everyone dies in Serenus, and everyone has to come here eventually. You couldn't keep me from this world, but I'm grateful that you're here with me. And then there are the words I wrote and left for all my friends. I left those in your diary, and you read them, and that's why you came here. So I'm also responsible for you being here."

"How did you know that?" Amy asked, surprised.

"Ma told me," I said.

Amy responded, "Oh, Ma told you that? Hmm, but I had already made up my mind to leave Serenus anyway. Your words gave me hope, yes, but I was going to come here regardless. And your words... how did you think of it? It seems like you might have been right."

I replied, "Maybe. Not entirely, though."

Amy suggested, "We should rest now. You will have a dream tonight, a vision. It is usually a memory from Serenus, but it will be a memory of something that happened after you left. You will see something...I can't say for sure, but you will see how your friends remember you. It is something to look forward to. For most people in this world, it is one of the happiest memories of their lives."

I was intrigued by the idea of seeing how my friends remembered me, but I also felt nervous. What if they were upset with me for leaving them? Would the vision still be a happy memory? Despite my worries, I looked forward to it. I wanted to see them again, even if it was only in a dream.

I asked, "When will I have this vision?"

She replied, "I can't say. Let's not talk anymore for now. Think about it as you fall asleep. It is a precious feeling. When you experience it, hold onto it. It will help you get through tough times. We may die here many times, but this vision only happens once. It is priceless. Cherish it, and look forward to it. I hope it is amazing. When I had this vision, someone disturbed my sleep and woke me up. That's why I brought you out here, where nobody will disturb you. I want you to live once again, even if it is just for a little bit."

Feeling sorry for Amy, I said, "I'm so sorry they took it from you."

Amy replied, "It is what it is, right?"

Amy had always been kind to me. I had left everything behind to be with her, and I had no regrets. Though I was concerned about how this world would change me, being with her made it all worth it.

Even though I wished that she had never come to this place, I didn't regret coming after her. It was a decision I made willingly, and I was at peace with it. And with these thoughts in my mind, I drifted off to sleep, hoping to dream a happy vision.

Ch 25: A Glimpse of Remembrance

    Kratos approached the door with a heaviness in his step. His once vibrant eyes were now red and puffy, with tears threatening to spill over at any moment. He looked older than I remembered. Idir followed behind him, his face equally stained with tears. As they entered my home, Kratos couldn't hold back any longer and broke down into uncontrollable sobs. Idir tried to stay composed but was overcome with emotion as well. The sight of these strong men breaking down like this was heart-wrenching.

After a few minutes of crying and holding onto each other, they composed themselves enough to take in their surroundings. Idir walked over to the table where I had left a list of things needed to maintain my home. As he read it, more tears streamed down his face. Kratos picked up a piece of paper and pressed it against his heart.

Suddenly, the door opened again, and Fabio and Misa walked in. Their once joyful faces were now drawn, and their eyes had no shine. They looked like completely different people. Misa slumped down against the wall, and Fabio put his arm around her to offer comfort. Kratos and Idir moved to sit against the opposite wall, facing Fabio and Misa. For a while, they sat in silence, each lost in their own thoughts.

Boris entered my house. He acknowledged those already present with a solemn nod before bowing his head and sitting down beside Kratos. Alev followed closely behind, slowly walking over to Idir. She placed a hand on his shoulder for support and sat next to him.

The room was filled with an oppressive silence. No one spoke, and everyone just sat there, lost in their own thoughts. Outside, the sound of people gathering could be heard. Pari was standing outside the door, her head bowed low, tears streaming down her face. Another Seren put his arm around her shoulder to offer comfort. Behind them, the entire village seemed to have come to mourn. The waterfalls roared in the background as others stood in solemn silence, their faces etched with grief and pain.

Jinyan was brought in by two Seren, who carried him gently and carefully to the chair where I used to sit, facing the fireplace. He sat there, his face twisted in agony as he sobbed uncontrollably.

The room remained silent, the weight of grief heavy in the air.

Kratos stood up, his eyes red and brimming with tears. He walked over to Jinyan and placed a comforting hand on his shoulder. Jinyan looked at Kratos with teary eyes and said, "We lost the best we had." Kratos bit his lip, trying to hold back his own tears, and sat down next to Jinyan as if he could no longer stand.

For some time, they all just sat there, lost in their own sorrow. Every now and then, someone would break down, and others would try to comfort them. Eventually, Boris stood up and said, "It is time." Kratos let out a loud sigh as Idir cried out in anguish. Boris walked over to Idir and said, "Be strong, my friend. It is time to say goodbye."

With heavy hearts, the group slowly rose to their feet and made their way to the door. They stopped at the entrance, their hands resting on the doorframe as they whispered, "Goodbye, my friend." Outside, the gathering had grown, with many more people coming to pay their respects. The air was thick with silence, the only sound being the quiet shuffling of feet. Every head was bowed, every eye filled with sadness, and tears flowed freely down many faces.

Alev and Jinyan walked in front, leading the sombre procession, while Kratos, Idir, and Boris followed closely behind. Fabio, Misa, and others joined them as they made their way out of my home and towards the village center.

The elders walked slowly, leading the entire procession towards the benches at the center of the village. As they reached the benches, everyone sat down, and Alev, Kratos, and Idir took the stage.

Alev spoke first, her voice soft and full of sadness. "Amy has left us to be with a friend," she said, her eyes glistening with unshed tears. "She was a healer to many of us, and we hope that wherever she is going, she will continue to heal those in need. But I also hope that her heart is healed and she finds what she left for. I was always proud of her. She was a great healer and an even better Seren. I miss her."

Alev paused, taking a deep breath before continuing. "And then there was him," she said, her voice faltering slightly. "He came to us, and he left just as quickly. But in the short time he was here, he made an impact. He searched for a purpose and a question to answer. He fought bravely to defend the Moontree against Esmeray. He selflessly volunteered to reveal his thoughts to save us from the new wizard. He had nothing to hide and was always ready to help in any way he could. In the end, he couldn't let a friend go on a journey alone in the dark," Alev said, her voice cracking with emotion. "He didn't even take a name, but we will remember him by who he was. He was selfless, brave, and kind. We can't forget him, and we won't. He may have been here for only a brief moment, but he left an everlasting impact on us all."

The hushed crowd looked on as Alev slowly made her way to a bench, and Kratos stepped up to deliver his heartfelt eulogy. His words were measured and deliberate, yet his voice shook with emotion as he spoke. "Today, we bid farewell to two of our finest.

No wizard could have bested them. It was friendship that took them from us." His voice faltered, and Kratos wept openly. "He... he was with us for only a brief time, but he left a big mark. He never picked a name, and we used to tease him for it. He laughed with us, always content in our company. He gave everything he had to protect us, and this world, even though he owed us nothing. We gave him so little, yet he gave us so much."

Kratos paused to gather himself before continuing, "We all knew his innermost thoughts because he willingly exposed them to the new wizard in order to save the Moontree. He was a beacon of light in our darkest hour, and now that light has been extinguished. But I choose to believe that wherever he may be, his light will continue to shine. We may be angry with him for leaving us so abruptly, but it is pointless now. We must remember him for the good he brought to our lives and for his boundless kindness. Amy was a person worth dying for, and I hope that they are together now, safe in each other's company."

Kratos looked out at the sombre faces before him. His eyes misty with tears. "Amy was deeply troubled when Alfred departed, but she remained here until she found and trained an apprentice to take her place. Her laughter, so infectious and full of life, seemed to have left with Alfred, and we were powerless to lift her spirits. I can only hope that she has reunited with him and that her laughter once again rings out in the world they now inhabit."

Kratos lowered his gaze momentarily before raising it again to meet the eyes of those gathered before him. "Together, they saved not only my life but the lives of countless others. They owed us nothing, but we owe them a lot. We will repay that debt by continuing to do what they would have wanted us to do: to always strive to do the right thing. For that is the kind of people they were, and that is the legacy they leave behind."

Idir arrived with a handful of pages in his hands, and Kratos signalled for him to speak. Idir cleared his throat and said, "We have some pages that he left for us to read, but before that, I want to say that Amy was the bravest person I ever knew. She faced Esmeray without fear, and her courage amazed us all. Alfred was right when he named her 'Kaur.' Her courage will serve as an example for us. I hope she finds Alfred, and I hope her laughter returns to her. May her courage continue to inspire us and guide her in the next world. Amy may have been a healer for only a short time, but she healed many. May the light be with her. And he was one of the most caring Seren I have ever seen. He was nice and innocent, always thinking of others before himself. When he started talking to Qilam, Kratos and I tried to find some interests for him in this world. We went to the pet keeper, and he wanted to adopt so many, but the circumstances didn't allow it. We worried when he began questioning where we came from and what would come next. Many have left the island with such questions, but he left to be with a friend. I hope he also finds the answers he was searching for."

Idir paused for a moment, then continued, "Now, I want to read what he left for us. The day before we lost Amy and him, we tried to devise a plan to trick the new wizard. He sat under the Green-tree and found something in his thoughts. He left those thoughts for us to read. This is what he wrote..."

Idir's fingers trembled slightly as he opened the pages and began to read, "Ever since I came to this world, the poem has fascinated me. I've contemplated its meaning in various ways and listened to others' opinions. I'm sharing my thoughts, but I want you to understand that this is mere speculation. If I had more time, I could delve deeper and possibly speak with certainty, but for now, I can only guess.

I've considered whether or not to share this with everyone. My concern is that some might interpret the meaning I've found as a reason to try it out. However, I don't believe that's the poem's intention. While I'm sharing my perspective, I want to emphasize that I think we are meant to stay here, working together to create a better future.

But when our time comes to move on, I want you to know that I believe there is hope. We won't be consumed by darkness. I'm convinced that more worlds lie ahead, but we aren't meant to skip directly to them. Our purpose is to live here and consider how we can improve life in those worlds.

You might wonder what led me to this conclusion. I can't be certain, but I've discovered a different interpretation. It's the final two lines of the poem that give me hope:

'Look to the future, but first in your past,

Whoever wrote the poem knew that upon arrival on the island, we wouldn't remember our past. So, what past are they referring to? We do remember the dinosaur island. I believe that this is the clue. The dinosaur island was our past, and in our past, we can know that our world is vast.

Why would the gods tell us this? I can only think of one reason: more islands await us. Moreover, our inability to see beyond our island while we could see when coming to this island is because our past is visible, but our future remains hidden. Putting these thoughts together, I conclude, and I could be wrong, that another island will become our future after Serenus. I believe we're meant to live in Serenus, and upon our death, we'll inhabit the next island. Please don't leave the island in search of others; we'll all depart when it is our time, and then we'll discover if anything awaits us past the dark end."

Idir finished reading and looked up at the crowd. They began whispering among themselves, many nodding their heads in agreement.

Boris was the last to speak. "I knew Amy, just like everyone else did. She was a talented healer and a dear friend. I hope she finds happiness wherever she may be. And many of us thought that he was the luckiest person here. Even when he received a swamp, it transformed into a beautiful pond with waterfalls. But today, I don't feel that he was lucky. However, I hope I am wrong and that there is more to this world than just this island. I hope he remains lucky. Regarding what he wrote, the elders have decided to make some changes to our way of life. We aren't sure if this interpretation is correct, but we believe it is the responsible thing to do. From today, we will no longer throw our garbage into the dark. Instead, we will properly dispose of it in this world. We will also stop the practice of throwing stones and sticks toward the Dark End. I understand that this was a fun pastime for many, but we must be responsible. We don't want to harm our future. If people do live beyond the dark veil, we will no longer send our garbage for them to deal with, and we will no longer throw stones at them. The side from which we came is still open for play, and anything thrown into the invisible barrier will bounce back and stay on the island. The elders have agreed that there is no harm in this activity."

Boris nodded and stepped back, and Kratos, and Idir walked back to the benches with him. As they did, solemn music started playing, and everyone stood up and bowed their heads in respect.

A peculiar sensation swept past my mind, and I attempted to push it away. Yet it persisted, probing deeper into my head, as if searching for something. This bizarre energy it generated felt unnatural, and I desperately wanted to stop it. But it continued, leaving me no choice but to wait for the sensation to dissipate.

Amy shook my shoulders vigorously. "Wake up, wake up."

Blinking open my eyes, I sat up. Black dust fell from my clothes, and I found Amy looking at me with concern. "What happened?" I asked.

Amy asked, "Did you have a bad vision?"

I shook my head. "No, not at all!"

"Oh," Amy said, a hint of relief in her voice, "Did I wake you up in the middle? You were... shaking."

I reassured her, "No, you didn't disturb it. I saw the vision. You were right. It was... a memory I will always remember."

Amy's eyes widened, curious. "Yes, I saw a smile on your face, but then, in the end, something changed. What happened?"

I hesitated, trying to find the words. "Something happened after the vision was over. I don't know what, but there was a... like a presence inside my head. I could feel it... doing something. I tried to push it away, but it wouldn't leave me. It's good that you woke me up."

Amy looked puzzled. "Oh, that's very strange. Have you felt that before?"

I shook my head. "No. It was really weird. Maybe like when Alia was testing me."

A few people nearby were still sleeping. As I spoke to Amy, they raised their heads and shot angry looks in our direction. I quieted down and whispered, recounting the vision in detail. It was a happy memory for her, even though she couldn't see it for herself. I tried to repeat precisely what Alev, Kratos, Idir, and Boris said so she could remember all the details. She looked happier listening to it.

Amy smiled warmly. "They are too generous."

I grinned and replied, "Well, it's true what they said."

Amy's smile broadened. Then I told her what Boris said in the end.

Upon hearing this, Amy was shocked. She jumped up and exclaimed, "What??? No more stones?"

"No more stones?" A voice asked from nearby.

With a gleeful bounce in her step, Amy responded to the voice, "NO MORE STONES."

"No more stones? What?" More voices joined in as more and more people started getting up from their sleep. As they rose, they shook their clothes, and Black Dust spread everywhere. The light particles stayed floating in the air, making everyone look like they were surrounded by a black cloud. Many people ran toward Amy and bombarded her with questions: "What are you saying?", "How do you know?", "No more stones? Are you sure?"

Amy pointed to me, beaming. "He did it. He stopped the stones."

Two rather intimidating men approached me. "No more stones?"

I glanced at Amy for help. She just smiled back. Everyone around me had a peculiar smile on their faces. It seemed like they had forgotten how to smile, but they couldn't contain the happiness inside them. Their faces appeared healthier and less droopy.

Amy patted my shoulder, her eyes gleaming. "You have no idea what you've done for these people. The garbage and stones from Serenus were a major problem, plaguing them for as long as they can remember. The stones we threw from Serenus landed on their heads. As the stones began to fall, everyone would take shelter and hide away in the Keep or behind a wall. You have given them hope. Just look at their faces."

I didn't fully comprehend what I had done for them, but their expressions spoke volumes. They were no longer indifferent like the day before. Instead, they stood in a group, jumping, clapping, and even dancing.

"No more stones. No more stones." People started chanting as a few picked me up on their shoulders.

I nearly tumbled off. Amy trailed behind us, laughing at the unexpected shift in the atmosphere. Together, we walked back to the Keep, continuing the chant, "No more stones. No more stones."

As we passed the guard's checkpoint, the guards inquired, "No more stones?" The crowd responded with a resounding, "NO MORE STONES." The guards, jubilant, joined the throng. Upon reaching the Keep, the news spread like wildfire. Everyone gathered around us. Those who hadn't even looked up the day before were now beaming. All their troubles seemed to have receded to the back of their minds.

"HE IS THE ONE!" A loud cry erupted from one side. Then another, "He is the one!" Many joined in the chant, "He is the one. He is the one." Amy stood in front of me as guards approached and ordered her to step away. Uncertain of their intentions, she glanced back at me and then questioned them. They moved her aside and positioned themselves beside me, separating me from the crowd.

"Amy!" I called out, "Stop it, let her come."

The guards glanced at me, then searched for Amy and gestured for her to approach. This time, they allowed her to remain by my side. The crowd's noise level intensified. Someone found pots and pans and used them to play music reminiscent of what we'd heard in Serenus. Amy looked at me with astonishment, and I returned her look. What had just happened? Things had transpired so swiftly that I could scarcely believe what I was witnessing. The people were still dirty, their clothes saturated with Black Dust, but their eyes sparkled, and their faces were learning to smile again. It felt too easy. From the suffocating atmosphere of the previous night, the faces that had forgotten to smile were now illuminated. It felt surreal.

"He is the one! He is the one!" The chanting persisted. I didn't know what they meant by it, but the guards made certain that no one was allowed near me any longer. They pushed the people away, who cooperated and stepped back without protest.

More guards materialized and encircled Amy and me. They guided us away from the Keep and the crowd. From every direction, people emerged, each vying for a glimpse of the unfolding scene. The chanting, the crowd, the guards, and the transformed ambiance... it was astonishing.

Amy and I were undeniably anxious. We didn't know what they meant by "he is the one," nor did we know what they intended to do next. The guards appeared to be shielding us from the crowd, who, in turn, made no attempt to break their formation. This eased our nerves slightly.

When enough guards arrived to form a protective circle around us, the people sat down, creating a bigger circle around the guards. No matter which way I looked, I saw people sitting quietly, their eyes fixed on me. I didn't know what they expected or what would happen next.

Amy whispered, "I see hope in their eyes."

I responded, "Yes, but what does it mean? What's happening?"

Amy hesitated before replying, "I have no idea, but it doesn't look bad. I think they consider you to be... their saviour."

"Saviour?" I exclaimed. "Me? I know nothing about them."

"Still," Amy explained, "you solved a problem they've faced forever. I'm pretty sure they think of you as a special person who will rid them of their troubles. Just look at how they're looking at you."

A Black Dust storm arose from one side, in the distance. Within the dust cloud, I saw fire flying toward us. Amy said, "It's the Fire-horses. These creatures have fire in their bellies. They have no flesh; they're only made of bones. These creatures are used for riding and aren't dangerous, but I worry that the men riding them could be the king's men."

The crowd grew quiet and anxious. Amy was right. The riders on the Firehorses were the king's men. They demanded to know the reason for the commotion.

The guards told them, "No more stones."

The riders scanned the sky all around them, then asked the guards, "What?"

The guards repeated, "No more stones. The one has arrived." Then they pointed to me.

The riders grew visibly upset at this. One of them yelled, "There's only one saviour, and he is Shikongo, the king. Who is this pretender?"

The crowd rose to their feet and became agitated. They started chanting, "Wizard king, wizard king, wizard king."

The guards couldn't allow the chanting to continue. They threatened the people, but the crowd didn't stop. The guards and riders were vastly outnumbered, and the crowd seemed to swell even larger.

Before things spiraled out of control, the guards and riders decided it was best to retreat. They headed toward the castle as people came close and hoisted me back up on their shoulders. A few others lifted Amy, and they carried both of us back to the Keep.

Once inside the Keep, the doors were locked and braced. As Amy and I were taken to a platform above them, the people sat on the ground. A few of them stood near us as guards, and all eyes looked up at me with a mixture of desperation and hope. What were they expecting from me? I knew far too little about this world to even address them.

Amy understood my predicament and spoke to them, "He needs time. Go on about your lives today. We will gather again tomorrow."

I glanced at Amy in surprise. What was I going to tell them tomorrow? She signalled for me to stay quiet, but the crowd was unhappy with her announcement.

"The king's men will be here soon. We need to be ready," one person said.

Another stood up and yelled, "With the one on our side, the wizard king can't defeat us."

The crowd's energy began to build again. I didn't know what they were thinking of me. The king had the magic of the lost scroll. I had merely experienced a... lucky break.

Amy interjected, "Send a group of elders and we will talk in private. He will announce the next step after discussing it with the elders."

Voices from the crowd asked, "What elders? We don't have elders." They were clearly unhappy with Amy's suggestions. I could feel their frustration growing, so I decided to address them directly. As they sensed my willingness to speak, the crowd fell silent, all eyes on me.

"Listen, everyone!" I began, "I just arrived here a day ago. I'm new to this world and still learning about it. I need time to understand. Please help me. Send some wise men and women who can introduce me to the realities of this dark land."

The people exchanged whispers, and after some discussion, they selected two men and a woman to introduce me to their world.

Ch 26: The Burden of Leadership

The first man, wearing a long white shirt, stepped forward and introduced himself. "I am Shahzor, the Stable Master and Keeper of Firehorses. I've been here for a long time and know this world better than any other. I am even allowed inside the castle to train the king's riders." Shahzor had black hair and brown eyes, and his imposing stature reminded me of Kratos.

The second man approached, his attire unusually fancy with many pockets. "Kallar, The Sneaker, at your service. I can infiltrate places without being seen. I know the secrets people hide, and I understand the hearts of men and women."

Next, an older lady with a kind face and blonde hair introduced herself. "My name is Ariana. People confide in me and share their stories. I listen and offer advice."

And so, with this council assembled, our first meeting began.

"Ariana," I inquired, "what do the people expect of me?"

"People have been waiting for 'the one,'" she replied. "They believe they've found that person in you. They think you will solve all their problems."

"All their problems?" I gulped nervously.

Kallar interrupted, "Are you truly the one? What powers do you possess?"

I hesitated, unsure if I should tell them about my ability to know when I was wrong. Instead, I said, "I don't know if I have the power to solve your problems, but if we unite, we can overcome any challenge."

Shahzor nodded in agreement. "Indeed, you've already resolved a long-standing issue in our world. No more stones and garbage from our past means we can clean up this world, and we no longer need to hide under walls twice a day. How did you accomplish this? How did you know what to do?"

Once again, I spoke the hard truth. "It was luck. I discovered an interpretation of the poem and left it for my friends in Serenus. They accepted my interpretation, and stopped throwing stones."

Ariana smiled warmly. "Your people accepted your interpretation and acted on it. Your people trusted you. This means we can trust you."

"But what do you need me to do for you? What other problems do you have?" I inquired.

Kallar replied, "Fulfill the prophecy. Open the door to happiness and lead us out of this living nightmare."

"What is the prophecy?" I asked.

Kallar explained, "The prophecy tells of a chosen one who will come to save us all. If you're that person, you can pass through the door. Let's go and open it."

Ariana, noticing the confusion on my face, elaborated, "There's a door that no one can go through. In Serenus, when you went to the edge of the island, there was a dark veil. In this world, there is a door. Water falls off the edge into unseen depths below. We can't leave the island by water. Just before the cascading water, there are steps that ascend above it, and at the top of the steps lies the door. This door is our escape from this wretched place. Everyone who has tried to go through it has been thrown back by an invisible force. We call it the door to happiness. We believe that once we can enter the door, our troubles will end, but we've been waiting for the one who can go through."

Shahzor chimed in, "It's either the door to happiness or the door of misery. As long as the door remains closed, people believe they can't be happy, so they aren't. If the door opens, even if it doesn't lead us to another island, at least we'll know we aren't meant to wait for it. If you are the chosen one, you can pass through the door."

Amy concluded, "So we just need to try the door. If he can pass through... what if only he can pass through?"

Kallar countered, "No, the prophecy states that the chosen one will open the door for all of us. If he can pass through, we all can."

I stood up, determined. "Let's go to the door, then."

Ariana grasped my hand and gently pulled me back down. "Think before you act. Sit down."

Surprised by her insistence, I sat down and listened.

Kallar cautioned, "If you can't go through the door, hope will wither once more."

Shahzor added, "Look at the faces of the people. I've never seen them so optimistic. If you can't open the door to happiness, what will become of them? Let them savour this happiness for a while. There's no need to rush."

I nodded, understanding their concerns.

Ariana wondered, "But how do we tell the people that he won't try the door?"

Shahzor proposed, "We have to stall. Distract them."

Amy disagreed, "I don't like that. We can tell them the truth."

Kallar addressed me, "Your friend is naive. We must consider the greater good. The truth won't work here. People have awaited the door's opening for generations. They don't want to wait any longer."

I challenged Kallar, "Why can you wait longer?"

Kallar smiled, "Because I don't think the prophecy is true. I believe it's just a story. You stopped the stones, but that doesn't mean you'll solve all our problems."

Shahzor nodded thoughtfully. "I don't believe the prophecy is true either. What we have here is a unique opportunity. Your position of power, stemming from people's perceptions of you, offers the chance to unite them. Having solved two of their problems, you can bring them together to tackle even more challenges. We've been waiting for someone who can truly lead the people. Shikongo wields magic but has no interest in the Keepers. You, however, could guide the Keepers. With us as your council, you'd be able to accomplish what no one else could—lead the people. You've instilled hope in them, so don't attempt to open the door. If you fail, their hope will wither, and you'll lose your influence."

Amy glanced at me and shook her head. "No, this isn't right."

I recalled Ma's words: "Steady improvement is better than drastic action." Had she been preparing me for leadership? Did she foresee my role in guiding these people? Was it my destiny? Ma had never mentioned a door; she'd said I was meant to change the system in this world, not to find a way out. If I could lead

these people, inspire them to improve their world, we could establish rules and restore civilization. In doing so, I could rebuild
Serenus. But why did Amy object to the idea? I needed to understand her perspective.

"Amy, what's bothering you?" I asked as Kallar, Shahzor, and
Ariana stared at her.

Amy hesitated for a moment, then responded, "What this council
is essentially suggesting is to avoid trying the door because it might
not open, and should it remain closed, you'll lose your power
over the people. I believe that's wrong. People will value honesty.
You can attempt to open the door after informing them that the
prophecy's validity is uncertain. Tell them you think we can transform this world into Serenus rather than fleeing it. And let them
know that even if the door doesn't open, hope isn't lost."

I turned to the council. Kallar vehemently shook his head,
Shahzor remained silent, and Ariana appeared lost in thought.

Shahzor spoke up, "What your friend says seems reasonable, but
it won't work. Doing what feels right isn't always the best course
of action."

Ariana added, "Your friend has a valid point. Her words make
sense. However, the people here are desperate for a swift escape
from this world. If you ask them to mend their surroundings,
they'll lose interest. Many have tried and failed in the past. Why
haven't they acted to improve their conditions? Because they
don't believe they're meant to be here. They've always looked to

the door to happiness as their escape from this hellish existence. Sometimes, doing the right thing isn't the right thing to do."

I looked back at Amy, who remained unconvinced.

Kallar interjected, "Your friend isn't the one who needs to make this decision. It's up to you. She hasn't lived here long enough to understand. I've never seen her before. I know the people, as do Shahzor and Ariana. Make the right choice. Don't just follow what feels morally correct; do what will work. Pursue the greater good."

I felt torn. I appreciated Amy's perspective, but I couldn't disregard the council's advice. They knew the people and their circumstances. Listening to them seemed wise, but it also meant leading with a lie.

Kallar's agitation at my indecision was evident. "To lead people, you must make difficult choices. You have to do what's uncomfortable, and in return, you'll gain power over them. It's not all about tough decisions; you'll also earn their respect. You'll sleep in the cleanest place we can find and enjoy the finest food. We'll ensure your comfort. Be pragmatic and seize this opportunity. Do good for the people and enjoy the benefits that come with power. We know this world; we've suffered here. Keep us as your council, and we'll guide you every step of the way. We'll make most of the challenging decisions for you. You can reap the rewards, while we'll think and execute your commands. Consider it. Look around. This is hell, and you have the chance to live like a king."

Kallar made my decision easier. I knew exactly what I needed to do—not live like a king. But Shahzor couldn't stay silent. "You don't have to live like the king. You can be kind to the people and genuinely improve their lives. Morality holds little value in this world, and it means even less to Kallar. Don't do it for the benefits of clean living or better food; do it for the peace of mind that comes from knowing you've made a difference in countless lives."

Ariana nodded in agreement. "Kallar is a sly one. Don't do it for his reasons; do it for the greater good."

Their words made it seem like I had a clear path, but in reality, I didn't understand what they meant. "What exactly would I do for the greater good? If I announce that I won't try the door, won't they simply stop believing in me? How can I lead them then?"

Shahzor replied, "We can think of something. We can tell them... how about we say you had a vision? We can present something that convinces them attempting the door isn't the right path—a magical reason that will impress them."

Ariana chimed in, "A vision is a good idea. People often have visions on their first night. We could claim you had a vision that revealed the course of action. You could say the door will open eventually, but we have to accomplish something first. This way, you can motivate them to improve their lives."

"So, you mean herd them like sheep?" I asked.

Amy responded, "That's not you. They may know the people,

but I know you. You can't do that. Just be yourself. You're the one who stopped the stones and garbage, not them. Don't listen to them. Trust yourself."

"Just listen to myself?" I echoed, recalling Ma's words. She had advised me to be myself but had also warned against drastic actions. How could I know which guidance to follow in this situation?

Below us, the people grew restless. More and more of them stood up, casting questioning glances our way.

Shahzor concluded, "You've consulted your council and heard your friend's advice. The people won't wait much longer. It's time to make a decision."

Kallar and Ariana nodded in agreement, and the three of them left the platform, leaving Amy and me alone. I still didn't know what to do. Amy took my hand, "Just be yourself."

As the people noticed the council meeting had concluded, they grew even more restless. Their whispers intensified, turning impatient. I walked to the edge of the platform and gazed at the crowd below. They raised their faces to look at me, and I felt like I was their provider, with them as the needy. They wanted something from me, and I had to decide what to give them: a lie that could improve their lives or a truth that could shatter their hope. No, there was a third option; I could trust that they, too, were capable of understanding and reasoning. I would tell them the truth but in a way that would maintain my power to improve their lives. But how could I do that?

As I remained silent for a few moments longer, many eyes began to turn away from me, and they looked at each other disappointedly. Shahzor signalled for me to say something.

"People..." Once again, dead silence enveloped the area as I spoke, causing my confidence to waver slightly. "People, I am not superior to you. I am not more than you are. I tried something that made sense in Serenus, and it worked out. Your wise elders have informed me of a prophecy. I don't know its origin, whether it's a fabrication or the truth. However, I do know that if we try, we might succeed. I know that if we keep our hopes alive, there's a chance. I know this world is filled with suffering, but the actions of my friends in Serenus have just eliminated two of our biggest problems. Those issues were impossible to solve by the ones who had already arrived here, but those are resolved now. What we have before us is a world that we can mend."

As the crowd began shaking their heads, Shahzor, Ariana, and Kallar lowered theirs in disappointment. I could feel my power fading, my authority and influence over the people evaporating. I could see it in their expressions and in their eyes. Their faces transformed, and instead of looking at me with admiration, their eyes turned angry. Fear crept in, and I suddenly felt that Amy and I were vulnerable. Desperate to regain my power, I continued, "People, it is what it is. You can either run from it or do something about it. I can try to open the door, but I don't believe that just because I played a part in solving two of your problems, I'll be the one to solve all of them. However, I do believe that together, we can. I'll attempt the door, but if I can't go through, should we abandon all hope? What problem is so big that we can't solve it if we work together? We can do it."

"Does he want to be our king?" someone asked from the crowd.

"Are you the one or not?" Another person yelled, followed by a hissing sound.

Many others joined in the hissing. I remembered Ma's words:

Hiss at the hunters.

In an instant, they had transformed me from a saviour into a hunter preying on them? A felt a chill enter my body.

"Let's carry him to the door, I say!" someone else shouted. I noticed Kallar sneaking away from the crowd. Shahzor and Ariana stood up and tried to pacify the people. "Listen to him. He knows better." The crowd hissed at them. Some began moving toward the platform, yelling, "We'll throw him through the door if he doesn't go right away!"

Ariana attempted again, "He had a... vision... listen to him."

The people stopped and looked at her. "Vision? What vision?" Many asked simultaneously. "What did he see?"

The hissing ceased, and Ariana walked to the front of the crowd. "He had a vision last night. He is the one, but to open the door, he must first complete a mission, a challenge. The door will open, and he will be the one to open it, but it's not as simple as walking through it. Ma hasn't been kind to us. We need to follow him, listen to what he says. Do that, and the door will open. That... is the vision."

People glanced around, unsure of what to do. Then, one of them asked, "But the prophecy said the one who stops the stones and sticks will be the one allowed through the door to open it for all to follow."

Many heads in the crowd nodded in agreement, murmuring, "Yes, that's the prophecy."

Ariana appeared troubled, but she maintained her composure and tried again. "For all to follow. It's the way the gods phrase things that confuses us. The prophecy means we have to follow him, and then the door will open. Think about it. Do you know better? He's already stopped the stones and sticks. He knows what he's doing. If you knew better, why haven't you opened the door yet? Follow him, and the door will open."

The crowd seemed uncertain and undoubtedly disappointed. They had hoped their suffering would end, but the news that they had to do more was not what they wanted to hear.

"Let's try the door. Maybe it will open," an older woman from the crowd suggested.

"Yes, let's try the door first," someone else chimed in.

More and more people joined the chorus, "Yes, let's try the door first."

I had no issue with trying the door, but I understood my council's concerns. If I was unable to go through the door, the prophecy would be invalidated, and the people would lose faith in me.

Shahzor joined Ariana and spoke forcefully, "Have you gone completely mad? We've found this opportunity, and you want to ruin it because you can't wait a little longer? Haven't you waited lifetimes here? Can't you be patient and do the right thing? Follow him! He will open the door. Don't force his hand, or the prophecy will be broken by you, not by him. Is that what you want? He will go through the door when the time is right. If you don't follow his word and force him, the door may never open. Think... you've suffered enough. Don't destroy an opportunity that has already come too late. Can you wait for another? Who else will fulfill the prophecy if the stones and sticks are already stopped? There is no second chance. This is it. Be wise. Be patient. Don't ruin a good thing like we've ruined so many good things before."

Shahzor's stern words had a profound effect on the crowd. They fell silent, uncertainty and fear evident in their eyes. My heart ached for them; they had endured so much and had been waiting for salvation for so long. Now they were being fed a lie. There was no vision, no way of knowing if the door would open even if they followed my instructions. Was I meant to stall them until we repaired this broken world and eliminated the need to seek refuge beyond the door? But what if the door truly opened for me? What if the prophecy was real, and we could bypass the arduous task of fixing our world? What if stepping through the door would create a path for others to follow, leading us to a heavenly paradise? Was it right to deny them this possibility?

I decided I would attempt to open the door in secret, to see if a miraculous escape from our hellish existence was indeed possible. As I pondered my thoughts, a woman in the crowd began to cry. Soon, her tears were joined by others, an outpouring of sadness and desperation. I was taken aback by the intensity of their desire to leave this place.

Amy came to stand beside me and whispered, "It is what it is. We're lying to them, but at least you tried. What can we do if they're not ready for the truth?"

"How long will it take, according to the vision?" A tearful man's question caught me off guard.

I hadn't lied to them yet, but by answering this question, I would be. Should I reveal there was no vision? Doing so would endanger Ariana and Shahzor and might lead the people to force me through the door. If I failed, our chance to unite them could be lost forever. The prophecy had already been partially fulfilled; no one else could take my place. But should I perpetuate the lie? What could I say? I had no idea.

Amy resolved my dilemma by saying, "Patience, my friend. It is what it is."

"It is what it is," the people repeated through their sobs.

From my vantage point on the platform, the weeping crowd appeared vulnerable and powerless. They were being deceived and manipulated, and I hoped it was the right thing to do. Shahzor, Ariana, and Kallar joined me on the platform. I glanced at Kallar, raising my eyebrows, and he offered a sly smile. It seemed he, too, had rejoined the council. By embracing the lie, I had gained control over the people, but my council now held power over me. They could expose me at any moment. At least Amy, with her worried expression, was a true friend.

"What do we do now?" A man asked, his eyes searching for answers.

My knees felt weak. There was no time for planning or meetings; I had to reveal what the vision required us to do to open the door.

Shahzor stepped up, "We need to form a civilized society. We need to establish rules."

"What for? We're not living here forever," another person shouted, wiping away tears.

Kallar chimed in, "We need a well-functioning system. An efficient one. The task ahead is substantial, but it's not insurmountable. We can achieve this with the right rules and discipline in place."

Ariana continued, "We will create laws that treat everyone fairly, ensuring that all have access to the basic necessities of life, just like in Serenus. Everyone will contribute, and all will benefit from this system. Give us a day to draft the laws. Life will improve now. The one who will open the door to happiness is here; even before that door opens, he will bring joy to this world. You can have hope and safety now. Your lives will improve even before the door is opened."

Ariana's words instilled hope in the crowd. Their expressions brightened, and I could sense hope all around.

"Why doesn't he speak?" Someone from the crowd yelled.

"What's his name?" Another asked.

"Yeah, what do we call him?" A third voice inquired.

Kallar, Shahzor, and Ariana looked at me as Amy said, "He has no name. Call him what he is - a friend. A friend to all."

"Thank you, friend!" One man said, followed by another, then another. Many pledged their loyalty, promising to stand by me until the end. Some simply nodded, accepting me as their leader.

I felt thirsty and suffocated. I whispered to Amy, "I am so thirsty. Where can I get some water?"

Amy addressed the crowd, "We will gather again tomorrow." She gestured for me to follow her as she walked away.

Behind me, I heard Shahzor address the crowd, "Celebrate the arrival of the one who will open the door to happiness. Be happy, dance, and celebrate today. Tomorrow we will start the work."

Amy and I returned to the three falls. We drank water and shared a piece of bread that she had hidden in her dress. As we ate, we tried to come to terms with the immense responsibility now resting on our shoulders.

"I woke up today as a nobody with no responsibility, and now I have to lead them to happiness? I am not ready for it, but I am so happy that you are with me," I confessed, and Amy nodded in agreement.

Amy replied, "Maybe it's for the best. If we can get them to focus on improving their lives in this world, we are doing something truly great here... I don't like being part of a lie, and it will weigh on our hearts, but perhaps it's the sacrifice we have to make."

We lingered near the falls, wishing to stay longer, but people began to gather around us. They pointed and whispered amongst themselves.

I shared Ma's words with Amy, explaining how Ma had known I would be in a position to change this world. She had prepared me for this. I was destined for it. Amy was pleased to hear it, and in my heart, I felt this was the role I was meant to play – to lead the people back to Serenus. After resting a little longer, we headed back to the Keep.

Shahzor greeted us outside the Keep and said, "Let's go to the stables. There's no comfortable place to sit here. I've invited Kallar and Ariana to join us there."

Amy and I followed him, observing numerous people sitting on the ground. They seemed somewhat happier, but I couldn't understand why they weren't taking any initiative. Why were they just waiting for things to be fixed? It made no sense to me, so I asked Shahzor.

He smiled and replied, "You're new here. When you've lived a meaningless life countless times, things lose their meaning. Sitting in a chair or on the ground feels the same. Why should they get up and do something when there's no hope? No one wants to live here. They want to escape, and they're waiting for the path ahead to open."

I was baffled by his response. They were living here regardless, so why not make it better? I couldn't grasp their reasoning.

Upon reaching the 'Go Like Thunder Stables,' Shahzor proudly pointed to his Firehorses. "I have many Firehorses. You're welcome to stay here and enjoy the ride." Then he glanced at Amy and smiled, "You too, my friend."

Shahzor seemed like a level-headed man. "How do you manage to stay sane in this world?" I inquired.

"Because I'm passionate about Firehorses. They keep me busy. I don't care when the door opens. I have my own mission. These Firehorses are extraordinary creatures. It's said that they can travel as fast as lightning. I'm searching for a horse capable of that. This pursuit keeps me occupied, and my hobby keeps me sane. The king knows of my passion and calls me to train his riders. I'm living in hell, but, honestly, it doesn't feel like hell to me."

A hobby kept him sane. Perhaps if I could find hobbies for every-one else, they would also become more invested in life. I sudden-ly remembered Kratos and how he had sent Idir to persuade me to adopt a pet. Now I understood that he was trying to help me find something to connect with that world, rather than talking to Qilam and wondering about the next.

Shahzor opened the door to a stone building and gestured for us to enter. Now, we needed to wait for Kallar and Ariana. We sat, gazing at the Firehorses through the window. Shahzor began explaining their various characteristics. "They're loyal creatures. Once they bond with you, they'll give their lives to save yours," he said.

Amy stood and approached the window. "Can they fly?"

"Yes, they can fly," Shahzor confirmed.

"Faster than an arrow?" Amy asked.

Shahzor looked at her with concern. "What are you thinking?"

Amy smiled and shook her head.

Shahzor walked to the window and stood beside her. "They can fly faster than any arrow, but the king also has Firehorses." He gave Amy a meaningful glance, and she lowered her eyes.

"I told you I could help you find Alfred. When I visit the castle next time, I'll try to locate him. I have friends there, so I can... he'll know you're here, although I don't know if he can come to see you. Wait for the king to invite me. Until then, don't do anything you'll regret."

I wasn't sure what laws we would create during this meeting, and I felt unprepared. I had lived in Serenus and knew its laws; perhaps we could implement similar ones here? I needed time to not-think. "Can I have some time alone until they arrive?" I asked Shahzor.

Shahzor nodded, leading me to an adjacent room before returning to speak with Amy. I sat down, attempting to clear my mind. It took a few moments to push away all the thoughts. Once I felt lighter and my mind was empty, I waited for any notifications to surface. Amy's words echoed in my head: Faster than an arrow flies? Why did Amy ask that? Was she planning something? I made a mental note to consider this later and cleared my mind again. Kallar had left when the crowd wasn't listening to us, only to return once Shahzor and Ariana had regained control. I realized I couldn't rely on Kallar during difficult times, but I could trust Shahzor and Ariana to act in the people's best interest. Satisfied with this conclusion, I waited for any other insights to arise. Nothing came, so I focused on my breathing and listened to the sound of each breath, feeling a bit sleepy. I hadn't slept well the previous night. Who could have thought that on my first night in Forsaken Serenus, I'd be sleeping exactly where my home used to be in Serenus?

When no other thoughts surfaced, my mind wandered back to Serenus. I indulged in these happy memories, recalling the forge and the sound of the hammer striking metal. It felt like a reward from my mind. I remained lost in these beautiful memories until I heard a commotion in the adjacent room. Someone was arguing with Shahzor. I quickly rose up to see what was happening.

Four men clad in shiny armour barged into the room, looking out of place. Shahzor pleaded, "What do you want? Tell me!"

One of them looked at me and said, "By the king's order, you must come with us."

Shahzor tried to argue, but the other guards pushed him aside. Amy hissed, "Why? What does the king want?"

The commander shoved her away, gripping my arm and dragging me out of the room as two guards restrained Amy. Outside, a crowd of angry people rushed toward the stables, hissing and yelling at the guards, "Wizard king, wizard king!" as if it were a curse.

The commander mounted his Firehorse, and we took off before the crowd could reach us. The other guards followed, and the people ran below us. The commander didn't fly too fast, ensuring the crowd could keep up. Why? What were they planning?

After some time, we arrived at the island's edge. There was no dark veil like in Serenus, only an endless drop beyond the land. Water cascaded into the unseen depths below. A single door stood atop a set of stairs above the water. The guards landed near the door, waiting for the people to gather below. I spotted Amy and Shahzor among the crowd.

As the gathering crowd grew, the commander proclaimed, "Be aware, all of you, there is only one rightful ruler in these lands. He has discovered the lost scroll and holds the power to unlock the gateway to the next world. Your so-called leader is nothing but a fraud, a pretender, and I will demonstrate this truth to you now, in this very moment."

He shoved me toward the door, saying, "Go on, go through the door."

I hesitated to try the door. One of the guards opened it, and with a creak, it revealed nothing but endless darkness on the other side. The guards dragged me to the door and pushed me in. I vanished into the void, feeling as if I were floating. I looked all around to find something, but all I could see was an impenetrable darkness. I couldn't see a single thing. Suddenly, something grabbed me, lifted me up, and hurled me back through the door. I landed at a guard's feet.

The crowd gasped. I rose slowly as the guards flew away. The hopeful glimmer in the people's eyes vanished.

"Pretender!" someone yelled.

Another hissed, and more joined in, chanting, "Pretender! Pretender!"

I descended the steps, not daring to meet anyone's gaze. My eyes remained on the ground as the furious chanting continued: "Pretender! Pretender!"

As I passed by, people hissed and shouted, "Pretender!" Amy joined me, and we left the chanting crowd behind. Some of them now sat on the ground, their hope stolen by the king. They were angry and hurt, but their spirits were so broken that they didn't resort to violence. We continued walking, wanting to be anywhere but near these disheartened people.

Word spread quickly that I was a pretender and a liar. Amy and I could no longer visit the Keep; we didn't know what they would do to us if they saw us there again. There was only one place where we might find some semblance of safety – the vast, open world roaming like the Miserables. We snuck past the checkpost and ventured into the land of the Miserables.

Ch 27: Miserables Ahead

Why did Ma do this to me? I thought I had found my path. I thought I knew what I was supposed to do. Did I fail in leading the people? Did this happen because I stood with a lie? All these thoughts kept me busy for the evening. What happened was so... stunning. The people saw me as their saviour. I thought I did nothing wrong... I wanted to help them, but now they saw me as a liar who could never be trusted again. If I could explain it to them... but how would I even gather all of them in one place? I had lost all power. It is what it is. This was the only conclusion I could reach. What next? What now?

Even Amy couldn't go to the Keep anymore. She was badly disheartened. She had hoped to find Alfred with help from Shahzor.

Now that felt unlikely. This world was taking everything away from us.

We roamed the black, dry, deserted land for the rest of the evening until we reached the baker's home. The baker was a kind-hearted Keeper. He didn't care who he was feeding; his goal was to help, not to judge. He brought enough rations from the Keep to provide for any Miserables who showed up at his home, some of whom were his permanent guests. He wouldn't allow anyone inside his home, but he was okay with the Miserables sitting outside. The Miserables, too, respected the baker and never gave him any trouble.

Amy and I stayed outside his home for the night. He gave us water and bread. We thanked him and sat away from his home. It was very quiet. There wasn't even the sound of a cricket. The wind moved the dry Black Dust around, and that made some sound, but other than that, it was complete silence. We had nothing to say, but our heads were full of thoughts. We stayed quiet and just sat in the barren, cold world. When we got tired of sitting, we lay down, looking at the beautiful sky above us. It was one thing that was out of our reach. No wizard could destroy the stars, or they would have done that.

"Amy!" I called out.

"Ya?" she replied.

"We will find a way to reach Alfred. Don't worry," I reassured her.

"Yeah," she responded, but I had nothing else to say, and she clearly wasn't in the mood to talk, so I stayed quiet.

In a little bit, she laughed and said, "You are the luckiest unlucky person I have ever met."

I laughed, "And what about you?"

Amy laughed again and said, "I think we are in the right place now. Miserables. That's who we are."

"Miserable, Amy," I quipped.

Amy chuckled, "Miserable... for light's sake, pick a name."

I sat up and told her about the conversation with the guards. They named me N53. "N53 is as good a name as any."

Amy laughed again, "Not really! I am not calling you that."

We stayed quiet for a bit, then Amy said, "Fifty-three, I can get used to that."

I smiled, "Miserable Fifty-three it is, then."

Amy began, "Once upon a time, Miserable Amy and Miserable Fifty-three were sitting in a miserable world...."

"They were really miserable," Fifty-three added.

We laughed again.

Amy said, "Imagine if Fabio and Misa were here. Of course, we don't want them here, but if they were... they were fun."

Fifty-three replied, "Yeah. I miss them a lot."

Amy continued, "Did you know Alfred is a lot of fun too? He used to be. I don't know what this world has done to him."

"I know," Fifty-three said.

"You know?" Amy asked.

"Yes, Fabio and Misa told me. They said you were a lot of fun too."

"Yeah, good old times," Amy sighed.

"You changed so much when Alfred left?" Fifty-three inquired.

Amy's voice trembled as she said, "I... I never felt like... no one really knew me like Alfred did. We were always together, and when he left, I was in shock. I... I felt like I couldn't have a friend again. I didn't feel I could fit in."

"A lot of people cared for you," Fifty-three reassured her.

"Yes, I know. I think when you have such a good friend for a long time, and then you lose them, it feels like no one else can fill that gap," Amy explained.

"Yes, I understand," Fifty-three said.

"It's not that I didn't appreciate all my friends in Serenus. I did. I... let him down by not going with him," Amy admitted.

"But he didn't want you to go with him," Fifty-three reminded her.

"Yes, because he thought I didn't believe in what he believed in. Maybe I should have believed in... whatever he believed in," Amy said, trailing off.

"That's not..." Fifty-three started.

"I know... Well, I am very lucky I met you," Amy smiled.

"Yes, that we can agree on," Fifty-three said.

Amy laughed, "When you came to Serenus, and you asked me those questions about where we came from, I felt like I was talking to a younger version of Alfred. I got upset at your questions that day. Did you notice?"

"Yes, but I felt care. When I talked to Qilam, and then you came to warn me that Qilam was not... I knew that you cared," Fifty-three said.

"Yeah, about that. There is something I need to tell you," Amy said hesitantly.

"Me too, but you go first," Fifty-three replied.

"Okay, so Ma told me," Amy began.

"That Qilam was not lying," Fifty-three finished her sentence.

"Yes, she told you too?" Amy asked.

"Yes," Fifty-three confirmed.

"Can you believe it? That's so strange," Amy said, bewildered.

"Actually, I can. I felt like the entire village had one impression of Qilam, and I had a different one. Of course, I thought he was making up stuff or was crazy that he heard these voices in his head, but..." Fifty-three trailed off.

"You thought he wasn't bad. That he meant well," Amy concluded.

"Yes," Fifty-three agreed.

"I see that now," Amy said, nodding.

Fifty-three asked, "Did Ma also tell you what convinced him to go into the dark?"

Amy replied, "Yes, how crazy is that? You thought he was the wizard, remember? You asked me when I came to warn you about him. And he thought you were the wizard."

Miserable Amy laughed, and Miserable Fifty-three laughed with her. I looked up and saw Ma smiling above Amy.

I questioned, "Wait... how did that happen? How am I back with you? What's going on?"

Ma asked, "What does it feel like?"

I answered, "It... it feels like Fifty-three is separate from me. It feels like I am here with you, and Fifty-three is there with Amy. But I was... I was just there, and now suddenly, I am here with you. What happened?"

Ma explained, "You will live with me now, and Fifty-three will live in that world. I have created a copy. Your copy was sent to that world. You have been experiencing everything that your copy experienced. You saw through his eyes. You read his thoughts. You were him, except you were not. Now he will do what he will do. He has the freedom of choice. You can observe him, and you can feel for him, but you will stay with me."

Fifty-three spoke, "Did you ever think that maybe there really is no wizard? I mean, we thought Esmeray was the wizard because she was the enemy. Then we thought the new wizard was the wizard as he, too, had magic and wanted to attack us. What if there is no wizard?"

Amy replied, "I think there is a wizard, or the poem wouldn't say catch the wizard, but yes, maybe we never knew who it was."

Fifty-three agreed, "Yes, Miserable Amy, you could be right."

Amy laughed, "Thanks, Miserable Fifty-three!"

Fifty-three said, "You know, it's not too bad here. Not when we are together."

Amy added, "I was just about to say it. Hell doesn't feel like hell when you are with a friend."

Amy and Fifty-three talked for a while before they fell asleep. I explored my new reality and talked to Ma.

What was that about?

Ma responded, "I know what you are talking about. That was a good attempt on your part to bring the people together, but too bad it didn't work."

The king is... he is...

Ma completed my sentence, "Cunning."

And he has the lost scroll?

"Yes."

He has it, really?

"Yes, he has it."

It doesn't feel right.

"I know what you mean. He has the lost scroll, but he doesn't act how the finder of the lost scroll should act."

Why?

Ma responded, "That is for you to find out."

Why don't you just tell me?

"Because it is more interesting this way. You will enjoy this better if I don't tell you right now."

Why are you keeping the people in so much misery in hell?

"I am not. It is the world they created."

No, they didn't. They left Serenus, and you sent them to hell. They didn't do that to Serenus.

"Not any single one of them, but together, all of them did this. I didn't interfere. Everyone who leaves Serenus comes to me, and their copy goes to a future Serenus. That future Serenus is what the actions of their parent copy made it to be."

But what is the point? Why keep them in so much pain?

"I am not keeping them in pain. Yes, there are problems, but I am not keeping them."

They were being pelted with stones twice a day. The stones came from Serenus. How could they stop it?

"They threw the stones themselves when they were in Serenus."

But they didn't know that those stones were falling on the people on the next island. That is very cruel, Ma.

"I know. I agree that it is harsh, but it is the Protocol. If I find a better way, I will change it. I can't just remove the stones and let other actions influence the future. I am not supposed to interfere. And I had no idea they would start throwing stones at their future when I made the world. I did not design it to be cruel."

But there is a lot of room for improvement.

"Yes. Well, the stones have stopped now, so that trouble is over."

So what will they do now? I mean, Amy and Fifty-three?

Ma teased, "That is for you to find out."

I sighed. Are you not going to answer any questions?

"Questions that will be answered in the future, we will witness them together as the answer is found. You can talk to me about what has already happened."

Was I right about the poem?

"Partly. Many people have been right before. In part. No one has yet found the full meaning."

What will... oh.

"Yeah, no questions about the future."

Is there really a prophecy about the one who will go through the door?

"There is a prophecy, but the real question is whether it will come true or not. A prophecy foretells an event to happen in a certain way. I am very interested to see if it comes true."

Where did the prophecy come from?

Ma sang,

"A chosen one shall come our way.

With grace and love, to light the way.

Wise and kind, with a heart so bright,

He'll stop the stones and bring delight.

The door to happiness, once shut tight,

Will be unlocked with the hero's might.

For all to follow to a world of light,

Where happiness reigns, and all is right.

This is the prophecy. Someone made it up to give their friends some hope."

Oh... So, it is just a made-up thing.

"Yes, but that doesn't mean it may not come true."

How did the king find the lost scroll?

Ma smiled, "Okay, so this one has happened in the past, but I think you will enjoy it more if I don't tell you right now."

I laughed. That's not fair. You said I could ask about things that have already happened.

Ma teased, "Nothing is fair. You are welcome to cry a little to move past this bad feeling."

Do I still have a choice? I mean, what am I now? Am I dead? Will I go to a world? What happens to me now?

"You will stay with me as your copy goes through the world. We will be together watching his journey. If he succeeds, he will open the door to happiness, and then everyone will leave hell."

What if he doesn't succeed?

"Then he will stay in that world until someone else succeeds."

So going through the door is a must? I thought we could make that world back into Serenus. I thought that was the mission.

"Maybe the door will open when the world becomes Serenus again."

When it becomes Serenus, the door will open? That doesn't make sense. Can people always leave a good place? Is that the rule? That's cruel.

"Well... that is the system."

It doesn't make any sense! What's your reasoning?

"It does make sense. You are not able to see it yet, but you will."

I am starting to think you are not a good Ma.

"I'm sorry. I know I am not what I can be. I am always working toward it."

I don't think so. I just told you that your system is faulty. You have no explanation for it, and still, you keep it this way. Is this a joke? When the world becomes Serenus again, then they can leave it? But they have to stay to suffer?

Ma explained, "I know what you mean. I understand why you think like this, and I understand why it feels totally unreasonable from your point of view, but I can tell you that there is a reason, and once it is time, you will know it. And you will agree that it was the right thing to do. And at that time, if you tell me a better way, I will change the system, but until then, your judgment is faulty. You are correct in what you are saying, but there are things you don't know which will make it incorrect. Wait till you know the rest, and then tell me what you think. Until then, just trust me."

I believe in what makes sense to me, and this does not make sense to me.

Ma laughed and teased, "Do you, really? What if I told you that this is just a vision you are having and there is no other copy, and whatever I am saying is what you are imagining in a dream? What if I say you are not really talking to me, you are dreaming."

I gasped. What? Is it a dream?

Ma clarified, "No, but what if it was. You are believing many things that I am telling you... I am just pointing out that there can be many things that you believe in, and think that they make sense even when they don't. Don't think too highly of yourself. You know very little."

Then tell me. I have a mind. I can understand. I am capable. Tell me, and I will believe it if I see the reasoning.

Ma explained, "You don't understand. If I tell you reasoning that makes sense, does that mean it is the truth? What if I make up reasoning that is not true but makes sense to you? I am quite capable."

But are you a liar too?

Ma admitted, "I lie all the time."

What? How can I believe anything you tell me?

"Didn't you say you had a test to filter out what was the truth and what wasn't? The test to see what makes sense and what doesn't?"

You're a liar? I don't believe that.

"I am a liar, and by saying this, I have proved myself to be a liar. If I am not a liar, why am I telling a lie?"

I groaned. I feel like my head is spinning.

Ma laughed, "I'm sorry. I was just teaching you that there can be things that make sense to you but are not true, just as there can be things that don't make sense to you but could be true."

Okay, I can't win an argument with you, but I really need to know... Are you a liar?

"I am sorry, but I am. But you can trust me. I will not lie to you. I promise."

How can I trust a liar?

"You can. You can trust me, and I won't lie to you."

I don't know. You will have to earn my trust."

Ma smiled, and everything around me grew vibrant. Now, how did she find this funny? She was definitely weird, and I didn't feel like talking to her. I was having such a nice moment with Amy and Fifty-three, and she came in the middle and totally ruined it. I knew she was listening to my thoughts, and I wanted her to listen. She had done it, after all.

Fifty-three woke up before it was light and felt thirsty. He looked at Amy and found her covered in Black Dust. He shook his head and went to the baker's home to get some water. He found a clay water container outside the home and drank from it. From beside him, a man with a very long beard coughed.

The man looked wild and dangerous. Fifty-three was frightened. He stepped back a few steps while keeping his eyes on the scary-looking man. He made no sound, but the man opened one eye and stared right at him. It was really creepy how he opened only a single eye and moved his eyeball around to stare at Fifty-three.

Fifty-three froze. He didn't know if he should run. The man looked very weak. He probably couldn't catch Fifty-three, but who knew. It was a place for Miserables... thieves, criminals... who knew what this man was capable of. Then the man stood up and opened his other eye. With the gesture of his hand, he called Fifty-three to come close. Fifty-three wanted to run. The man signalled for him to come close again. Reluctantly, Fifty-three walked a step forward. The man wanted him to come even closer. Fifty-three stepped closer while keeping his eyes on the man's hands. There was no weapon in the bearded man's hand, but that didn't mean he wasn't dangerous. The man signalled again, and unwillingly Fifty-three stepped another step forward.

The creepy man pointed to a side as if to show something really important and whispered in Fifty-three's ear, "It's me. Over there. You see that? That's me."

Fifty-three looked in the direction the man was pointing, but he couldn't understand exactly what the man was pointing at. He turned his head back to the man to see what he meant. The man was pointing in another direction now, saying, "It's me. Over there. You see that? That's me."

Fifty-three stepped back a few steps nervously. What was wrong with this man? What did he mean by that? It's me. Over there? What did that mean? Was he... crazy? Fifty-three stepped back a few more steps and slowly walked away. The man sat down, closed his eyes, and went back to sleep.

I asked Ma, "Ma, What's with the creepy old man?"

Ma replied, "Just wait and see."

Fifty-three returned to Amy, who was still asleep. He sat by her but kept an eye on the man. He could hardly see him from this far, but he made sure to keep checking every now and then.

Finally, Amy woke up, and Fifty-three told her about the scary man.

Fifty-three said, "I don't think we can stay here. That man... something's really wrong with him. What kind of people live here? The ones who are not accepted by the Keepers or the Seekers. It is dangerous to be here. Is there no other place that we can go to?"

Amy, still brushing the dust off her clothes, creating a black cloud of dust around her, responded, "I don't know. We can't go to the Keepers. We are not allowed to enter the castle. This is the only place left."

Fifty-three suggested, "We need a way to protect ourselves. We need to get some weapons. I don't feel safe here."

Amy asked, "Where will we get weapons?"

Fifty-three replied, "I don't know. Let's ask the baker."

Amy agreed, "Okay, I will ask him."

They walked to the baker's home, carefully checking their surroundings. They knocked at the door but got no response. After waiting for a while, they decided to come back another time.

There was nothing to do, and there was nowhere to go. They sat at the side of a dirt path. It was windy, and the dust was in the air, making it harder to breathe. Fifty-three tore a piece of his shirt and gave it to Amy to cover her face. Then he ripped another piece and tied it up on his face to breathe through the cloth. It felt much better with such a small change.

After sitting for a bit, Fifty-three said loudly over the noise of the blowing wind, "We can't just sit here."

Amy didn't know what to say. She just looked back at Fifty-three and raised her shoulders.

They stayed quiet for a while, then Fifty-three said, "Let's find some cover before this gets worse."

They walked away from the path in one direction, but it was really hard to see. They had no idea which way to go, so they sat back down and waited for the wind to calm down.

Fifty-three suggested, "Let's go back to the path. At least we will see the baker when he comes back."

Amy nodded, and they walked back to where they thought they had been sitting earlier. The path was nowhere to be found. After going around in circles for a little bit, they sat down again. Now they were really worried. It was hard to keep their eyes open, and they were only peeking from behind the eyelids at this point. Covered in Black Dust, they looked really miserable now.

Ma, what's going to happen? I asked.

Ma replied, "Patience."

Please take care of them.

"I don't interfere except by creating a thought in their head. Let's see if they will listen to me."

Amy suggested, "Maybe we should sit facing away from the wind and just wait it out."

Fifty-three turned to face away from the wind and slumped down to wait it out.

I asked, "That's it?"

Ma replied, "It's better than before."

Fifty-three asked Amy, "Miserable Amy, how are you feeling now?"

Amy responded, "Miserable Fifty-three, I am totally miserable now."

They shook their heads, smiled, and slouched down even lower.

Fifty-three inquired, "Are there mountains nearby?"

Amy answered, "Yes, I have been there with Alfred in Serenus."

Fifty-three asked, "And are there any caves that we could shelter in?"

Amy replied, "Yes, until we figure out where to go, maybe we should find a cave to hide in."

Fifty-three agreed, "Let's do that after talking to the baker."

Amy said, "Okay."

Finally, the wind died down, and they looked at each other and laughed. They looked wilder than the wild man Fifty-three had seen early in the morning. Walking back to the baker's home, they tried to get rid of the dust from their hair, but it was stuck. There was no way they could get rid of it without a proper bath or two.

The baker was home when they arrived. After looking at their sad faces, he said, "You have no idea how to live out here, but at least you covered your faces. What are you doing here? You can't survive like this."

Fifty-three replied, "We can't go anywhere else, so we are miserable."

The baker said, "You don't belong in this place. The weather is not the only enemy out here."

Amy explained, "We don't belong anywhere. We can't go to the Keepers, and we can't go to the Seekers. There is no other place for us to go."

The baker, looking like a kind man, shook his head. "You won't survive out in the open. Stay at my home until I can find another place for you."

Fifty-three and Amy were speechless at the kindness of their new host. He also gave them soup to drink. After a shower, they looked and felt much better. The baker became busy with his chores, and the two of them helped as best as possible. He was happy to have the help.

I asked, "Did you do that, Ma?"

Ma replied, "The baker is kind, but if they came to him looking better than they were, they wouldn't have found a place to live."

I questioned, "So you helped them?"

Ma answered, "Yes and no. You won't understand it yet."

The baker introduced himself, "My name is Nuno. I will get you some supplies from the Keep tomorrow and show you where you can live safely."

Fifty-three and Amy stayed at Nuno's place for the rest of the day. In the evening, someone knocked on the door. Nuno opened a small window in the door and handed out bread to whoever was outside. This happened several times, and most of the time, Nuno didn't even know who he was feeding. He didn't care about that; if someone needed help, he helped them. When Fifty-three saw an unusually dirty hand through the window in the door, he recognized the man. It was the creepy man from the morning who could open one eye and look around.

Fifty-three told Nuno, "I saw this man today when I came for some water. He is very scary."

Nuno nodded, "Yes, Faqeer can be scary. I will introduce you to him tomorrow. He is not dangerous."

Fifty-three was scared; he didn't want to meet Faqeer, but he stayed quiet. After that, he didn't ask about any other hands. He kept his head low and just helped Nuno. Amy remained quiet throughout the conversation, not even asking about Faqeer. Something else was on her mind.

Once Nuno finished his work for the day, he left the house to meet someone. Fifty-three asked Amy what was bothering her. Amy wouldn't tell him. She was definitely upset, but she didn't want to talk about it. After that, she stayed a little reserved for the rest of the evening. Fifty-three was taken aback by this change in her behaviour. He wanted to know what happened so he could maybe try to fix things, but Amy wouldn't say. At night when Nuno came back, they went to bed.

In the morning, Nuno headed out for the Keep to bring them

some supplies so they could leave the bakery for their new destination.

Amy was still keeping to herself. Fifty-three asked, "We are going to find a new place for us to shelter in, and you are very quiet. Is everything okay? I have a feeling that something is bothering you. If you like, you can share with me."

Amy hesitated, struggling to find the words. Something was definitely bothering her, but she was finding it hard to express it.

Fifty-three tried again, "Do you not want to go? You know we can't go back to the Keep, but we can try to get into the castle if that's what you want."

Amy shook her head, "No, I don't want that. It's dangerous. I don't want to put your life in danger."

Fifty-three asked, "But you want to go to the castle? You just don't want me to come with you? Is that it?"

Amy nodded, "But I can't leave you alone either. And don't even try to convince me. I won't. But yes, this is making me sad that I am going away from Alfred, and I don't know when I will be able to come back. He doesn't even know I am here, or he would have found a way to meet me."

Fifty-three nodded, and Amy said, "I just want to know he is okay."

Fifty-three nodded again, but in his head, he was thinking of a way to make it happen. How could he solve this problem? Amy wants to meet Alfred, but she doesn't want him to come with her, and she doesn't want to leave him alone.

He thought about it for a while but couldn't come up with anything. Then they ate food as he stayed lost in his thoughts. What could he do?

After their meal, he sat alone in the yard and closed his eyes. It was time to let his mind wander. He stayed there for some time until he had a plan, though he didn't tell Amy about it. He wanted to be sure it would work, and only then would he tell her.

Fifty-three and Amy busied themselves cleaning up Nuno's house. They wanted to leave it better than when they arrived. Nuno still wasn't back, so they did some of his chores for him. They had seen him work the previous day, so they did what they thought would help him.

When Nuno returned, Shahzor accompanied him. He was happy to see the two of them were safe. He said, "Nuno is a blessing on this land. I am so glad you found him."

Nuno was full of praise for Shahzor as well, "And what of the blessing that keeps Nuno going? I couldn't do anything if I didn't have your help."

As it turned out, Shahzor and Nuno were very good friends. Shahzor had told Nuno the entire story of yesterday's events, and together they decided that Fifty-three and Amy should be sent to the Tree Circle.

"The Broken Circle?" Amy asked.

Fifty-three inquired, "What is the Broken Circle?"

Nuno answered, "No, the Broken Circle is the name for the Tree Circle in Forsaken Serenus. The Tree Circle is a group of people living in a secret place. They named themselves after the Tree Circle in Serenus. They left the Keep in search of a place suitable for growing the Moontree again, but when they couldn't grow a Moonseed, they formed a small community in the only place where a Moontree could be grown. Very few people know about this place, and we need to keep it that way. We can't destroy it by crowding too many people in there. I will send you two with a letter, and they will allow you to enter."

Nuno looked through his bookshelf and found a map. He explained, "Beyond Sere, the land is tough to travel. It is very rocky. When you get to this rocky place, look for two mountains whose peaks bend toward each other. You see this on the map; this is where you will find the Tree Circle... or I should say, they will find you. You won't be able to find them, but they keep a watch to keep intruders out. They will find you, and if you show them this letter, they will take you in. I trust you with their location because Shahzor says you are good people. Do not destroy our last hope."

Amy promised, "We would never do such a thing. You can trust us. Tell them, Fifty-three!"

Shahzor interrupted, "Fifty-three? What kind of name is that?"

Amy laughed, "The guards gave him this name because he didn't have a name in Serenus."

Shahzor laughed, "And why didn't you have a name in Serenus? What did people call you there?" For some reason, he found it really amusing.

Fifty-three replied, "They called me No-name."

Amy cackled, "Or 'This-one.'"

"This-one?" Shahzor and Nuno cracked up.

Nuno said, "Why don't you pick a name? Come on, we can't call you Fifty-three. Let's think of a name now."

Someone knocked at the door, and Nuno went to check who it was. Amy and Shahzor suggested many names for Fifty-three to choose from.

Nuno's voice called from the door, "This-one, come here. I want you to meet someone. Amy, you too."

We left the room and approached Nuno as the creepy old man whispered something in his ear. This-one stayed a couple of steps away from them while Amy and Shahzor went closer and greeted the man.

Nuno introduced the whispering man, "This is Faqeer. He is a very gentle fellow and my good friend, and he has a secret to tell you. Come on, This-one, don't be shy, come closer."

This-one walked a couple of steps closer. The rest of the distance was covered by Faqeer, who came very close, pointed to a stone on the ground, and whispered, "It's me. Over there. You see that? That's me." Then Faqeer walked to Amy, pointed to a tree trunk, and whispered in her ear as if telling her a big secret, "It's me. Over there. You see that? That's me."

Shahzor asked Faqeer to tell him the secret. Faqeer went to his ear, pointed to... there was nothing there, and said, "It's me, over there. You see that? That's me." Shahzor nodded and hugged Faqeer, "Yes, I see that." Faqeer became very happy at the acknowledgment. With a grand smile, he pulled out a small hand-held musical instrument from his robe and tapped on it with one finger as he walked away to a tree trunk. Once he reached the tree trunk, he began to go around it in circles as he tapped his finger on the Kalimba, keeping it close to his ear. Lost in a world of his own, he kept going in circles and tapping on the instrument.

Amy and This-one were unsure of what was happening. Nuno explained, "Faqeer is lost in his mind. He plays the Kalimba and shares his secret with everyone who listens. He has never hurt a soul. You don't have to be scared of how he looks. He is harmless."

We watched him go in circles around the tree trunk as Shahzor said, "He stays near the bakery. If you see him, go listen to his secret. He won't remember he's told you his secret before, and then just acknowledge that you see him over there, wherever he points, that will make his day. A piece of bread and some acknowledgment, that's all he needs from us."

This-one felt bad for Faqeer, though he wondered if Faqeer had an easier life than most. Faqeer had no needs, no missions, and was able to be happy if someone just acknowledged him - a simple life.

Ch 28: The Puppet Master

Nuno suggested, "Let's go back inside. I will show you what supplies I brought for you to make the journey."

Shahzor responded warmly, "I have to leave now. It was nice meeting you again. And on behalf of Ariana and me, I want to apologize for what happened two days ago."

This-one reassured him, "That's okay, though I have found something amazing, and I can't really leave yet."

Amy looked puzzled, having no idea what he was talking about.

This-one continued, "If only I could somehow meet Conrad, just to be sure before I share it with everyone."

Shahzor, who was about to leave, had his interest piqued, "Conrad? I know him. He is a great thinker. I've met him a few times in the castle."

This-one sighed, "Yes, he is a great thinker, and he would know what I am talking about. If I could just somehow send word to him, he would leave everything and come meet me."

Nuno asked curiously, "Are you sure? He is a very busy person. What is it? Tell us, and we can tell him."

This-one shook his head and produced a folded paper from his pocket, "Not yet, I need to be... but how would I... yes, if this message could somehow reach him, he would be so intrigued that he would have to come."

Shahzor, Nuno, and Amy were all eager to know what was on that page.

Unable to control his curiosity, Shahzor offered, "If you give me the message, I can get it to him."

This-one replied, "But you'll have to wait till the king calls you. I can't wait that long. I need a faster way."

Shahzor said hurriedly, "I can do it. Give it to me, and I will make sure it reaches him."

This-one asked, feigning surprise, "Really? You can do it?"

Shahzor repeated confidently, "I can do it. I'll make sure it reaches Conrad by tomorrow. I can do it."

This-one nodded, "Okay, I trust you. Here you go."

Shahzor took the page and couldn't wait to open and read the message. He glanced at the page, then back at us, and said, "Okay, I will leave now." With a wave of his hand, he bid us goodbye and left in a hurry.

This-one watched him go. Shahzor really couldn't hold himself too long. He was reading the message as he walked away. Then he stopped and turned his head back to us. His face was full of wonder. He stood there for a couple of moments, looking back at This-one, and then left.

Nuno was eager to know what was in the message, "What is it? Can you tell me? What is it about?"

This-one laughed, "Shahzor knows it now, and though he may not understand what it means, I'm sure he will tell you."

Nuno laughed in response, "Yes, he can't keep it from me. Come, I will show you what I brought for you."

Nuno opened a small cloth bag and handed us two water bottles, a map, and some clothing. "You will need to carry water on you. The map will show you the way, and... try this on. This is the proper clothing for the journey."

Amy spread out the cloth. It was a headscarf.

Nuno explained, "And this face cover is for when you are traveling through dust storms. It will protect you."

Amy donned her scarf and covered her face, leaving only her eyes visible.

Nuno continued, "This is the proper way to cover up if you live in sandy regions or places with dust storms. Make sure to cover your entire body. Wind can carry sand at high speeds, and it hurts on exposed skin."

This-one put on his scarf, feeling protected and hidden from the world. No one could tell who they were because only their eyes were visible.

Nuno remarked, "You still need to see, so you can't cover your eyes. I wish we had something that would cover the eyes while still allowing us to see through it, but I don't have anything like that."

Amy expressed her gratitude, "This is great. Thank you so much for this. It will help keep us safe on our journey. We really appreciate it."

"So you will be waiting to hear from Conrad before you leave? You are welcome to stay here as long as you want," Nuno offered.

Amy thanked the baker and turned to This-one. "Let's go out and try our new cover-up."

This-one knew she was confused and wanted to know why he delayed the journey. As they walked outside, they felt safer. They were covered and hidden not just from the wind but also from onlookers. No one could tell who they were, making it possible for them to walk around without worrying about bumping into a

Keeper.

Amy inquired, "What are you up to? What was the message? Why are you delaying?"

This-one explained, "I want to meet Conrad before we leave."

Amy pressed, "Why?"

This-one revealed, "So I can ask him to tell Alfred you are here."

Amy's eyes smiled, "Ohhh... Thank you. But how did you convince Shahzor? What's in the message?"

This-one laughed, "A line in the line of thought. It thinks what I think."

Amy was still puzzled, "The line from his tree wall in Sere? What does it mean?"

This-one confessed, "I don't know. I knew Shahzor would read it and not understand it, and I... believe Conrad will come to meet us to find out who we are."

Amy considered, "What if he doesn't?"

This-one reassured her, "Then we will try another way. And now we know that if Shahzor is properly motivated, he can send word inside the castle without waiting for the king to call him."

Amy's eyes smiled again, and she nodded. "Where was all this clever planning two days ago?"

This-one laughed, "I was overwhelmed and couldn't think

straight."

Amy and This-one walked around for a while. No longer needing to hide since they were already covered up, they decided to visit the three waterfalls.

Sitting near the falls in their headscarves, they could finally relax out in the open again. The wind picked up, and Black Dust rose from the ground, hovering in the air. They squinted their eyes as they walked back to the baker's home.

Upon their return, Nuno commented, "I saw you did so many chores for me. You really are good people. How was your walk in the headscarves?"

Amy and This-one removed their headscarves, and the three of them laughed. They were entirely protected from the Black Dust, except for a horizontal band around their eyes.

This-one remarked, "The headscarves work wonders in this place. Not only did they protect us from the wind, but we could also walk around without fear of being identified. We went to the three falls."

Nuno nodded, "Yes, the three falls formed when the river changed direction. It's said that it was the home of a thinker who used to sit in his boat, thinking about the mysteries of the world while enjoying the sounds of the waterfalls. Who knows if it's true or not, but... people here make up all kinds of stories. There's too much free time and little to do."

Amy and This-one exchanged glances and smiled, then This-one added, "I have heard that the thinker had a friend who liked to sleep in the boat, watching the beautiful night sky while enjoying the sound of the falls."

Nuno observed, "They would have to tie the boat somehow."

Amy chimed in, "I've heard they did tie it."

Nuno nodded, "Imagine sleeping like that and waking up in the morning without layers of Black Dust on us, feeling the fresh morning wind. Oh, what heaven they lived in."

Amy and This-one smiled again and nodded. Then they washed off the black band from their eyes and helped Nuno with his baking.

I felt much better knowing that Amy and This-one were safe. "It's not so bad for them now," I said. "They're finding new friends and learning new ways to live in that world."

Ma replied, "Yes, they are in good spirits and in good company. I am very happy."

Curious, I asked, "Can we do something here?"

Ma responded, "Yes, of course. You will experience what they're going through, but you can do stuff in the Sandbox to keep yourself occupied."

I thought about it for a moment. What should I do? All I had to do was think, and the thought would become real. There were unlimited possibilities, but it felt like once I could do anything I wanted, I didn't really want to do anything. It wasn't real.

Ma questioned, "What is real?"

Things that actually exist.

Ma inquired, "Exist, how?"

Physically exist so that we and others can touch them or know that they are real.

Ma asked, "Does touch make them real?"

No, if we can see it, we can know it's real.

Ma continued, "Is it our ability to sense that decides whether a thing is real or not? What about things that we cannot yet sense? The tiger could sense a trail that you couldn't, but the trail was real."

Yes, but whatever I do here, that's just here, not real.

Ma countered, "Whatever someone is doing in Serenus is just there, not here. How is that real and this not real? That place is temporary. This will last forever. You think that was real, and this is not?"

So does that mean it's actually this place that is real and that... Serenus was not real?

Ma concluded, "Anything that exists in any form is real, even if it exists in someone's thought. It's the existence that makes it real, not someone's ability to sense it. Serenus is real, this place is real, and Forsaken Serenus is real. Whatever comes next will be real too."

Curious, I asked, What comes next?

Ma replied, "That is for you to find out."

I laughed, Of course.

I turned my attention back to This-one. He was asleep and dreaming.

In his dream, Amy donned a headscarf as she left the baker's home. She passed by the Keep and continued to the stables, moving as if on a secret mission. Stealthily, she approached a Firehorse and mounted it. The Firehorse began to gallop, gradually gaining speed before soaring into the sky, speeding toward the castle.

As soon as Amy reached the castle walls, warning bells sounded inside. High in the sky, she searched for Alfred but couldn't spot him. Diving down, she soon found herself pursued by several guards on their own Firehorses. Skillfully, she dodged and zigzagged through the castle's streets, people leaping out of her way as she desperately searched for Alfred.

Amy led her pursuers on increasingly longer straight runs, then took sharp turns to throw them off course. All the while, she continued calling for Alfred.

Guards from all the watchtowers unleashed a hail of arrows at Amy, who nimbly dodged them as she flew past. The ringing bells in the castle, the swarm of Firehorses pursuing her through the streets and sky, and her desperate cries for Alfred finally drew him out of a watchtower and onto a wall. Recognizing her, he shouted for the guards to cease fire. To her astonishment, they obeyed.

With the Firehorses no longer chasing her, Amy could finally hover in place above Alfred. More guards appeared behind him, but he ordered them not to attack. Then, voices rang out, "Who is it, Alfred? Is it her?" "Is Amy here?"

For a few moments, Alfred simply stood with a broad smile on his face, while Amy froze in mid-air, gazing back at him. Arrows from a nearby tower narrowly missed her.

Infuriated, Alfred turned to the archers and yelled, "STOP FIR-ING! IT'S AMY!" Someone shouted back, "We have orders to fire. We can't allow her to enter the castle like this."

Alfred looked at Amy and said, "Go, I'm coming." She pulled up just as more arrows whizzed by her.

Turning to the guards behind him, Alfred announced, "Amy is here. I have to go."

The guards nodded enthusiastically, "Go, Alfred, go!"

Alfred sprinted forward and leaped off the wall. As he hit the ground, he transformed into a puff of smoke and vanished.

Shocked, I asked, "Why did he do that?"

Ma explained, "Because the king won't let him leave the castle. He died because he knows he will come back, and this time he will choose to be a Keeper."

I reminded, "But he will forget everything. He will lose all his friends, he will come as if he came from Serenus, and he won't even know to be a Keeper. He will pick to be a Seeker again."

Ma pointed out, "I would say he is smarter than that. Look at his friends."

The guards were devising a plan to reach the river, ensuring Alfred would choose to be a Keeper this time. Or miserable. Anything but a Seeker.

Back at the stables, Shahzor was furious with Amy for using a Firehorse to reach the castle. He worried that this would breach his trust with the king and result in severe consequences. Despite Amy's repeated apologies, the damage was done.

Shahzor demanded that Amy leave the stables immediately and never return. As she departed, she was both happy that Alfred would come and guilt-ridden for betraying Shahzor's trust. Unbeknownst to her, several Firehorses from the castle arrived at Shahzor's stable and set it ablaze.

I shook my head, "No, this is not right. She can do it, but this is not the right way."

Ma nodded, "Let's hope Amy doesn't try this."

The next morning, This-one called for Amy. "Amy... Amy!"

From the other room, Amy replied, "Yeah."

This-one excitedly told her, "I had a dream last night. I saw you learn to fly Firehorses. It was really strange. It felt very real. I saw you ride a Firehorse into the castle to find Alfred. You found him, but after you left, he jumped off a wall and died because that was the only way he could meet you. And... and when you got back, the king's men burnt down Shahzor's stables... for letting you use a Firehorse to enter the castle."

Amy gasped, "This was your dream? I had this exact plan. This isn't a dream; it's a vision."

This-one nodded, "We can't do it like this, Amy."

Amy agreed, "No, we can't."

This-one suggested, "Let's hope Conrad will come, and then we'll find a way to get Alfred out of the castle. It has to be done secretly. We can't be so open about it that Alfred won't be able to sneak out anymore."

Amy nodded, "I hope you're right. I hope Conrad comes."

I looked at Ma, and she said, "Yeah, this happens sometimes. Very rarely, though."

Ch 29: A Mischief in the Dark

Nuno left home in the morning as usual. The smell of freshly baked bread wafted through the air, filling the room with a warm and comforting aroma. This-one and Amy finished their chores and set out. With water bottles full, some bread wrapped in a cloth, and headscarves in place, they planned to visit Sere.

Sere was a place in Serenus that had been devastated by the battle between Conrad and Esmeray. They wanted to visit Sere and travel slightly farther to spot the two mountains they needed to head towards to find the Tree Circle.

Together, they walked briskly. Amy had visited Sere multiple times; she knew the way, and Nuno's map helped. In Serenus, they would traverse a forest to reach a river, and beyond it lay the desolate, dark place called Sere. In Forsaken Serenus, there was no forest, and everywhere resembled Sere.

The journey to Sere was tiring, and the hot sun beat down on their heads, making them sweat profusely. Before midday, Amy and This-one reached the river, only to find it reduced to black mud. The bridge still stood, and they crossed it cautiously. They proceeded a little further, and the large tree loomed on the horizon. The tree looked almost exactly as it did in Serenus.

Inside the tree, the air was thick and musty, and the black dust coated everything, making it difficult to breathe. Numerous footprints in the tree room hinted at frequent visits, although it didn't appear that anyone was living there. No books or scrolls adorned the broken shelves. Amy placed her hand on the wall, and This-one moved closer to see what it was. A line in the line of thought, it thinks what I think. This line now had emotional significance for them, especially for Amy. She hoped Conrad would come and that she would be able to find Alfred.

They didn't spend much time inside the tree. Consulting the map, they went past the tree to spot the two mountain peaks. Their view was obstructed; the dust in the air reduced visibility. They continued following the map until midday, at which point they sat down and drank some water.

This-one asked, "Should we go a little farther?"

Amy replied, "We could go a little, but I worry we may not make it back before daylight runs out. And if the wind picks up, then we definitely can't make it back."

This-one suggested, "Let's give ourselves some extra time and head back now."

Disappointed at not spotting the two mountains, they returned to the baker's home. Fortunately, it wasn't windy, and they made it back with plenty of daylight to spare. The journey had shaken their confidence, so they sought Nuno's help in deciphering the map. Nuno pointed out the landmarks they should look for and inquired if they had seen any. They confirmed that they had.

Nuno comforted them, "The visibility is really bad, but I believe you were heading in the right direction."

This-one and Amy nodded, but they were not satisfied.

Nuno shared, "I have good news. Shahzor was able to send the message to Conrad."

Their faces lit up with smiles, and Nuno asked, "What is it that you have found? What does it mean?"

This-one explained, "It was in Conrad's tree room, where he used to think. We saw it when we were in Serenus. Only Conrad can explain what it really means."

Nuno smiled, "But you said you found something?"

This-one responded, "I found his writings."

Nuno remarked, "But that was in Serenus. You sounded like you found something here."

This-one hesitated, avoiding Nuno's gaze, and said, "I didn't say that."

Nuno laughed, "Why do you want to meet Conrad?"

Amy recounted how she had tried to persuade Shahzor to send a message to Alfred, but he wouldn't do it until the king himself called him to the castle. Thus, they devised a plan for Conrad to deliver the message instead.

Nuno smiled, "This was your way of motivating Shahzor? But he didn't need any motivation. He couldn't send a message to Alfred until the king called him, because Alfred is a commander in the King's Guard. Sending a message to Conrad is easy. He is usually at the Sanctum of Knowledge. Reaching a King's Guard is not an easy task. Shahzor didn't mean to stall you. He genuinely couldn't help you until the king himself called him to the King's Hall, where he would find Alfred."

This-one kept his eyes on the floor, "We didn't know."

Nuno reassured them, "It's okay. You're just trying to find your friend, and you don't know who you can trust here, but I can tell you that you can trust Shahzor."

Amy replied, "We trust you and Shahzor."

Nuno continued, "And your trick may have actually helped you after all because Shahzor didn't think of it, but Conrad can reach

Alfred. Conrad has access to the King's Hall, as he is one of the most notable thinkers in the Sanctum of Knowledge."

This-one responded, "Oh, well, that's great then. If he comes..."

Amy inquired, "What is the Sanctum of Knowledge?"

Nuno explained, "It's a library that contains all the knowledge of this world. All poems, scrolls, and interpretations of the poem are also kept there. Many Seekers work there, with their job being to find new mysteries with the ultimate goal of opening the door to happiness. All their findings are stored in the Sanctum of Knowledge."

Amy asked in a surprised tone, "So the king does want to open the door?"

Nuno replied, "Shikongo is just like us, stuck here. He wants to get out of here as much as anyone else. He is living a life of luxury but also a life of responsibility. And his ways are not kind, but he is very... motivated. The pursuit of knowledge is his life's mission, which is why he was able to find the lost scroll."

This-one inquired, "Where did he find it?"

Nuno explained, "In the Troll Cave. At least that is what he claims, though no one knows why he doesn't have the power of gods if he has the scroll."

Amy asked, "So he claimed he found the lost scroll and was made king?"

Nuno confirmed, "Well, his claims were backed by... enough proof... that there is no choice but to believe him."

Amy recalled, "Alfred used to think there was a Troll Cave in Serenus. Of course, most thought it to be a fairy tale."

Nuno responded, "No, there really is a Troll Cave, but accessing it is a challenge."

This-one mused, "It appears all stories that we ever heard are true... to some extent."

Nuno agreed, "Yes, there's probably some truth to all the tales, but as they are passed on from mouth to mouth, the tales are transformed, exaggerated, and translated incorrectly."

Amy reasoned, "Alfred wanted the scroll. If the king has it, then that is why Alfred reached the level of a commander in the King's Guard."

Nuno added, "Your friend is quite motivated."

Amy smiled, "He's always been like that."

Just then, someone knocked at the door. Nuno picked up a loaf of bread and went to answer it. Amy and This-one waited in silence for Nuno to return.

Nuno announced, "Conrad? Please... come in."

Amy and This-one jumped with joy and ran out to greet Conrad. Conrad looked at Amy and immediately recognized her. He playfully messed up her hair and said, "You were quite young the last time I saw this happy face."

Amy was ecstatic when they returned to the room and sat down. She couldn't keep her feet on the ground.

Conrad asked, "And who is this? I don't believe I met this one in Serenus."

Nuno and Amy laughed as Conrad looked at them curiously. Nuno replied, "This is This-one." Amy and Nuno burst into laughter.

Conrad looked at This-one and said, "This-one?"

Amy answered, "Yes, that's his name."

This-one smiled and said, "You can also call me No-name, Fifty-three, or N53."

Conrad smiled back, "Interesting. By not taking a name, you have taken many names. Let me guess, you were a thinker, am I right?"

Amy and Nuno laughed again as This-one nodded with a smile.

Conrad inquired, "So you sent the message? Do you know what it means?"

This-one shook his head, "I don't know what it means, but we need your help."

Conrad responded, "Oh, this was your way of getting my attention. Well, you have my attention. Tell me, what can I help you with?"

Amy asked eagerly, "Have you met Alfred? How is he?"

Conrad turned toward Amy, "Alfred is doing fine, better than fine, I would say. He is a commander in the King's Guard. A nice fellow, though a bit too serious... and ambitious."

Amy spoke softly, "He was my friend. I left Serenus to find him." Conrad's expression grew serious as he listened.

"Oh, I see," Conrad said, "So you want to meet him? Is that why I am here?"

Amy and This-one nodded, and Conrad leaned back in his chair. "Hmm, a tricky business. I'll see what can be done. Give me some time."

Conrad then turned his attention to This-one, "And why did you leave Serenus? Are all the thinkers still going after the lost scroll?"

This-one shook his head, "No, I... I came after her. I couldn't leave her alone."

Conrad's face lit up, "A good friend." He looked at Amy, "You are lucky to have found such good friends."

This-one said, "But I am not a thinker. Ma said I'm not so good at it."

Conrad raised an eyebrow, "Oh, then what did she say you were good at?"

This-one felt his cheeks flush with embarrassment, and he hesitated before answering. He looked down at the floor, "I can know when I am wrong. That is my ability."

Conrad leaned forward in his chair, his eyes fixed on This-one, "You can know when you are wrong? How does it work? Tell me more."

This-one was taken aback by Conrad's interest, "I don't know how it works. I never realized it in Serenus that this was my ability."

Conrad turned to Nuno and said, "Keep him safe." Then he turned back to Amy, "Protect him at all costs and keep him away from the king. His ability... it is special. I have read about it in the Sanctum of Knowledge."

Conrad's words left This-one in shock, "My friend, you might just be what we've been looking for."

Conrad then turned to Nuno, "Take him to the Tree Circle. Don't leave him alone until he is safe there." And then back to Amy, "I will let Alfred know, and we will need to sneak him out to come to see you. Stay here in the baker's home. He will come to meet you soon. Feed the needy while the baker is away."

Conrad stood up and looked at Nuno, "Any questions?" Nuno shook his head, and Conrad nodded before hurrying out the door.

Nuno and Amy turned to look at This-one, their eyes wide with wonder. This-one didn't know what to say. Amy and Nuno continued to stare, and after a moment, This-one spoke up, "Can you please stop staring at me?"

Amy looked apologetic, "I'm sorry. I just... You look... I mean, there is a lot inside you that still needs to be understood."

This-one asked, "Do you understand yourself fully?"

Amy's eyes widened with excitement as she spoke, "No one ever told me I have hidden powers inside me. Remember what Alia said about you? What if you're the wizard? We use the word 'wizard' as a curse, but maybe Qilam was right. Maybe you are the wizard, and wizards aren't necessarily evil."

This-one furrowed his brow and replied, "I can know when I'm wrong. I don't see how that's such a special ability. And Ma said I'm not the wizard."

A sudden knock at the door startled them, and Nuno went to offer the visitors bread. Instead of a friendly face, two guards appeared. They pushed the door open, rushed in, and quickly closed it behind them. Nuno tried to resist, but they dragged him into the room. Amy and This-one attempted to help Nuno, but one of the guards raised his hand and said, "Conrad sent us to protect you. We're not here to hurt you. Our orders are to travel with you until you reach Sere. We have to leave right now." He then looked at Amy and continued, "You can't come with us. We're to transport these two."

The guards allowed them no time for discussion. When Nuno tried to argue, they responded firmly, "We have our orders. We need to leave right now. The two of you, come with us."

Nuno protested, "At least let me take some food and water for the journey."

Relenting, the guards gave him a few moments to gather supplies.

Amy stood by This-one, her eyes full of concern. "I will come for you. Don't worry. I won't leave you alone."

This-one shook his head, "No, I'll be okay. Remember what Conrad said. You have to wait here."

Amy nodded in agreement.

Nuno hurriedly packed a bag, wrapped some bread in a cloth, and filled water bottles. Turning to Amy, he said, "Wear your headscarf and go to Shahzor. He will bring you enough supplies to run this place. It doesn't matter who comes to the door. They shouldn't go hungry."

Amy promised, "Don't worry about that. I'll take care of it. Please take care of my friend."

Nuno replied solemnly, "I'll die before I let anything happen to him. I promise."

The guards ushered them out of the house, their headscarves concealing their faces, and they set off toward Sere. Evening was settling in, and darkness enveloped the landscape. The guards, carrying lanterns and seemingly knowing the way, led them forward without stopping for even a sip of water.

Upon reaching Sere, Nuno asked the guards for a weapon. They handed him a knife, a bow, and some arrows, saying, "Anything for Conrad. Be safe now."

The guards departed, their mission complete. Nuno and This-one remained outside Conrad's tree room.

Nuno whispered, "We can't stay inside. If someone is following us, that's where they would expect us to be. We'll camp outside, but make sure not to make a noise. There are... things, enemies out here that don't differentiate between friend and foe."

Nuno drove four charred sticks into the ground and draped a cloth over them. He and This-one crawled underneath, shielded from the dust and hidden from potential harm.

This-one felt fear. He didn't want to leave Amy, and the haste with which Conrad had sent them away only intensified his anxiety. He wondered when he would see Amy again, and as he drifted off to sleep, his heart remained heavy with uncertainty.

When This-one opened his eyes, he discovered that Nuno was nowhere in sight. He crawled out from under their makeshift shelter and scanned the surroundings. He couldn't see Nuno, but he did notice footsteps in the overnight-gathered Black Dust. The prints suggested that multiple people had been walking around their camp. Fear gripped him, and he wondered if something had happened to Nuno.

This-one approached the tree cautiously and peeked inside. He found Nuno busy reading the tree walls.

This-one asked, "What's going on?"

Nuno replied, "Nothing. I just... I woke up early and was reading Conrad's writings on the wall. The words are very thought-pro-voking, don't you think?"

This-one nodded, "Yes."

Nuno continued, "His words are deep, though I don't fully un-derstand what he means... in a few places."

They left Sere, setting off to find the two mountains that would guide their journey.

This-one inquired, "Have you ever been to the Tree Circle be-fore?"

Nuno responded, "Many times. I'm part of the Tree Circle. Shahzor is too, and so is Conrad."

This-one remarked, "Almost all the people I've met so far are part of the Tree Circle? But you said it was a secret. How come so many people know it?"

Nuno explained, "Only the right ones know it. The ones that the Tree Circle thinks can be of use and won't destroy the only place where a Moontree can be grown again. You're lucky you met the right people."

This-one recalled, "I didn't feel so lucky for the first two days."

Nuno smiled, "Yes, of course. It's quite a shock coming to this world, and Shahzor told me about your attempt to bring everyone together. They're not ready to wait one moment longer. They only want the door to open."

This-one sighed, "Shahzor and Ariana were able to convince the people, but the king ruined everything."

Nuno nodded, "Shikongo doesn't want to share power. He doesn't want more leaders to emerge. He wants to be the only one who decides the fate of this world."

This-one noted, "He's clever, too. He made sure people saw that I couldn't go through the door."

Nuno agreed, "Of course he is. If he wasn't clever, he wouldn't be the king."

This-one said, "I wonder how he knew where to find the lost scroll."

Nuno speculated, "I think he just looked everywhere he could and eventually stumbled upon it."

"Yeah, maybe."

"Did you learn to use weapons in Serenus?" Asked Nuno.

This-one replied with a smile, "No, but I can point a bow at a target. We used blacklight bows to fight Esmeray."

Nuno raised an eyebrow, "Esmeray?"

This-one clarified, "She was a... we thought she was a wizard."

Nuno inquired, "But you don't think so anymore?"

This-one shook his head, "I don't know."

Nuno offered, "I can teach you how to use weapons. You never know when they'll come in handy."

This-one agreed, "Okay."

Nuno demonstrated how to use a bow. This-one shot numerous arrows at a target, but missed every time. Nuno reassured him that it was okay and that improving any skill required lots of practice.

Next, Nuno taught This-one how to use a knife. He advised, "If you're in a knife fight with someone, you've already lost. Try to stay away and use a bow and arrows, but learn to use the knife just in case."

After practicing for a while, they continued their journey. When they finally spotted the two mountains, evening had set in.

Nuno didn't want to camp there, "It's not safe to stay here at night. There are creatures here that will hunt you down in no time. You can't run from them; they can see in the dark. It's very likely that if something attacks us, we won't even see it. They can see the heat in our bodies, so they don't need light. It's easy for them to hunt at night."

This-one, feeling afraid but trying to appear brave, asked, "Okay, so what should we do then?"

Nuno sounded scared as well, "We can hope that they won't find us."

"That's our plan?" Asked This-one in shock.

Nuno replied, "There's no plan to escape these creatures. If they see us, we're dead. Just stay low, don't make a sound and hope none come this way."

Nuno and This-one lay down. This-one was unhappy and angry. He didn't like the fact that Nuno hadn't mentioned this danger before. He and Amy were supposed to travel on this journey, and Nuno never mentioned such a threat. He had thought Nuno was a wise person, but perhaps he was mistaken.

Nuno remarked, "The sky looks so beautiful."

This-one questioned, "Is it okay to talk? Can the creatures hear us?"

Nuno replied, "They can hear, but I don't see any here. We can talk for now."

This-one countered, "You said we won't see them coming. I think we shouldn't talk."

Suddenly, something moved behind them, and they fell silent. This-one's heart raced with fear while Nuno remained completely still.

A scraping sound emanated from nearby, and Nuno whispered, "It's digging for something."

This-one hushed him, "Shhh."

Nuno apologized, "Sorry."

The scraping sound ceased, and they heard the footsteps of an unknown creature. The sound grew closer and closer. This-one pressed himself further into the ground, while Nuno stayed motionless.

The footsteps came close and stopped at a short distance. This-one closed his eyes and waited. The creature sniffed the air and came nearer. It stopped and sniffed the air again, then advanced even closer. This-one's heart raced with fear, and he felt his breath growing louder. Nuno remained absolutely silent, and This-one tried his best to quiet his breathing, but it seemed louder than ever. The creature inched closer. It halted again, sniffed the air, and this time, it pinpointed their location. It charged toward them. This-one was certain there was no escape.

I exclaimed, "Ma?"

"Patience," she advised calmly.

"...Now is not the time for patience. We need to do something," I urged.

"Patience," she repeated.

The creature was now dangerously close to This-one and Nuno, likely able to see their body heat. They stayed low, and then Nuno picked up a stone and threw it away from them. The creature dashed after the noise in pursuit.

Nuno whispered urgently, "Run before it comes back."

This-one whispered back, "You said not to run."

Nuno didn't wait for This-one's response. He was already sprinting away.

Feeling misled and abandoned, This-one didn't know what to do. Before he could act, he saw the creature chasing after Nuno. Maybe he would be okay. Maybe the creature would go after Nuno. He quickly dismissed the thought. No, I have to do something to help Nuno.

This-one stood up and hurled stones at the towering creature. One stone hit its mark, causing the creature to stop chasing Nuno and turn around. It charged toward This-one, who now stood helpless. The creature hissed and lunged at him.

I yelled in desperation, "Maaaaa?????"

"Patience," Ma's voice advised.

This-one fell to the ground as the creature landed its paws on his chest. He wasn't injured, but the force knocked him down. The creature then stood up and began to laugh. From behind it, Nuno appeared, joining in the laughter.

This-one gaped in disbelief as Shahzor and Nuno laughed uncontrollably.

"Look at his face," Shahzor said between chuckles.

Nuno laughed heartily, "We got him real good."

This-one exclaimed, "What was that? I thought you were wise people."

Shahzor approached This-one, staring him straight in the eyes, "This is payback for tricking me into sending a message to Conrad."

Shahzor and Nuno continued to revel in their cruel prank while This-one sat fuming. He longed for his previous companions, feeling that these two were insane.

For some time, Nuno and Shahzor teased This-one, who remained in a sour mood.

Shahzor reassured, "Come on, it was just a little prank. You weren't in any danger. There are no creatures here."

Nuno added, "No, not here."

Shahzor continued, "You know how I felt when I found out you played me? Not good. This is just payback. You're fine. Stop pouting."

This-one relented, "I'm sorry I did that, but you really scared me."

Nuno placed his hand on This-one's shoulder and said, "At least now we know we can rely on you. You threw stones in an effort to save me. That was very brave of you."

This-one shook his head in disbelief, "You two are insane."

Shahzor grinned, his eyes sparkling with mischief. "Come on, we're in... this place. There's nothing wrong with having a little harmless fun. Come on, sit with us. You've proved yourself. You were willing to put your life in danger to save ours. We won't let it come to that. We won't let anything hurt you."

Nuno nodded in agreement, "You're a good friend, but you deserved that for what you did to get to Conrad. Don't do that again. Talk to us. We're your friends. You don't need any manipulation. Just tell us what you need. If we can do it, we will. If we can't, we'll let you know."

This-one sighed and sat down beside them. "I'm sorry I did that. I needed to help Amy, but I didn't know who I could trust."

Shahzor's expression softened. "And we're sorry we did this, but you can trust us."

This-one looked at Nuno, curiosity in his eyes. "How did you know Shahzor was going to... do this?"

Nuno smiled, the corners of his eyes crinkling. "Shahzor caught up with us near Conrad's tree room. We planned it when you were asleep. He's been following us all day, and you didn't see him. You need to be more aware of your surroundings. You need to have eyes in the back of your head if you want to survive here."

This-one frowned, "I thought Shahzor was supposed to help Amy with supplies."

Shahzor waved a hand dismissively, "That's taken care of. She'll have everything she needs."

This-one nodded, relieved.

Shahzor grinned, "So, where were we at picking a name for you?"

Nuno chuckled, "We're calling him This-one for now."

Shahzor laughed, "This-one? No. Tonight we are picking a name... I mean you are picking a name. Otherwise, we'll pick one for you."

This-one thought for a while but couldn't choose a name. Finally, he conceded, "You pick a name for me."

Shahzor suggested, "How about Daniyal?"

This-one considered it, "It's good."

Nuno shook his head, "Nah, don't take the first option. Let's hear some more."

Shahzor offered another name, "Magoro?"

Nuno raised an eyebrow, "What does that mean?"

Shahzor shrugged, "I don't know."

Nuno insisted, "No, we have to know the meaning. How about something that means over-thinker, the one who can't pick a name for himself?"

Shahzor and This-one laughed, the sound echoing through the night.

This-one said, "How about you two not worry about my name. When I find a name I want, I'll let you know."

Nuno ignored This-one, "How about Huan? It means happy."

Shahzor smirked, "I'm pretty sure that's a girl's name."

Nuno frowned, "Oh..."

This-one yawned, "I'm going to sleep."

Shahzor offered another name, "Ashwin. I like how it sounds."

Nuno asked, "And what does it mean?"

Shahzor replied, "Horse tamer, I believe."

Nuno shook his head, "Nah, it doesn't fit our friend's personality."

This-one drifted off to sleep as Shahzor and Nuno continued brainstorming names for him.

Ch 30: Keepers of the Forest

In the morning, they were awakened by a man from the Tree Circle. Nuno rubbed his eyes and greeted him, "Dante, we brought This-one to... this place on Conrad's orders."

Dante nodded, sunlight glinting off his silver hair, and signalled for This-one to approach.

Shahzor offered his parting words, "Turns out it's not so easy to pick a name for you. It was very nice to meet you again."

Nuno chimed in, "Good luck, This-one."

Shahzor and Nuno left to head back, and Dante studied This-one with a furrowed brow. "This-one? Is that your name?"

This-one sighed loudly, "Yes, or No-Name, or Fifty-three."

Dante smiled, "I am Dante. Nice to meet you."

This-one returned the smile, "Nice to meet you too. Tell me a name that you like."

Dante replied, "I like Dante."

This-one chuckled, "Yeah, but that's your name. Tell me another name that I can use."

Dante pondered, "What is your personality like? A name should define you."

This-one laughed, "I am good at knowing when I am wrong."

Dante looked at This-one for a moment, then thought for a while. After staying quiet for another few moments, he said, "I'll get back to you on this."

Dante led This-one to an opening in the side of the mountain. They walked through the tunnel for a bit and then came upon a whole new world. It was a lush, green landscape filled with trees, plants, grasses, and birds. The sudden change from near silence to the cacophony of an entire living, thriving place was astonishing. A massive waterfall cascaded from the top of a mountain in front, splashing into a valley where flowers of various colours spread as far as the eye could see. The mountains surrounding them formed a steep barrier that could only be breached by Firehorses, but they'd have to be right on top to see the green paradise below, as it wasn't very wide.

Dante and This-one walked along a grassy path as the scent of this living place enveloped them. This-one was nearly moved to tears by the sight of so much life.

Dante smiled and nodded, "Who knew, right? Anyone who comes here for the first time feels overwhelmed. It's quite a striking experience, but only a lucky few can come here."

This-one asked, "Do you have magical trees?"

Dante shook his head, "No, the Moontree doesn't grow. We tried many times and wasted so many Moonseeds. We have no more Moonseeds to try, and there's no point in repeating the same failed attempts, but we keep this place safe until it becomes possible, if ever. That's why this place must be kept a secret. We can't let it be destroyed. That's why there's no name for it. Having a name means people can talk about it more easily."

This-one nodded, scanning the area but saw no homes like in Serenus, "Where do you live?"

Dante explained, "We live in the caves. We don't use wood to build anything, and stone buildings would reduce the available space for trees to grow. We are the protectors of This-place."

"Where are the others?" This-one inquired.

"Follow me," Dante replied, leading the way.

They entered a cave where an older woman with long braided

hair sat alongside a young girl. Dante introduced them, "This is Mosi, our elder, and next to her is Jaci. We are the Tree Circle."

Mosi spoke firmly, "Keep This-place a secret, okay?"

"Yes, I will. I promise," This-one assured her.

"Good, good," Mosi replied, nodding.

Dante turned to This-one, "You can clean up in the waterfall. I'll bring you some food."

This-one ventured outside and headed towards the waterfall, feeling a sense of security. The place reminded him of Serenus. He swam under the waterfall for a bit and then came out to lie on the grass. He no longer needed a headscarf here, and the freedom felt invigorating. He could feel the breeze and the touch of grass on his skin once more. He stayed there for a long time, enjoying the sounds of the birds and watching squirrels scamper up and down the trees. He observed rabbits and chipmunks. The tree trunks were not as large as those in Serenus, but many living creatures made their homes inside them. For the first time since arriving in Forsaken Serenus, he could think of normal things again.

Dante returned, carrying food. "Magical, isn't it? Being able to feel the grass in this world?"

This-one nodded, savouring the meal—a salad made with various fruits and leafy greens sprinkled with pepper and salt.

Dante reminded him, "Eat the fruit, spread the seed. That's how we live here. We don't kill anything. We don't hunt. Occasionally, we get bread from Nuno, and we live happily. We have never felt we need more. We are blessed to be here." His eyes filled with tears, "We are living here when everyone else..."

This-one nodded and invited Dante to sit down. "When did you come here, Dante?"

"A very long time ago," Dante replied.

"You're young, so it wasn't too long ago, I guess?" This-one asked.

Dante smiled, "Okay, not that long ago. It's not like we can count days by looking at the Moon like we did in Serenus."

This-one furrowed his brow, "Why not?"

Dante laughed, "What? How long have you been here?"

"Maybe ten days," This-one answered.

"And you never noticed?" Dante inquired.

"Never noticed what?" This-one questioned.

"The moon is always half-moon," Dante explained.

"Oh, really? I... no, I never noticed," This-one admitted.

"You don't look up at the sky at night?" Dante asked.

This-one felt his cheeks redden, "I do. I don't know how I never noticed that."

Dante chuckled, "You don't really look. You glance, and you say how beautiful it is, and then you look away. To look is to really observe all the details and to let it form an image in your head."

"Were you a thinker in Serenus?" This-one asked.

"No, I was a healer," Dante revealed. "The goal of This-place is to regrow the Moontree. Only healers understand the magic of trees."

"My friend, Amy... She is... was a healer. She will come here soon, I hope," This-one shared, a hint of longing in his voice.

Dante nodded in understanding.

"Why doesn't the Moontree grow here?" This-one inquired.

"We don't know," Dante said. "No one grew the Moontree in Serenus. It grew by itself. Here, when we plant a Moonseed, it grows into a sapling and then dies. We don't know what to do."

"Is Mosi a healer too?" This-one asked.

"Yes, and she came from Serenus at a very old age, which means she was a healer for a long time, but even she can't understand the mystery. Maybe this world is too messed up. Maybe magic isn't allowed here," Dante pondered.

"Maybe the soil isn't good," This-one suggested.

"We've tried everything we can think of. And now, we don't even have a Moonseed to work with," Dante said, frustration evident in his voice.

Just then, Jaci ran over. "Hi, I'm Jaci."

"I am... you can call me This-one," he introduced himself.

Jaci giggled, "Yes, I heard. I think it's a good name."

"Really?" This-one asked, surprised.

"Yes. If you live here, you'll be This-one of This-place," Jaci explained with a smile.

"Hmm, most people I meet think I should pick a proper name," This-one commented.

"This-one is special. No one has ever been named This-one before," Jaci insisted.

"What did you do in Serenus?" This-one inquired.

"I was a healer," Jaci replied.

"I have a friend who was a healer in Serenus. I think being a healer was one of the best jobs," This-one mused.

Dante turned to This-one, "What did you do in Serenus?"

"Not much. The elders thought I was a thinker, but I couldn't really think of anything new," This-one confessed.

Jaci laughed, and This-one joined in. "Yeah, they thought I was a thinker, but Ma said I had another ability that I failed to realize. It was funny that I lived there doing the wrong job, but it's even funnier what my real ability was."

Jaci asked curiously, "What was your real ability?"

Dante giggled as This-one answered jokingly, "I can know... when I am wrong. That is my special ability."

Jaci laughed, and Dante and This-one laughed with her.

"So what does that actually mean? Did you ask Ma?" Dante inquired.

"I can learn better because I can know where I am wrong," This-one explained.

Jaci nodded. "Some people find their abilities early on in Serenus, and some just stumble upon it by chance. I'm sure your ability was amazing. Too bad you couldn't use it."

"But why did Conrad send you here? You weren't a healer," Dante asked This-one.

"I don't know that. I didn't know only healers could come to This-place," This-one admitted.

Jaci reassured him, "No, that's not true. Others are allowed too. But yes, mostly healers."

Dante nodded in agreement.

"Did you ever experience something in your life that felt... out of place, extraordinary?" Jaci asked.

"I can't think of... oh, yes. Do you know what a Mirror is?" This-one asked, his brow furrowing in thought.

"No," Jaci replied, shaking her head inquisitively.

"It's a special ability. We had a Mirror in Serenus who could... bring one's feelings out in the open, so those nearby could feel those feelings as their own. It was used to test what someone felt about a certain thing," This-one explained.

"That's an amazing ability," Dante chimed in, his eyes wide with fascination.

"Yes, it was really something," This-one agreed.

"So, what about it?" Jaci inquired.

"I was tested by the Mirror, and she said I had something in my head that she couldn't understand," This-one revealed.

Dante laughed, "Maybe she couldn't understand why you didn't pick a name."

This-one laughed as well, "No, she said there was a power inside me."

"Then..." Jaci urged him to continue.

"Then, nothing. That's it," This-one admitted.

"You didn't explore what this power was? You didn't try to find out?" Jaci questioned, disbelief in her voice.

"I didn't get a chance. A powerful wizard threatened to attack the Moontree unless I left Serenus with him," This-one explained.

"Why did a powerful wizard want you to go with him?" Dante

inquired, genuinely curious.

"Because he thought I was the wizard the poem talked about," This-one replied.

"And... are you?" Dante asked hesitantly.

"No! Ma said I'm not the wizard. I had a... friend in Serenus who thought we could be a wizard and not know it and that it wasn't necessary that the wizard was a bad person. He thought I could be the wizard," This-one clarified.

"So you left Serenus with the wizard to save the Moontree?" Jaci surmised.

"Ah, no... my friends found a way to catch the wizard and send him to the Dark End," This-one corrected her.

"Then why couldn't you explore your ability?" Jaci pressed.

"Well, my friend, the healer, she left Serenus in search of her friend. And I had promised her that I would follow her if she left," This-one explained.

"So, your healer friend went after her friend, and you went after her?" Jaci summarized.

"Yes," This-one confirmed.

"And is someone coming after you?" Jaci asked, grinning.

We laughed out loud.

"And where is your healer friend now?" Jaci asked.

"She's waiting to meet the friend she left Serenus for," This-one answered.

"And what are you doing? You left Serenus for her. She finds her friend, and then what will you do here? You didn't think it through," Jaci pointed out.

"Well, I... came for a friend. I was there with her. I helped her find her friend, and now that she is waiting to meet that friend, Conrad sent me here," This-one explained.

Jaci nodded, "Interesting."

Dante laughed, "So Jaci? What's the judgement then?"

Jaci snapped at him, "Shut up, idiot!"

Dante laughed, "Jaci likes to ask so many questions as if in the end she's going to announce a verdict, but then she just ends the conversation."

Jaci laughed with him, "I ask questions because I have a curious mind, and I like to know things."

This-one looked at Jaci in surprise, eyebrows raised. Dante and Jaci continued their playful bickering, but he stayed quiet.

Dante changed the subject, "Okay, so now we're waiting for Conrad. What should we do to pass the time?"

Jaci suggested, "You could go out and make sure no one is near This-place."

Dante laughed, "Oh... yeah, I didn't complete the round. I'll see you guys later."

Jaci jokingly retorted, "You don't have to."

Dante picked a small stick and playfully tossed it at Jaci before disappearing into a nearby cave.

Jaci turned her attention to This-one, "So, what do you like to do when you're free?"

This-one hesitated, "... I ... I don't know. I haven't really been free a lot."

Curious, Jaci asked, "What did you see in this world?"

This-one recounted the story of his meeting with Ma, how he came to this world, how he attempted to unite people, how the plan fell apart, and how he had to hide in the baker's home until he was sent to the Tree Circle. "That's all. Now you know my entire life story," This-one concluded.

Throughout the narration, Jaci asked many questions, making sure she understood the reasons behind every action. Afterward, she said, "I ask questions so I can understand better. I think I understand you. You're a good friend and a kind person. You want to do the right thing, and it hasn't been working for you so far. But you always land on your feet somehow, so you're very lucky too. And I think we're lucky that you came to us."

Jaci's kind words warmed This-one's heart, and both Ma and I were once again thrilled that he had landed on his feet again. He was in good company.

Ch 31: Now is the time for you to shine

Over the next few days, This-one spent his time exploring This-place. The mountains were riddled with caves, each serving various purposes. A myriad of trees and plants adorned this hidden world, creating a serene atmosphere.

Dante and Jaci had an interesting friendship. They often argued and annoyed each other, yet they remained close. Jaci was unique. Not only was she curious and eager to understand things in detail, but she also had a peculiar habit of talking to plants and trees as if they could hear her. Each time she approached a tree, she would say hello, place her hand on the trunk, and nod. She made sure to visit all her tree-friends regularly, and if she didn't see one for a few days, she felt compelled to pay it a visit. Dante and This-one would accompany her, sitting nearby as she greeted each tree with a genuine sense of having missed them.

Dante never commented on this behaviour, but This-one found it quite intriguing. When no one was around, he even tried it himself. He placed his hand on a tree trunk and said hello, imagining that the tree was a friend who could understand him. Thinking of a tree as a living being capable of feeling seemed right. However, he never practiced this in front of others.

Dante and Jaci reminded This-one of his friends back in Serenus, particularly Fabio and Misa. He shared his stories and listened to theirs. They were easy to talk to. Dante and Jaci had lived in Serenus at different times, but upon meeting in Forsaken Serenus, they quickly became close friends. Mosi had been a Keeper for many years before leaving to find a place where the Moontree could grow. Jaci and Dante accompanied Mosi on her quest. Together, they eventually found This-place. Nuno was the next member to join the Tree Circle, and on his advice, they shared its location with Shahzor. Conrad had only recently become a part of the Tree Circle, brought in by Shahzor after they met at the castle. The group was extremely cautious about who they brought in. They had tried growing the Moontree multiple times, but the saplings would never survive beyond a few days. They didn't know what else to try, so they kept This-place a secret, hoping one day they would finally figure out how to grow a Moontree. This-one found Mosi's conviction and determination to find This-place quite inspiring.

In their free time, This-one, Dante, and Jaci often sat in the trees. The branches offered various opportunities for leisure and play. Within a few days, This-one felt stronger, able to hang, swing, and sit comfortably in the trees. The view from above provided a different perspective of the world—more expansive and somehow more satisfying than what could be seen from the ground.

Both Jaci and Dante were surprisingly strong, despite their lean frames. This-one guessed it was due to their frequent tree climbing. They could pull themselves up with ease, a skill that This-one initially struggled with but was gradually improving. Sometimes, while perched on a tree branch overlooking the waterfall, This-one would wonder, "Why don't we live in the trees? I understand we couldn't do that in This-place because the trees are too precious, but why didn't we spend more time in the trees in Serenus? The trees were all around us, waiting to be climbed, and the view from above is... undeniably better."

Jaci agreed with This-one, feeling completely at home among the trees. Dante would often hang upside down from a branch, playfully challenging This-one, "You can do it now. Stop thinking. Start living. Come, hang with me."

One day, while This-one was picking fruit, Conrad finally arrived. Dante and Jaci were overjoyed to see him, as he had secured a special place in their hearts. Later that day, Conrad spoke to This-one.

Conrad, with a glint in his eye, said, "I have a theory that I want to test. Come with me."

This-one, concerned about his friend, asked, "How's Amy?"

Conrad answered, "Amy is happy. She is with Alfred. Now, come."

Relieved that Amy was finally with Alfred, This-one followed Conrad to where Mosi and Jaci sat. They both looked at This-one and smiled warmly.

Curious, This-one inquired, "What's going on?"

Conrad urged him, "Tell us what Ma told you about your ability."

This-one hesitated, "She said I can know when I'm wrong."

Conrad prodded, "And?"

This-one continued, "And that this ability enabled me to learn."

Conrad encouraged him, "Don't be shy. Say it."

This-one gathered his courage, "Ma said because I could know when I am wrong, I could correct myself. She said because of this, I was better at learning than others."

Conrad pressed on, "Jaci told us about your experience with the Mirror. Alia said you have a power inside you. But you don't know what that power is, right?"

This-one corrected him, "Was. What that power was. Yes, that's right."

Conrad laughed, "And the elders thought you were a thinker?"

This-one replied, "Yes, but they were clearly wrong."

Conrad explained, "Learning is an ability that everyone has. We can all learn. What's so special about you?"

This-one admitted, "I don't know. I never felt I was better at it."

Conrad requested, "Tell us all your experiences in Serenus."

This-one was taken aback, "ALL experiences?"

Conrad clarified, "All unusual experiences."

This-one began, "Well, we fought Esmeray and defeated her."

Conrad asked, "What was unusual about that?"

This-one explained, "She was a powerful wizard. She killed you, but we defeated her."

Conrad shook his head, "No, that's not what we're looking for. We want to hear about things that happened that you couldn't explain. Things that others couldn't do, but you could."

This-one thought for a moment, "I always believed Qilam wasn't bad, unlike others who thought he was useless and dangerous. I enjoyed talking to him."

Conrad probed, "Why?"

This-one elaborated, "It made sense what he said. I mean, he said things that were unbelievable at the time, but he never pretended to know for sure. He told me he wasn't sure about it and worried he could be wrong. That made me feel like he wasn't lying. And his actions ultimately helped Serenus."

Conrad pushed further, "Okay, something else?"

This-one was at a loss, "I... don't know."

Conrad prompted, "Okay, tell us what Alia said about you."

This-one recounted, "She said I have a power inside me that she couldn't access. There was something, a piece of information, hidden inside my head that she couldn't reach. She wanted to know it and tried her best, but she couldn't find out."

Conrad inquired, "This was the only unusual thing about you in Serenus?"

This-one confirmed, "Yes."

Conrad requested, "Okay, tell us all the details of this event. How did it start, what happened, everything."

This-one recounted the entire event, and as he did, Conrad's face lit up, reminiscent of his expression back in the baker's home. Mosi, too, sat up a bit taller as This-one finished telling the story.

Conrad exclaimed, "So, Alia tried to probe your mind, but she couldn't. When she used too much power, she weakened. You were about to collapse, but then you started sensing Alia's feelings. You became the Mirror. You are a learner. You learn from experience. You learned her ability!"

This-one's mouth hung open, his knees nearly buckling under him for a moment.

Mosi chimed in, "This-one has come to This-place, and it is good."

Jaci laughed, and Conrad approached This-one, who was still lost in thought. He said, "My friend, you are a learner. From any experience you have, you can learn. You can even learn abilities from other people."

Jaci interjected, "But how is that useful now? There are no abilities left."

Conrad explained, "Yes, all our magical abilities vanish when we leave Serenus, but... I think whatever he learned will stay with him. He can't learn now because he lost his special learning ability, but what he learned could still be inside him."

Jaci wondered excitedly, "So he could still be a Mirror?"

Conrad nodded, "Yes, I believe so, but a Mirror needs Moonlight to probe a mind, and we don't have a Moontree to collect Moonlight."

Mosi shook her head, her voice tinged with sadness, "Moontree doesn't grow here."

Conrad approached Mosi, "Don't lose hope, Mosi. There is

more. This-one is terrible at realizing who he is." Then he turned to This-one, "Didn't Amy capture Moonlight in your presence? Didn't you experience that?"

This-one almost screamed, "I did!"

I looked at Ma with wide eyes, "Wow, Conrad is good."

Ma smiled, "Yes, he is."

Conrad continued, "It's possible that you learned the ability to capture Moonlight."

Jaci stood up in excitement, "And if we have Moonlight, we could feed the sapling and keep it strong."

Conrad nodded, "So? Can you? Capture Moonlight?"

This-one was unsure. No, he felt as if he knew nothing. Then he started laughing with tears in his eyes.

Conrad asked, "What?"

This-one, now caught between laughter and tears, replied, "I am so... ignorant. And you know what? Kratos once asked me what success in life meant, and I... I told him."

This-one laughed in fits as tears streamed down his cheeks. The others watched him with concern. "I told him, I answered that question... As if I knew... I didn't even know what life is, and I thought I could tell him what success in life meant." This-one shook his head as he cried, "I am the biggest idiot who has ever lived."

Conrad placed his hand on This-one's shoulder, "No, my friend. You are capable, but not all-capable. You can do things that no one else can, but you struggle with certain other things. That's true for everyone."

This-one shook his head, "I am just lucky. That's my ability."

Conrad replied, "Well, that can be said for everyone who has an ability."

This-one said sadly, "I wish I knew who I was, what I could do. I wish I knew it in Serenus."

Conrad nodded thoughtfully, "I understand you feel like you failed, but I think this was meant to be. Your journey unfolded in such a way that you could arrive here — exactly where you are needed. Where no one else can make a difference, you will play your role. You've been preparing for this very moment, and your time starts now. It's time to realize your potential. Now is the time for you to shine."

I glanced at Ma, who had tears in her eyes. Ma nodded in agreement.

This-one composed himself and said, "I need a thinker like you to be my guide, to show me what I can do and how to help."

Conrad smiled warmly, "All the thinkers of this world are nothing compared to what you are. You represent hope. I will be with you, and everyone who wants to turn this hell back into heaven will be with you too, but you will lead us, not me. I will advise you and share my knowledge, but you have to be yourself, and that's enough. All this time, we were waiting for you."

This-one inquired, "But how did you know Amy captured Moonlight when I was with her?"

Conrad replied, "When I brought Alfred to her, I asked her to tell us everything about you. Oh, and Alfred wanted me to tell you that he would do anything to help you. Whatever you need. He was very grateful that you were there for Amy when he couldn't be."

This-one nodded, "Amy is my friend. I didn't do it for Alfred. He doesn't owe me anything, and I am happy that they are together. Tell me what you need. What can I do?"

Mosi smiled, "Capture Moonlight!"

From that day on, This-one's life revolved around capturing Moonlight. The healers shared as much information as they could until, eventually, he succeeded. He caught his first Moonlight.

On that day, This-place was filled with joy, hope, and life. This-one placed the tiny Moonlight string in a tiny stone vial. He gifted the vial to Mosi, who wore it in a necklace, tears welling up in her eyes as she put it on.

Conrad announced, "There is only one place where we can find a Moonseed: The Sanctum of Knowledge. We need to steal it. I will do that. I will return with the Moonseed. Don't leave This-place. Gather Moonlight and wait for me."

This-one promised, "I won't leave. This is who I am now."

Conrad left to steal a Moonseed from the castle while the Tree Circle worked harder than ever before to make as many containers as they could. Unable to use wood, they crafted containers from stone. This-place buzzed with unseen energy as This-one honed his skill at capturing Moonlight from the half-moon that appeared every night. It had always been there, but only now could they harness its light and benefit from it.

Days passed, and stone containers filled with Moonlight, but Conrad didn't return. Mosi was certain they needed more Moonlight to nourish the sapling daily. She often said, "More is good." So This-one captured as much as he could.

The cave where the Moonlight containers were stored began to fill up. This-one would refill the containers that lost their glow, and over time, there were so many containers that he couldn't fill new ones. All his time was spent refilling those that lost their Moonlight.

They prepared as best as they could, but many more days passed without Conrad's return.

One day, Shahzor arrived with terrible news. "Alfred left Amy and returned to the castle."

This-one's eyes widened, "Oh... why? Where is Amy now?"

Shahzor shook his head, "I don't know. She just walked away, and I have no idea where she went. I came to see if she came here."

This-one sighed, "She didn't come here. Where could she go? There is nowhere else to go."

Shahzor replied, "No, there are places to go, but I thought she might come to you."

This-one's heart ached, "Why did Alfred leave her?"

Shahzor explained, "He is a Seeker. He left her already in Serenus. He left her again for the same reason. He wants to find the lost scroll."

This-one lamented, "I wish I could be with Amy, but I can't. Where is Conrad?"

Shahzor shook his head, "I haven't heard from him in a while."

This-one pleaded, "Shahzor, I need your help. Please find out what happened to Conrad! He had to complete a crucial task."

Shahzor nodded and left. This-one's life became difficult. He wanted to leave This-place, but he had a duty. His friend or his duty? He had to make a decision, and for the first time in his life, he didn't choose a friend. He stayed, though it weighed heavily on him. He refilled the containers with Moonlight as if it was the purpose of his life now.

Dante and Jaci stayed with him, trying to distract him with whatever they could think of, but This-one was hurting. Every day that he chose not to search for his friend was a day spent in misery, yet he remained. He felt guilt, but his decision was firm. "I won't leave until the Moontree grows," he would tell Jaci and Dante when they looked at him with concern.

Nuno paid them a visit and told them that there was still no sign of Amy. No one knew where she went. Conrad was still at the castle but had no luck stealing the Moonseed.

"What if we tell the king that This-one could grow the Moontree again?" Dante suggested.

Nuno shook his head, "No, This-one has already stopped stones. If Shikongo finds out he can do more, he will not let him. The king will not cooperate. If he knew that a Moontree could be grown here, he would take This-one and make him grow a Moontree, but he would be the only one who would benefit from it. And he would use the Moonlight to tighten his grasp on the people."

This-one inquired, "What if growing the Moontree opens the door?"

Nuno replied, "We can't be sure. What if it doesn't? We can't risk losing you to the king. The king must not know. We need to grow the Moontree, and that is the way to strip him of his power. People will see that it is not the king who is solving their problems. Until that time comes, you need to stay hidden."

Jaci nodded, "The king must not know."

Nuno repeated, "The king must not know."

Nuno left, and This-one remained burdened with guilt. A part of his existence was intertwined with Amy, and that part was lost somewhere in this forsaken world. He worried for her, and it was tearing him apart from the inside.

I was lying on the back of a giant Snow Owl as it gracefully soared through the night sky of the Sandbox. The breathtaking sight of stars and galaxies above me was my favourite view, and I often indulged in this activity to contemplate various matters. I found myself thinking about This-one and what he was going through. I could understand his thoughts and feel his pain as if it was my own. What This-one experienced in Forsaken Serenus, I endured in the Sandbox. I couldn't solve his problems for him, but I thought about them all the time. It wasn't really a choice. If This-one was thinking something, so was I. That was how Ma's system functioned.

The more I reflected, the more it seemed that the king was the root of all problems in Forsaken Serenus. But what kind of powers did he possess? I wished Ma would tell me about the king, but she insisted it would be more interesting if she didn't.

Ma? I said.

Ma appeared, "Yes."

Why is the king such a... problem?

"That's who he is. That's what his path made him."

Okay, but you must dislike him a lot, right? He is causing so much pain.

"Yes, he is causing pain, but he is also keeping the world together."

No, he is not.

"He is. Do you know what the world was like before he became king?"

Tell me.

"Anarchy. Now there is a system. He controls everything and causes a lot of misery for his own selfish reasons, but it is still a better world than before he became king. He wants to open the door, so he needs peace. He has gathered all the knowledge in the Sanctum of Knowledge. This is a great service to the people. He did it for his own reasons and not to help others, but it did help others."

But you dislike him, right?

"No, I pity him. He does things with the wrong intentions, even good things, so he doesn't get any credit."

But you dislike him for what he does to others when he causes pain, right?

"I don't dislike anyone. I can understand why someone is the way they are. That doesn't mean I think they are right, but I don't dislike them. It is the system I created. They are the product of this system. Right actions or wrong actions are all my doing."

But you do get angry sometimes, right? Like when they are doing something bad, don't you get upset with them?

"Yes, I do get upset, and I cry."

And then you punish them?

"No, if someone is doing wrong, they are already hurting themselves. I don't punish them. I try to help them become right. I speak to them in their thoughts, but they choose not to listen to me."

When someone does something really, really bad, don't they deserve punishment?

"When someone does something bad, they are already being punished by themselves. Their own judgment is punishing them. I don't punish them. What they do to others, they are also doing to themselves."

Esmeray attacked the village. She destroyed homes and hurt people. She did that to others, not to herself.

"What are others?"

Others, you know... not her, the rest of the people.

"I know. Others need to be protected from her, just like you would protect a healthy thing from a diseased one. But the diseased one is not to be disliked or hated. It is to be healed, helped, and treated."

How could we treat Esmeray?

"If you couldn't, then you could limit her ability to hurt others."

That's what we did.

"Yes, but you didn't have to send her into the Dark End."

We had to. There was no place we could keep her in. She would have attacked us again.

"Maybe. I understand your reasons, but she could also change. Sending someone into the Dark End should only be done if there is no hope left."

How could we know if there was hope or not and if she was capable of change or not? We can't leave ourselves vulnerable.

"Yes, I understand. Those who create bad experiences for others should receive bad experiences, so they can be deterred from repeating their mistakes. But your focus should be on protecting yourself and others instead of punishing them or sending them into the Dark End. That takes away their chance to change."

I don't think Esmeray could change. And we couldn't keep her anywhere. We didn't have an option where we could protect ourselves from her and not send her to the Dark End.

"How long did you think to defend against her attack, and how long did you think of finding a place to keep her to stay safe from her?"

We didn't. We didn't think about it because we didn't want to take a chance.

"And did you know where you were sending her? What if there was no Loop of Black Tears, and she went to another island? You didn't want to solve the problem. You wanted to get rid of it. And I can understand your reasons, but if you ask me, you shouldn't take away one's chance to change. Yes, protect yourself and others from the disease, but don't take away their right to heal."

Hmm, I'm sorry. I didn't think like that.

"I am sorry too."

If someone is dangerous, we should protect against them, but we shouldn't take away their right to change.

Ma nodded, "Yes."

And we should help them heal.

"Yes. And I think it is time to tell you a secret."

I sat up. What secret?

Ma smiled, "There is no them. It's only us."

What do you mean?

Ma repeated, "There is no them. It's only us."

What? I don't understand.

"I know. I want to leave this thought in your mind, dangling unresolved, bothering you. I want to see if you can figure it out."

Figure what out? It doesn't even make sense. There is no them?

Ma teased, "Yes, now you get it. There is no them."

No, I don't get it. What do you mean it's only us?

Ma asked, "Which word are you having trouble with? 'Only' or 'us'?"

Maaaaaa!

"Patience. Let it sit in your mind. Let's see what it comes up with. Until then, leave it unresolved. It is okay to leave things unresolved. Don't be so quick to reach a conclusion. Sometimes, just tell yourself, I don't have enough information about this, so I can't reach a conclusion. There is no rush to pick what feels like the best option. You can wait for the right one."

This-one's thoughts pulled me to him. "I am failing her. What is she going through? When will Conrad come back?" This-one said to himself as he placed another container that he had refilled with Moonlight. Then he sat down in despair and said to himself, "I am feeling so bad... what should I do? Oh... Ma said I should cry... maybe that will help."

Tears ran down This-one's cheeks as he allowed himself to cry. He knew what he was doing was right, there was no change needed, but he had to let out the frustration. He was alone in the cave and he let the tears fall for a few moments.

Ma said, "Poor This-one. He has been so sad, so stuck."

As This-one finished crying, he wiped away his tears. He stayed there for another few moments and wondered how much lighter he felt after crying. He heard footsteps and quickly cleaned his face with his shirt.

Jaci walked into the cave and asked This-one to go with her. She was smiling. This-one felt better and smiled back, "What happened?"

Jaci replied, "Come on, let me show you."

They walked out of the cave as This-one hoped it was Conrad who had come back. He followed Jaci with quick steps.

Jaci walked into another cave, with This-one right behind her. Dante and Mosi were already there, and they were holding candles.

Mosi greeted him, "This-one has come. Good, good."

Dante came forward holding a candle, "A ray of hope."

Jaci picked a candle, smiled, raised the candle, and said, "is what you are."

Then they sang together as This-one watched in surprise.

> "A ray of hope, is what you are,
>
> What you have brought, and what you are.
>
> We lived in Serenus without concern,
>
> Left problems for our future, let our world burn.
>
> When we left Serenus, we were shocked!
>
> The door to happiness... was locked!

We were covered in mud, and we drowned in a flood,

But we didn't care for that; we were growing a bud.

We tried all we could, and were eager for some hope,

Nothing really worked, we were rolling down a slope.

We could face all suffering and suffer all the pain,

But without any hope, we couldn't try again.

Our hearts were dark before you came,

We had scary thoughts, but then you came.

A ray of hope is what you are,

What you have brought and what you are

We can see your pain; we can see it in your eyes,

Your friend needs your help, and your heart cries.

But you stay steadfast, and you gather Moonlight,

We thank you a lot and are with you in this fight.

Our light in the dark, you are doing what is right,

There's always an end, though it isn't in our sight.

Our hearts feel pain when it aches your heart,

We can feel your pain; We are tangled, not apart.

We are here for you; rely on us,

Accept our shoulder, cry on us.

We can listen to your problem and say we understand,

If we can't carry your burden, we can hold your hand.

Our light in the dark, you are doing what is right,

There's always an end, though it isn't in our sight.

A ray of hope is what you are,

What you have brought and what you are."

This-one had tears in his eyes as they hugged him, patted him on the shoulder, and messed up his already messy hair, saying, "Thank you." He felt like his problems became easier and simpler. Their words made him stronger. He was not alone. They understood his pain and acknowledged his sacrifice.

This-one's eyes shimmered with gratitude as he said, "Thank you, this means a lot. I hope we can regrow the Moontree. I hope it proves to be useful."

Mosi, her voice warm and gentle, replied, "You are trying. Trying is good."

This-one nodded, determination evident in his tone. "Yes, I am doing what is right."

Mosi smiled. "Doing the right thing is good. Appreciating when someone does the right thing... that's good, too. And saying thank you... also good."

With a mischievous glint in his eye, Conrad entered the cave with a Moonseed in his hand. "And stealing... also good?" he asked playfully.

Mosi laughed and shook her head as his arrival infused This-place with renewed energy. Dante, Jaci, and This-one jumped with joy.

I was ecstatic. I jumped around and danced involuntarily. Ma was also happier than usual. She joined me in the dance as This-one watched the Tree Circle select a spot to grow a Moontree.

Dante brought 'The Book of Trees', and they carefully planted the seed. Now it was time to wait. Conrad stayed at This-place to see if the tree would grow again. This presented an excellent opportunity to talk to him and learn from his thoughts.

The next morning, after checking on the Moonseed, This-one and Conrad went for a walk. This-one asked, "What does it mean? A line in the line of thought."

Conrad thought for a moment before adding, "It thinks what I think."

This-one repeated, "Yes. What does it mean?"

Conrad explained, "It's a thought I had while sitting under the Greentree once. The idea is that we are just a thought in a long line of thoughts."

Intrigued, This-one asked, "And who is the thinker?"

"Ma," Conrad responded.

"Oh, I see," said This-one, with a nod of understanding.

Conrad continued, "Yeah, at the time, it felt very amazing, and I wasn't really sure if it was correct. But then I asked Ma, and she said it was right."

This-one wondered, "So, we really are her thoughts?"

Conrad confirmed, "Yes, thoughts that she acted on and made us, or... just thoughts."

This-one pointed out, "You didn't ask Ma if she acted on the thoughts and made us or if we are just the thoughts."

Conrad shrugged. "Our manner of existence doesn't matter. Whether we exist as thoughts or as things she made as a result of thoughts, what difference does it make?"

"Hmm," This-one mused.

Conrad smiled, and This-one laughed, "And the elders thought I was a thinker."

Conrad replied, "You are. Everyone is a thinker. Some think about what they can do in this world, and some think about who they are and why they came here."

This-one complimented him, "But you are so good at it."

"Meh, not really," Conrad said modestly. "I haven't thought of a single thing that could help our world. You stopped stones. I didn't. You defeated Esmeray, I couldn't. And I have been trying to bring down the king, but I am yet to have some success, though I see hope in you."

This-one recalled, "Nuno said we could take the king's power if people were on our side, if we could regrow the Moontree."

Conrad spoke thoughtfully, "Yes, we may be able to do that, but I'm not sure it's the right way."

This-one furrowed their brow, asking, "Why not?"

Conrad explained, "Anarchy is not the way. There is a system in place. What will we replace it with if we bring it down? Any system is better than no system."

This-one countered, "But this only helps those who are close to the king."

"And those are people too," Conrad reminded. "Our goal is to make the system work for more people than it is working for today. We don't want it to stop working for those it already benefits. We don't need to punish them because they have what we don't. We need to have it too. The king has his followers, and they will fight if an effort is made to dethrone him. Who will suffer in the fight? The ones who are more vulnerable. We have to do it smartly. We have to... find a way to make things better. Anarchy and chaos are not better. Steady improvement is better than drastic change."

This-one inquired, "Why? If all the problems could be solved at once, wouldn't that be better?"

Conrad shook his head, "If all the problems could be solved at once, that would be better. But it's not possible. There will always be problems. Our goal is to make tomorrow better than today, not to break it down and build again."

This-one asked, "So how will we do that?"

Conrad proposed , "First, we need to find the source of the king's power. If we could take that from him without a fight, that would be a good start."

This-one's eyes widened, "You mean to steal the lost scroll?"

Conrad replied, "No, the lost scroll didn't give him powers."

"I heard he got his magical powers back because of the lost scroll," This-one insisted.

"He may have," Conrad conceded, "but the real source of his power is what he claims to have accomplished."

"What is that?" This-one asked, curious.

"To die and come back as if he didn't die. To become invincible," Conrad explained.

This-one thought out loud, "Maybe he got this power because of the lost scroll. The scroll was supposed to make us a god. Maybe he can do that now, because he is..."

This-one hesitated, unable to finish his sentence. Conrad probed, "You couldn't finish your sentence. Why?"

"I don't know. It doesn't feel right," This-one admitted.

"Exactly," Conrad agreed. "If he has the power of gods, why is he afraid? He couldn't have you as a leader of the Keepers because he felt insecure. Why does he fear? Is the power of the lost scroll not enough to satisfy him? Why does he need more? Who wants more?"

This-one answered, "The one who thinks he doesn't have enough."

"Or the one who lies about what he says he has," Conrad added.

This-one's eyes widened, "You think he's lying?"

"I'm sure he's lying. There's no other explanation," Conrad confirmed.

"But why can't he die then?" This-one asked, puzzled.

"Exactly," Conrad nodded. "That is the mystery we need to solve. How is he able to live through death?"

"How can we find out?"

Conrad sighed, "I don't know. I've spoken to many Seekers who don't believe the king has the lost scroll. No one knows how he can live through death."

This-one raised an eyebrow, "Many Seekers think he doesn't have the lost scroll? So they accept him as king knowing he's a liar?"

"Yes," Conrad nodded, "it gives them an opportunity to live a better life here and to keep working in the Sanctum of Knowledge."

Conrad looked at This-one with a smile, "I have a plan, though it's risky, and you'll have to... take the risk."

This-one inquired, "What is it?"

"I'm still working on it. I'll let you know once I have it figured out," Conrad promised.

This-one nodded, "Okay, but first, I have to find Amy as soon as I can leave here."

Conrad shook his head, "No, stay here. Let Amy figure things out by herself."

This-one protested, "No, I can't leave her alone."

Conrad insisted, "Some alone time is good for her. She needs to realize that Alfred is on a mission. He's a Seeker at heart. He can't live away from it for too long."

This-one asked, "What if we could find a way to send Amy to the castle, so they could be together again?"

"No, that's not what Alfred wants," Conrad replied.

"But what about what Amy wants?" This-one argued.

"She needs to learn that Alfred's highest is finding the lost scroll. He left her in Serenus because he knew she wasn't interested in the scroll," Conrad explained.

"But she's alone, and who knows where she is and what troubles she's in," This-one worried.

Conrad pressed, "What you have to do is far more important than what one person needs."

"A friend, what a friend needs," This-one persisted.

Conrad countered, "She's still just a person."

This-one wasn't happy with what Conrad was saying. They stayed quiet for the rest of their walk, and Conrad respected their silence.

They checked back on the Moonseed and found Dante and Jaci sitting there. In a little while, Mosi came and sat by it too. They knew the Moonseed would take time to grow, but they couldn't stay away from it.

Over the next several days, everyone sat by the Moonseed whenever they had free time. Mosi would even talk to it. They had grown Moonseeds before, so they were very hopeful that it would grow. The real challenge was keeping it alive. This-one kept busy collecting Moonlight every night.

As days passed, the Moonseed grew into a sapling. The Tree Circle was happy. Soon they would find out if magic would return to Forsaken Serenus. Mosi poured Moonlight on its delicate little leaves as others watched curiously. The sapling drank the Moonlight and grew stronger. More days passed, and the sapling grew into a healthy plant. It was regularly fed with water and Moonlight. This-one couldn't keep up with the needs of the plant. He collected Moonlight whenever the moon was in the sky, but the containers were emptying.

Mosi was hopeful. She thought once the plant established its roots, it would need less feeding. As more leaves grew, they would glow in the Moonlight as if taking the Moonlight directly from the moon.

This was very encouraging, and Conrad was sure it would grow. He even started planning to grow more Moontrees outside of This-place. Soon, he returned to the castle.

The Tree Circle carefully measured and drew a circle around the Moonplant, envisioning a place for The Seven to grow around the Moontree. However, it was too early for that. The plant's roots hadn't reached that far yet, and it needed to become a tree first.

Weeks passed, and the Moonplant grew, nourishing their hopes. This-one collected Moonlight non-stop. He was overjoyed that the Moontree was growing, but his heart remained tangled elsewhere.

Ma and I observed everything, hoping it would all work out, and it seemed like it would. We felt that things could improve. The people in Serenus had stopped throwing stones, the garbage had ceased piling up, and a Moontree was growing in Forsaken Serenus. Things were good, except for the fact that Amy was alone, which bothered This-one, but there was nothing to be done.

Months went by, and Dante and Jaci left a few times to find Amy, but they returned without any news of her. They would sit with This-one and offer hopeful words, though they secretly worried that she might have encountered trouble.

Ch 32: There is no them

Ma? I thought.

"Yes?" she responded.

You said you created many worlds. Can you tell me about your other worlds?

"Yes, I made many worlds, and each runs a different line of thought — a different experiment, exploring various possibilities."

Can you show me one of those worlds?

"Yes. Let me see... which one should I tell you about. Hmm, okay, I know. There's this one world where the systems are very close to how they are in this world. You'll understand that one more easily."

What is it called?

"I call it 'reality'," Ma replied.

But you said all worlds are real; then why did you call that one 'reality'?

"Because the system in that world was designed to show everyone the 'reality' of their actions once they reached Forsaken Serenus. In that world, the watch on your wrist plays a much bigger role in life in Forsaken Serenus," Ma explained.

I glanced at my watch. It was blank. What does it do?

"When someone leaves Serenus, the watch shows them how people in Serenus remember them."

Like my vision on my first night here? When my friends remembered Amy and me?

Ma clarified, "Yes, but it's not just once. The watch shows them visions all the time - whenever someone thinks of them."

Why don't we have that? That sounds amazing.

"It is amazing if people were happy with you, but not always. Let me show you instead of telling you."

Ma changed the world around us into Forsaken Serenus. We were on top of the keep, looking down at everyone. It appeared very much like the Forsaken Serenus I had seen. Well, upon closer inspection, this one was worse. I saw a person hitting his head on a wall.

What's going on? Why is he hitting his head on the wall? That looks painful.

"Yes, he received a memory on his watch. It's a painful memory."

What did he see?

"Someone just remembered how he caused pain. Someone remembered him with disgust and hate."

What is hate?

"Hate is a strong feeling of dislike. Your world doesn't have this feeling. The man you saw is hitting his head on the wall to punish himself," Ma explained.

That's horrible. Didn't they go through... The Loop of Black Tears? Did they not forgive themselves?"

"They did, but when their watch shows them memories, they can't help it. They experience pain and misery, and they end up hurting themselves."

That's too much, Ma. Isn't that excessive punishment? They can't die, they can't fix their mistakes, and even after going through The Loop of Black Tears, they still get punished? That's too much. Please, Ma, help them.

"That was the system in that world, but look, he was not alone. Observe how he has others to help him. They have a support group. They talk to each other, they remember the horrible things they did, and they repent, which helps them cope with these memories."

What did that man do?

"His name is A. He caused a lot of pain in Serenus, and now he gets memories when people remember him. They recall him with harsh words. Those words didn't have any impact on him when he was doing all the bad things, but once The Loop of Black Tears stripped away all the pretense, the layers of lies, and the entitlements... once all delusion is washed away, they see the reality, and it is painful."

But he has others... the support group to help him deal with it. Look, the man next to him is consoling him.

"Yes, that is B. He consoles A because he knows what A is going through."

He sounds like a good guy.

"Yes, he is doing a good thing now, but how does he know what A is going through?" Ma asked.

Because he goes through the same?

"Yes. B started wars that hurt millions in his world. He had a circle of 'friends' around him who would cheer him on. He pretended that he was doing the right thing as if tricking enough people into believing he was doing the right thing would make it so."

Amy said many people think they are doing the right thing even when they are not. Is that correct?

"Yes. B destroyed villages, evicted people from their homes, and rained fire down upon them from above while his 'friends' boasted about the good they were doing for their world. They thought that if they lied loudly and frequently enough, their lies would become the truth."

But no one believed it, of course, right? They could see what was happening, right?

"Well, you would think that, but not really. His friends were skilled at lying and twisting words. They convinced many, and those they couldn't convince, they threatened, discredited, and humiliated. They believed they were so adept at their propaganda that no one would see them for who they were, but they were wrong. History remembers them for who they truly are. Like the Black Dust that hovers in the air before settling to the ground, their lies could only cloud the air for a little while. A lie needs to be fed constantly, or it falls apart. The truth remains afloat."

So a small group let him do horrible things?

Ma explained, "Yes, a very small group supported him because they benefited from the war. A much larger group around him was made up of fools who he had convinced that he was doing the right thing, and an overwhelming majority of that world saw him for who he truly was, but they had their own interests. They didn't want to stand up to him."

That sounds awful. I'm glad I'm not in that world.

"It is horrible," Ma nodded sadly.

So the ones he was fighting against, were those the good people?

"No. In many ways, they were worse than him. They had less power, but they shared the same mentality: to use any means to gain more resources and control over their part of the world. Their tactics were different. They would start wars, claiming that I had told them to do so."

There's no way people fell for that, right?

"Well... many did and joined them," Ma replied.

WHAT? Don't people in that world have their minds?

"They do, just like in your world, but the liars concoct stories to convince others that they are good and the other side is evil and that they are fighting against evil," Ma explained.

Both sides think they are good and fighting evil?

"Yes, and many fall for their traps. They join their battles and die for them, believing they are dying a glorious death."

That world is insane. Wow... I thought we had problems in Serenus. I... I still can't comprehend why people don't see through these lies."

"The ones who do are in the majority, but they are not violent. That world is controlled by violence, not logic. Those who can inflict the most pain are the ones who get to decide the fate of others."

They don't have elders? Wise people?

"When you were in Serenus, the elders needed to be carried around. Why?"

Because of their old age, they didn't have much strength in their bodies.

"But why were they still elders? Why would everyone still listen to them?" Ma asked.

We didn't listen to them because of the strength of their muscles. We listened to them because of the wisdom of their ways.

"In 'reality'... in that world... people don't listen to wise ones. They listen to strong ones," Ma said.

That's so sad. So... so many must be suffering there, then.

"Yes, far too many."

It's sad... but it's kind of funny too. How do they not see what they are doing?

"The liars in that world are very convincing," Ma said. "They create divisions. Even when there isn't an enemy, they find one. They create one. They define one, and then they draw circles and lines, and they claim the people on this side are good, and those on the other side of the line are bad."

Lines? I asked, puzzled.

"Yes, they've quite literally drawn lines on their world map. They say the people who live on this side of the line are 'us,' and the people who live on the other side of the line are 'them,'" Ma explained.

Is it a magical line? What does the line do?

"Nothing... it's just a line they drew as if you picked up a stick and drew a line on the ground," Ma said.

I laughed. That's absurd. Do all of them spend too much time under the Yellowtree or something?

"They don't have a Yellowtree," Ma replied.

I sighed. Ma, this world makes no sense.

"It is what it is."

Okay, and who is that guy bringing water for... B?

"That guy is C. He's the one B started the wars against."

They fought each other, and now he's bringing him water?

Ma explained, "Yes, after going through The Loop of Black Tears, they are exposed. They have nothing to hide behind, and when all their clever schemes and costumes are washed away... beneath all those layers, they share the same interests, agendas, personal goals, and mentality. They wore different masks and fought each other, causing millions to suffer, but when the masks were removed, they were so similar that they became friends in Forsaken Serenus. They understand what the other is going through, and now they are part of the same support group."

And what about that one... the one without a shirt on... The one riding a Firehorse. What did he do?

"That... yeah, that one. He puts his arm in the door and closes the door to cause himself pain," Ma said.

Ouch... Why? I asked, wincing at the thought.

"He's also a friend of A, B, and C. He, too, wore a mask in Serenus, a mask of delusion. He, too, created a lot of misery. He thought his decisions held more weight, even if they caused millions to suffer. He invaded them, forced them to leave their homes, and ordered their killing. And he, too, believed that he had a valid reason for doing this as if there ever is a valid reason to do this."

But wars are fought by... lots of people. One person can't fight a war. Why are they the only ones hurting themselves?

"You're right. They were products of their system. An entire system stood behind them and supported them, but they were the foolish ones who took responsibility for all the atrocities. They were the gullible ones with inflated egos. They were easily manipulated and agreed to shoulder the entire burden of the system. Others who were more cunning stood behind them and cheered them on."

Why would they take all the responsibility?

"They were easily swayed and cheap to purchase. A little encouragement and a bit of praise were enough to win their hearts. And they had these delusions of grandeur. They were easy to convince that they were destined to achieve something great," Ma explained.

What about those who suffered at their hands? Why couldn't they identify them as cheap and delusional? Why did the others join them? Why did they fail to see the truth?

"Their lies were based on values that others held dear—values like fighting for what is right, sacrificing for your land, and even the desire to make me happy."

That's ridiculous. They even fought to make you happy?

"Yes, that's what they told themselves and others."

I tried to make sense of their world for a moment and then asked, "Maybe they had some magical ability. Were they incredibly skilled at persuading others? Could they make others do whatever they said? I don't understand why others joined them."

"Not only did they join them, but they also made them their leaders and gave their lives for them. All of them gained their power from the same source: division. To fight someone, they need to elevate an enemy. They create a terrifying, evil image of an enemy who is out to destroy you, consume you, and erase you from the face of the earth," Ma explained, her face contorted with disgust. "They draw lines not only on their world map but also in their minds. Anyone who lives on this side of the line, or thinks like this, is 'us,' and on that side of the line, or thinks like that, is 'them.' They need 'us' to deceive and exploit for their schemes, and they need 'them' to frighten 'us.' All of them work like this. They create a division between 'us' and 'them' and ignite conflict. As 'us' fights 'them,' believing we are doing the right thing, these manipulators gain more and more power and control. And they create this division based on the most trivial things, like the colour of one's skin."

What? Just when I thought it couldn't get more absurd.

"Yes. In your world, Idir's skin colour was darker. There are many places in that world... in 'reality' where Idir wouldn't be welcome just because of the colour of his skin," Ma said.

That's... I can't believe it. What about height? Fabio is tall. Would he be in danger in some places?

"Not yet, but you can never be sure with them," Ma replied.

What if someone speaks a little differently?

"Yes, they've used that too," Ma confirmed.

And they always find fools who believe them? They always find an 'us'?

"Too often, they do," Ma sighed.

Are the people too soft-headed in that world... in 'reality'?

"No, there are very smart people. People who can figure out complex aspects of how their world works still fall for these lies."

So these... liars, these tricksters, the clowns in costumes, are they much... sharper? Much more capable than others?

"They believe that, but when they get a chance to govern a place and act like an elder, they run it into the ground. They aren't intelligent; they're cunning. They aren't wise; they're deceitful. They excel at trickery but lack understanding."

So, what benefit do they get out of it?

"They amass a lot of resources that they snatch from 'us' and 'them.'"

Do they need more resources than others to survive? Are their bellies bigger?

"No, but they enjoy hoarding as much as they can. They believe they deserve more than others," Ma said.

Why? Nothing you've said suggests they deserve more.

"When they hunt someone down, they have those around them who praise them. They crave praise. They want more and more of it. They love to hear that they are better than others, and when many people tell them this, they form a delusion. They accept it in their minds. They start thinking of themselves as superior. They believe they deserve better. They think they matter more than others. They start talking louder than others and addressing gatherings of people. They convince themselves that they know best while others don't."

But why do others listen? How come they always fall for it?

"Once someone becomes part of 'us,' once someone picks a side between 'us' and 'them,' then they are easy to deceive."

So they need an 'us,' and they need a 'them.' So everyone who talks like that, who creates division, is like them? Is that how people can identify them?

"Yes. And anyone who helps them create division is their friend, not mine. I created all, and I love all. I don't take sides. There are no sides. There's only one side, my side. There is no 'them.' It's only 'us.' If you find someone who says otherwise, they're not my friend. Hiss at them because they are hunters. And they're not just a handful you saw. There are many... too many... way too many, and as long as people keep falling for the trick of division, more and more will use the trick," Ma warned.

Then Ma opened the door to the Keep, and I sighed in disgust. It was full of people hurting themselves. Their watches would vibrate and ding, and they would see a memory of how people remembered them and then inflict pain upon themselves.

I was beyond shocked. I didn't know what to say. I definitely couldn't look anymore.

Please stop it, Ma. I can't bear to see it.

Their world vanished but left me shivering.

"Your hell doesn't feel so horrible now, does it?" Ma asked.

I pleaded, "Ma, please remove their watches. Please, they've gone through The Loop of Black Tears, and now they can't fix anything. They can't die. They can't escape. This is too much, Ma. Please... Please remove their watches."

"I understand what you mean. In that world, I didn't originally have The Loop of Black Tears. Forsaken Serenus was the place for them to learn what they did using the memories from their watches. Then I created The Loop of Black Tears and sent all of them through it. When they came out, they hurt themselves when they saw a memory from Serenus. What you saw was a past system. They aren't hurting anymore. I have removed their watches."

Ma... I don't want to talk about that world, that... 'reality.' That world is... please never show me that again.

Ma apologized, "I'm sorry. The world of 'reality' is far more painful than yours. I didn't mean to traumatize you."

I closed my eyes, but the haunting scene of 'reality' popped into my head again. I shook my head, trying to dispel the terrifying thoughts. It was too scary, too real, and far too painful.

Ma? I murmured.

"Yes," she replied gently.

That's why you said... when you told me a secret... There is no 'them.'

"Yes," Ma confirmed.

But what about these hunters? Are they not 'them'? Are they not the enemy?

"No, they are 'us' too," Ma explained.

I nodded. I didn't want to talk about 'reality' any longer. I yearned to return to the simpler world, the world where This-one was growing a tree of hope. I never wanted to hear about 'reality' again.

"I'm sorry, but I hope you learned something from it."

Yes, division is wrong. There is no 'them.' It's only 'us.' I understand.

Ma nodded, and I turned my focus to This-one.

Ch 33: The Awakening of the Trees

This-one was now part of the Tree Circle. He had lived there longer than I had lived in Serenus. The Moontree was a small tree now, and around it grew six more plants. These were not the Seven that would surround it later. These were the trees that would grow a Moonbulb.

Jaci read from 'The Book of Trees' and said, "It is going to grow six Moontree trunks, and once those are able to survive on their own, they will grow tall, surround, and cover the first one. Under their shade, it will die away, leaving a place where branches from the six trees will grow a Moonbulb."

Dante exclaimed excitedly, "Then the magic would have returned to Forsaken Serenus!"

Mosi corrected him, "The magic has already returned. With This-one. Now it will heal everything."

Jaci laughed, "And is that good?"

Mosi chuckled, "Yes, Good... good."

This-one listened to their conversation and wondered when he would be able to go look for Amy. He still needed to collect Moonlight. Mosi said he would have to do that until the six other trees had grown, and that could take months. But there was no one else who could do this, so he had to stay. And while he felt very bad about it, he kept reminding himself that he was doing the right thing.

I asked Ma, "Why do we feel guilty even when we are doing something right?"

"It's not guilt," Ma explained. "It's a bad feeling that arises when even the best choice available isn't what you hoped for. When circumstances limit your possibilities, you pick the best one, knowing that your heart wanted something better, but it wasn't possible."

Nuno visited them often, bringing as much bread as he could carry. Those visits were times of celebration. Although they had access to fruits and made various jellies and soups, they eagerly anticipated the bread.

One day, Jaci took This-one on a tour of the outside. He hadn't been to the desolate land in a long time, and the absence of any sound surprised him once again. The lifeless terrain seemed to yearn for greenery, and the dry Black Dust covered him whenever the wind blew. His work with the Moontree felt even more crucial after witnessing the outside world again.

Beyond This-place, there was a mountain range with peaks taller than the ones surrounding their haven. Jaci told This-one of a place where the land reached so high into the sky that the dust couldn't touch it – the top of the world. This-one longed to see it someday. Jaci had never seen it either, having only heard stories. This-one believed in the possibility; if This-place could exist in Forsaken Serenus, anything was possible.

After spending the day outside, they returned to This-place, needing a thorough shower before rejoining the others. The outside world was still suffering, and his efforts were the only hope they had. The trip helped This-one feel better about himself, making it easier to stay.

Conrad visited again and told This-one his plan to expose the king.

"It's risky, but only you can do it," Conrad said.

"What is it?" This-one inquired.

"Have you heard of the Troll Cave?" Conrad asked.

"Yes, that's where the king found the lost scroll," This-one replied.

"Exactly. You have to go to the Troll Cave and uncover details of what happened when the king went there," Conrad explained.

"You won't come with me?" This-one questioned.

"No, only one person can be allowed in the Troll Cave," Conrad said.

"Who?" This-one asked.

"The one who can fulfill their need will be allowed to enter," Conrad revealed.

"What do they need?" This-one inquired.

"They need to heal. Whoever can heal them will be allowed to enter. This is the information I've gathered so far. The king found the Troll Cave and went to them. They wouldn't let anyone enter until their need was fulfilled," Conrad shared.

"The king can heal?" This-one wondered, his curiosity piqued.

"No, that wasn't their need at the time," Conrad explained. "Back then, they needed to fulfill their purpose, to give the lost scroll to the one who found them. The king was the first to find them. They allowed him to enter, and he discovered the lost scroll there. We don't know how he did it, but he left them disappointed. A mysterious illness has now taken hold of their kingdom. They will only allow the one who can heal them to enter."

This-one asked, "And you think I can heal them with Moonlight?"

"Moonlight heals by itself," Conrad said. "Whoever carries

The Lost Scroll   600

Moonlight with them can heal them, but there's another reason why only you can do this."

"What is it?" This-one asked.

"I'll tell you once you return. You have to trust me," Conrad replied.

"Okay, I can trust you," This-one agreed.

"But it's risky, and there's a chance that what I'm saying could be wrong," Conrad cautioned. "You have to take the risk. The king is the only one who knows more about the Troll Cave. I don't know what they will do to you once their need is fulfilled."

"That's the risk?" This-one questioned.

"Yes, but I have a plan that... may work," Conrad continued. "You can only carry a small amount of Moonlight, which won't be enough to heal many trolls. You can tell them that if they let you return unharmed, you can bring them more Moonlight."

"Understood," This-one said.

"But for any of this to work, first, we need to test if Moonlight still heals in this world. And we can't use any while the Moontree still needs it. So, this is a task for after the Moontree no longer needs you," Conrad explained.

"Any news of Amy?" This-one inquired.

"I've sent friends after her. They're searching for her. As soon as I hear anything, I'll come and tell you myself," Conrad reassured.

"Okay."

This-one walked away as Conrad watched him with worry. Something was different, and Conrad felt it.

Later, Jaci and Dante approached This-one. "What was Conrad talking to you about?" Jaci asked.

This-one shared Conrad's plan with them.

"We'll go with you," Dante declared.

"You can't," This-one insisted. "Only one is allowed to enter, and you have to be here with Mosi."

"We'll go with you," Jaci persisted. "If they don't let us enter, we'll wait outside."

"No, you need to be with Mosi," This-one said firmly. "And who knows how long it'll take to return? I need to find out what the king discovered there. I can't come back until I have the answers."

Jaci and Dante were visibly unhappy with this.

"There's still time," Dante said. "We'll find a way."

With that, they returned to their work.

Conrad left the next morning but promised that he would return as soon as he had any news of Amy. This-one sat outside with Mosi, listening as she spoke to the Moontree.

Suddenly, Jaci came running and yelled, "The cave is flooding! Come help me!" This-one sprinted towards her, and they entered the flooded cave together. Water gushed in from one side, quickly filling the space. Dante was already there, trying to plug the opening with mud.

"It must have rained a lot nearby," Jaci said, her voice filled with alarm.

Dante nodded as he struggled to stop the water flow. This-one joined in to help. They did their best to create a channel for the water to flow in and out of the cave.

Once they successfully diverted the water so it wouldn't flood the cave, Dante voiced his concern. "What if it rained on the mountains too? A lot more water will come from the waterfall and flood the valley." The terrifying thought made them all extremely anxious. The Moontree could be flooded.

They hurried to Mosi to inform her and then raced to the top of the mountain to assess the situation.

"We can't stop the water. We have to divert it away from the valley," Dante declared.

"But only if more water comes this way. We need the waterfall," Jaci said.

After brainstorming, they devised a plan to create an alternate path for the water. It would flood the lifeless lands nearby, but their priority was protecting the Moontree. They spent a full day working tirelessly until they were satisfied with the results. They ensured that only the overflow would go into the new channel and the waterfall would continue to flow as usual if there was no extra water.

"That's the best we can do for now. I hope it's enough," Dante said, exhausted.

The trio returned to Mosi and updated her on their progress. She had stayed by the Moontree all day, worrying and hoping it would survive. As night approached, they held their breath and waited. This-one couldn't waste any time, so he captured Moonlight while Dante, Jaci, and Mosi anxiously anticipated a potential flood.

The night passed without incident, but they now faced a new concern. Jaci lamented, "If only we could grow the Moontree where it used to be. It was safe there."

Dante comforted her, "It will be okay. This-place is a safe haven for it, especially now that we have dug up a new channel for the floodwater."

Exhausted, they laid down to rest. It would take months, and there were many threats, but hope remained.

The four of them stayed vigilant, nurturing the Moontree and tending to its needs. One day, This-one shared the story of Amy's ring, the one with the Moonlight inside, with the others. He recounted the wizard's attack and how Amy gave him the ring for protection.

Mosi smiled broadly as Jaci explained, "Mosi wore that ring for a long time. She would replenish the Moonlight as it faded. She kept it until she died. It's special because it contained the first Moonlight ever captured, and when This-one captured the first Moonlight in this world and gave it to Mosi, she told me about it. She feels very lucky to have held the first Moonlight from both worlds."

This-one hadn't realized how much the gesture would mean to Mosi when he gave her the vial, but now he was overjoyed that he had done so.

The Tree Circle now had a new member: the tree itself. Sitting around it, Jaci once said, "Now we are a proper Tree Circle."

Dante shook his head. "No. The real Tree Circle was in Serenus."

Mosi placed her hand on Dante's shoulder and explained, "Anywhere people sit under a tree is a Tree Circle."

Jaci nodded in agreement, "A tree circle is a group of people sitting under a tree. Everywhere a tree grows, a tree circle may form."

Dante and This-one nodded in understanding.

What was once only hope was now becoming a reality. The Moontree's six tree trunks grew big enough to shade the original tree, causing it to wither. This-one asked Mosi if they could now use some Moonlight to test its healing ability. Mosi agreed.

Jaci suggested, "Moonlight takes time to heal. If we hurt ourselves to test the healing ability, we won't be sure if it was the Moonlight that healed us or our bodies' natural healing process. And we don't want to hurt ourselves so badly that it can't otherwise be healed. There is only one way. We have a Mirror here, and we have Moonlight. If This-one can use Moonlight to expose our feelings, that means Moonlight can be used in this world."

Dante chuckled, "And Jaci will happily volunteer for this because she has nothing to hide."

Jaci laughed, "What about you? I think you're the best candidate."

Dante countered, "Why me? Why not you?"

Mosi said, "Exposing your inner feelings is not good."

Everyone laughed, but then Mosi offered, "Use me."

Dante insisted, "No, it has to be me."

Jaci exclaimed, "Oh no. I will be the first in this world on whom magic will be used."

Then Dante smiled and said, "This-one, you have sacrificed a lot, and the three of us have long been ready for you to test us."

This-one hesitated. He had something else on his mind, "I think we can wait. There is no hurry."

Jaci reassured him, "What happened? We're okay with it."

This-one said, "I don't know. Let's wait for a better option."

Dante argued, "There is no better option."

This-one continued, "If I have to use Moonlight to heal the Trolls, then I think we should test its power to heal something. My friend Idir once told me a story of how a Seren hurt his wing, and it was healed with Moonlight. It couldn't have healed without it. If we could do something like that, that would be proof that it works."

Jaci smiled, "You're a good friend, but we have long been ready for you to test us. Don't worry. We've lived together so long that we already know a bit too much about each other."

Dante laughed, "And we don't mind if you find out something about us that you don't already know."

This-one finally agreed, "Okay, I won't probe too much. We just want to see if it works."

Jaci grinned, "Of course, you don't want to discover all the idiotic stuff in Dante's head."

Dante laughed, "Why are we assuming it will be me? This-one, you choose."

This-one thought for a moment and said, "Dante, it looks like it will be you."

Dante smiled confidently, "I knew you would pick me. I'll focus my mind on the most disturbing thoughts to reveal. I'm not going to make it fun for Jaci."

They sat by the Moontree and gathered the necessary materials to perform the mirror test. Jaci carefully filled a vial with Moonlight and placed a Moonleaf inside it. The vial began to swirl ferociously, the liquid churning and shimmering. This-one cleared his mind and sat by the vial. Dante placed his hand on the vial as the Moonlight calmed down. This-one closed his eyes and placed his hands on Dante's hands, then tried to remember what it was like to probe Alia's mind. The thought was an old memory, and he wasn't certain exactly what his mind had done. He attempted for a bit but couldn't probe Dante's mind. He tried to sense a path to Dante's mind that went from his mind to his hands to Dante's hand to Dante's mind, but he couldn't feel a path.

Jaci reassured him, "Don't worry. I'm sure even a Mirror took time to learn this skill. Take your time."

This-one tried again, but nothing happened.

Mosi advised, "The connection isn't through the hand. It's through the Moonlight. Sense the Moonlight, and the Moonlight will probe the mind."

This-one adjusted his hands to place them on the vial instead of Dante's hands and tried again. This time, he focused on sensing the Moonlight, and his mind could feel the energy pulsating inside it. He opened his eyes and said, "I can feel it. I'm sure it's magical. We don't need to test Dante."

Jaci protested angrily, "How do you know? If you don't reveal Dante's thoughts, I don't think we can be sure that it works."

Dante laughed, "Go on, friend, she has this opportunity, and she's not going to let it go."

This-one smiled, cleared his mind again, and attempted to reach Dante's mind through the Moonlight. A sliver of white flame appeared on top of their hands as he felt a connection form. The flame twisted and flickered as Dante looked at Jaci and smiled, his head starting to turn left.

Jaci yelled, "Stop it!"

This-one pulled his hands away, and the flame disappeared. Everyone sensed what Dante felt for Jaci: a strong emotion of affection and care. Beneath all their arguments and mock fights, they cared for each other deeply. At least Dante did, and there was no better way to show it to Jaci than to be tested by the Mirror.

Jaci approached Dante, "You are such an idiot."

For a few moments, they completely forgot that they had confirmation that magic had returned to Forsaken Serenus. Everyone just smiled, including Ma and Me.

Then Mosi declared, "This-one has brought magic to This-place, and that is..."

This-one, Dante and Jaci yelled in unison, "Good!"

Ma couldn't contain her excitement. She danced around the Sandbox and played the flute. I sat there, watching unreal energy replenishing everything around me.

Ch 34: Peak of the Black Sea

In just a few days, Conrad returned, and the plan to send This-one to the Troll Cave was set in motion. There was still no news of Amy, and This-one was eager to fulfill his responsibilities so he could go look for her.

Conrad provided a thorough briefing and pointed to various locations on a world map, "You must go to the Peak of the Black Sea. The entrance to the Troll Cave is on the north face of the mountain. Once you're there, you'll find it. I'm planning our next steps, and things are moving fast in the castle. It's time to uncover the truth about the king. Remember my words; it's risky, but we have to take that risk. I'm not sure what will happen, but there's no other way. You have to take the risk."

Jaci and Dante wanted to accompany This-one, but then no one would be with Mosi, and the Moontree also needed their attention.

Conrad had to return to the castle, so he prepared a bag for This-one and handed him the map, "Head to the highest peak north of here. It'll take three days to get there, but it shouldn't be a problem. Use the map."

Jaci was holding a piece of bread that she was about to eat. She placed it in the bag with the rest of the food. This-one smiled, and she smiled back.

"We have lots of fruits here," Jaci said. "You need all the bread we have."

Dante inquired, "How will you find out what the king did there?"

This-one responded, "I'm hoping if I can heal them, they'll answer my questions."

Jaci suggested, "Take some Moonleaves with you. If they're truly grateful, they might let you read their mind."

This-one nodded, and the three of them walked out of the cave toward the Moontree. This-one picked three leaves and expressed his gratitude, "Thank you, Moontree!"

The trio set off. Dante and Jaci accompanied him for a while before turning back, wishing him the best on his journey ahead.

This-one donned his headscarf and continued walking as the

wind picked up. When it became too dusty, he covered his face and continued with his eyes barely open.

There was no path to follow. He had to climb the mountain range to reach the highest peak. Climbing uphill was difficult, but doing so in near-blackout conditions was even more challenging. It tested his resolve. At times, he slipped and fell, narrowly escaping dangerous falls, but he persevered. His goal was to move as quickly as the situation allowed so he could search for Amy later.

After three days of walking, he finally reached the summit. He was close to the peak but hesitated as he saw someone sitting on a rock ahead. It didn't resemble a Troll, but he couldn't be certain.

This-one concealed himself behind another rock and scanned the area to see if anyone else was nearby. It was growing dark, and visibility was poor. He decided to remain hidden for the night.

As the wind picked up, the Black Dust engulfed the world below. Around him, he saw a breathtaking view of the night sky, and beneath it, an endless black. It appeared as though the part of the mountain surrounding and above him was the only thing under the vast starry canopy. It had to be his destination: the Peak of the Black Sea.

The world became simpler, with only a handful of things visible.

Ma marvelled, "Isn't it beautiful?"

I couldn't agree more. I imagined what the Black Dust concealing the world below would look like in daylight.

Ma said, "Like a black sea."

A beautiful black sea of dust. Hell isn't so bad from up here.

"It hasn't been so bad for This-one."

Who is it sitting above This-one?

Ma teased, "Guess what?"

Patience?

"Yes, patience."

This-one remained hidden throughout the night. He had been capturing Moonlight every evening for many months, and these past few nights felt as though they stretched on endlessly. Later, when he was too exhausted to stay awake, he fell asleep.

I was eager to see who was sitting near him.

Ma said, "You worry for him so much."

It's natural, isn't it?

Ma nodded, "It is. He was you, and then he became something else, but you've watched over him all this time and experienced what he experienced. It's natural to care for him, to not want him to get into a bad situation, but he has his own free will, and he chooses his own direction, and you can only watch."

And hope.

Ma agreed, "Yes, watch and hope that he's going in the right direction."

Yes.

Ma continued, "And there will be times when it feels like he's caught in a storm or is in danger, and it's difficult to watch, but after the storm, he meets the baker, and after the danger, he reaches This-place, and you feel you worried for no reason."

Yes, but he could have been in real danger, so it was right to worry.

Ma conceded, "Yes, it was right."

And I will worry next time too.

Ma smiled, "And that's how I feel for all my creations, just like you feel for This-one."

* * *

It was still early morning when This-one woke up. He looked around but didn't find anyone nearby. Carefully, he walked to the top, and an old man emerged from behind a rock.

The old man said, "I thought you were still asleep."

This-one asked, "Who are you?"

The old man responded, "I am an old man."

This-one said, "Yes, I can see that."

The old man inquired, "Did you bring my food?"

This-one replied, "What? No, I didn't bring your food. What do you mean?"

Old man shook his head, "Nothing. I thought you brought my food."

This-one wondered, "Was I supposed to bring your food?"

The old man shrugged, "How can I know that?"

This-one questioned, "Then why did you ask me if I brought your food?"

The old man replied, "Because I am hungry."

This-one asked, "What are you doing up here?"

The old man said, "I am reading a story."

This-one worried for the old man. "You can't read the story down there? You are an old man. Is it safe to be here all alone?"

The old man assured him, "I have been here a long time. There is no danger here."

This-one inquired, "Ok... do you know where the entrance to the Troll Cave is?"

The old man pointed to a path and said, "Follow that path. It will take you there. But they won't let you in."

This-one thanked him, "Thanks, but I don't think you should be here. On my way back, I can take you with me to live with the people."

The old man smiled, "I have lived with the people long enough. Now I live here."

This-one questioned, "How long have you lived here?"

The old man responded, "Not too long."

This-one asked, "And how do you survive here?"

The old man said, "There is a pond nearby for water."

This-one pointed out, "You can't just survive on water."

The old man explained, "Yes, the food comes to me."

This-one asked, "Someone brings you food?"

The old man confirmed, "Yes."

This-one smiled, "Oh, so that's why you asked if I brought your food. What do you do here?"

The old man pointed to the world under them, "I am reading a story. Look, the story is playing out in front of us."

This-one looked at where he was pointing but didn't see anything happening there. Then he remembered Faqeer and thought maybe the old man was also lost in his head. He acknowledged just as Shahzor had done with Faqeer, "Oh yes, I see a story playing out."

This-one wanted to move on to find the entrance to the Troll Cave, but he felt the old man may need help. He sat by him to wait for whoever was bringing him food to make sure it was okay to leave him alone.

The old man pointed out, "You see that dust storm? It is moving to the king's castle. He will be upset soon. He doesn't like dust."

This-one nodded.

Old man continued, "It rained a lot over there. That is where the Keepers grow their crops. The fields may have flooded."

This-one nodded with worry.

The old man mused, "The king will be cleaning the dust from his halls while the people worry that they won't have food to eat. Both will be upset, though their problems are very different."

This-one turned to face the old man and nodded in agreement.

The old man continued, "You see there, the Black Dust is carried by the wind and moves like a stormy sea. It will move over the mountains slowly and turn them black."

This-one nodded again.

The old man added, "When it rains, it will wash the dust off the mountains and send it back to the lands below. The dust will dry out in the plains, and the wind will pick it up again."

This-one nodded, intrigued.

The old man said, "The wind wants to blacken the mountains, but the rain keeps the mountains clean. The two have been fighting this battle, and none gives up. Sometimes the rain comes late, and all the mountains turn black, and sometimes the wind is not quick enough, and the rain keeps all mountains clean."

This-one nodded.

The old man pointed out, "Look at that eagle. It has a fish in its talons. It has found a place where fish still live. It has always known, even when the people didn't know."

This-one nodded.

The old man continued, "If you follow the eagle, it will take you where it nests. And if you follow it back, it will take you to where it catches fish. And the people will live down there and fight over food, but the eagle is able to feed itself. The eagle lives on the peaks that are clean, it answers to no one, and it doesn't worry about rain or dust. Isn't the eagle living a better life than the king and the people?"

This-one nodded, considering the old man's words.

The old man mused, "The eagle has a small head and has no room for problems. We have big heads, and our heads are filled with worries. The eagle drinks water, and it eats food just like we do, but it is enough to make it happy. When our worry about food and water ends, we find more things to worry about. Isn't a small head better than a big head?"

This-one nodded and asked, "Were you a thinker in Serenus?"

The old man replied, "I don't remember."

This-one opened his bag and gave the last piece of bread to the old man, saying, "I have to go to the Troll Cave. When I come back, you can come with me. I will take you to a baker who will feed you every day."

The old man took the bread and warned, "If the Trolls allow you to enter, you will not come back."

This-one questioned, "Why not?"

Old man explained, "They won't let you leave."

This-one replied confidently, "I have a plan for that."

This time the old man nodded, and This-one moved on to find the entrance to the Troll Cave.

Ch 35:
Keepers of the Scroll

On the north face of the mountain, there was a huge cave entrance. It had to be the entrance to the Troll Cave. This-one entered the cave. Inside, a partially visible barrier blocked his path. When he tapped on the barrier, a Troll appeared and said grumpily, "Who wants to enter?"

This-one replied, "I am This-one."

The Troll questioned, "Can you fulfill my need?"

This-one asked, "What do you need?"

The Troll answered, "Heal me."

This-one assured, "I can heal you."

Troll was suspicious, "I trusted once. I was tricked once."

This-one insisted, "I am not tricking you. I can heal you."

Troll demanded, "Prove it."

This-one explained, "I have magic. I can heal you."

The Troll made a scratch on his leg with his long nails and said, "Heal it."

This-one said, "I will have to come to you, and it will take some time."

Troll was firm, "You can't enter if you can't prove."

This-one reasoned, "I can't heal if I can't enter."

Troll dismissed him, "Go away then. You can't enter."

This-one pleaded, "I really need to, and I can heal you, please!"

The Troll walked away. This-one stared at the empty cave in front, wondering what to do. He couldn't go back. He had to somehow cross the barrier, but the Troll needed proof, and he couldn't heal the Troll without crossing the barrier. What if he scratched his own leg and showed the Troll that Moonlight could heal? But then he remembered that that's not how Moonlight worked. It took time. The effect of The Seven was immediate. Moonlight took time to heal, which is why they used the Mirror test to see if magic could be used in this world.

This-one walked out of the cave and returned to the old man to rethink his strategy. The old man was still sitting there. He had only eaten half a piece of bread, and the other half was on the rock beside him.

The old man saw This-one coming back, "Come, look... the Black Storm is about to hit the castle. The king will be really mad soon."

This-one sat with the old man and watched the storm, but his mind was stuck on thinking of a way to cross the barrier.

The old man said with excitement, "Almost there. Look, almost there."

This-one nodded.

Old man inquired, "How did your story go?"

This-one replied, "Nothing interesting happened. The Troll wants me to prove that I can heal, but I can't heal till I cross the barrier."

The old man smiled, "Interesting. A barrier to cross. The one who needs healing is behind the barrier. The one who needs to cross the barrier can't prove he is eligible to cross. Very interesting. Will you give up, or will the controller of the barrier give up?"

This-one answered, "I am trying to think of a way to cross it. I can't give up."

Old man suggested, "How about you find a middle ground?"

This-one asked, "Middle ground?"

The old man replied, "When the two sides don't want to give up, finding a middle ground is usually how the story continues."

This-one thanked the old man, got up, and ran back to the Troll cave. He knocked on the barrier, and the Troll appeared again, still in a grumpy mood.

Troll grumbled, "You again? You can't enter."

This-one proposed, "But can you come out?"

Troll questioned, "Why?"

This-one said, "So I can prove that I can heal you."

The Troll walked out of the barrier and put his leg forward, "Prove it."

This-one put his bag down and pulled out the container with the Moonlight. He picked a strand of Moonlight and placed it on Troll's leg. The Troll was mesmerized by the magical strand. This-one adjusted the strand on the Troll's leg, and the Troll shivered with anticipation.

The Troll inquired, "It is... What is it?"

This-one explained, "It is Moonlight. I have magic. I can capture Moonlight and use it to heal."

The Troll was curious, "What is it doing? It feels good."

The Troll was fascinated by Moonlight, and his leg needed time to heal. This-one needed to impress the Troll, so he would allow him to cross the barrier. There was one thing that he could do that created a magical light show.

This-one offered, "I can show you more."

The Troll had never seen magic before. No one had in this world. This-one asked him to sit down, then looked inside his bag for the Moonleaf. He unwrapped the cloth containing the Moonleaf and placed it in the container. The Moonlight started to bubble and swirl around. The Troll's eyes almost popped out. He was totally impressed by the show, but that was nothing. A lot more was coming to blow his mind.

This-one instructed, "Okay, now put your hands gently over here."

The Troll put his hands on the container eagerly.

This-one placed his hands on the container and closed his eyes. As the bubbling mist calmed down and the glow of Moonlight surrounded their hands, the Troll sighed in anticipation.

This-one looked at the Troll and then closed his eyes again. He searched for a path to the Troll's mind through the Moonlight. As he found it, the Troll giggled, "It tickles my mind."

This-one hushed, "Ssshhh!!!"

This-one searched the mind and found emotions of awe and amusement. The flame appeared over the Troll's hand, and the Troll laughed, "Yes...."

This-one needed to direct the Troll's mind to a certain thing to find what the Troll felt about that. This-one asked, "Now you believe me?"

The Troll felt a sudden feeling of gratitude, "I have not laughed in a long ... I have not felt this good ... You can heal. You can surely heal."

This-one ended the magic show and asked the Troll to open the barrier, "I can heal all of you if you allow me to enter."

The Troll didn't even look at his leg, "Yes, come. We have waited so long."

The magic show had an uplifting effect on the Troll. He wasn't grumpy anymore. This-one was surprised that he didn't care about the scratch on his leg and still allowed This-one to enter.

The cave turned and twisted and ended at a cage with ropes attached to it. The Troll entered the cage and called This-one in. This-one was not sure; he looked around, but there was no other way.

As This-one approached the cage, the Troll beckoned him, saying, "Come, we need you." Reluctantly, This-one entered the cage, and the Troll closed the door. Inside, This-one felt really awkward, as the cage was not very big, and the Troll just stood there staring at the door. This-one copied the Troll's actions and stood by him, also staring at the door. For a few moments, they just stared at the door, and This-one was unsure what they were doing. He peeked at the Troll, turning only his eyes. The Troll stood there staring at the cage door. This-one brought his eyes back to the front and stared at the door even harder, wondering if there was something he needed to see. The door was quite an ordinary door, and there was nothing special about it, but the Troll seemed very interested in it and just looked on. This-one also looked on, though he couldn't understand what he was supposed to see.

Suddenly, the door opened, and the Troll stepped out. This-one was confused about what the point of going in the cage, staring at the door, and then coming out was. But then something magical happened. More Trolls appeared outside the door, and they were all grumpy. They called him out, and This-one wondered if they had magic.

There was nowhere else to go, and This-one was in the world of the Trolls now. He stepped out of the cage and saw a huge dome above him. The ground was completely flat, which looked unnatural to This-one. He had never seen a floor so flat. Around This-one were giant, curious, and grumpy Trolls. They walked behind him as the Troll with the glowing leg walked him to a stone structure in the middle of the very flat land. Tall pillars held a smaller dome up, and under it sat a larger Troll with a Lion by his side. There were no trees, no other life form, nothing. Just Trolls on flat land with bricks under their feet and bricks above their heads. The Lion looked so out of place, and This-one wondered what he ate and what the Trolls ate.

The Troll with the glowing leg addressed the bigger Troll, "King-troll, this one can heal us."

The Trolls gasped with joy, and Kingtroll asked, "Come forward. Who are you?"

This-one replied, "I am This-one. I have come to heal you."

Kingtroll asked, "But not just to heal us. What do you want?"

This-one replied, "I want answers, Kingtroll. Another one like me came to you...."

Kingtroll interrupted furiously, "The liar. A liar came to us."

This-one nodded, "Yes, the liar. I want to know what he did here."

Kingtroll replied grumpily, "Tell him what he did."

Everyone sat down and signalled for This-one to sit down as well. This-one sat down, and the Troll with the glowing leg stayed standing as he narrated the story, "We are Trolls. We have lived here since Avis created us."

This-one interrupted, asking, "Who is Avis?"

The Trolls got upset and shushed him, saying, "SSshhhhh! Don't talk in the middle." The Trolls then asked This-one to stand up, and This-one stood up apologetically.

The Troll with the glowing leg started again, "We are Trolls," he said, his voice low and gruff. "We have lived here since Avis creat-ed us. He gave us a mission to keep the lost scroll safe till the one who found us would relieve us of our duty. We lived and waited, and waited, and waited..."

Another Troll let out a sigh and muttered, "And waited."

Suddenly, Kingtroll's Lion let out a loud roar that echoed around the domed room, and many of the Trolls growled in frustration at the interruption. The Troll who had spoken out stood up, head bowed in embarrassment. This-one watched the exchange, feeling equally embarrassed.

The Troll with the glowing leg shook his head and started once again, " We are Trolls. We have lived here since Avis created us. He gave us a mission to keep the lost scroll safe till the one who found us would relieve us of our duty. We lived and waited, and waited, and waited. We lived and waited, and waited, and waited, and waited, and waited," he said, his voice heavy with sorrow. "But no one came. We waited and waited until... the liar, the liar came to us."

The Trolls became furious, their anger palpable as they breathed heavily, nostrils flaring. "He lied to us. We gave him the lost scroll, but he refused. He refused!"

"He took the scroll," the Troll with the glowing leg continued with a heavy sigh, "but he didn't say the words."

This-one was curious and waited patiently for the Troll to continue, but he seemed to be taking his time. Finally, the Troll sighed again and said, "He refused. Liar!"

All the Trolls exhaled loudly, and This-one kept his head down in silence.

"The liar took the scroll, but he refused to say the words," the Troll with the glowing leg said. "He didn't say it. I can't believe it. Ohhh, but I feel it."

This-one remained quiet, listening as the Troll continued. "He left us. We failed. He left us failed. We failed Avis."

The Trolls shook their heads in despair, and one of them even sobbed. Kingtroll and the lion both shook their heads slowly.

"He gave us his word," the Troll with the glowing leg said, his voice trembling with emotion. "But once he had the scroll, he didn't say it. He took the scroll, and he left. Left us failed. We have been miserable since then. We failed our purpose. We failed... A sickness spread in us. All of us are mad. We are grumpy. We... feel so bad. We wanted to go out. Go after him. But Avis said we were not allowed to go uphill or downhill. So we sit here, and we wait. And we are grumpy. The liar left us. He took what he came for and gave us a need. He left us failed."

The Trolls let out a collective sigh, and Kingtroll spoke up. "And now you will heal us? Take away our pain?"

This-one looked around, making sure it was okay to speak. Seeing everyone standing up, This-one took it as a sign that he could speak. "What was the liar supposed to say that he didn't say?"

Kingtroll responded, "We are not allowed to say those words, but the words are written on the lost scroll. He was supposed to read them. Avis said when we hear those words, our mission is complete. He didn't say the words. He refused."

This-one was even more curious now. "Why did he refuse to say the words?"

Kingtroll looked at This-one with a sombre expression and spoke in a deep and solemn voice, "The liar said it wasn't the lost scroll. The liar called us liars, even though we have kept the scroll safe since the beginning of time. He was the only one we allowed in, and we gave him the scroll, but he refused to believe it was the one he was searching for."

This-one's eyes lit up with curiosity and hope as he asked, "What if I say the words?"

Kingtroll asked skeptically, "Do you know the words?"

This-one shook his head and said, "No, you can tell me, and I can say the words."

Kingtroll shook his head and replied, "No, Avis forbade it. Only the one who finds the lost scroll can say the words."

The Troll with a glowing leg said, "Kingtroll, what if we give him the lost scroll? Then he can read the words."

Kingtroll jumped in his chair with excitement, "Will you do it? Then you don't need to heal us."

This-one was confused. "You still have the lost scroll? I thought the king took it?"

Kingtroll replied, "He held it. He read it. He has it now, but he can't take away the scroll itself."

This-one replied with almost a scream, "Yes, I WILL DO IT! Give me the scroll, and I will say the words."

Kingtroll nodded hurriedly, and the other Trolls became very anxious and uneasy. They rubbed their hands and looked at This-one with such gratitude in their eyes.

Kingtroll gestured to the stairs to his right and said, "Go on, hurry, up the stairs."

This-one followed the Kingtroll to the stairs, feeling a sense of anticipation and thrill. The trolls waited as he ran up the stairs. As he reached the top of the stairs, he saw a tiny room with a table in it, and on the table was a scroll. This-one rushed to the table and picked up the scroll.

The scroll had a strange texture, and it was old and worn. This-one could feel the roughness of the paper under his fingertips as he carefully unrolled the scroll.

He read the words with diminishing excitement:

> "Your vessel is sinking; Survive the tides.
>
> The end is coming; open your eyes.
>
> Live and think, but don't you stall!
>
> Catch the wizard; go past the fall.

The prophecy is cruel and very clever.

The fruitless war goes on forever.

Look to the future, but first in your past.

Know that your world is oh so vast!

Congratulations, you have found the lost scroll. Now thank the trolls and say, 'your purpose is served,' and the Troll Cave will disappear. You will be sent back to Forsaken Serenus."

This-one sat down with his hands on his head. He felt his head spinning. How could this be the lost scroll? Everyone had this already. Was this a trick? A puzzle? What did this mean? He sat there thinking as his head ached in disappointment. This was not the lost scroll.

The Trolls yelled for him to hurry up, urging him to say the words and complete their mission.

As he sat there holding the lost scroll, he began to have a realization. Maybe finding the lost scroll meant understanding the lost scroll. Did that mean they had it all along, and they just didn't understand it? He couldn't be sure.

If only Conrad were here, he would know what to do. Now he realized why the king didn't say the words. This world would disappear upon saying those words. He couldn't say it. This was too big a matter. He couldn't decide for everyone.

This-one carefully picked up the scroll and examined it from every angle, hoping to find some hidden clue or puzzle. He then walked towards the stairs and asked, "Is this the lost scroll?"

Suddenly, the Trolls fell silent and glared at him with angry eyes. Kingtroll quickly intervened, pleading, "Yes, this is the lost scroll. Avis placed it there, and we were not allowed to go up the stairs. This. Is. The. Lost. Scroll!"

This-one lifted his head and looked around the room, scanning every inch of the ceiling and walls, but found nothing out of the ordinary. The Trolls begged him to say the words, but This-one ignored their pleading and searched the room over and over again. He examined every corner, every surface, up close, from far away, from different angles, but found nothing.

Now, tears flowed down Kingtroll's face as he put his hands together and said, "You have the lost scroll, now say the words." This-one understood the king's dilemma; he couldn't say the words. The Trolls were suffering from a sickness of the mind, and no magic show or moonlight could heal them. The despair of their failure was the cause of their suffering, and the king had betrayed them.

This-one stayed in the room, contemplating his options. He knew that all the options were bad, and he didn't want to make any decisions. However, the Trolls kept begging him, and he couldn't ignore them anymore. He went to the top of the stairs and said, "Listen to me. When I came to this world, I had a poem in my pocket. I have read that poem hundreds of times. This scroll is the same poem that I had in my pocket, that everyone has with them when they come to this world."

Kingtroll and the others were disappointed, and they sat down and began to sob. This-one continued, "I want to help you, but I can't say these words. The world outside is suffering too, just like you are. They have been waiting for the lost scroll to heal them, to take away their fears, to make them god. If I say these words, your suffering will end, but so will this place. What if there is a clue hidden somewhere that I am not able to see? What if I am missing something? My world is waiting to heal. I can't take this risk. I can't say the words."

Kingtroll shook his head and sat down with the others. His lion walked up to him in a slow, sad walk with his head bowed and nose almost touching the floor. The lion sat beside the king, trying to comfort him. This-one felt their pain and cried. He sat down with his back against the wall as the Trolls sighed, sobbed, cried and grieved under him. He felt a heavy burden on his chest and whispered, "I can't take the responsibility... I can't decide for everyone. I can't take away the possibility. What if I am missing something?"

Then, a new thought struck him. "Oh... it could be a test." Maybe if he said the words, it would result in finding the lost scroll. The king didn't say the words, so he didn't get the scroll. What if he said the words? But he didn't want to give the Trolls false hope again, so he thought about it in his head. He wished Conrad were there to help him decide what to do.

What would Conrad do? "He is a thinker. What would he do? He would think, and he would find... no, Conrad said he hasn't solved a single thing. I stopped stones. Conrad said I was the one who had to come here. He said there was a reason he would tell me later. He said it had to be me... Conrad already told me that I have to be the one to decide."

Conrad had placed this heavy responsibility on This-one's shoulder. This-one remembered his words, 'I have a plan, though it is risky, and you will have to take the risk.'

This-one wondered, 'Was that Conrad's way of telling me that I am supposed to take the risk? Why me? Because no one else could heal... But wait, anyone could come with a Bluelight vial and make the Trolls feel better... Then why me? ... Did Conrad not want to wait for the Bluetree to grow? Or did he not want the responsibility? If I say the words, the Troll cave will disappear. Can I take this responsibility? Can I take the risk? ... Conrad is selfish... he wants me to take the risk... What would happen if I risk it? ... All the information I have says this is the lost scroll. And I did tell the Trolls... that I would say the words if they gave me the lost scroll... It feels right... I should say the words... And Shahzor... and Ariana would say I should think of the greater good... What is greater good? By saying the words, I will end the suffering of the Trolls... but I may leave my friends in endless misery. What if the lost scroll opens the door to happiness?'

This-one didn't know what to do. He wished it wasn't him who had to make this decision. He wished anyone else could take his place.

Thinking out loud, This-one said, "Amy would say to do the right thing. She would say... listen to yourself... Just be yourself... Who am I? What do I want? What do I think? It feels right, that's what I thought... I think it is right to thank them... Just be myself."

With newfound resolve, This-one stood up and said, "Just be myself. Just do the right thing... Take the risk..."

Walking to the stairs, This-one said, "I will say it. I will say the words."

The Trolls stood up and squeezed closer. Kingtroll and his lion also stood up with hopeful eyes.

This-one felt all eyes on him as he walked down the stairs, looked at the Kingtroll, and said, "... Th... ..." Lowering his head, he continued, "I can't say it."

The Kingtroll pleaded, "Please, please... say it..."

The Trolls stood there with their eyes begging him. This-one remembered the Keepers, who had stood just like this when he became their leader. The Keepers needed something from him that he couldn't give, something he didn't have. And now, the Trolls needed something from him that he couldn't give either. Could he? No, he couldn't eliminate the possibility. He couldn't decide for everyone. He had to leave this door open. But the king had already done that, and it didn't work. Maybe taking the risk was the right thing to do.

This-one closed his eyes tightly, bowed his head, and said it,

"Thank you! Your purpose is served."

A deafening and guttural roar reverberated throughout the dome, sending shockwaves through the ground and rattling This-one's bones. The walls groaned and twisted, as if they were about to collapse. The air grew thick with an intense sense of danger, and a terrifying sense of foreboding washed over This-one.

In an instant, everything plunged into pitch blackness, leaving This-one alone in the darkness. The Trolls disappeared before his eyes, leaving their last expressions etched into his mind - an expression of gratitude, success, and satisfaction that comes only from fulfilling one's purpose.

As the darkness slowly receded, This-one found himself alone with the lion. To his astonishment, the lion was smiling, its eyes glowing in the dim light. The lion bowed its head, then looked up at This-one. It lifted its front right paw, and with one swift, deadly swipe, killed This-one.

The sound of This-one's final scream echoed through the dome, a mournful wail of anguish and disbelief.

I screamed in shock, "MAAAAA??????"

Ch 36: I found myself

I screamed, "Maaaaaa!" My mind raced as I struggled to process what had just happened.

Ma tried to console me, saying, "It's okay. Everything will be fine."

I couldn't believe it. "Did he just die?" I asked.

Ma responded, "No, he is heading back to Forsaken Serenus...in a moment. Everything is fine. There is nothing to worry about."

"But why did the lion kill him?" I wondered aloud.

Ma laughed and said, "Him?"

Confused, I asked, "What's so funny?"

Ma replied, "Everything is fine. You will see...and it is time for you to learn my next secret... You never asked me what I look like."

I asked, "What do you look like? Why does it matter?"

Ma explained, "I appear to you in the form of a person, but I don't really look like a person. Look around. This is what I look like. I am everything. Whatever you see around you is me. I am the existence itself."

Stunned, I asked, "What? All of it is you? You are a... what are you?"

Ma replied, "I am Ma, The Maker. You can also call me The System or...the thing that exists...or thingymajig." Ma laughed.

I was amazed. The existence itself was talking to me, joking with me, and it was so cool. Ma was friendly and kind, but also faulty, and accepted her faults and failures so openly. Of course, it did. What was it scared of?

Ma laughed and said, "She/her. Those are my pronouns. Don't call me it."

I took a few moments to process everything. The entire existence could speak to me? I pointed at a stone and asked, "That stone, is that you?"

Ma replied, "Yes, I am the stone."

I then pointed at a nearby tree and asked, "And that tree?"

Ma replied, "I am the tree too. I am everything."

I asked, "A stone is dead. It cannot move or feel. Are you...are parts of you dead?"

Ma responded, "Are your nails alive? Aren't parts of you 'dead'? And what is it that you call life? Isn't it just a form, a system, a sequence? Put things in this order, and they can act like a small system. You call it life as long as the system holds. When the system breaks, you call it death and you say death is permanent. If you knew how to put the system back, it would be alive again. Then was it really dead? That stone is not dead. It is alive. It has systems inside it that are working all the time. Changing over time. It responds to its surroundings. It gets hot when the sun shines on it. There are others that don't do that. It has an internal system that is in motion. Small parts of it are doing what they are supposed to be doing. It looks still, but there are things spinning inside it. Tiny little things. When you see the stone, you see a constant object without any activity—one that cannot do anything or change. When I look at it, I see a crowded mess of activity. It is buzzing with change. Come back in a while, and you will see how it has changed. It changes differently than you realize, but it is still alive. As alive as you. You just don't know how to detect this life."

I could feel the ground beneath my feet start to tremble as I asked, "Everything is alive? Everything is changing?"

Ma smiled at me as she replied, "Yes. Everything is alive and is changing. And the entirety of it, the whole thing, that's me."

Suddenly, the stone I was standing on started to move. I struggled to maintain my balance as it quickly stabilized and rose up into the air. The stone flew around the Heart of the Forest, and I found myself enjoying the ride.

Something spoke to me inside my head, asking me if I wanted to go faster. Faster... I thought. The stone sped up, and I had to sit down to avoid falling off. As it moved even quicker, I could feel the wind on my face, pushing my hair back. I turned my head to look at Ma, but she had disappeared.

As the stone carried me higher and higher, we left the Heart of the Forest and flew around the entire forest. I looked down and saw the expansive collection of things that were parts of existence, parts of Ma. The trees, the land, the water, the air, everything - all of it was Ma.

I flew faster and faster; I felt myself turning into an orb of light. I went through stars in the sky, the galaxies that spread out, and the black holes that looked like they were devouring everything. Everything was in motion, alive with change. How could I call it dead?

The stone carried me farther and farther as we zipped through a blur of lights until everything was left behind, and I saw threads and waves - endless waves, twisting, vibrating, and curving into themselves, visible in some parts and invisible in others. Endless waves in an endless motion.

And then, in a single instant, everything wrapped up, and I was back on the ground, standing on the stone with Ma in front of me.

Ma explained, "All of that is me. And all of it is alive. It is changing, and all changes are recorded in time. I can read all the changes, finding patterns and clues. And through this system, I am looking, searching..."

I couldn't help but ask, "For what? What are you looking for?"

Ma replied, "I am looking for my purpose, the reason for my existence."

I was amazed and asked, "You are so powerful. You are everywhere. You are so capable, then why don't you intervene? Why do you let bad things happen? Why did you let Esmeray kill Conrad? Why did you let Amy be so sad? Why do you let people suffer?"

Ma explained, "It is part of my Protocol. To try all the possibilities, I have to let all possibilities happen. I have to let change happen. There is no such thing as good change or bad change. There is no success, and there is no failure. Change is just change. It is based on a formula. The change will happen the way it becomes possible. Some changes don't feel good to you, and you desire that I remove those changes, but then I would break my own Protocol. I can't remove some lines of thought. Then I might fail. I would not be able to try all the possibilities. And I have seen that some changes that don't feel good initially, can eventually lead me to a path of amazing discoveries."

I was troubled and asked, "But what about us? You make us suffer for your own good? I thought you were good. You let bad things happen to us so that you can find what you are looking for? It serves your purpose, so you let it happen? Did I say it right?"

Ma replied, "Yes. I don't know a better way. I don't know how to remove the bad possibilities and still try all the possibilities."

I was frustrated and argued, "That is what YOU want, to try all the possibilities. I don't want that. We don't want that. I don't care if all the possibilities are tried or not. I would rather Esmeray was good. You don't care about how your creation feels? You just want to find your purpose?"

Ma smiled, "How did I make you?"

I replied, "What? I... I don't know how you made me. You never told me that."

Ma smiled, "Yes... but think about it. If I am the entirety of existence, how did I make you? How did I make the waves you saw? How did I make this stone? Out of what?"

Perplexed, I asked, "Out of... what? Huh, if you are the one that exists, what did you use to make us?"

Ma answered, "I used myself. That's all I had. Everything is made by me, with me. The waves are at the root of everything... What is a wave? A disturbance, a change in a constant, a distortion of a still line. In the form of those waves, I twisted and turned myself to make all that I could. I used my own 'body' to create everything. And I can feel my body, sense what it feels. When you feel bad, I feel bad... I feel worse. I'm better at feeling than you are. I made you from myself. You're a part of me. That's how I can read your thoughts. When you're hurt, I hurt. When you cry, it's a part of me that's crying - I'm the one crying. And the part that made me cry? That was me too. My system isn't perfect. There are parts of me that make me cry. There are people like you who help others and people like Esmeray who cause pain. You are me, and Esmeray is me too. I am good, and I am bad. I tell the truth, and I lie. I am everything. When I allow bad things to happen, they happen to me. It hurts me too. Actually, it only hurts me because you are nothing. You're not a separate entity; you're a part of me, a part that's hurting. If a part of you was hurting, say your shoulder, wouldn't you be the one hurting? I feel bad when bad things occur, but I let them happen so I can explore all possibilities. I am desperate. I hurt myself to try to get what I want... my purpose. So I did what made sense; I made you to find my purpose, and I made all the others too. You are my thought - a line in my thought, capable of conversing with other thoughts and with me. And I am the entirety of the thought. I am everything. I am every person, every thought, every action, and every consequence. We are all connected, and our choices affect each other in ways we cannot imagine."

Ma continued,

> "Looking for something, in wanderings alone.
>
> Disturbance in nothing, to flesh and bone.

Head raised high, my passion knows no limit.

The depths of the ocean, or a perilous summit.

It is all me. And I am looking for the reason for my existence, and I created you and others to serve me... to find that reason."

After a moment of contemplation, I said, "Hmm, I never thought about it like this. You're everywhere and everyone. So you're doing everything that's happening... I am you, and you are me, and that's why you're so close to me. That's why I feel this connection with you... Oh, and that's why when you're happy, I'm happy. But what if there are thoughts outside of you too? What if you, too, are a thought of someone else?"

Ma's voice carried a hint of wonder. "I want to know if there is someone who made me, but I have never seen anything that I didn't create. I never heard a thought speak to me in my head like I talk to the thoughts I created. Or maybe I'm not as adept as Qilam at listening and identifying the voice in his head. I'm open to the possibility that there could be more than just me, and I'll keep searching until I discover the truth. I haven't given up. I'm seeking all answers. To try every possible thought, I made everything unique. You think in a way that no one else can. Everyone begins with a different set of parameters. You can't all think alike, which is why I said, I don't want you to follow Amy. I want you to be you. Together, one day I will find out."

Intrigued, I asked, "One day in the future? But you created time. Why don't you read what will happen later? Can't you read any part of time?"

Ma explained patiently, "That's not how it works. Time stores what has happened up to now. I know everything that has occurred so far, but I don't know what will happen next. I have a way of finding out, by trying it out. And I'm doing that, so I will find out, but I can't skip ahead. You're thinking about time incorrectly. Time doesn't yet contain the record of changes that haven't occurred. And I have given you freedom of action. You can choose which path to take. You will decide where I will go."

I thought about what she said. "So, I will take you forward?"

Ma smiled gently. "Yes, but in reality, it will be me taking myself forward because you're a part of me. You don't say 'my legs walked me today.' You say, 'I walked.' I will say 'I went forward,' but yes, it could be through you."

Feeling empowered, I asked, "I have the freedom to do whatever I can? You won't stop me? I can do anything? And you don't even know yet what I will do?"

Ma replied, "Yes, yes, yes, and kind of yes."

"But I never felt like I was in control. I mean, I never realized that I could do whatever I wanted."

Ma clarified, "You can do whatever you can, not whatever you want. Whatever becomes possible for you to do, you can do it. What is yet impossible for you to do, you can't do that. You are bound by fate."

"Remind me again, what is fate?"

Ma explained, "Fate is your circumstances. It is what has already happened and set your direction. It has determined your possibilities before it's time for you to choose a path."

I nodded in understanding. "So all of us are trying different paths to find our purpose... your purpose?"

Ma replied, "Yes, all of you are my thoughts. Each thought is unique, taking different paths. That's why I said nothing is fair and competition is flawed. No two things can be judged based on a single test. Nothing is superior to the others; they're simply different. Some differences prove more useful in certain tasks, while others do not. Choosing the right set of abilities for a task is not wrong, but pretending any comparison can be fair is deceptive. When a world becomes wise enough, it realizes this and eliminates competition for survival. It creates systems that allow everyone to live and explore their possibilities. It discovers ways to share and remove division. If I am a tree, you are my leaf. If a cluster of leaves on one side fights a group of leaves on another branch, who suffers? A branch cannot win while the tree loses. There is no competition among my branches. We're all in this together. As I said, there is no 'them.' It's only 'us.'"

I thought about her words for a moment. "So we have freedom of choice, and our bad actions can hurt you?"

Ma nodded. "Yes, I constantly feel the consequences of all my actions. Remember when you asked if I face the repercussions of my failures? I do—all the time. When you fight, you hurt me. When you kill someone, you kill a part of me. When you hurt someone's feelings, you hurt mine. And when you spread good experiences, you make me happy."

I empathized with her. "When we fight... that must be very painful for you?"

Ma's voice quivered, "Yes, I cry when my creations kill me. When they destroy countless possibilities, I weep in pain. But it is all my own doing. It is what it is."

My heart ached. "I'm so sorry."

Ma offered a sad smile. "I'm sorry too, and now you know why."

I connected the dots. "Because I am sorry, and I am a part of you. If a part of you is sorry, it's you who is sorry."

Ma affirmed, "Yes."

"I thought we were all separate, but we're all part of one. We're all... you."

Ma confirmed, "Yes."

"And can you die?"

Ma shook her head. "Not at the hands of my creation, at least not yet. I believe I will find my purpose one day."

I asked, "What do you think your purpose could be? Do you have any theories? What is your best guess?"

Ma responded thoughtfully, "My best guess is that I am a thought. Whose thought, I don't know. For a thought to exist, there has to be a thinker and an unknown. Maybe a thinker is thinking through me to discover what is not yet known to them. I believe this is who I am, and I made you to be similar to me."

I considered her words. "I am a thinker... everyone is a thinker... trying to find one unknown at a time?"

"Yes," Ma agreed. "Your mind receives information about your fate from its senses, then analyzes it using learnings from past experiences. If the past experience was good, the mind wants things to keep moving the way they are. If not, it wants to take action so the next thing that happens feels better. That's how your mind decides what it should do next. It tries to improve your fate—one thought at a time. If you think about it, it's just receiving new information, understanding it based on past experiences, and generating the next action. In an even shorter way, you could say that it is a processor of thoughts. It's a tool that enables my journey from not-knowing to knowing. With every new understanding, there's one less thing left to figure out. Will there always be a next thing to figure out? I don't know. That's why I said,

> What is the point? Where am I going?
>
> Coming to an end, or am I still growing?
>
> I'm thinking it right, or in the wrong context?
>
> Is there a stop, or always a next?"

Conrad thought that. It was on his tree wall.

Ma smiled, "If Conrad thought it, doesn't that mean I thought it? Conrad is me—a part of me. If he thought it, I thought it."

I nodded, "Yes, of course."

Ma concluded, "So my best guess is that I am a processor of thoughts. And I will always have something to think about—until the day every answer is known. That would be my death because there would be nothing left for me to do. I would have found everything I needed to, and then I wouldn't need to do anything. And what do you call things that just stay still, not thinking or doing anything?"

"Dead!" I realized. "You think you will die when you have found all the answers?"

Ma shrugged, "It's a theory. I don't know what will happen. I want to find out. I believe I will, eventually."

I couldn't help but ask: "Are you not scared of death?"

Ma shook her head. "No! Death is peace. It is the end of the struggle. It is the finding out of all the answers. It is the escape. A flattening out of a disturbance in existence."

"But what if there is another world for you to go to?" I proposed. "Just like I didn't know what would happen to me after I die, maybe you too are unaware, and there will be things that will happen after you die. What if you have to face consequences in the next world?"

Ma's eyes widened slightly. "If you're trying to scare me, it's working. Not that I haven't thought about it, but I have suffered so much already that it feels like my death would be the end of suffering."

I continued, "That's how you would feel, that's how I felt. I didn't think Serenus was a great place to live. Not until I left it. I thought there was always some trouble, one problem after the other. One wizard after the other attacking the trees. We didn't think we were living in heaven, but compared to Forsaken Serenus, I would say it was heaven. Maybe you will go to a place so bad that you will think this place was heaven."

Ma held up her hand. "Okay. That's enough for now. I have stressed over it enough already. I have found that there is no way to know, so it's better not to stress over it."

You are just like me. That is exactly how we think. You are more powerful and more capable but faulty and scared... like me, like us.

Ma nodded. "Yes, I don't deny it, though I would say it differently. I would say my creations are very much like me. I made things that are very much like I am because that's all I know."

Agreed.

Ma continued, "One last thing... I told you how the mind works... by receiving new information, checking its existing experiences, and then generating an action... You can only ever choose one path... it is decided by your fate and past experiences as well as other factors like the presence and balance of different chemicals in your body... At any point, your mind generates only one possible action... it takes the only path that it thinks is right based on the available data."

I frowned. "But that would mean I have no control? And then no one can be blamed for anything. They are only doing what becomes possible..."

"Yes... so what should we do then?" Ma asked.

I thought for a moment. "Nothing... things just happen... whatever is possible, only that happens? Then I don't have any control... Esmeray did what she could based on her fate... there is no point in feeling guilty or worrying... there is no point in being afraid... what's going to happen will happen. But you said we had control to pick a path."

"Yes... I said that. And you have control. You are the one picking the path, but you are picking the path that your mind gives you. And it gives you what it thinks is the next right thing to do in your reality... in your circumstances."

I shook my head, still not fully grasping the concept. "There is no point in doing anything?"

Ma corrected me. "That's not right. You are alive through me... you are experiencing things... you are going through it, so there is a point. One thought at a time, you are trying to improve your fate. If you stop trying, you may have to suffer a worse fate. What you need to understand is how you have control. What variable you can change to adjust your direction. You need to understand that the mind generates the next action based on its past experiences. If the experiences are good, its actions will be good. This is the only thing that matters. Experience and feelings. Nothing else matters. And if we have come this far that we have figured it out, we should use this knowledge to live better, to make our tomorrow better than today."

"So then the point is to have good experiences?" I inquired.

Ma nodded. "Exactly. Have good experiences and spread good experiences. And if your mind does what it does, and everyone's mind does what it does, then what can we do to improve the experiences?"

I paused for a moment. "We tell them, we tell everyone about it. If everyone's mind has this information, then they will choose a different path. So sharing this knowledge is what will create good experiences? Is this the most meaningful thing I can do?"

"Exactly," Ma nodded. "And now that your mind has reached this understanding, its next actions will be different... its next actions will do what will create more positive experiences... we are blessed to have reached this learning. We have found this pattern, and this learning is going to create a lot of good in the world. Just spread this... tell everyone... once it reaches their mind, they are more likely to create a world that cares for others because their mind knows that there is no them, it's only us, but also because a world that gives good experiences is a world you will have a good experience in. Do it for yourself, not for others. There are no others."

"Okay, I get it now," I said. "Sharing our understandings is our way of controlling our direction."

Ma smiled. "I couldn't have said it better. I read time, I read all the changes to find such learnings and patterns. And then I use these to improve. You are my extension. Do the same. This is the best way I have found so far. Do this till a better path becomes available."

"But what about the lost scroll?" I asked, still uncertain.

Ma laughed heartily. Then she tried to stop and asked, "What was the lost scroll supposed to give you? What is the lost scroll?"

I hesitated, unsure of what she meant. "The lost scroll is the knowledge that makes one god and removes their fears."

Ma laughed again. "And what were we just talking about?"

A sudden realization hit me. "Ohhhhh..... oh... Ohhhhhhhhhhhh-hhhhhhhhhhhhhhhhhhhhhhhhhhhhhhh. So that's what it means." I nodded with an open mouth, astonished.

Ma smiled. "You have the lost scroll now. The intervention is over. It is time for you to play your role now. Go into the world and tell everyone about it. Tell them how we are connected. Tell them how we can make the world better. Share this knowledge! This is pure. This is balanced. This is reasonable. This power cannot be used for evil. Spread this."

Ch 37: Welcome to Forsaken Serenus

I woke up and found myself in the boat, gently swaying as it made its way toward Forsaken Serenus. This time, no garbage accompanied my boat, but there was enough filth on the sides to make me hold my breath for as long as I could. The stench was overwhelming, and I felt my nostrils flare with discomfort.

As I anxiously waited to reach the spot where I could disembark, my thoughts drifted back to the conversation with Ma. I had the lost scroll, but it didn't grant me powers or magical abilities. Instead, it gave me knowledge that could heal the world. So, did the king possess this knowledge? He sought power to control the world, but instead discovered this profound truth. I couldn't help but laugh at the irony of the situation – how the king must have felt when he wanted powers to rule the world but was presented with knowledge that showed him he wasn't meant to dominate others.

But the king remembered everything when he returned, whereas I was told that when someone died in Forsaken Serenus, they came back without any recollection of their past life here. I also remembered everything just like the king. Both of us didn't get a magical ability from finding the lost scroll, but the people say he has magic. Oh... he is a learner. Just like me. If he has magic, it is what he learnt in Serenus. I shook my head. He was nothing but a liar, a trickster – a clown in costume.

As the boat moved on, I spotted a crowd of people gathered around the guard's checkpost. Upon noticing my approach, they rose to their feet, their eyes fixated on me. Though they maintained their distance, their interest was piqued. Many pointed in my direction, exchanging whispers among themselves.

My boat finally reached a clean spot, and I stepped out onto solid ground. To my surprise, someone had cleared a path, making the walk much more bearable than before. As I moved forward, I caught sight of Conrad, Shahzor, and Nuno in the crowd. Their faces lit up as they recognized me, and they ran toward me with excitement.

Conrad inquired, his voice tinged with hope, "Who am I?"

"You are Conrad," I replied with a warm smile.

Overjoyed, Shahzor and Nuno began dancing exuberantly as Conrad exclaimed, "He remembers!"

"He remembers?" The words rippled through the crowd in a chorus of astonishment.

The three guards I had encountered during my first visit to Forsaken Serenus rushed toward me, eager to know, "Do you remember who we are?"

I laughed, responding, "Yes, you are... not nice."

At my words, they burst into laughter and joined the others in their jubilation. Behind them, the entire crowd erupted into a celebratory frenzy, chanting, "He remembers!" Someone started banging pots and pans together, providing a makeshift rhythm for the people who danced with wild abandon. The guards hoisted me onto their shoulders, carrying me through the throng of merrymakers.

Everywhere I looked, I saw pure elation, satisfaction, and hope. Their eyes glistened with tears of happiness as they continued to chant, "He remembers!"

Conrad couldn't contain himself, his body convulsing with an unbridled dance that seemed to defy any traditional steps. He simply allowed his body to express his joy, and it responded with a dance of sheer delight. Shahzor, Nuno, and more people from the crowd joined him, forming an ever-expanding circle of dancers.

As the festivities continued, I noticed Firehorses approaching from behind the crowd. No one else seemed to pay them any mind, but I couldn't help but worry. Were they the king's men? As they reached us, the riders dismounted and inquired of Conrad, "He remembers?"

When Conrad nodded, their stoic expressions dissolved, and they forgot their duties as guards, joining the crowd in celebration. Their exuberant shouts breathed new life into the gathering.

As the celebration raged on, I wondered why they were so ecstatic. When they finally allowed me to walk on my own, I pulled Conrad aside.

"Conrad? What's happening?" I asked, my expression a mix of surprise and amusement.

Conrad nearly shouted, "We told everyone that you were able to enter the Troll Cave. We have taken the king's power. You remember just like he does. We did it!"

Then, leaning in to whisper, Conrad asked, "Did you find the lost scroll?"

I nodded, but before I could say anything more, he gestured for me to remain quiet.

Conrad cautioned, "Not here. Not where people can hear you. Let's talk about it later. First, we have to do something important."

Raising his voice, Conrad announced, "We've taken the king's power."

He didn't seem to mind the guards' presence as they danced alongside the people. I glanced at them with concern, but Conrad reassured me, "They are people too. They want the same thing. And they, too, are happy."

With that, Conrad instructed the guards to fetch a table. They hurried to the checkpost and returned with the table they used for their games. Conrad placed it in front of him, climbed atop it, and called out, "My friends!"

It took a moment for the crowd to settle down and lend him their attention.

Conrad began, "My friends, we have found another who remembers just like the king. And this one is from us. He cares for you. He wants you to have a better life, and he wants to help you."

The crowd responded with enthusiastic whistles and applause.

Motioning for silence, Conrad continued, "And we have more news for you. The magic has returned!"

Astonishment rippled through the crowd as they struggled to process Conrad's words. "What?" they murmured, their eyes wide with disbelief. They stared as if they had heard something beyond the realm of possibility.

Conrad raised his voice, passionately announcing, "The magic has returned, and we are planting a Moonseed tonight!"

It took time for the people to accept this astonishing news. They exchanged glances, their faces etched with uncertainty.

"Clear this place! Clear the Broken Circle! Clean it!" Conrad commanded. "Tonight, we will plant a Moonseed. The Tree Circle will return to Forsaken Serenus!"

The crowd came to life, moving like a synchronized swarm. They used their hands, the guards' weapons, and anything they could find to clear away mud and garbage.

Conrad approached me, explaining, "We have Moonseeds. We need to grow more Moontrees. The magic will return and, with it, people's hope. Tonight, you have to show them that you can capture Moonlight. The seed doesn't need Moonlight until it grows into a sapling, but we need to demonstrate that the magic has returned with you. You must capture Moonlight and pour it on the Moonseed once it is planted in the ground."

"Where's Amy?" I asked, concern clouding my expression.

Conrad's face darkened. "We don't know. We've looked everywhere, but there's no sign of her. We don't know what to do."

My voice resolute, I declared, "I can't stay here for months to grow another Moontree. I need to go find her."

Conrad pleaded, "What will you do? Where will you look for her? We have looked everywhere we can. People who know this world... I have sent them to look for her. You can't search for her any better than they can... you are needed here. This world needs you."

Tears welled in my eyes as I gazed at the people around me, fully aware that I was needed there. But I couldn't embark on another time-consuming endeavor. Could I find Amy more effectively than the others? Once again, all options seemed bleak. I had hoped to search for her, but the world required me to stay right where I was.

Conrad hugged me, saying, "I know what you're going through. I'm trying my best to find her. Please... you are needed here."

I nodded, my heart heavy with sadness even as I committed to helping an entire world. Once again, I had to prioritize the needs of the many over my own desires.

As night fell, the Broken Circle had been cleared. Everyone gathered around as Shahzor and Conrad stood where the Moontree once grew. Shahzor dug a hole in the ground, an entire world watching with bated breath.

Before we could plant the Moonseed, we saw fire approaching in the distance. The flames raced through the darkness, drawing ever closer. People glanced nervously at the king's riders but did not retreat. They gripped whatever weapons they had, prepared to defend themselves.

The Firehorses drew nearer, and we waited, tense and watchful. The king's guards arrived, their gleaming armour radiating an aura of intimidation. Yet no one yielded, refusing to grant them passage. The line of Firehorses reached the crowd and split into two, forming a barrier in front of the people. From behind the line, a larger Firehorse emerged, its rider crowned with authority. The people gasped nervously, but none retreated.

With a fluid motion, the king dismounted his horse and strode confidently toward the gathered people. He signalled for his guards to stay behind, choosing to approach the crowd alone. His tall, imposing figure commanded respect, and his self-assured demeanour made it impossible for anyone to meet his gaze. Instead, they looked down as he drew nearer. Unfazed by his proximity to the crowd, he continued to move forward.

As the king came face to face with them, the people reluctantly stepped aside. His authority was so great that he seemed unconcerned by their overwhelming numbers. He pressed on, and the crowd parted before him, their eyes averted. Finally, he reached us.

Shahzor and Conrad stood protectively in front of me as the king demanded, "Conrad, show me the magic."

Conrad hesitated for a moment, visibly affected by the king's authority. Then, he nodded and placed the Moonseed in the hole in the ground. Shahzor covered it with soil, and Conrad urged me, "Show them the magic."

I had never seen the king before. His pristine, elegant armour and the way everyone reacted to his presence left a deep impression on me. He had such command over the people, as if he harbored no doubt that they were insignificant. How did the king wield such dominance and control over everyone? What power did he possess?

Conrad whispered in my ear, "We have Shikongo right where we want him. We have an audience, and we have everything we need to prove him wrong. It's time. Capture Moonlight."

I nodded and looked toward the moon. Capturing Moonlight was something I had done every night for months, so that wasn't the issue. What truly concerned me was the king's demonstration of authority. I knew I had to strip him of that power and control, but today wasn't the day for that. Today, we merely needed to do something he couldn't do. I had to fight one battle at a time.

I captured the Moonlight, and the lightning bolt flickered for a moment, healing the hopeless hearts around us. Holding the Moonlight string in my hand, I placed it where the Moonseed was buried. The soil absorbed the light, and the crowd erupted with elation.

Conrad turned to the king and declared, "The magic has returned. It's time to heal the land."

The king approached me and locked eyes with mine. I held his gaze, unflinching. He hugged me, whispering in my ear, "Come to the castle. We have much to discuss and much to do."

This unexpected invitation took me aback, but I wasn't the only one. No one had anticipated such an act from the king. Shikongo mounted his Firehorse, casting one last glance at the crowd before soaring away, leaving everyone bewildered. The celebration resumed.

Conrad turned to me and inquired, "What did he say?"

"He asked me to come to the castle," I replied. "He said we have much to talk about and much to do."

Conrad nodded in agreement.

The night passed in jubilant celebration. Ariana approached me, asking how I had been. I told her I was faring better than expected, and she was happy to hear that.

Nuno brought bread, and Shahzor, Nuno, and I sat by the Moonseed. Conrad joined us and asked, "Okay, so what is the lost scroll?"

I began recounting the tale of the Troll Cave and my conversation with Ma. My friends listened intently, their eyes fixed on me as the flickering firelight danced across their faces. When I finished, Conrad mused, "It's simpler than I thought. I assumed it would be a difficult-to-understand enigma that would elude us. But this... it's so straightforward."

Shahzor and Nuno nodded but remained silent, lost in their thoughts. Conrad finally broke the silence, "We need to tell everyone."

"Yes," I agreed, "Ma said that's the point - to share the knowledge with everyone."

Shahzor chimed in, "After our meeting with the king, let's gather everyone in one place and tell them."

We sat there, enveloped in a comfortable quiet for a long time. Around us, many others lingered, whispering and pointing in our direction. All of us felt an invisible tether to the Moonseed, unwilling to leave its side. We knew everyone experienced this connection, yearning to remain close. The Moonseed would take time to grow, but we couldn't bear to leave. Eventually, we relaxed and fell asleep in a circle around the precious seed.

Morning came, and Shahzor left to fetch Firehorses while Nuno returned to his bakery. Conrad and I waited for them as people gathered to see the Moonseed's planting site. Conrad instructed them to clear a larger area around the Broken Circle to accommodate more visitors. This would be our gathering place. Eager and hopeful, people began cleaning in ever-expanding circles around the Broken Circle.

As visitors arrived in groups, they spent time near the Moonseed, hoping and praying for its growth before joining the cleaning efforts. Shahzor and Nuno returned with three Firehorses, and Shahzor showed me how to mount the majestic creature. After some struggle, I finally managed to sit on the horse without tumbling off. That was all we needed for now. Shahzor, Conrad, and I set off to meet Shikongo in his castle.

The castle was huge and so beautiful. I had never been inside the castle before, and I couldn't stop looking around. It was an unbelievable sight. Meticulously designed channels managed rainwater, and neat streets lined with houses resembled a proper village like Serenus, albeit crafted from stone and devoid of greenery. As we passed the Sanctum of Knowledge, I marvelled at its stunning architecture, tall minarets, domed roofs made of stone, and intricate glass windows. Seekers bustled about, clad in clean robes.

We continued toward the king's hall, and the castle's interior stirred deep thoughts within me. The residents enjoyed a level of comfort that starkly contrasted the lives of those outside the castle. Within the walls, people appeared respectable and honourable, greeting one another with dignity and politeness.

The further we ventured, the more it felt like a different world. I couldn't have fathomed the beauty hidden in stone or the happiness radiating from the castle's inhabitants. The sights left me awestruck.

Throughout our journey, Conrad stopped to speak with various people, all of whom treated us with respect and kindness.

My preconceived notions of the castle had been shattered by the time we reached the king's hall. I felt disoriented and uncertain, realizing that I knew nothing about the lives of those within the castle walls.

As we approached the king's hall, we were greeted by a representative of the king, standing poised at the entrance. "Please follow me," he requested, and Conrad gave a nod of agreement. We trailed behind him as he led us to an exquisite stone building. "Make yourselves comfortable," he said, "The king will receive you in the king's hall this afternoon." Handing us clean clothes and robes, he continued, "You must be tired. Please freshen up, and I'll send for some food." Before departing, he added, "If you need anything at all, inform the guards outside. They'll attend to your needs."

Shahzor's face lit up with a broad smile, showing his happiness at returning. The way he moved around indicated that he had been there many times before.

Conrad noticed my astonished expression and remarked, "Don't judge a book by its cover. Give it a chance. It may surprise you."

"But I assumed the castle would be a terrible place," I replied, "I thought the king was cruel. Yet this looks great."

Conrad smiled, "No one is entirely good or entirely bad. The king has done much good for his people. The issue lies in how he treats the Keepers."

"Why should he treat them differently?" I asked, "They just sit outside, contributing nothing. The king and his men built all of this through hard work. They must think, 'Why should we let them enjoy the fruits of our labour?' Look at this place. They have a system in place. They are civilized people. Is it wrong that they don't want everyone to come in here?"

Conrad responded with a gentle smile, "It's not wrong, but he doesn't have to steal from them. This stone came from a mine built by Keepers. The guards' weapons are forged from iron discovered by Keepers. You're unfamiliar with the history. The king considers himself honourable and respectable, and based on what he's created here, it seems justified. But if you look back further, you'll see that this place was built on the backs of the Keepers, who were then denied entry. The king doesn't even allow them to have a leader. He sabotages their efforts to form a society, fearing that if the Keepers worked together, they could challenge his authority. He doesn't want rivals; he wants to subdue them, ensuring they can never compete with him. And he doesn't have the resources to provide for them or share with them. He wants to take whatever he needs from the Keepers without giving anything in return."

"Why can't Keepers and Seekers be friends and work together?" I inquired.

Conrad explained, "In Serenus, everyone lived together; there were no Keepers or Seekers. The king, however, is a Seeker, and he believes Seekers are superior. He thinks they deserve all the resources to find the path ahead. In his view, those who simply want to live comfortably are a waste of resources."

"But the resources aren't his to decide that," I countered, "Ma created the world. Everyone owns everything equally."

Conrad nodded, "But he doesn't think like that. He believes

Seekers, who are working toward a purpose, are the ones doing something useful. Keepers, in his mind, are just... living. He sees life in this world as pointless. The goal is to maintain discipline and systems working toward a single objective: to open the door. Every Seeker in the castle is focused on finding ways to achieve that goal, and the king provides them with all the necessary resources because, in his eyes, they are useful. He has nothing to offer the Keepers, whom he perceives as lesser beings. He wields power and makes decisions for everyone, but he refuses to share that power or those resources."

I nodded. "At least he's kind to the Seekers."

"Yes," Conrad agreed, "that's why our aim isn't to topple the system. Seekers are people too, and if they're benefiting, half our job is done. We need to find ways to improve the system so Keepers can benefit as well, without taking away what the Seekers have. To achieve that, we need someone to replace the king - a leader who considers everyone's needs."

After changing into clean clothes and enjoying a delicious meal, we were escorted by the king's guards to the king's hall.

Upon entering, I was awestruck by the hall's beauty. Elegant pillars flanked both sides, with numerous stone benches situated between them for visitors to sit. An open space dominated the center of the room, and at the far end, a series of steps led to a raised platform where a single, imposing chair stood, with the king seated proudly upon it.

Guards lined the hall, and it was clear that everyone was well-trained and disciplined. They moved with purpose, each knowing their specific duties and performing them efficiently.

There was a long line ahead of us as we reached the hall. Conrad and Shahzor walked to the end of the line, and I followed. We stood there, waiting to be heard by the king. However, only a couple of moments passed when a guard approached us and invited us to have a seat at the nearby benches.

My eyes roamed the hall, taking in its stunning design and the orderliness of its occupants. It was obvious that a well-executed plan had been followed to create such a magnificent and functional space. I couldn't help but be impressed. Who was the mastermind behind it all? Could it have been Shikongo?

In the midst of my admiration, the king asked the court jester to entertain the hall. The court jester was a man in brightly colored clothing standing in a square filled with sand. As the jester turned, I recognized his face - it was Duncan. I felt a pang of sympathy for him, standing there so humiliated.

Duncan, however, seemed to savour the attention and spoke excitedly, "Your majesty, let me tell you the tale of a Celestial Gardener and a Mighty Worm."

Everyone laughed. The king raised a hand, and silence enveloped the hall.

With a mischievous grin, Duncan began spinning a new yarn,

"Your Majesty, long, long ago, our world was a barren and lifeless place, devoid of the wonders we see today. Suddenly, a towering creature appeared from the heavens, its very presence filling the void with a sense of possibility. This celestial being reached into its pouch and sprinkled seeds of life across the lifeless expanse. And so, the first inklings of life began to stir. One of these seeds, surrounded by a protective bubble, learned to harness the resources around it. Each time the bubble burst, it reformed, stronger and more resilient than before. As the bubble continued to grow and evolve, it sprouted more bubbles around it, gradually transforming into a wriggling, thriving worm. Over time, the worm encountered other beings that had evolved from the same seeds, each with unique shapes and abilities. One day, the worm met a mysterious jellyfish, floating gracefully through the air. The jellyfish landed on the worm, its tentacles piercing the worm's skin to make contact with its primitive brain. Through this extraordinary connection, the worm and jellyfish learned to communicate, forming a symbiotic relationship.

The worm used the jellyfish as its eye, feeding it in exchange for a view of the world outside itself. Together, they explored their surroundings, encountering other bizarre creatures and learning from each experience.

Eventually, the worm came across another of its kind, and the two decided to join forces. The two worms merged, their bodies combining in a single form, their minds intertwined, and they discovered the joy of conversation. They argued, debated, and reasoned with each other, becoming smarter and wiser with each exchange.

As their intellect grew, so did their success in the world. They learned to hunt better, to defend themselves from those who sought to bring them down, and to adapt to the challenges life threw at them. They continued to grow and evolve, absorbing the strengths and abilities of the creatures they defeated.

In time, the mighty worm and its jellyfish companion rose to become the undisputed rulers of the world, the Alpha Beings. Their dominion over the land was unparalleled, and they ruled with a firm yet fair hand.

Yet, despite their power and wisdom, they never forgot the origins of their existence. They gazed at the sky, searching for the celestial creature that had planted the seeds of life so long ago. They hoped that, one day, it would return to reveal the purpose behind their creation and bestow upon them the ultimate knowledge.

And so, Your Majesty, the tale of the Celestial Gardener and the Mighty Worm teaches us that our origins, no matter how humble, can lead to greatness."

The King's court erupted into laughter at the absurdity of his story. Duncan's eyes lost their shine, and he felt disappointed.

However, amidst the laughter, the King raised his hand once more, and silence fell. He looked scornfully at Duncan and said, "While you may have hoped to entertain us with this ridiculous tale, you have only managed to make a fool of yourself. What a preposterous story! A worm and a jellyfish ruling the world? Your attempt to convey a message has failed, and you have only succeeded in making us question your position as our jester."

With the King's words, the atmosphere in the court grew cold. The laughter turned to whispers of mockery, and the faces of the audience showed disdain for Duncan's tale. The jester, feeling utterly humiliated, hung his head low, his confidence shattered.

I couldn't help but wonder. There was so much beauty and incredible planning, yet at the same time, such ignorance. There was no care for the Keepers and no respect for Duncan. It felt as though people were divided into classes. Some were respected, while others meant nothing. That was the problem with this system. It was undeniably beautiful, but it lacked heart. The creators didn't care about how it affected others. The king did what he believed was right and thought he had the authority to decide for everyone. Who granted him this authority? How could he decide who should live well and who should be miserable? No, this wasn't right. This system would work wonderfully with a good king, one who would care for everyone. However, it would be cruel under a wicked ruler. One person shouldn't be the sole decision-maker. One person shouldn't hold the entire system in their hands. This was wrong.

I remembered Serenus again. The elders decided on all matters, but they weren't cruel. They made decisions based on what they thought was best for everyone. But what if their idea of "good" wasn't truly good? What if they believed someone should be a thinker when that person was actually a learner? Was no system perfect? Conrad said we had to replace the system with a better one. What could be better than this? What if we always found a good person to be king? Then that person would do good things. But what if someone pretended to be good, and once they were made king, they weren't good? No, even after becoming king, they should remain good or be removed. Yes, that felt better. Once we found a good king, we could keep them for as long as possible. And what about a queen? Yes, it could be a queen, of course. When the people felt that the king or queen was no longer serving as a good leader, they could find a replacement. This felt even better. It felt good to more of me.

I decided to discuss this with Conrad later. For now, I focused on the events unfolding around me.

The king listened to people's requests and passed judgments, either granting or denying them. It was all up to him. He could do as he pleased. If it felt right, he allowed it; if it felt wrong, he denied it. No one could argue or protest. The king's word was final. He sat there, deciding everything for everyone.

Now, I observed the king himself. The way he sat, the way he moved—it was all so... graceful. Almost too graceful. Who moves like that with such authority and confidence? Every time he spoke or shifted in his chair, he maintained a perfect posture. Even the slow, graceful movement of his neck seemed unnatural. I had never seen anyone move like that before. It felt like it was part of the plan, just like the way the guards moved. Everything was done for a reason. The king wasn't acting like he would normally act, nor was he sitting as he would if he were alone. No, it was all a performance designed to appear graceful. And it did look grace-ful. Each movement was planned to build his image, to make him seem grander than he truly was.

I had never spoken or moved like that. I mimicked Shikongo, moving my head from right to left the way he did. A smile ap-peared on my face as I tried it, and indeed, I felt more graceful. Yes, a slow, graceful movement. It was easy to imitate. I straight-ened my back and sat at the edge of the bench, just like the king. It was challenging to maintain this posture for an extended peri-od, but it did make me feel more... upright and elegant. So, all of this was well thought out, and there was a reason behind it. Wow. Even the tiniest details had a purpose. How much planning must have gone into it? How to sit, how to move, how to talk. It was all an act designed to make him appear better than he truly was, so those around him would think highly of him.

I realized the king was wearing a shell, a carefully crafted persona that he donned whenever he was with others. Like clothing, the king created a personality that demanded respect and command-ed authority. This was the king's secret, and a glance around the hall confirmed its effectiveness. Everyone looked at the king as if he were something beyond their reach.

If I wear a shell like the king, I thought, I can make others treat me differently. I can pretend to be more than I am, better than I am, and that would deceive others.

I smiled as I planned to try it with Dante and Jaci the next time I saw them. I chuckled inwardly, imagining Jaci and Dante looking at me with respect as I acted gracefully. This-one has found the lost scroll, and now This-one commands respect. I chuckled again. Conrad elbowed me when he heard my stifled giggle. I refocused on the events in the hall.

The next person to speak to the king wore elegant robes and appeared knowledgeable. As he addressed the king, his words were full of praise. I listened to how he spoke.

The person in the elegant robe said, "My gracious king, we at the Sanctum of Knowledge are blessed to have you. My king, you are wise. You know what is right and what deserves attention, and the pursuit of knowledge is of utmost importance. My king, you have provided for us, enabled us, and supported us in our time of need. My king, our needs are small; your abilities are vast. My king, we need more. We need to expand... to make room for more knowledge and experiments. You are the provider, my king. We cannot turn to another. We are blessed to have you as our ruler..."

The man continued to praise the king and request the expansion of the Sanctum of Knowledge. I listened to the way he spoke and thought about how it affected the king. Then I realized something else. They spoke to the king with such dignity and respect, praising him and asking for his assistance. He was just a king. Yet, I had been talking to Ma, the Maker of worlds, and I had never praised her. I had never addressed her in such a manner. She deserved far more than the king. Was I uncivilized? Did Ma consider me someone who lacked grace in speech? If anyone deserved to be spoken to like that, it was Ma. But I had never addressed her in that way; I simply called her Ma. Was I lacking in manners? Perhaps I should speak to her the way she deserved to be addressed.

Suddenly, I found myself in the Sandbox again.

I was sitting on a tree with a beautiful waterfall in front of me and a setting evening sun. This was one of the scenes I preferred and often created to enjoy the beauty. I thought about what words I should use to address Ma. I needed to show her that I was not a wild thing, that I could speak to her as they were speaking to the king. Yes, I needed to at least try it.

After thinking for a bit, I said, "Ma?"

Ma appeared in front of me with a curious smile on her face. Something amusing must have happened elsewhere because around me, colours were more vibrant, and the tree swayed with happiness. I didn't know what it was, but I felt the energy and enjoyed it.

Then, I addressed Ma the way she deserved to be addressed, "Oh Gracious Ma, O Maker of the Worlds, O Ma, You are the provider, You are the enabler, You are... You are the one... who has blessed..." I ran out of words. That was all I had prepared, but it felt like it was not enough. I needed to add more.

I paused for a bit and added, "O Ma, The Maker...."

No, I had already said that. I was very nervous. In an attempt to show Ma that I, too, could address her properly, I was failing. I didn't have the words, and I hadn't prepared enough.

I tried again, "O Ma, O Gracious Ma, The Maker of the Sandbox, The Maker of Serenus, The Maker of Forsaken Serenus, The Maker... of all the worlds, O Ma, you are...."

And Ma just couldn't hold it anymore. She burst into laughter. She laughed and laughed and laughed. She would point at me and then laugh. She just couldn't control it, she laughed, and I loved it. I was embarrassed, utterly embarrassed, but I loved it. And I loved the energy I felt when she laughed.

When she still couldn't stop herself and went into another laughing fit, I pleaded, "Ma?"

She closed her lips and tried for a moment but couldn't control her laughter. She said, "I'm sorry..." and then laughed again.

"Maaaaa!!!" I felt very nervous now and wanted to know what was so funny. Was I that bad at addressing her? In an effort to impress her, did I actually prove that I was a fool who didn't know how to speak to her? If that was it, she should teach me how to speak to her.

Finally, she was able to speak again. She came close, looked into my eyes, and said, "Talk to me like you talk to yourself. I am closer to you than anyone can be. I am you. You are me. I know what you think, just like you know what you think - even better. Words don't mean anything when you can read someone's thoughts. You don't need flowery language; you don't need to praise me. I am not your king. I am not your queen. I am your friend. Talk to me like a friend. Talk to me like you always did. When you say 'O Gracious Ma' in an appeasing way, I don't fall for it. When you call me Ma, I don't feel you don't respect me enough. I know how much love you have in your heart for me. When you know what's in someone's heart, you don't need to listen to their words. I like it when you call me... when you say Ma, and I say Yes? Isn't it beautiful? What could be better than that? Imagine what I think of those who work against me, create division and hurt me, but when they talk to me, they talk as if... they pretend... as if I don't know? Do you think I fall for their pretending?"

No. You know better. You know all.

Ma smiled, "Speak to me like you are talking to yourself. But if you ask me, I love the way you say Ma."

"Oh," I said and nodded. "Ma?"

Ma smiled, "Yes."

I smiled, "This is simpler. I like it too."

I lay down on the branch, watching the waterfall. My words echoed in my head, "O Maker of this and maker of that and... oh and don't forget gracious ma," I laughed again. The tree laughed again.

"Ma," I said.

"Yes," Ma said.

This time... it is different. I feel like I am This-one, and I am also here.

Ma answered my thought, "Yes. You are This-one now, and you can talk to me anytime. You can live in both worlds. In your head, in the Sandbox, you can imagine and create, and at the same time, you can live in Forsaken Serenus. Now you know what I would sound like. You can identify me in your thoughts. I sound like you. Now you can talk to me whenever you want. Once you find the lost scroll, all copies become one."

I felt happy and nodded.

Ch 38: A Duel of Diplomacy

Then, I brought my attention back to the king's hall. I was still waiting for the king to talk to me.

Conrad whispered, "The king is making us wait. It's a power move. The longer he makes us wait here, the more kingly he feels about himself."

I nodded. I had already figured out that this was all an act to appear more than he was. He couldn't be himself here. He had to hide behind a shell, a persona. One that he thought he needed in order to be respected. And who needs a shell to hide behind? The one who has something to hide. The one who thinks less of themselves than they want others to know. Why does the king think less of himself? Why can't he talk to people like normal people talk? I didn't know him enough, but I did know that he was a learner with a shell of lies and a carefully crafted personality to impress others and maintain his command.

I didn't care that the king was making me wait. I could expose Shikongo anytime I wanted, but that was not my goal. I was thinking of a way to improve his system. I wasn't interested in starting a fight with the king. My goal was to somehow make things better than they already were. And I needed to preserve all the hard work that had been put into the system already.

I whispered, "Conrad?"

Conrad whispered, "Yeah?"

I asked, "Did Ma talk to you about improving the system?"

Conrad nodded. "Did she talk to you?"

I nodded.

The king stood up, and everyone around us stood up suddenly.

The king said, "This is enough for today. I will listen to the rest tomorrow."

The king walked away, and the people got up and started heading out of the hall. We looked at each other's stumped faces as we wondered if we were supposed to come back the next day.

"Follow me. The king will see you now." A guard came to Conrad and said.

I walked with Shahzor and Conrad to the adjacent room with a huge table. The guard pointed to the stone chairs on one end and said, "The king is not-thinking; he will be with you shortly." The guard left, and we waited.

When the king finally arrived, he sat at the far end of the table. A guard brought a bowl and placed it in front of him. The king picked some fruit and pushed the bowl toward us, saying, "Have some fruit."

I was surprised. The king no longer had a shell. He was acting like a normal person now. He even sat back in the chair and scratched an itch on his belly.

Shahzor thanked the king, took a piece of fruit from the bowl, then passed the bowl to Conrad. Conrad, too, picked a piece and forwarded the bowl to me. I took a smaller piece and pushed the bowl back to the king. As the bowl slid on the table toward the king, Shahzor and Conrad gasped. I realized then that maybe this was considered to be disrespectful.

The king didn't mind. He caught the bowl and picked another piece of fruit. Then he asked me, "So, did you say it?"

I looked at Conrad and then back to the king, "Say what?"

"In the Troll Cave, did you say the words?" the king asked.

I nodded.

The king nodded back, took another piece of fruit, and slid the bowl to me. I took a piece and passed the bowl to Conrad. Conrad took a piece and passed the bowl to Shahzor. Shahzor picked a piece, then picked up the bowl, walked to the king, and placed it in front of him respectfully.

"So, what happened then?" the king inquired.

"It turned dark as night, and the Trolls disappeared. When the light returned, it was just the lion and me, and then the lion killed me," I explained.

The king nodded thoughtfully. "I always wondered what the lion was for."

"Then I was with Ma again," I said.

The king nodded again. "And she gave you the lost scroll."

I nodded.

Then the king took the last piece of fruit from the bowl and yelled, "Guard!"

A guard walked in respectfully. "More fruit," the king commanded.

The guard bowed and left with the bowl.

"What did it feel like? What changed when you got the lost scroll? When Ma shared the knowledge with you, what changed in you?" the king asked.

"When I found the lost scroll, they became us," I answered.

"Huh... Is that what you were looking for?" the king questioned.

"No. I thought it would be a magical power," I admitted.

"What happened after that? When you left again?" the king continued.

"I woke up in the boat," I replied.

"And you came back to the island and remembered everything?"

"Yes."

The guard returned with more fruit, placed the bowl in front of the king, and left. The king took a piece and pushed the bowl toward Shahzor. Shahzor picked a piece and passed the bowl to Conrad. Conrad took a piece and passed the bowl to me. As I picked a piece, Shahzor and Conrad watched me uneasily. I pushed the bowl toward the king.

The king laughed. "So that's who you are. A rebel?"

Shahzor lowered his head, and Conrad said, "He is a friend at heart and interacts with everyone like friends do."

The king spoke calmly, "I know him." Then he yelled, "Kallar!"

Kallar walked in, bowed, and sat near the king, turning to face Shahzor.

Shahzor stared at him but didn't speak.

Then the king asked, "Did you pick a name?"

I shook my head. The king smiled and said, "Why won't you pick a name?"

I replied, "A name doesn't matter. It is not important. You can call me This-one."

The king nodded and said, "You have lived a good life. In Serenus, you received a home with waterfalls in your front yard, and you had friends like Kratos, Amy, and Idir. You tricked Esmeray and saved Moontree. Then your friends risked their lives to save you from the new wizard, yet you left because Amy left. You gave up Serenus for a friend. You stopped stones and garbage. You are the one who brought magic to this world. And now you have found the lost scroll and can't be killed."

I looked at the king with an open mouth. I did not expect him to know this much about me.

Then the king said, "And you don't pick a name. Everyone picks a name, but you don't. You are okay with being different. You know what you have?"

Conrad lowered his head.

"What do I have?" I asked.

The king nodded. "You have a story. A story you can tell, and the people will like you. They will follow you. They will listen to you. You have never hurt anyone, so you are likable. You brought magic back, and now you are growing a Moontree — something no one could do. People will like you. They will want you to lead them. The question is... what happens next in your story?"

I stayed silent. I didn't know what to say.

The king smiled. "If I didn't know you, I would think you want to be king. But I know you. You will want to do the right thing. And that is why I called you here. I want to know what, in your mind, is the right thing to do."

Shahzor and Conrad looked up at the king as I asked, "How do you know me?"

The king yelled, "Qilam!"

Qilam walked in with slow steps. He bowed and sat by the king and turned to face Conrad.

I stood up and walked to Qilam.

Qilam stood up. I hugged him and said, "I'm very happy to see you again." Qilam nodded and sat back down.

The king looked at Qilam and then stared at me as I took my seat. Conrad smiled.

"So Qilam, what will No-Name do?" the king asked.

Qilam cleared his throat, "No-Name will want the Keepers and the Miserables to have the same comfort as Seekers have."

The king nodded and asked, "And do they deserve it? To be brought into the castle?"

Qilam shook his head. "No, my king. They do not deserve it.

They are wasting their time and their lives, and they will be a burden on the resources. The mission to open the door is more important than their comfort."

"What do you say to that, This-one?" the king asked.

I shook my head. "Nothing is more important than feelings. Creating a system that provides everyone with the surety of survival, a good experience, an opportunity to explore their possibilities, and a way to contribute using their abilities is more important than opening any door."

The king yelled, "Alfred!"

Surprised, I turned my head to watch as Alfred walked in, bowed to the king, sat by him, and turned to face me.

"Alfred, is providing a good experience more important than opening the door and finding what is next?" the king asked.

Alfred spoke firmly, "The point of this world is to open the door. Those who are working on it deserve more resources. The system doesn't owe anything to those who are here to just waste their time."

I shook my head. "No, the system owes them because this system has taken from them. You have stolen from them, and you owe it back."

Alfred shook his head, and the king laughed, "Even your friends don't agree with you."

I said a bit harshly, "I have talked to Qilam a few times and heard stories about Alfred, but they have never been my friends."

The king nodded and then yelled, "Amy!"

I stood up in shock and turned to see if it was really Amy who the king was calling. I believed with all my heart that Amy could not be on the king's side.

Amy walked in, her silky dress rustling with each step. She bowed to the king and sat by Alfred.

I was still standing and looking at Amy, but she didn't look back at me. She kept her eyes down. I didn't understand what was happening. I kept staring at Amy as Conrad said, his voice laced with concern, "Amy, are you okay?"

Amy replied without looking up, her voice barely audible, "I am fine."

"Amy?" I said, but she didn't look up. Her face was... like a stone. As if she didn't even hear me.

The king said, "Amy, do the Keepers deserve to live in the castle?"

Amy shook her head.

I was very upset now. "If opening the door to happiness is the goal, then you should be spreading happiness. I am not asking to allow them to live in the castle. I am asking that they be allowed to improve their lives. I am asking that you stop stealing from them. I am asking that you stop pretending that you have a right to decide for them."

King refused. "The resources are limited. Whatever we have, we need to use to open the door."

I shook my head, my anger building. "No, whatever we have does not belong to you to decide that. Every comer has as much right as you have. Every one of them is as important as you are. You live in a stone castle with all this extravagant use of resources, and you say they don't deserve to have these? How many houses can be built with the stone that is used to build just your hall where you sit and decide people's fate?"

King smiled, "There it is. So you would destroy the hall? You would take the stone and build their homes? Is that what happens next in your story?"

I replied quickly, "No, I wouldn't destroy anything. A lot of hard work and planning has gone into it, and I think it is very beautiful. I want you to stop pretending that you own the world. There is more stone in the ground, and everyone can build if you stop looting them."

King said, "There is one more person I want you to meet." Then he yelled, "Erasmus!"

An old man walked in with slow, careful steps. I knew this man. He was the old man from Troll Mountain.

As the old man took a seat, the king said, "This is my friend Erasmus. He tells me there is a place where fish still swim in the water. He says eagles still find uncharred sticks to build their nests. He says there is a place on this island where trees still grow, and he says there is a Moontree growing there."

The old man nodded as Conrad and I looked at each other with worry.

I gasped, and the king said, "I have known about This-place for a while now, but I never intervened. I hope reviving the trees opens the door. We couldn't do it without you, but now we can try this possibility. You can be the leader of Keepers and revive the Tree Circle. I will not come in your way, and you give me your word... you will not come in my way. We can be two kingdoms, and we can live side by side. Seekers and Keepers. You can be the king of Keepers, and we can be friends."

Conrad looked at me, his eyes shining with excitement, and nodded happily. I was not happy. I wanted to bring back Serenus, and Serenus was one people, not two. I didn't like the division. Having two kingdoms meant there was a possibility of war between the two. I wanted to unite everyone. I didn't want to create lines... what was the word Ma used? Ma whispered in my head, 'Borders.' Yes, I didn't want to create borders.

I thought quietly for a bit.

Then I offered a counter-proposal, my voice clear and determined, "I don't want to be king. Keepers and Seekers are one people. If we start dividing the people like that, next, we might have to divide healers and thinkers. This is not the way. We are one people, and the Tree Circle is the center of our kingdom. Send your builders to teach Keepers how to build their homes. Once Keepers have their homes, open up the castle. Let people meet, and live where they want. I will work on restoring the Tree Circle while you treat every comer to this island the same as you treat a Seeker. If you accept this, I will bow to you. You can be the king of the entire island."

All eyes turned to the king, who was in shock. His eyes widened. He said, his voice wavering, "You will bow to me in front of everyone?"

I nodded. "If you accept this, you are my king."

The king jumped up, his face flushed with excitement, "I accept."

Shahzor screamed in a whisper, "Yes!!!"

The king ate a piece of fruit from his bowl, and pushed the bowl to me. I handed a piece to Shahzor and another to Conrad. Then I took a piece for myself. Then I picked up the bowl and walked to the king to place it in front of him respectfully. The king placed his hand on my shoulder. I looked at Qilam, who was smiling, his eyes twinkling with approval.

The meeting ended, and I left the castle with Shahzor and Conrad. We went to the Tree Circle and then to the Keep. We informed everyone that the island would be one kingdom again. The people were unsure, their eyes filled with doubt. They didn't think the king would care for them. They wanted me to be the king of the island because I had proven to have magic. I shook my head, and they became quiet. The people had their doubts, and their distrust of the king was evident.

Then I went to the Tree Circle with Shahzor and Conrad, and Nuno joined us there. We sat by the Moonseed as others sat nearby.

Nuno asked, his voice tinged with curiosity, "Why did you do this? Why not be a king of Keepers and work for what they need?"

Conrad smiled warmly as I answered, "The king is a good planner. He has already demonstrated the ability to build a system. A lot can be improved, but there is a system in place. If that system is working only for Seekers, an improvement would be to make it work for Keepers as well. And I am not a king. I can't do what he can. And if I am going to be growing a Moontree, I will need months of work. I can't be a king while I work on this. The king can be a king. He is a good king for the Seekers. We just needed him to be a king for all of us. And we got that. Who knows how the door will open. We will work here as he works there."

Nuno nodded.

Under the glittering stars, we stayed near the Moonseed for the night. As did many others.

I looked at Ma and asked, "Did I do the right thing?"

Ma smiled, her eyes soft, "Steady improvement is better than drastic change. Being together is better than being divided. Instead of being a second king in the land, you made the king work for you. The king is happy. You are happy. It is a win-win, and I am happy."

It was too late, so Conrad said we would tell everyone about the scroll the following day.

In the morning, the king sent guards to stand around the Tree Circle. The guards said people could sit nearby, but no one was allowed to walk near the Moonseed. Later in the morning, the king himself rode a Firehorse and came to talk to us. I made sure to bow to him when everyone was watching.

The king stood by as Conrad and I sat on the ground. We discussed plans to train the Keepers and mine stones for building their homes. The king gave Conrad the task of overseeing new construction and asked Shahzor to plan logistics with his builders. They needed more Firehorses to bring stone from the mine, and Shahzor knew how to get more Firehorses.

As the king left, a Keeper bowed to him. A smile appeared on the king's face, his eyes lighting up with satisfaction. He reached his Firehorse, then turned and called me to him. "This is my favourite Firehorse. I brought it as a gift for you." I thanked him, and the king left with his guards.

Shahzor shared tips on how to ride the Firehorse. I practiced riding and then requested that Shahzor keep the Firehorse in his stable.

Everything was working out, but there was something that was still bothering me. I couldn't understand why Amy was with the king. I asked Conrad if he could send word to her that I wanted to see her. Conrad was also very upset with Alfred. All this time, Alfred knew where Amy was, and Conrad was searching for her all over the island.

Ch 39: The Dawn of Ma

Shahzor informed us that everyone was gathering to hear about the lost scroll. We assembled where the village center used to be. Nuno invited me to speak. Everyone settled on the ground. I sat in front of them and began:

"I met Ma when I died in the Troll Cave. And Ma gave me the lost scroll. It is a piece of knowledge. A knowledge so pure that it cannot be used for evil. The lost scroll makes us god and takes away all our fears. Now, I am going to share this knowledge with you. This knowledge has the power to transform our world into heaven, but only if it is shared. I am sharing it with you. Your job is to share it with those who are not here."

The villagers nodded, their eyes reflecting a newfound wonder.

I continued, "Ma is everywhere. Look around you. What do you see?"

Many heads turned to survey their surroundings, then turned back to me with questioning eyes.

"Everything you see and what you cannot see – a stone, a tree, a person, a thing or energy, even a thought – whatever the manner of existence, the entirety of existence is Ma. Ma is all-powerful. She can do whatever can be done. Not only can she do it, she is the one doing it. She is around us and inside us. We are a part of existence. We are a part of Ma. And Ma knows what we think, and Ma can feel what we feel. Just like we can feel what our body feels. She is better at it than us. She can even feel what we can't feel."

A villager stood up. She raised her hand and looked at it. She asked, "This is Ma? Am I Ma?"

I replied, "You are Ma. I am Ma. All of us are Ma. All of us are the same. And all of us are different because of our fate. She made us different for her need. We are finding one unknown at a time for her. Ma connects us all. Ma is what is common in us. She created us from the fabric of her own existence. And she cares for us like one cares for themself. When we do something good and make someone happy, we make her happy. When we hurt someone's feelings, we hurt Ma. She feels pain, and she feels happiness. She laughs, and she cries. She dances, and she sings. In me, in you, in birds, in flowers, in things we have no knowledge of. It is okay to be happy. It is good to be happy. Ma says, 'to be happy is to be thankful.' It is okay to express yourself. And it is also okay to cry. Crying is not complaining. Crying helps us move past the bad feeling. We are all equal in her eyes. Whether we do good things or bad things, Ma still loves us. Even if we hurt her, she doesn't dislike us. When we forgive ourselves, we find her with open arms. We judge each other, and we say this one is better than that one, but it's not true. We are just different. No one is better than others, except in the feelings we spread. Those who spread good feelings make Ma happier than those who don't. Ma is not our King. Ma is not our Queen. Ma is our friend – a friend who understands us like one understands themselves. No one can understand us better than Ma. And when we talk to her, we can talk to her like friends talk. Ma is cool. Ma is funny. And Ma is reasonable. When one discovers Ma, one springs warmth and shares positive energy. If everyone focuses on creating good experiences for each other, our world will transform into heaven. If we believe in Ma, we will go to heaven. No, heaven will come to us. Our world will become heaven."

The people gasped, their eyes wide with astonishment.

My words were altering their perspectives. I continued more passionately, "Who are we? If we believe we are merely what is contained within the confines of our bodies, then we die when our bodies fall apart. But if we believe we are part of Ma, we live as long as Ma exists—forever. I cannot predict the form we will inhabit, but I know we will live on. In our current form, we have the freedom to act. Parts of me will become dust in the future as they have in the past, and my freedom will be limited. Today, however, I can take action and seize this opportunity to contribute. Now is our chance. We can transform this world into heaven, making it Serenus once more. Conflict and troubles will always be there, but the more believers we have, the greater the chance that our world will be filled with happy experiences."

The woman who had been standing remained on her feet. She said, "This doesn't sound complex. It's very simple. Why did it take us so long to realize this? We should have discovered it sooner." Many in the crowd sighed, nodding in agreement.

I continued, "Ma is reasonable and open to the possibility that she, too, could be someone's creation. Perhaps there is more to existence than her, but she has not yet uncovered it. Seekers wish to explore whether there is more than Ma, and there is nothing wrong with that. Ma encourages them to search, and she wants us to uncover all unknowns. If Ma is all there is, then all paths will lead to her. Let everyone search in their own way. If there is more, she wants to know. She is not scared of questions. If Seekers find something that was not known before, they do her a service. If they don't, then whatever path they go on will eventually lead them to her."

I paused to catch my breath, noticing a newfound sparkle in their eyes. "Ma doesn't intervene. Our world is filthy, but Ma will not clean it for us—except through us. We have the power to clean it, and in doing so, we act on her behalf. Prayer is not asking for someone to come and do something for us; rather, it is wishing for something, working towards it, and then hoping that our efforts will be enough. Ma doesn't perform miracles or rescue a drowning person. She has entrusted us with control. She watches us. She feels for us. And she hopes for us, but she doesn't interfere.

This is our time to act, and our lives are in our hands. We have freedom, but our freedom has boundaries. We cannot escape our reality, as our fate defines the limits of our freedom. However, we can change our fate, as every change is a change in fate.

If we seek happiness, we must eliminate negative possibilities and try to make positive outcomes a reality. If we burn a tree and then pray for fruit, our prayers will go unanswered. Try it. It won't work. We must plant a tree, nurture it, and, if our effort was enough, it will bear fruit, answering our prayers. The key to happiness lies within us; no one can bring joy into our lives but ourselves. What causes you sorrow? Work to eradicate that possibility and change your fate. Imagine a world where everyone around you tries to make you happy. How incredible would that be? Such a world is possible—one that fosters positive experiences, establishes rules and systems that promote happiness, replaces competition with cooperation, and recognizes that everyone is unique and equally deserving of the world's resources.

Ma says when a world reaches this understanding, they eliminate competition for survival, allowing everyone the freedom to explore their own possibilities without fear. This is the point of making systems. This is why systems exist, and a system cannot function without contributions from everyone. In Serenus, I could not have been a successful material researcher as I had no interest in it. My way of thinking did not align with that pursuit. Choosing the right abilities for a task is not competition, but a system that rewards certain abilities with abundant resources while others receive little is ignorant, spreading negative experiences and creating division.

Imagine if you didn't have to worry about survival; wouldn't you pursue your interests? Wouldn't you do better in a thing that interests you? Wouldn't your contributions to the system be more valuable if you did what you were good at? We all share the same basic needs: shelter, food, companionship, and acknowledgment. We can work individually to achieve these or implement a system that addresses these needs, allowing us to contribute in more meaningful ways. Serenus was better; Forsaken Serenus is not. So why are we living like this? Together, we can do better.

When you speak to someone, speak to them as you would speak to Ma — with respect. When you need help, ask as if you were asking from Ma. Serenus no longer throws garbage our way, so we can clean this place together. And when we start cleaning, don't look to those who aren't contributing, and don't stop because some aren't participating. We are not doing this for them; there is no "them." Do it for ourselves and for Ma. In Ma's name, do what you can, contribute what you can, and then cast aside all negative thoughts, living free from fear, pride, jealousy, and doubt. With an open heart, contribute what you can. Can we not make this world Serenus again? We can, and I know that I will try, as will my friends and many of you. Let's offer this prayer; let's wish to bring Serenus back; let's work to bring Serenus back; and then let's hope that our efforts will be enough to bring Serenus back. Once we have done our part, it will happen or it won't—there is no fear or worry, for it is what it is. If we fail, we will try again. Failure is not bad; rather, it is the ladder to success. Ma told me that all I needed was to be myself and to correct my course once I realized I was wrong. That is all we need to do. Can we try it? Is it worth a shot?"

No one answered. I didn't need their response to know what they thought. They were already on their feet, moving like a swarm without needing to be told what to do. Conrad winked at me from afar, while Shahzor ran to me, hugged me, and said, "This-one can speak!" I laughed, and then we joined others in the work.

Everyone had common sense. We knew what needed to be done, and we did it. Wherever someone found a place they could contribute, they did so, working as if it were for themselves. Over the next few days, we cleaned up the area around the Tree Circle. Conrad, Shahzor, Nuno, and I dug up many areas, burying garbage in holes and covering it with soil. Others followed suit, and within a few days, the foul smell disappeared. Some people gathered stones from the land and arranged them around the Tree Circle, creating benches for people to sit on. Hope and direction returned to the people once again.

It became a tradition to work all day and then celebrate around the Tree Circle in the evening. Songs and dances returned to Forsaken Serenus, as did whistling and cheering. Many people found various ways to play music, and life returned to their hearts. A once-missing positivity was restored, thanks to Ma.

When the Moonsapling sprouted its first leaves, people were overjoyed. They couldn't believe their eyes. They cried and laughed, sang and danced. Ma didn't mind the singing and dancing; in fact, Ma danced with them, within them, and sang through them.

The king often sat by the Moontree; his guards placed a large stone for him to sit on as others sat around him on the ground or on smaller stones. The king never joined in the dancing, but I was certain he wanted to. His position simply prevented him from mingling with common people, and at times like these, I felt pity for Shikongo that he felt he needed to stay in the shell.

In all the planning, it was evident that Shikongo prioritized aesthetics, just as he had with the interior of his castle. He desired functionality and beauty and didn't mind investing more resources to achieve it. He believed that spending more for a beautiful appearance was worthwhile. Conrad, too, was very pleased with the design of the homes for the Keepers.

As the Moonsapling began to sprout leaves, I busied myself with collecting Moonlight. The nearby checkpost now served as storage for Moonlight containers. To everyone's surprise, one day, Nuno brought some grass from This-place. He never revealed its origin, but he planted it near the Moonsapling. No one stepped on the grass; instead, they sat on the ground beside it, tenderly running their hands through the blades as if it were the most precious thing they had ever encountered. People took turns sitting by the grass, feeling its texture, while others would shout at them to handle it more gently. Everyone wanted to sit on the grass, but no one ever dared. They watered it and wished for it to spread as they gathered around the Tree Circle each evening. They wished for it, worked for it, and hoped it would be enough.

Ma whispered, "You were right. This is prayer: to wish for something, to work for it, and to hope it works out." I nodded quietly and looked around.

Nuno saw me and asked, "What are you nodding at?"

I smiled and replied, "Something Ma said."

Nuno was in shock, "You can still talk to her? Even in this world?"

I replied, "Yes, you can too."

Nuno asked, "How?"

I explained, "I don't know how Qilam could do it, but I know how I can. I know who Ma is, so I know what she would say. When I hear a thought in my head, I can tell if it's Ma or not. Ma wouldn't speak of division or competition. Ma would say what is good for all. Once you know Ma, finding her in your thoughts is easy."

Curious, Nuno asked, "What does she sound like? Her voice from Sandbox?"

I laughed, "No, she'll sound like you. You won't hear another voice, a different voice, because she isn't separate. She is you. You'll hear your own thoughts."

Nuno continued, "Then how do I know it's her?"

I responded, "You are her. Every thought in you is her thought. I don't know how to teach you; it's something you have to do yourself. You have to find her inside your heart. And once you know who she is, you'll know which thought is her. You will know what makes her happy. And then you will be happy."

Nuno and I sat in silence for some time, contemplating my words. I wasn't sure if it was I or Ma who said it. I had never really thought about it like that. When Qilam told me he could hear a voice in his head, I believed he was crazy. When Ma spoke to me, it felt entirely normal.

Ma? I thought.

Yes, I replied.

Both thoughts 'sounded' like my own. Was I going insane? I mulled over that idea for a bit, and perhaps Nuno was doing the same. No, I shook my head vigorously, so much so that I lost my balance. As I regained my footing, Nuno looked at me quizzically.

I lied, "I almost fell asleep."

"Oh," Nuno laughed.

Time passed, as it always does—carefree, altering our fate with each change. It continued its course, recording our actions while we worked diligently. We cleaned and prayed.

The Black Dust storms still dampened our spirits every now and then, and we still woke up covered in dust, but it couldn't damage our morale too much. We learned to look past this one thing that we couldn't fix for a long time. We needed the ground to be covered with grass and trees to finally eliminate the Black Dust, but that wasn't going to happen for years.

One day, the king arrived with a large sign that read "Serenus." His builders had carved it in beautifully polished marble. The guards placed the sign where Serenus Kitchen used to be. People would come, sit by it, and sing songs reminiscent of their time in Serenus. It almost felt like Serenus at night. During the day, we could see all the black surrounding us, which saddened everyone, so we worked harder and harder to get rid of it. Some of us busied ourselves making torches for the Village Centre. Indeed, it became a village center like the one in Serenus.

Once Conrad finished digging channels for rainwater, he asked people to find small stones and make a path from the Tree Circle to the Keep. And they did.

Then the rains came.

Forsaken Serenus was a place of hostile elements. Just as the Dust Storms made being outside unbearable, the rains caused mud, landslides, and floods. We protected the Moontree as best we could, but elsewhere, much of our work was destroyed. Water overflowed the channels and ruined the paths. Everything became muddy again. Those were challenging days, but we kept fighting the rain. As it destroyed something, we rebuilt it. Eventually, the rains stopped, and we celebrated our victory. We succeeded in maintaining equilibrium—a balance of Ma's elements around us—so that we avoided the negative possibilities. Our effort was enough, and our prayer was answered.

The Moontree was safe and growing strong. It was now a small plant and the center of every celebration. People treated it as if it were the most delicate thing. They were afraid to even touch a leaf, but it was resilient. It grew stronger and stronger amid the Black Dust and rain.

Conrad managed to send word to Amy and Alfred, but they didn't come. I couldn't understand why. One day, I decided to go to the castle and speak to them in person, but Conrad said it wasn't a good idea. If they didn't want to see me, maybe we shouldn't pursue them.

I felt like Conrad didn't want me to get involved with Amy and Alfred. He wanted me to focus solely on the Moontree. It bothered me, but I tolerated it. I didn't go to the castle but hoped one day Amy would come to see me. I often wondered what could be the reason she didn't visit, but I couldn't think of any plausible explanation. It made me sad, so I practiced not-thinking and humming when no one was around.

Dante and Jaci couldn't leave This-place because then Mosi would be alone for days, and no one else knew about This-place.

We still wanted to keep it hidden. I couldn't wait to meet them again. Nuno had visited and told them about the lost scroll. He said they were delighted. I was happy that they were happy.

When I met Nuno in the evening, he wanted to discuss something that was bothering him.

Nuno said, "I've observed that those who believe in Ma work selflessly. However, those who don't are just there to benefit from others' work. I'm afraid this will weaken the resolve of the believers. I overheard a group discussing believers and non-believers should live separately. They argue that non-believers shouldn't reap the benefits if they don't contribute."

Shahzor, sitting next to me, replied, "Are they true believers if they say this? They are Ma, and those they call non-believers are also Ma. If Ma benefits from their work, do they have a problem with that? Their hearts are still closed. They haven't really grasped the concept yet. Ma is against division. Now they want to divide themselves into believers and non-believers? That's entirely missing the point. They need to think of Ma more often. They need to be reminded of what believing in Ma means."

Conrad and I nodded in agreement. Nuno smiled, "I'll tell them. If you're a believer, you don't worry about whether someone else is putting in the work or not. You do it for yourself and for Ma. And they are Ma too. If they benefit from your work, you're doing great."

Conrad thought for a moment and then said, "Not only do we

need to share this knowledge, but we also need to keep reminding each other. We should talk about it often, so we don't forget, and our belief stays strong."

I talked to Ma almost every day in the Sandbox and inside my head. I started seeing things differently. Everything was Ma. Everyone was Ma. Whatever happened around me was Ma's doing. If I ate something, it came from Ma. I thanked her. If I spoke to someone, I spoke to Ma. I spoke with respect. My world looked different; people around me felt different. I felt connected. If I helped someone, I didn't feel like I did them a favour; I was only helping Ma. When I asked for help, I only ever asked from Ma. She was the provider, and everything came from her—through a part of her, but still from her. When something good happened, I was grateful for all the changes that made the good thing a possibility. When something bad happened, I accepted it.

I tried, whenever I could, to remove negative possibilities, and when I failed, I understood that it was beyond me. I felt lighter. Acceptance of my fate was such a relief. I did what I could and then stopped worrying. My burdens lightened, and life became simpler. When I felt sad, I cried, not to complain, but to move on. When something good happened, I laughed. Little things brought more happiness than I imagined, and big problems didn't feel like burdens. I could only try, and it would work out, or it wouldn't. It is what it is.

And then, one day, it clicked. The words of Faqeer ran through my thoughts. "It's me. Over there. You see that? That's me." Had he found Ma already? Had he figured out the concept? How did he know? And why did he leave everything once he learned it? Did he not care anymore? Did nothing matter anymore? Would the finder of truth become like Faqeer? No, that didn't feel right. He wasn't useful. He was... just alive. Enjoying the feeling that he was Ma. Not sharing it with others would be... selfish? Was he selfish? No, it didn't feel right, either. He was lost. Yes, he was lost in the knowledge and couldn't contain what it meant. He found the lost scroll without even going to the trolls? Could we do that? What if we could all find the scroll without the need to visit the trolls? Could all of us, inside of us, find Ma? Maybe.

I met Faqeer many times. I wondered how he figured it out, but he wouldn't say anything except, "It's me. Over there. You see that? That's me." I would sit by him, watch his old wrinkly face and messy beard. I would just watch his expressionless eyes and wonder who he was before he found Ma. And whether he knew he was right. Of course, I told him many times. But he would only say, "It's me. Over there. You see that? That's me." I hoped he knew it in his heart. I hoped for him, but also for me. I wanted him to know. I liked him, and I wanted him to have the satisfaction of knowing. Maybe it was my need more than his. He didn't really need anything. And when someone doesn't need anything, you can't give them anything. Bread. Of course, I could give him bread. Or, to say it properly, Ma gave him bread through Nuno.

Everything moved well for months. The Moontree in the Tree Circle grew six trees around it, and the grass spread. Around it, in a spiral, the construction of new homes was moving at full speed. People started taking showers more often. They started combing their hair. They felt better and were getting back to normal. They would laugh and spend time with each other. Food was still too little, but it was getting better. A lot more people would now tend to crops. Everything went well, except Amy and Alfred did not come to visit the Tree Circle.

And as everything was going so well, I knew that bad possibilities were still possible. There was nothing to worry about, no real sign of any danger, but I had this feeling in the back of my head that something bad could happen anytime. As if my story could not have such a happy ending. I worried about it, and then it happened.

Alfred came to talk to me, and he had this look of despair as if he was in a cage and he couldn't do anything about it. He asked me to go somewhere we could talk in private. We walked to Nuno's home and then walked a bit further until we were out in the open with no one around as far as we could see.

Before Alfred could tell me what he wanted to talk about, I asked him, "What is the common ground?"

Alfred raised his eyebrows and said, "Common ground? Oh... You read that?"

"Yes," I replied, "Amy showed me the letter you left for her. What did you mean by common ground?"

Alfred explained, "An idea that everyone could adapt and believe in. I wanted to find a story that could unite us... A story that everyone could call theirs. And I believe it had to be based on common ground. Such a story would have no room for division or hate. It would have to appeal to everyone... not be targeted at some and leave others out."

"And did you find it? A story that everyone could find theirs?"

Alfred laughed, "Really? Are you still asking me that? Don't you know now? You found the lost scroll. You know the common ground, the story that has a place and acceptance for everyone... a story where the beacon of light is not tilted to one side. It spreads its light evenly."

I nodded.

Alfred continued, "I need to talk to you about something else but promise me what I am about to tell you, you will never tell anyone."

"How can I promise that? I don't know what you are about to tell me," I replied.

Alfred insisted, "It is about Amy, and I need your help, but I can't tell you unless you promise."

"Okay, I promise. What is it? Is she okay?"

Alfred hesitated, "I don't even know where to start. Okay... first of all, when the king went to the trolls, he found the lost scroll, but he refused to thank the trolls."

"Yes, I know that," I said.

Alfred continued, "And the trolls killed him. When he woke up in a boat again, he remembered his life here... he remembered everything."

"Yes, I know."

Alfred added, "That is why he was chosen to be king because he claimed to be invincible, and he had found the lost scroll. But it's a lie. He is scared of death because he can be killed. And so can you. He knows it, and you have to be careful because if you die, and I believe he plans to kill you, you will come back thinking you just came from Serenus. You will not remember anything."

"No, that's not right. We are both learners. We can learn from death. That is why we remember our past even when we come back," I explained.

Alfred shook his head, "No, anyone who dies in Troll Cave comes back with their memories. There is no other way to leave the Troll Cave. But if you die here, you will forget everything you learned in Forsaken Serenus. You will lose all your friends."

"How do you know this?" I asked.

Alfred nodded, "I had my doubts. I wondered why the king needed guards if he was invincible. If death is just an inconvenience to him, then why is he scared? I have stood outside his room to guard him, and I can tell you, when you came back, he was scared. And he plans to get rid of you, but he doesn't know what to do. Erasmus is his most trusted advisor. They are planning to get rid of you."

"How do you know this?" I asked again.

"I am in the king's guard, and I hover around the king, trying to find his weakness. Trying to figure out what powers the king has. And I heard them talking," Alfred revealed.

"But he is helping us rebuild..." I countered.

"That is how he deceives," Alfred's voice was firm as he spoke. "A hunter appearing to be a friend. He considers you a threat. Before you found the lost scroll, Seekers used to talk openly about whether the king actually had any powers. He knew it, but didn't care. He didn't feel threatened. Now, he is scared. Now no one is allowed to speak on this topic anymore. When kings feel scared, they curb freedom of expression. He is scared of you. He is looking for a way to get rid of you and keep Keepers and Seekers under his control."

"Those who believe in Ma are set free. No king can rule them now. I am not worried. But... when I met the king, I don't understand why you and Amy were on his side," I asked.

"We are trying to hunt the hunter, so we need to appear to be his friends," Alfred explained.

"Oh... and that's why I can't tell anyone," I realized.

"Yes, by being close to him, I can find out things about him that I can use to bring him down." I nodded, and he continued, "Amy and I are playing a dangerous game, and now, it has gotten out of hand."

"How?" I asked.

"Our original plan was to find what the king found from the scroll, but since you got involved, Amy worries that the king is going to get you killed soon. Now she is picking a riskier path," Alfred revealed.

"Oh no. Please stop her," I pleaded.

"I have tried, but I can't. And that is why I came to you. Help me stop her," Alfred implored.

"What is she planning to do?" I inquired.

"She is looking for a weapon. A weapon that turns everything into Black Dust," Alfred replied, concern etched on his face.

I didn't know what to say. I couldn't have imagined such a weapon existed.

Alfred sighed, "The king is not just looking for ways to open the door. He is looking for all kinds of powers to subdue others. His Seekers figured out how Serenus was destroyed and have long been working on finding a weapon that could do that. And now they have it. Look around, all this Black Dust. Serenus was destroyed with this weapon, and now we have it in this world too."

"And Amy is trying to get that weapon? What does she want to do with it?" I asked.

"Yes. She... I don't know. You need to stop her. I know she is talking to Seekers. I know she is looking for the weapon, and I know that she wants to... save you from the king. She is willing to take desperate measures," Alfred admitted.

Desperate to help, I asked, "Tell me what to do."

Alfred urged, "Talk to her. Tell her not to use such a weapon on this world again."

"I will talk to her, but what do I say?" I asked.

"Tell her that you are just one person. Tell her that even if you are killed, Amy and I cannot expose ourselves. We have worked so hard to get close to the king, and... everything will go to waste if Amy finds that weapon," Alfred explained.

"Okay, I will talk to her. Should I come to the castle? I don't want Amy getting involved with such dangerous weapons," I said, worried.

Alfred shook his head. "She is strong. She doesn't need you to protect her from danger. She stares into the eyes of danger, and she doesn't feel fear. But she can't see you getting hurt. She thinks you are here because of her, and she can't let anything happen to you."

"That is the Amy I know," I said, nodding.

"Good, then come with me. Let's go talk to her," Alfred started walking away.

We were still some distance from the castle when we heard it: a sound so loud that we temporarily lost our hearing. Both of us wore expressions of extreme fear. Then, gathering courage, we ran toward the source of the sound and watched a huge castle wall collapse. As we got closer, we saw a hole inside it. A part of the wall had simply disappeared, but there was no debris. A pile of Black Dust was all that remained.

Guards ran toward the wall while others fled from it. Alfred shook his head, "She tricked me. She knew I was away. She chose this time, so I wouldn't stop her."

"What do we do now?" I asked.

Alfred raised his shoulders and said, "We can't do anything... except..."

Alfred lifted his face, lost in thought, and then said with a new-found resolve, "Come with me. We need some Firehorses." Alfred started running toward the stables.

I ran after him. People saw me running and heard the sound of the weapon. Fear was etched on their faces. I knew the look; it was on Alfred's face too. Things were going so well, but how could they? We were in hell, after all—a place of misery, not happiness. A place of bad possibilities.

We reached the stables and found Shahzor standing there with a worried look. "What was that sound? Did you hear it?" Shahzor asked.

"Yes, stay away from it. As far away as you can," I yelled as I ran toward the Firehorses.

Shahzor yelled back, "Where are you going?"

We didn't answer. I didn't know where we were going; I was just following Alfred. Alfred mounted a Firehorse, and I jumped on another one. Then we flew toward the sky. I followed him. As we soared higher, we saw another Firehorse in the sky. It was Amy. Behind her, many more Firehorses were chasing her.

"Are they attacking Amy? Shouldn't we go help her?" I yelled.

Alfred shook his head, "Amy doesn't need our help. She has the weapon. Nothing can stop her now. Not those Firehorses, not arrows. It's only you and me now. We have to stop her."

We flew toward the Door to Happiness. Alfred landed at the top of the steps near the door, and I landed beside him, wondering why we had come there. He pushed our Firehorses, and they flew away. Then he looked at me and said, "She is coming here."

My heart sank as I asked, "Why?"

Alfred glanced back toward Amy and the Firehorses behind her that were getting closer. He spoke urgently, "She will be here soon. We need to stop her. She is going to destroy the door."

"What?!" I exclaimed.

"She is going to destroy the door," Alfred repeated.

"Why... would she... What? Why?" I stammered.

"She calls it the Door of Misery. As long as seekers look toward this door for happiness, no one can be happy," Alfred explained.

"But what if this is our way out of here?" I protested.

"I know, but she doesn't... Listen... there is no time. Think of how we will stop her. She is coming," Alfred urged.

"What can we do? How can we stop her?" I asked desperately.

Alfred shook his head, "We can beg... we can plead... but I don't think it will be enough."

"I will not let her destroy the door. I will stand in her way if I have to. I will not let her," I declared.

"That's why I brought you here. To stand in her way. This is the only thing that may stop her now," Alfred explained.

The loud bang rang in our ears again. Some Firehorses got too close to her, and Amy fired the weapon at them. They moved back just in time. Amy looked scary, holding a two-pronged staff.

I gulped as she got closer. She was moving without any fear, just like when she had faced Esmeray. Then we saw two Firehorses approach us. It was Shahzor and Conrad. They landed near us, and we saw the horror in their eyes.

Amy fired the weapon again. Now, no one was trying to get close to her. The vibrations from Amy's staff carried on for some distance, and although they weren't dangerous after a certain point, they still rang in our ears like bells. It was painful, but Amy's face showed no pain.

Alfred and I turned to Shahzor and Conrad simultaneously, and Alfred said, "Get out of here. She is not going to stop. We are our best hope. Don't come in her way."

Shahzor and Conrad refused to leave. Conrad then said, "This-one's life is too important to risk. You can try and stop her, but we can't let This-one come in the way."

I turned to them and shook my head aggressively. "No! You don't know. She is... She will not hurt me."

Shahzor pushed me on the shoulder and pointed to her, "You think you know her? Look at her. Look at her! Does it look like she will stop?"

It was too late to leave now. Amy was at the steps. She got off the Firehorse and moved up swiftly.

Shahzor pushed me back toward the door and said, "She will have to go through me before she can hurt you."

Conrad stood in front of Shahzor, "She will have to go through me to get to you."

Alfred moved to the front, "And before she hurts any of you, she will need to go through me."

So that was our line of defence against a friend. And we watched her climb the steps, her feet not slowing down. She moved with such intensity that it felt like she wouldn't stop for anything.

Alfred begged her, "Please, Amy... Amy, don't do this. Amy... listen to me. Please... don't do this."

Conrad and Shahzor pleaded, and I moved closer to the door. My back touched the door as I placed my hands on both sides of the doorframe. If she was going to destroy the door, she would have to kill me.

Amy reached Alfred and hit him with the stick part of the staff. Alfred fell off the steps into the water below. Then she swung the staff effortlessly and pushed Shahzor and Conrad, making them fall off as well.

She leaped forward and reached me. I looked down at where Alfred, Shahzor, and Conrad were in the water. They were trying quickly as they could to get back to the steps.

Amy stopped next to me and smiled, "Hello, I missed you."

"I missed you, too," I said. "Please don't do it, Amy." I tightened my grip on the doorframe.

"It will be okay. Trust me," she said confidently.

"No, Amy. You can't take away this possibility... Please don't do it," I pleaded.

Amy rested the staff on the step and said, "It's time to end the games. The king thinks there is someone above Ma. He says this door will take us to them. Ma doesn't interfere. If there is someone above Ma, and they want us to reach them, they need the door."

"You can't decide for the entire world, Amy," I begged.

"That world?" She pointed to the horde of people gathered near the steps watching what was happening. "That world is suffering... it is waiting... If there is someone above Ma, why can't they just come out and say it? Why can't they give us clear-cut instructions that no one will doubt? Why can't they show, out in daylight, a sign that no one can deny? Why can't they tell us what they need from us? Then we could all move forward together and with a single focus."

I begged, "I don't know the answer, Amy. But that doesn't mean we should eliminate this possibility."

Amy shook her head, "You don't understand. I am not eliminating the possibility. I am... exploring it. Ma doesn't intervene. If Ma is our god, then we can destroy the door. We can destroy anything. But think about it... this door here... it makes no sense in Ma's story. In Ma's story, the door to happiness is already open. It is through our hearts. Why would Ma put this door here? Maybe the king is right. Maybe there is a sneaker. Someone above her... who is controlling her... who is making her do things... who is hiding. And if there is someone, and they want us to go through the door..."

"Then they can't allow us to destroy the door. Then they will intervene," I nodded slowly.

Amy smiled. "Exactly, it's time to end the games... it's time to find out if there is someone who will intervene, who will show their hand and not let things get out of control."

Alfred reached Amy and said, "I will not let you do it, Amy."

Amy looked at me, and I said, "Alfred, if we can destroy this door, then we can live here happily, and if we can't destroy this door, then we will know there are gods above Ma... Alfred, the gods don't need our protection. They can protect themselves. If they need the door, we can't destroy it."

Alfred wasn't sure, but I moved out of her way. Amy moved to the door and pointed the staff at it. A loud bang made us close our eyes.

The End

This has been a story of magic.

...

Imagine finding a tether that's not one-sided,

A belief beyond doubt, to finally bring about,

A beacon of hope that's not lopsided.

I've heard the rumours and hoped against hope.

They tell me I'll find it

In the lost scroll,

An idea,

A message,

A beautiful goal.

The real deal,

No tricks,

No lump of coal.

To unite us where needed, but allow our differences,

Leave room for possibilities, but erase all distances.

Wholesome and wise conduct for a world exquisite,

Where goodness is a product, not a prerequisite.

The idea of an open mind, not vengeful and punishing,

Accepting all and being kind, beautiful and ravishing.

...

I believe in myself; I'll find the scroll.

...

Then,
Together we will stand
On the other side,
With the scroll in my hand,
But no fear and no pride.

...

In every newcomer,
Of white or black colour,
In pursuit of the secret,
As Khan or as Egret,
In their longing
And their passion,
Whether a he
Or a she,
You will always find me.

I will be missing you until we meet again.

Credits

Author:	Malik Khalid Ejaz
Co-author:	Tahira Ejaz
Editor:	A.I.
Cover design:	A.I.
Copyright:	Fact and Lore Publishing Inc.

Contact

Email:	khalid@factandlore.com
Instagram:	@factandlore
	https://www.instagram.com/factandlore
Twitter:	@FactandLore
	https://twitter.com/factandlore

Manufactured by Amazon.ca
Bolton, ON

33357938R00423